RAINBOW IN A BOTTLE

DISCLAIMER

Rainbow in a Bottle is written as a fictional story.
Even though it is based on research of actual people
and events, the facts cannot be substantiated.

Published by Brolga Publishing Pty Ltd
ABN 46 063 962 443
PO Box 12544
A'Beckett St
Melbourne,VIC, 8006
Australia

email: markzocchi@brolgapublishing.com.au

National Library of Australia
Cataloguing-in-Publication data
National Library of Australia Cataloguing-in-Publication entry
     Rainbow in a bottle / Joan B. Cooper.
     9781922175601 (paperback)
     Subjects: Aboriginal Australians--Queensland--Fiction.
               Australia--Race relations.
               Australia--Social life and customs--1891-1901--Fiction.
               Australia--History--1891-1901--Fiction.
     Dewey Number: A823.4

Printed in China
Cover design by Brolga Publishing, initial concept by Janette Wilson
Typesetting by Brolga Publishing
Painting (back cover) by Joan B. Cooper

BE PUBLISHED

Publish through a successful publisher. National distribution, Macmillan
& International distribution to the United Kingdom, North America.
Sales Representation to South East Asia
Email: markzocchi@brolgapublishing.com.au

RAINBOW
IN A BOTTLE

Joan B. Cooper

For Cameron and Ryan

AUTHOR'S NOTE

Contrary to popular opinion, the black and white races of Australia have been cohabitating since white men first stepped on to the shores of Australia. Not all white men raped and beat Aboriginal women into submission, nor did all black men shun the attention of white women.

Many such couples fought desperately against the bitter intolerance of those early days, just for the right to love, honour and cherish each other.

Although this book is fictional it is based on the life of my grandsons' GreatGreat Grandmother and Grandfather, two people who had the courage to fight the prejudices of this world.

They paid the price but left behind them a legacy of four generations of proud, achieving people; your people, Cameron and Ryan. May their story give you pride in their past and courage in your future.

This book is for you with all my love, Nanna.

PROLOGUE

The discovery of gold in far northern Queensland Australia in 1874 sent a stampede of ex-convicts, genuine prospectors and land-hungry free settlers scurrying north.

They struggled inland through the harsh wild country, driven by the promise of instant wealth and sheer greed, willingly suffering thirst, starvation and even death at the hands of local tribes fighting to protect their lands. In their ignorance, the invaders took to senselessly slaughtering any Aborigine they came across who stood between them and their Eldorado.

Along the sea route to this Mecca, small settlements sprang into being with the English sounding names of Bowen, Townsville, Cardwell, Cairns and Port Douglas. These towns existed to supply the endless stream of diggers with beef, stores, clothes and tools, all sold at exorbitant prices by enterprising businessmen.

The flood tide of people invading this vast, isolated northern region was further swelled by thousands of indentured Chinese labourers, sent by their oriental masters to re-pick the goldfields. By 1876, it was estimated that twenty thousand people were seeking their fortunes on the far north Queensland goldfields.

Aboriginal tribes were scattered from their land causing a complete breakdown of their traditional way of life. Only the more isolated tribes survived, still clinging to their old ways.

The dispossessed became the fringe dwellers of the gold rush shantytowns. Here they were exposed to all that was rotten in the white man's society – stealing, brawling, claim jumping and murder – that was the order of the day.

A never-ending supply of cheap, adulterated, often lethal liquor, and the scrapings of the Chinese opium pipes aided their degradation.

The black women were traded for these mind-destroying substances, to be abused and infected by the sex-starved male population of the goldfields.

By the early 1890s the gold had petered out. Disappointed diggers moved on to search for a new Eldorado. Some hardy souls stayed on to brave the tropical rainforest and mosquitoes, carving out farms for themselves around the north Queensland districts.

The fringe dwelling Aborigines soon found themselves diseased, demoralised, despised and thrown to the very bottom of the social scrap heap.

Then came the missionaries to save their souls with misguided European ideals of Christian charity. Under their parochial, patronising care, Aborigines were bribed, bullied or beaten into mission stations to be taught the error of their ways. Children were separated from parents and forbidden to use traditional language, food or lifestyle. Thus, within a couple of generations, the basis of Aboriginal culture was destroyed, leaving a race of confused, dispossessed, angry people.

This book is the story of two such people, one black, one white, who against all the racial prejudices of that time, found a deep and abiding love for each other, in this the most unlikeliest of places.

EPIGRAPH

The Legend of the Coloured Sands (as told to me by Aunty Shirley Foley).

Way back in the dream time there lived a beautiful aboriginal maiden named Murrawar, she fell in love with the rainbow who came to visit her in the sky.

One day Burrawilla, a very bad man, stole Murrawara for his slave wife, he beat her cruelly and made her do all the work while he sat and admired his terrible killing boomerang, which was bigger than a tree and full of evil spirits.

One day as Murrawar ran away along the beach, she saw Burawilla's boomerang coming to kill her, she cried for help and fell onto the sand. Suddenly she heard a loud bang and saw her faithful rainbow coming to save her across the sky. The wicked boomerang attacked the brave rainbow and they clashed with a roar like thunder killing the boomerang and shattering the rainbow to pieces. The rainbow lay on the sands and died and is still there, its colours displayed on the sand dunes for all to see. The Aboriginal women believed that if they sprinkled the coloured sands on their hair the rainbow would protect them always.

CHAPTER ONE

His clerical collar rubbed an angry welt that seared like a red-hot iron with every move he made.

Sweat dripped from under his wide brimmed straw hat, forming a rivulet down his spine, staining the back of his black linen jacket with a sopping wet crucifix shape. The rivulet became a stream as it poured down his legs to pool in his black leather boots.

Mosquitoes swarmed on every inch of exposed skin they could find, bloating as they greedily sucked his blood. Sheer dogged determination now kept him on his feet, as he hacked and slashed with his broad-bladed cane knife, at the mass of tangled mangroves and stinger vines that blocked his path. His disgruntled assistant had long since thrown down his knife in disgust, and stomped off along the newly cut track to their camp on the beach, cursing old Samuel Grimshaw and his crazy ideas.

Billy Bambry, the huge black South Sea Islander kept working at his master's side, dragging away the severed undergrowth. He shook his woolly head in despair at the condition of the little man he served. He seemed hell-bent on destroying himself in a fanatical fervour to establish his dream of a mission on these inhospitable shores called Fake Bay, nestled on the edge of the Great Barrier Reef of tropical northern Australia, in the year of 1893.

Billy had tried to persuade the old minister to wait a while, until he became acclimatised before attacking this wilderness, but no, Samuel Grimshaw had ignored the advice and begun to work immediately.

Their expedition had only arrived the day before, in the very unseaworthy little clipper *Goodwill* through weather that only a saint or a madman would have braved. With the most meagre of provisions and a few rusty tools, the old man had set himself the monstrous task of clearing a site for an Anglican mission beneath the towering Mount Venture Ranges, south of the tiny tropical port of Cairns.

'Hey, Beengoo, hurry up with the water,' Billy called to a spindle-legged little Aboriginal boy who struggled up the track from the camp carrying a large billycan, slopping water as he went.

'You wanna drinka water Rev'and?' he called, grinning to himself at the cleric's ridiculous outfit, completely unsuitable for the climate and the work – but Samuel Grimshaw had insisted on wearing it, just in case they came across any native tribes.

'They have to know I am a man of God, that I will not harm them, they must see the cloth immediately,' he explained, but they had seen no sign of Aboriginals. Samuel Grimshaw straightened his aching back and removed his small round wire-framed spectacles. Sweat stung his eyes as he peered towards the boys.

'Be with you in a minute,' he replied as he tried to polish the thick round lenses with his soaked handkerchief.

Taking the offered can he drank deeply, letting the tepid water trickle down his neat grey streaked beard. 'Ah that's better. It's this humidity that's the killer, Billy. Must remember to take some salt tablets tonight. Is Mr Tilburn still back at the camp?' he inquired of Beengoo.

'Yes, Boss, he drink from his rum bottle, he sleep.'

'Well, it's just not good enough. We could have got much further today if he had done his share of the work, and now the light is fading. We'd better pack up. Did you catch any fish, Beengoo?'

'Only that many little ones,' the small boy held up three fingers.

'They will have to do. Go and bank up the fire and we can make a damper as well.'

'We'll have to get the stores off the boat tomorrow, Rev'and,' the big islander said.

'Yes, Billy, but we'll have to go steady with them. They have to last,' replied the Reverend anxiously, knowing they would not be nearly enough. Walking wearily down the track, Samuel Grimshaw thought of his ill suited assistant. He realised now that he had been foolish to take the fellow on. He had seemed keen enough at the start but had caved in on the first day's hard work.

Nausea overtook the old man; his vision began to swim as he approached the campfire. He made it to a fallen log just as his knees buckled. Dropping his face into his hands, he rested for a few minutes on the log until the dizzy spell passed. Looking up he saw James Tilburn leaning against a tree, swigging from a rum bottle.

'I thought I told you there was to be no strong drink in this camp, Tilburn?'

'Och! It is for medicinal purposes, Reverend, a man has to have a dram in these God forsaken parts, to ward off the fever,' Tilburn slurred in his broad Scots accent, sliding his paunchy body down to the base of the tree, his red hair and beard glinting in the firelight.

'Rubbish! There'll be no alcohol on any mission of mine, and if you had done your share of the work today instead of sneaking back here to intoxicate yourself, we could have had that track finished by now. Give that bottle to me.'

Wiping his mouth on the back of his hand, the drunken Scot rose and approached the Reverend menacingly. 'Ye can kill yourself ya stupid old bastard! But ye'll no be the death o' me wi' your crazy ideas. You've no' enough stores to last ye the week oot, and the tools ye 'ave would no' build a dog kennel. You're mad, old man! Even your own bloody church thinks so. They'll no' be sending any money to help ye oot, will they? Mind yer ain bloody business. I'll take a dram whenever I feel the need.' So saying, he upturned the bottle and drank deeply in Samuel Grimshaw's face.

'Billy! Take the bottle from him.' Samuel Grimshaw ordered, shaking with rage.

Billy rose slowly, his powerful near naked black body, stark against the white backdrop of the tent, the firelight gleaming on his perspiring skin.

'Ye just bloody well try it ye dirty black bastard,' snarled Tilburn snatching up his razor sharp cane knife.

Without taking his eyes off Tilburn, Billy gracefully swayed to one side until his fingers curled around his own knife. The two men stood menacingly poised, the campfire flames dancing between them in the strong wind.

Beengoo, rolling his big eyes in fear, flung himself behind the log the Reverend had just vacated. A vivid streak of lightning followed by an ear splitting clap of thunder acted as the starter's bell, jolting the two men into action.

As Billy sprang across the fire to the blundering drunk,

Tilburn hurled the empty rum bottle catching the huge black man a glancing blow on the temple, knocking him off balance sending his right foot down into the red hot coals.

Roaring with anger and pain, Billy regained his foothold and sprang in front of the stunned Tilburn. Billy's cane knife flashed before the Scotsman's eyes and slashed open the side of his face.

His hand shot to the gaping gash, blood pulsed through his fingers and stained down the front of his shirt.

'Stop it. In God's name, stop it!' shrieked the old minister, running between the two men. Billy dropped his knife as the Scot bolted down the beach screaming.

'You filthy, rotten bastards. I'll get you for this, see if I don't,' he cursed as he disappeared into the blackness of the mangroves.

Shakily, Samuel Grimshaw sat down once more on the log. 'I don't think we'll see him again until morning. We'll have to sail him back to the Cairns hospital tomorrow, I suppose, but I don't want him back in this camp. I made a poor choice picking him.'

Beengoo cooked the fish and damper, but as the three started eating, huge spots of rain fell sizzling into the fire.

'Looks like the storm's building up, Rev'and, we'd better get the gear into the tent.'

The tent canvas flapped wildly as they stacked their few blankets and boxes inside. They were quickly soaked by lashing rain before they had everything in and the guy ropes tightened down.

The storm deepened as the night wore on. The wind became a roaring gale, the tent collapsed, and their few possessions were hurled off down the beach.

The three, miserable, wet and wrapped in blankets, huddled together behind a sand dune as the rain beat down on them. Mangrove trees crashed to the ground around them as the screaming wind ripped up everything in its path. Billy Bambry's arms ached, as he desperately clung onto the old man and the young boy, fighting the storm as it tried to rip them from his grasp.

*

The morning dawned grey and heavy; the Reverend peeled back the sopping blanket, and eased himself stiffly upright, to survey the damage.

In the misty grey light he could just make out the roots of fallen trees, clawing naked to the sky, and he thought he could see part of the tent flapping from a tree farther down the beach, but it was only when he let his eyes scan the edge of the pounding surf that the full enormity of their predicament dawned on him.

'The boat! Oh my God! The *Goodwill*! 'He groaned, and frantically shook the other two awake. 'Look, the boat's done for! All our stores!'

Billy staggered groggily to his feet, wiping sand and water from his face. He followed the shaking, pointing finger of the old man, until his gritfilled eyes made out the grey shape of the little clipper, laid on her side like a beached whale, covered in sand.

Samuel Grimshaw stumbled off down the beach to retrieve their camping equipment. He pulled down the tent from the tree which, though ripped, could be mended, and folded it ready to carry back. He found tin mugs half buried in sand, and one billycan flattened against a rock, before he spied his haversack swinging from the roots of a felled tree. His heart cheered instantly as he realised his bible was in the haversack, he scrambled happily over the fallen trunk to retrieve it.

As he slithered down the other side, his foot trod on something soft and slimy. Looking down, he saw protruding from under the log, the matted red hair of a broken skull, wedged between the log and the sand, blowflies and ants were already weaving a steady track in and out of the bloody cavity.

Vomit rose in his throat as he kicked sand over what was left of Tilburn's head, Beengoo scampered nervously along the log to retrieve the bible, the Reverend Grimshaw performed the first religious service of his mission. After which, he had Billy and Beengoo erect a large wooden cross at the foot of the track.

*

It took two days with only bare hands, to dig out the *Goodwill*, only to find most of their stores ruined by seawater and sand. Sugar, tea and flour were washed away. Waterlogged hardtack biscuits were reduced to a soggy slime, a round of cheese was saved and laid on a rock to dry, and a few rusty tins of bully beef also seemed intact.

They managed to salvage the sail and most of the now, even more rusty tools. With the mighty Billy roped and harnessed to it like a bullock, and the old Reverend and the skinny boy pushing with all their might, they managed to right and re-float the damaged vessel on the now calm tide. Exhausted, they spent the rest of that day laid on the beach nursing aching muscles and feet torn by sharp coral.

Next morning, the Reverend sat morosely eating bully beef from a tin with shaking fingers, as he miserably took stock of his problems. How on earth could he go on? The stores were gone! And there was no money to buy more, even if the boat would get them back to Cairns. He had spent his last penny financing this trip, and the Bishop had warned him not to rely on the church for further finance. But he couldn't fail again, not after Western Australia.

He had to keep going. His teeth chattered and his hands shook so much he could no longer hold the tin, fearfully he recognised the returning symptoms of malaria; his thoughts turned angrily to the quinine lost from the ship with the rest of the medical supplies. His condition worsened swiftly as the morning wore on, until he sank into a mindless delirium. Wiping his hands across his burning face to clear his blurring vision, he staggered to his feet, calling wildly to the two amazed Aboriginals.

'Come on! Up on your feet! We have to do the Lord's work. "Onward Christian Soldiers",' he sang in a croaking voice as he weaved his way drunkenly towards the newly cut track. Tripping in the deep white sand, he fell spread eagled on the beach, still singing loudly, dragging himself along on his hands and knees. He had nearly reached the foot of the track before Billy, taking pity on him, went to help him up.

'Come on, Rev'and, back to the camp. You can't work. You bloody sick man,' he coaxed, as the Reverend tried to fight him off.

'No. No! Have to work. Have to keep going. Promised the Lord you see Billy. Said I'd save the black heathens. Have to do it now. Promised I did, Billy.' The old man fought off the strong black hands. Rigours shook his body and he curled up in a defeated ball. 'Frozen, Billy. I'm freezing to death,' he stammered.

'Beengoo will find some dry wood. We'll make you a fire. You feel better then.' The south-sea islander placed one mighty arm around the frail old man and lifted him to his feet.

They lit a fire and covered the sick man with dried out blankets, but it was clear as evening fell, that the old Reverend was getting steadily worse. Delirious now, he ranted on about his mission and his God, thrashing off the blankets in burning fever one minute, only to lay freezing and shaking the next.

Billy pulled out the salvaged sail and tied it together as best he could to provide a shelter for the old man.

'We break camp at sun-up Beengoo. Got to get old Rev'and to white man's hospital. He's bloody sick, done for if you ask me.'

The crippled little cutter limped into Cairns harbour late next afternoon, and leaving Beengoo to guard the boat, Billy carried the sick old man like a babe in arms, through the muddy streets of the little town, and deposited him on the veranda of the small timber hospital, much to the amazement of the long-skirted, frilly capped matron.

'Rev'and Grimshaw, 'im bloody sick man, shaking fever, you fix 'im good, then I come get 'im.' So saying, he strode off back down the street, his huge black feet splashing through the mud.

The surprised Matron turned her attention to the ranting man, lying at her feet. His clerical garb was ripped and stained, the once white collar twisted back to reveal a wicked weal of bleeding chafed skin, around his sunburned neck. He lay with his eyes closed twitching and mumbling to himself, 'Must keep working. So much to do. Have to send for Henry. He'll know what to do. Must send for Henry. He's a good boy,

Henry.' The old cleric rambled on, unheeding, as the Matron half carried him into the hospital.

CHAPTER TWO

The young girl picked up the boiling kettle from the wood stove and poured the water into the big black china teapot. She arranged the crockery and, spying a chipped saucer, she changed it for a more presentable one.

Slicing the small loaf of cake, she was very careful to produce as many thin slices as possible, turning over the dry end slice to avoid any waste. Loading a large wooden tray with milk, sugar, teapot and cake, she carried it into the parlour where her mother was presiding over a meeting of the Ladies Guild. As she entered, she mentally counted heads, against slices of cake.

She placed the tray on the table covered with its red chenille cloth and she noticed some of the fringe was missing and tried to tuck the torn edge to the back of the table leg. Not that it bothered her, but she knew her mother didn't like visitors to see such signs of poverty in her parlour.

'Thank you, Ellen dear,' said her mother, approaching the table. 'Now ladies, would anyone care for tea?' The ladies gathered around waiting to be served.

'Really, Mrs Grimshaw, your daughters are growing up so quickly, I quite thought this was Amy,' Mrs Payton-Smith remarked as she accepted the offered cup of tea from Ellen. 'How old are you now dear?'

'I'll be sixteen next year,' Ellen volunteered, standing to her full height, and straightening her handme-down dress, which was rather faded and very cleverly patched.

Grace Grimshaw smiled at her daughter's exaggeration. She had actually turned fifteen four months previously. Looking at her slim young body and long, unruly, black hair, as she passed cups of tea to the assembled ladies, Grace thought again of her children's education. Time was slipping by so quickly and here they were, the two older girls into their teenage years, and still no signs of Samuel's financial situation improving enough to send them away to school, particularly since he had chosen to go off on this latest crusade of his.

Her pondering was interrupted by Mrs Moore. 'Have you anymore news of the dear Reverend yet, Mrs Grimshaw?'

'I'm afraid not, other than the letter we received from him on his arrival in Cairns, which was read out in church last Sunday.'

Mrs Moore shook her head gravely. 'Oh! The poor, dear man. He is so brave to take the Lord's word to those heathen blacks, and in such wild country. I do hear that they are actually cannibals and eat each other, and that no white gentleman could expect to live a year in such a climate, with malaria and the ague so rampant. I'm sure we all pray for his safety my dear.' The other ladies murmured in agreement.

Ellen finished handing out tea and retired again to the kitchen, her thoughts on her father. She wondered why he never seemed to be able to settle. In her young life she and her family had gone from one disaster to another, following her father's zealous attempts to interest the Church in his missions.

They had not long arrived in New South Wales, back from Western Australia, where he had been abused and ridiculed by the settlers of the area. She knew her mother had fervently hoped that he had worked the whole thing out of his system and would settle down in Gildbourne to a more ordinary way of life. But, no he had listened to a lecture by Baron von Mueller, given at the mission council, about his exploration of the wild tropical country north of Townsville. The only real toehold of civilisation past there was the small port of Cairns, and now he was off again, with very little support from the Bishop, to establish yet another mission in that inhospitable land.

Refilling the kettle, Ellen sat at the kitchen table, idly pressing her hand into the cake crumbs on the cutting board, and licking them from her fingers.

The kitchen door swung open and there stood her brother, Henry, looking dusty and tired.

'Henry,' she cried, 'What are you doing home?'

'Where's Mother?' he asked urgently, as he dusted his black jacket, and wiped the sweat from his clerical collar which was very grimy and limp.

'She's got a meeting of the church ladies league in the parlour. Aren't you supposed to be over in Tumburumba until next month?' she enquired curiously.

'Yes, but I received a telegraph from father.' He smoothed back his hair with his hand.

'Oh Lord, what's wrong now?'

'He's ill, and he wants me to go up to him and help,' Henry answered flatly.

'Oh, Henry not again. Are you going to go?' Ellen sympathized

'I've spoken to the Bishop and he has given me leave, so I can't see what else I can do.'

He was about to pull out a chair and join her at the table when the door opened.

'Oh, there you are, Ellen. I was just looking for – Henry! How nice to see you dear. How is the curate's life suiting you?'

'Very well, Mrs Moore. I find it very satisfying.'

'Come into the parlour dear. I'm sure all the ladies will be delighted to see how handsome you look in your clerical attire,' she reached for Henry's arm and propelled him into the next room.

His mother rose to greet her favourite, first-born son. 'Henry, dear, what are you doing home? How did you get here?'

'I rode into Tumburumba and managed to get the coach to Adelong. How are you Mother?' he said, kissing her cheek.

Quite a few sly looks passed from the assembled ladies to the tall young curate. Dark haired, like his younger sister, but with paler, harder blue eyes, he just missed out on being handsome. His newly acquired close-cropped beard made him look older than his twenty-four years, and his sixfoot, looselimbed frame, showed none of the usual curate's stance. He moved with the easy grace and muscular control of a manual worker, which he had been for most of his life.

While in Western Australia Henry had been the family's main financial support, doing any work available that paid enough. At the age of fifteen he had done the back breaking work of brick-making: hand cutting straw, treading it into watered clay, forming bricks and stacking, fourteen hours a day. In Perth, at the age of seventeen, he had opened a school for boys, and though the pupils were plentiful, the fees were not as forthcoming. Mining and vegetable gardening had built his frame and burnt his skin a deep tan, and work as a ringer and station hand, had given him the quiet poise and balance of a working horseman.

His personality had hardened with his muscles, he was practical, slightly arrogant, and found it hard to suffer fools gladly. His mother, who was perhaps the only person he had ever been close to, had encouraged his entry into the church. He found he was enjoying the life of a visiting curate among the outback families, with whom he had a lot in common, developing a great appreciation of their isolation and hardships.

'Is anything wrong, dear?' Grace Grimshaw was worried by her son's unscheduled appearance.

'Could you come into the kitchen, Mother, please?'

'Oh yes. Excuse me, ladies, if you would. Just carry on the meeting. I won't be a moment.'

Closing the door, Henry took the telegraph from his pocket and handed it to his mother.

BROKEN DOWN IN CAIRNS HOSPITAL – STOP – LEAVE EVERYTHING AND COME AT ONCE – STOP – FATHER

Expressions of concern and exasperation passed over her face, as she read it. 'When are you going?' she sighed, handing back the telegraph.

'I've seen Doctor Thomas. He has given me leave, and loaned me the passage money. I'm booked on the *Centa* leaving Sydney next week, but it's only for six weeks.'

'Just when you are settled doing your catechist.' she stated angrily. 'For once, doing something you want to do. You have spent most of your life following your father's wild schemes, doing most of the work plus supporting the family, and now this. I suppose you will have to go. Goodness knows what he has done to himself this time.'

'Will you be able to manage, Mother?' Henry asked with his usual concern for her welfare.

'Yes, don't worry about me. I have the little income from the church and this house rent free, though the children are in desperate need of clothes and shoes. Mrs PaytonSmith was saying she had some dresses that she wanted to donate to the mission. I think the mission donation will have to start here. You go. We'll be all right. Write to me as soon as you can and let me know how he is.'

Henry never ceased to be in awe of his mother's tolerance and fortitude. Even after all these years, and all the hardship, she still seemed to be able to pick herself up and struggle on. He had vowed to himself many times, that once he had secured a living somewhere pleasant and prosperous, he would offer his mother a permanent roof over her head, free from worry and constant poverty. Then his father could get on with his missionary dreams without sacrificing his wife and children to the cause.

Just then the baby in the back bedroom awoken from his nap, began to cry.

'Ellen, be a dear and get Barney will you? He'll need changing, and fill his bottle with water. It's so hot he's bound to be thirsty. What time did the others say they would be back from the creek?'

'Amy said by four-thirty Mother, she took some bread and jam for the little ones,' called Ellen as she walked down the passage to retrieve the now howling baby.

Grace turned to Henry 'I'd better go back in, Henry dear. Make yourself some tea. I won't be long. You look as if you could do with a rest.'

*

After the evening meal was cleared away, the younger children were bathed by Amy and Ellen and trooped, without protest, to bed. They were happy and tired after playing in the creek all afternoon, and making the long walk home.

Amy and Ellen took themselves out onto the front veranda and sat on the step, feeling the cool evening breeze on their faces as they gazed down the street at other houses like theirs, nestling in gardens, protected by dark, gently waving trees. Some windows showed the warm glow of oil lamps as the neighbours settled down for the evening.

'Henry is going up to Father. He's sick,' stated Ellen.

'Yes, I heard Mother telling Miss PaytonSmith,' replied Amy. 'I'm glad it's not us going. It feels so good to be in a town again and have friends. There's a social evening at the church next week. I'm going to ask Mother if I can go,' Amy tossed her straight mousey hair and pulled the bodice of her dress a little lower. 'I'm nearly seventeen and I don't see why I can't go to social occasions.' Amy pouted rebelliously. 'There's going to be dancing and supper afterwards.'

'Mother won't let you go. You haven't even got a decent dress,' replied Ellen, picking the dry gum leaves off a fallen twig. 'I wonder if Father is really ill or just wants Henry up there to help him? He is leaving tomorrow for Sydney. It will be weeks before we hear from him.'

*

Samuel Grimshaw sat in a squatter's chair on the veranda of the boarding house he had moved to after his discharge from hospital.

Although the sun beat down on the latticework screens, he wore his black jacket and had a light rug across his knees. He tried to rise as he saw his son walking up the steps towards the house, but couldn't quite get his balance. 'Henry! Henry old chap, how good to see you. I knew you'd come. Wouldn't let your old father down now, would you? Shall I send for some tea for you?' He held his son's hand in both his own.

'No, Father, thank you.' Henry parted his jacket tails and sat opposite the old man, noticing his sunken eyes and puffy yellow skin.

'How are you Father? Better, I hope? He never felt at ease with this man who could always manage to manipulate him.

Samuel beamed cheerfully. 'I'll be fine now. Just have to get a few things settled, and then I'll be back into it. I can't afford to let the grass grow under my feet. I have to show the Bishop that things haven't stopped and the mission will soon be ready to go.'

Henry stared at him in amazement. 'But you haven't even started yet, have you?'

His father airily brushed aside his doubts, 'Oh yes, got quite a bit of clearing done before this dratted malaria laid me low. Won't take long to have the place shipshape. Then we can start bringing in the blacks. Of course, it will be easier, now you are here.' Samuel Grimshaw's eyes glistened feverishly as he studied his son's reaction.

'I can only stay for six weeks, Father, I have to get back to my curateship,' said Henry, determined to lay ground rules.

'Oh! That? Don't worry about that. I'll write to the Bishop; tell him you're needed here. This is much more important.'

'I've only just started my training, Father. I have two more years to do yet, before I can be ordained. I must go back.'

The old man changed his voice to a pitiful whine. 'You can't leave me now, son! Not when I'm sick. There's so much work to do. I did try to manage on my own, but look where that got me, at death's door.

Henry tried again. 'Well, what about your assistant? Can't he carry on?'

'No, didn't you hear? The poor fellow died, in a storm you know. Had to carry on by myself then, would have made it too if it hadn't been for that storm, lost everything, I did. No wonder I became ill.' He tucked the rug more tightly around his knees.

'Look, Father, perhaps you should give the whole idea away,' Henry suggested hopefully. 'Come home. Leave it to a younger man. It's too much for you now.'

The old man glared at him belligerently, his hands shaking as his voice rose, 'No! Never! I will establish a mission! It is my life's dream son, my vocation, God's will!' The screaming voice dropped to a wheedling appeal for justice. 'It wasn't my fault I failed in Western Australia, you know. It was the squatters who drove me out. Frightened I'd take their blacks away. Worried they'd lose their free labour. They drove me out, Henry, and the church didn't support me enough. But not this time, with you here to help we can do it. It's my last chance, son. You will help me, won't you?'

Samuel peered feverishly through his small round eyeglasses assessing his son's reaction.

Henry sighed in weary defeat 'Father, I can't stay long but I'll help you all I can while I'm here. When are you going back?'

Samuel cheered instantly. 'Well, that's the point, son. I have to go to Townsville, to get some more money, you see? I will have to apply to the Townsville Synod for funds. I've spent every penny I have. You wouldn't have any, would you?' He looked hopefully at Henry.

Henry sighed, *Nothing ever changed.* 'I only have a small amount. How much do you need?' he asked begrudgingly.

The old man looked innocent. 'Not much. Just enough to pay my bill here, and the boat fare to Townsville. Oh! Then there's the hospital bill, but you can have my next salary cheque when it comes?'

'When will that be?' Henry asked suspiciously.

'A few month's time,' the old man answered evasively, 'but don't worry about that now. I'd better tell you what I want you to do while I'm away.'

*

The fishing boat dropped Henry in Fake Bay at low tide and he waded in past the little cutter anchored just offshore, carrying his carpetbag high to keep it dry. On reaching the beach, he looked around and saw the newly cut track through the mangroves, at the foot of which was a huge timber cross already leaning at a crazy angle.

To his surprise, he heard the sound of chopping, and as he came to the top of the track, he saw a small clearing cut out of the dense rainforest. A tent was erected by a fast flowing stream that bubbled noisily as it flowed out to the ocean.

'Hello! Anybody there?' he called loudly. The chopping ceased and, across the clearing strode the biggest southsea islander he had ever seen, followed by a small Aboriginal boy. The massive Islander stopped, arms folded, axe still in his hand, waiting, saying nothing, as Henry approached.

Nervously, Henry introduced himself 'I'm Henry Grimshaw, the Reverend Grimshaw's son. I've come to take over the mission for a while, until my father returns. You must be Billy Bambry, and this is Beengoo, I suppose?' he said, smiling down at the little boy, hoping for a warmer reception.

'When will Rev'and be back, Rev'and?' Billy asked, eyeing Henry's clerical clothes.

'Yes, well! I am not a Reverend yet, but hope to be one day. As for my father, he should be back in a month or so. He wants us to keep up the work while he is away. It looks like you have already been doing that, I'm glad to see. Now I'm here to help you.'

Billy eyed the stranger scornfully, wondering how much help this young white fellow would be. He looked well-built, same short-cropped beard as his father. Would he be as tough as the old man? *Soon bloody find out,* Billy thought, as he roughly handed the rusty axe to Henry. 'You can start alonga me, got to get clearing done before old Rev'and comes back.'

Surprised, Henry took the axe and seeing the challenge in the dark man's eyes, he stripped off his jacket and shirt and handed the clothes to Beengoo. 'Take these and my bag to the tent, will you, Beengoo. We have work to do.'

Naked to the waist, his white skin stark against the dark green jungle, he spat on his hands, rubbed the axe handle, and took an expert chop at the closest tree.

Splinters of bark flew as he chopped again and again, swinging into an easy rhythm. Billy stared in genuine surprise. Catching Henry's eye, he gave a big flashing grin of approval and picking up his cane knife, he too swung into the rhythm of Henry's chopping; a friendly competition between black and white commenced.

*

Over the next few days a bond developed between Billy and Henry. Billy came to respect the young white's knowledge of building and capacity for hard work. Between them they erected a sapling shed to store their odd assortment of tools, and also to use as an eating-place. Then they started on a tworoomed cottage.

Henry, ever conscious of Billy's critical eye, tried not to show concern at his blistered hands and mosquito bitten body. He went to bed most nights stiff and red raw from the sun and stinger vines, but he was determined not to let the black man see his discomfort.

Conserving the meagre supplies Henry had brought with him, they lived mainly off the land, shooting possums and birds and catching a plentiful amount of fish. One Sunday, craving some roast meat, they decided to hunt further a-field, closer to the looming Mount Venture Spur.

Setting off at daybreak, Henry followed Billy single file while Beengoo trotted behind carrying the water bottle. Henry had his rifle and Billy carried two spears. They travelled all morning through dense tropical rainforest, abounding with tree orchids and ferns. Brilliantly coloured parrots flashed in the tops of old gnarled trees, the whole place giving Henry the feeling of a Grimm's Fairy Tale.

They came at last into a wide clearing of plains grass. Billy signalled for them to stop and pointed to a group of wallabies grazing. As they watched, one raised its delicate little head and twitching its ears and nose in their direction, picked up their scent. Sensing danger, it bounded off on its powerful long back legs, triggering off the whole mob.

Henry only had time to take one shot before the wallabies disappeared into the scrub. The men spread out to search the long grass for the possible kill, and were hidden from each other's view.

Wading through shoulder high grass Henry thought he heard a noise and, pulling back the vegetation in front of him, he was just in time to see a black arm reach out and grab hold of the leg of the 'roo he had killed.

Primitive anger at being robbed of his kill, made him dive at the offender who wriggled and clawed in his attempt to get away, still clutching the carcass.

'Over here, Billy, quick, give me a hand,' shouted Henry as he hung on to a receding black leg.

Billy and Beengoo dived into the grass after the wriggling black native. Henry picked himself up in time to see Billy hauling the unfortunate youth out by his hair, while Beengoo dragged the wallaby in triumph.

'Don't hurt him, Billy! We don't want to frighten him off. Here, give him to me,' said Henry taking the quivering boy's arm.

Henry picked up his gun and the boy started trembling violently. 'No! I'm not going to shoot you,' Henry said. 'Here, look!' He gave the gun to the grinning Beengoo.

'No gun, you come with me? We'll take him back to the camp, Billy, and try to get him to lead us to his tribe,' said Henry, excited at this first contact.

Billy shrugged his shoulders. Swinging the dead wallaby over his massive back they headed towards camp.

Though tired after the long walk, Henry immediately whipped up a damper and threw it into the dying embers of the campfire while he opened one of the few rusty tins of bully beef. The Aboriginal prisoner watched every movement with intelligent mistrust, waiting his chance to bolt, but Billy, knowing the boy's mind, sat, rifle in hand, staring at him.

'Beengoo, come here. See if you speak his language.'

Little Beengoo stood shyly before the older youth, and spoke quietly in his lilting musical dialect. The puzzled look gave way, at times, to flickers of recognition as the youth listened to Beengoo but wariness remained.

'Does he understand you, Beengoo?' asked Henry as he offered the prisoner bully beef on a piece of hot damper.

The lad accepted the food and held it to his nose, sniffing it carefully before he took a bite.

'It's all right. It's good tucka,' Henry encouraged him. 'Why is he smelling it?'

'See if it got strychnine in it. Lotsa boss cockies round these parts give blackfellas white man's tucka, with plenty strychnine laced in it.'

'Good God! You mean they will purposely poison the food?'

'Yeah Boss, give 'em big bags flour, take back to tribe, kill bloody lot.'

Henry reached out anxiously, making the boy jump, as he took the sandwich and had a big bite. 'No poison, see? Me eat, very good,' he rubbed his stomach in mock enjoyment.

The lad grinned and polished off two more rounds, much to Beengoo's disgust. He only received one.

'Now Beengoo, tell him I am his friend. I want to meet his people. Ask him to take me to them.'

Beengoo stared at Henry in wonder but did as he was told.

'Do you think he understands?' Henry asked Billy.

'Dunno Boss, could do, but you better not go. He won't take you back to tribe.'

'I think he will. He trusts me, see!' The youth grinned as Henry handed him a roll of tobacco. 'You take me, give elders tobacco?' Henry said, holding out a wad. The boy nodded happily.

'Look, he understands.' I must go with him, it will be our first contact.'

'I'd better come too Boss, see you safe.'

'No, Billy, too many will frighten them. I'll be all right, I'm sure I can trust him now.'

Henry cut off one leg of the wallaby and wrapped it in an old cloth. 'I'll take this too, as a present. I should be back before dark. If not, don't worry, I'll stay if they let me.'

Leaving his gun and cane knife behind, Henry signalled to the boy to lead the way. Billy and Beengoo exchanged looks of distrusting doubt.

The black youth moved off swiftly, and for a while Henry thought he was trying to lose him, but he would turn, and wait for him to catch up, Henry was completely lost before darkness fell.

The youth signalled that they should rest for the night, and scraping together some dry leaves, he curled up on them and was soon asleep. Henry did the same but sleep eluded him. He tossed and turned for hours before finally falling into a deep sleep.

Henry awoke to the screeching of parrots as they fought for berries in the branches above him and he lay for a moment watching the sun filter through the dense canopy. Remembering the youth, he sat up and looked to find only an empty pile of leaves. There was no sign of the boy or the leg of 'roo meat, nor, when he felt in his pockets, the wad of tobacco. Disappointment filled him. He would have dearly liked to make contact with a tribe before his father's return. Oh well, it had been worth a try, he thought.

He stood, brushed down the leaves from his clothes, and relieved himself in the bushes. He thought about finding his way back to the camp. Shouldn't be too difficult, just turn round and march half a day. That should bring him to the coast again.

He set off briskly, and had walked for half an hour before realising that he couldn't get his bearings from the sun; the tree canopy was too thick and there didn't seem to be any high ground to take a bearing from. Looking carefully around, he decided he recognised a faint track through the undergrowth, and followed that.

After the first few hours, he was walking more slowly, feeling thirsty, he could hear running water, but couldn't find it in the dense undergrowth, which restricted his vision to a few feet.

He struggled on all day, each track and clump of fern looking exactly like the one before, seemingly a million trees every one different yet every one exactly alike. As the early tropical night began to fall he finally came to a clearing of sorts that seemed vaguely familiar. He looked around hoping to find something he recognised.

His heart sank to his boots as he spotted two piles of dry leaves. He had been walking in a huge circle and was back where he started! Fear griped him now, as he lay again on the leaves, trying to will himself to sleep, to escape his parched throat and gnawing hunger. He would have to try harder and be more observant tomorrow if he was going to find his way out of this damn place.

Next morning he was awake well before dawn and watched carefully for the first light of day. Aiming in the direction of the rising sun, he walked again. Rain started to fall about midday, gently at first, hardly soaking through the dense leaves above his head, but soon turned into a drowning tropical torrent.

He battled on for a while, slipping and sliding on the muddy vegetation, his vision impaired by the thick mist that enveloped him. The snatching branches and vines seemed to reach out as he rushed past, trying to bind around his arms and legs to make him a prisoner in this nightmare jungle forever. Panic filled him now, and he stumbled on in blind terror.

Finally, exhausted and terrified, he sank to his knees in the slimy mulch, sobbing. In his misery he crawled under some bushes, curled himself into a wet defeated ball, and slept.

When he awoke, he had no idea of how long he had slept. It was still dark but the rain had stopped and what little sky he could see winked with bright stars. He lay for a while taking comfort from them and praying for deliverance.

Easing himself up on one elbow, he glanced about but could see very little in the pitch blackness. He realised his legs felt heavy around the calves, raising himself a little higher, he peered curiously along his body. The mud splattered trousers seemed to disappear half way down his legs and he wondered if he was hallucinating. Something shining caught his eye, a pattern, and scales!

He stared in morbid fascination as his eyes picked out the twisted shape of a huge snake wrapped around his legs. He froze in horror, silent screams rent from his throat! Perspiration beaded on his forehead. He knew that one movement would be his last, and to panic would mean instant death.

He breathed deeply to try to still his pounding heart, and very gently lowered himself back onto the ground. He lay rigid, his mind frantically searching for a means of escape. While the snake, curled snugly around the conveniently warm stumps of his legs, slept blissfully on.

With corpse-like stillness he watched the stars slowly dim, and the first rays of dawn flicker into the sky. Soldier ants marched up his arm and tracked round his neck and over his other shoulder, some biting as they went, but he dare not move a muscle to brush them off. Mosquitoes began to swarm round his head and he laid, silent victim to their sucking, their high-pitched buzz making his petrified mind scream.

At last the day broke and the shrieking parrots descended once again for their breakfast of berries. It took Henry some minutes to realise that the weight on his numbed, cramped legs had lifted. Disturbed by the shrieking birds, the snake was slithering away across the leafy ground, no doubt in search of its own breakfast.

Tears of relief ran down his face as he painfully moved his legs and began to massage them, trying to bring back the circulation. He decided he had to escape this terrible place today, or die in the attempt. Hunger and thirst being his first concern, he cursed his ignorance of the rainforest. He knew there must be bountiful food all around him, but which was edible and which deadly poisonous?

He decided it was foolish to try and eat anything, but drink he must. Surely there would be a pool around after all that rain? He set off to find one.

Seeing birds flying mostly in the same direction, he decided to follow them.

Forcing his way through the dense undergrowth of ferns, and tripping over the roots of gigantic trees, he pushed on, his clothes now ripped and arms and face covered in bleeding scratches and swollen bites. He leaned to rest on the bark of a gnarled moss covered tree. The occasional shriek of a parrot and the constant ticking of cicadas was the only noise he could hear – or was it?

He listened carefully. He thought he heard running water. Yes, it had to be. Quickening his step, he followed the sound until it developed into a muffled roar. Climbing down a steep bank he slipped on the wet grass and rolled the last twenty yards.

Picking himself up, he clawed his way through chest high pampas grass until he stumbled head long into the bend of a fast flowing creek. After quenching his thirst he lay submerged, for as long as his breath could last, allowing the icy cold water to sooth his stings and scratches. Wading upstream round the bend, the roar became deafening, as torrents of white foam cascaded down over a fifty-foot waterfall. Dancing in the sun, a huge rainbow arched above it. Its beauty took his breath away, and he sat for a long time watching the water rushing past him while lazy eddies formed amber pools among the rocks at his feet.

The peaceful scene soothed his shattered nerves and slowly his sanity returned. He knelt and gave a prayer of thanks for he knew that he was saved. All he had to do was follow the creek, and it would lead him to the coast…

*

Next evening, Billy and Beengoo were cleaning their fish on the coral rocks, the dying sun warming their backs as it slid down behind the mountains. A gentle breeze blew from the sea and ruffled Beengoo's tangled hair, as he stood holding up his prize fish with a big grin on his face.

'Real big fella this one, Billy, good tucka tonight?' He

laughed; Billy pulled a face as he looked at his own small catch.

Beengoo paused as he thought he heard a voice calling. His keen eyes scanned the beach. 'Someone come up beach, Billy,' he pointed, his eyes grew rounder in fear the longer he stared. 'It bad fella red beard spirit, he come to get us, look!' his voice shook with fear.

Billy leapt to his feet following the frightened boy's gaze, he felt his own scalp tingle as the scarecrow figure caked in red mud staggered towards them. The giant of a man and the small boy both set off to run at the same moment until the frantic calling of the ragged apparition penetrated their terrified brains.

'Hey, Billy, Beengoo, it's me! Don't run away for God's sake. Help me!'

They stopped in their tracks and turned warily. 'It young Rev'and, Billy, he done come back,' exclaimed the little boy, now sprinting towards Henry.

They gently burned off all the bloated leeches that clung to his body, washed him, and changed his clothes. Beengoo then fed him delicate fillets of baked fish. 'That was marvellous, Beengoo. The best fish I've ever tasted. No, I'd better not have any more just yet. Give my stomach time to get used to food again.' Henry leaned back on the blankets that Billy had laid down by the fire for him. He sighed with contentment.

'I must write to my mother tomorrow. She will be getting worried but I'd better not mention the last few days,' he mumbled as he pulled the blankets cosily up to his chin, relief flooding over him as he slipped into sleep.

*

The letter arrived one morning as Grace was in the backyard stirring the boiling copper, at the same time trying to keep the baby from crawling into the hot ashes. Ellen was carrying the large cane basket to the clothes line, when Amy came running into the yard, colliding with her, knocking the basket from her hands and depositing half of the clean, wet, nappies onto the dusty clay earth.

'Amy. Amy! Stop charging around like that. Haven't I enough to do without you making more washing? And how many times do I have to tell you, young ladies do not run?'

'But Mother, Mrs Bennet gave me this letter for you at the post office; it's from Henry.'

Taking the letter, Grace dried her hands on her apron and walked into the house, calling over her shoulder, 'Pick up the baby Amy, before he burns himself!'

In the cooler darkness of the kitchen she sat heavily at the table, wanting, and yet not wanting, to open the letter. She sighed and slit the envelope.

18 Feb 1893
Dearest Mother,
    By the time you receive this letter Father will be in Townsville.
    He was discharged from Cairns Base Hospital a few days before I arrived, and was resting up waiting for me. He had suffered a severe bout of Malaria, and on top of his other health problems, this has left him very weak and quite ill. He was advised to consult with a doctor in Townsville who

has great knowledge of these tropical diseases; and is doing so while he is down there attending the Synod.

He has prevailed upon me to stay here at Mount Venture Ranges until his return. The land father has chosen for the mission is in area, about 80 square miles, reaching from Cape Conroy to the Rufus River, about 40 miles from Cairns, accessible only by boat. It is very beautiful, but wild, jungle country, the rainforest being very thick and impenetrable. I have with me, Father's two boys, Billy Bambry and Beengoo. As of this moment we have made no contact with the natives though signs have been seen of their existence. I fear there is a great deal of work to be done before Father can even think of making contact with them. The rainforest is very difficult to clear, and to date our only shelter is a tent, one small shed made of sapling walls and tin roof, which is used as our dining room, blacksmith's shop, and an unfinished cottage of two rooms. Father has set me the task of building a schoolhouse before his return. I am endeavouring to do this, though equipment and tools are in very short supply. I am also trying to establish a vegetable garden, as our stores, which we receive from the Townsville mission fund, by way of our little cutter *Goodwill* are of unreliable quality, and availability. I trust that you and the children are well, and would request you to pass onto Bishop Thomas my sincere apologies. May he rest assured that, on the return of Father, I will return to my parish at Tumburumba with all possible haste.

Your affectionate son, Henry

'Is everything all right Mother?' called Ellen from the door, the other children standing wide-eyed and solemn behind her.

'Yes dear, it's all right. I'm just a little worried about your father. He has had to go to Townsville to see a doctor, and Henry will have to stay up there for a while.' Grace folded the letter and straightened her shoulders. 'Right ho! We have to get that washing finished. They say that cleanliness is next to Godliness, so off we go.'

That evening as Grace sat winding her hair into curlers, Ellen's head appeared round the bedroom door. 'Mother, is Father very ill? How long will he stay up in Queensland?' she queried.

Grace shrugged her shoulders, and reached out to pull Ellen down on the bed beside her. She brushed strands of hair back from the worried face of her daughter and said. 'Come on now, don't worry. You know your father. He'll be all right, and once he gets things organised, and the mission running, he'll be back.'

'But Mother, after all the trouble in northern Australia, everyone against him as they were, why does he want to do it again? Remember that horrible poem they put on the church door? You know:

Old Bishop Pearson sent a parson here
Whose name was Pastor Grimshaw
Poor silly wretch, he damned himself
To save the Lord the trouble.
They said he had blacks on the brain.'

'Well, I suppose he has, but in a different way,' Grace tried to explain. 'I know your father really believes it is God's will, and his vocation, to do all he can to establish missions wherever he sees a need.

'There's so much cruelty and injustice metered out to those poor people, and they desperately need protection. Father feels he can save them by teaching them Christian ways, and educating them, so that their children will be able to find a place in white society.'

Ellen frowned and traced her finger round the paisley design on the counterpane. 'But Mother, those Aboriginals where Father is now, they have lived as they do for thousands of years, so aren't they happy living like that?'

'That's only because they don't know any better. Now, no more buts. Off to bed now, it's late.' Grace shooed her out, not having an answer, having puzzled over this question herself.

*

The family struggled on for another two months without a word from father or son. Then one day as Ellen walked along the street towards their house pulling Barney in the little dog cart that Henry had made for him, she saw a shiny black gig standing outside the gate. The horse, tethered to the fence, was nibbling the tops of the bushes. She looked behind, calling to Meg and little Sally who were wandering along drumming sticks against the neighbour's picket fence. Their bonnets, pushed back off their heads, hung like lopsided halos and Meg's apron had a stain down the front.

'Hurry up you two. Can't you try to keep up?'

'I want to ride in the cart with Barney,' sulked Sally. 'My legs are tired.'

'Never mind. We're nearly home. Look! We have a visitor. I didn't know we knew anyone who had a carriage so elegant as that.'

Curiosity was getting the better of her, and she pulled the little cart even faster. Barney wobbled about as the wheels hit the stones and ruts in the road, but his little face beamed and he giggled at every jolt.

As Ellen swung open the gate she stopped at the sight of a uniformed manservant, sitting on the bottom step of the veranda, smoking a cigarette and studying his boots. He looked up with a start, as the noisy cart and rattling sticks heralded the approach of the children. 'You'd better go round the back, miss. The Bishop is calling on your mother.'

'Doctor Thomas?' Ellen asked in amazement. She looked down at her dusty boots and crumpled dress, with sweat stains under the arms, and then to the stain on Meg's apron. She knew that her mother would be furious if the Bishop saw Reverend Grimshaw's daughters in such a state. 'Yes, I think I should,' she replied, and pushed the two little girls before her as she tried to quietly ease the cart around the corner of the house.

'You two sit out here,' she said. 'I'll bring you each a slice of bread and a drink of milk, but be quiet. Mother has a very important visitor.' So saying she swung Barney onto her hip and crept through the kitchen into the back bedroom, where she popped him into his cot and gave him his favourite rag doll. 'Be a good boy, Barney and have a sleep.'

Obligingly, the child shoved the arm of the rag doll into his mouth, and rolled over to pick at the paint on the bars of his cot.

Ellen moved silently into the kitchen. She sliced two

wedges of bread from the loaf and spread on them the last of the butter, which was rather melted and runny. Filling two small mugs with milk she took them out into the backyard, where the little girls were sitting in the shade of the house.

'Here you are. Have this, then play quietly until the Bishop has left.'

Returning to the kitchen Ellen noticed a pile of mending abandoned on the kitchen table. She absently picked up the needle already threaded and attached to the hem of Meg's dress. She remembered it had been hers, and continued to sew up the hem as her mother had pinned it.

She could hear subdued voices from the parlour, but could not make out the words, until she heard her mother quietly sobbing. She found herself leaning against the hinge of the door, holding her breath.

Doctor Thomas' voice was deep and consoling. 'Mrs Grimshaw, I would have wished myself the last person on earth to bring you this news, but when I received the telegraph from Townsville, I felt it my duty to come immediately to be the one to tell you.' His boots squeaked as he paced the floor.

'I have to tell you that your husband has been buried in Townsville, with full Christian dignity. I'm sure you will appreciate the need for haste in such a tropical climate. There will be a memorial service, of course, which I will conduct personally.'

Ellen stood in shocked silence. She found that her legs were shaking uncontrollably, she was unable to move.

The Bishop continued, 'The Townsville Synod has already contacted your son, and asked him to remain at Bibiringda, which is the name your husband chose for the mission. We feel it advisable, as the land has now been granted to the church, to keep somebody in residence there for the time being. You know I did my best to dissuade the Reverend Grimshaw from taking on this venture. If only he had waited until proper funding was available, this would not have happened. I must ask you for the names of the people who provided him with the funding to defray his personal expenses. They should be notified.'

Grace's voice was cracked and barely audible as she replied, 'I'm sorry, Doctor Thomas, I don't know from whom Samuel received funding. He approached all the influential people he could think of to raise the money, but I don't know who contributed.'

'Well, don't worry your head about such things now. I will make enquiries. You must realise though that there will be business to attend to regarding your husband's estate. If you could give me his documents, I will have my clerk do the necessary paperwork, and employ the solicitors who act for the church, to wind up the estate.'

No reply came from Grace Grimshaw, and Ellen had a mad urge to run into the room and throw herself into her mother's arms. How could the Bishop be so insensitive as to ask these questions now?

Ellen heard the desk drawers being opened and her mother saying, 'There isn't much. Samuel kept all our personal papers in this box. If you would take the box, as I don't feel I could sort things out at the moment.'

The sound of chairs scraping, followed by footsteps, brought Ellen out of her trance, and she fled outside. She could hear the Bishop and her mother at the front door.

'Again, my deepest condolences Mrs Grimshaw. I will send

word about the memorial service, and the legal transactions. Goodbye dear lady, God be with you.'

As the carriage moved off Ellen hurried to the front of the house to find her mother, her face ghastly white and blank, standing rigid at the door.

'Come inside, Mother, please. Please, sit down. Shall I make you some tea?' Fear made Ellen's voice tremble as if she was a little girl again, lost and terrified. 'Mother, speak to me, please,' she begged, tears rolling down her face.

At last Grace moved into the parlour and didn't resist being lowered into a chair. Ellen flew out to the back of the house and hauled the amazed Meg to her feet. 'Quickly go and fetch Miss PaytonSmith. Hurry! Now! Tell her Mother needs her.' She pushed the startled girl towards the back gate. 'Go on! Run.'

She grabbed little Sally by the arm and roughly pulled her into the kitchen. 'Stay there and don't move,' she ordered.

Back in the parlour, Grace was still sitting as Ellen had left her. Ellen knelt before her and taking her hands began to rub them gently, not knowing what else to do. She stayed in dumb confusion until the front door opened, and Miss Payton-Smith entered with Meg, red faced, and panting, trotting behind.

'My dear Grace, whatever is wrong?' she asked, easing Ellen away from her mother, and staring into the blank face.

'I think it's Father. He's dead, Miss PaytonSmith. The BBBishop was just here, and – and Mother was crying,' sobbed the helpless girl.

'Shock,' said Miss PaytonSmith, 'Get the smelling salts, and make strong sweet tea. Hurry girl.' Pull yourself together.'

Ellen rushed to her mother's bedroom, and returned with

the smelling salts.

Taking the top from the bottle, Miss PaytonSmith waved the acrid ammonia fumes under Grace's nose. After a few seconds, her head pulled back and she began to cough. Awareness crept back into her eyes.

'It's Samuel,' she whispered. 'He's gone! Dead! Two weeks ago and I didn't even know. I didn't even know.' Huge sobs shook her body and her teeth started to chatter uncontrollably.

'Quickly, Ellen, where's the tea?' called Miss PaytonSmith. 'Do you have any brandy in the house?'

Ellen remembered her mother having a small bottle of brandy that she used to rub on Barney's gums when he was teething. She reached into the top of the pantry for it, knocking other bottles over. She stumbled back to the table, emptied the brandy into the teacup, added a heaped spoonful of sugar and poured the strong black tea in. Her shaking hands slopped the liquid onto the saucer as she carried it to her mother.

'Come, Grace, take a hold of yourself and drink this,' Miss PaytonSmith held the cup to Grace's trembling lips. 'That's right, dear. Now some more, it will make you feel calmer.'

Ellen noticed the younger children huddled in the corner, silent and white faced. She knelt down and put an arm around each, hugging them. They watched Miss PaytonSmith gently lift their mother to her feet and walk her out of the parlour into the bedroom.

When she returned to the parlour, Miss PaytonSmith sat in the chair and called the children to her.

'Now, children, you are going to have to be very brave. Your dear father has been called to heaven, and you will have to help your mother by being quiet and good. Ellen, you must draw the curtains throughout the house to show respect for the dead, and stay indoors. Where's Amy?'

'She went to visit Mrs Moore's Alice. They are working on the new altar cloths together.'

'Well, I will call on my way home and send her straight back. The ladies of the church will be here tonight to help, so don't be frightened, just get out your prayer books and read quietly. I must go now.'

By evening the ladies had organised the family. The two smallest girls had gone to stay with Miss PaytonSmith; Mrs Moore had swooped upon Barney and borne him off, protesting loudly. The other neighbours had brought the evening meal for the older girls, and a bowl of chicken broth for their mother. The postmistress had taken what washing there was to be done.

The house was strangely silent as Amy and Ellen sat at the kitchen table, not knowing what to do or what to say to each other. The loss of their father seemed so unreal to them, with no funeral to think of, no ritual in process. Finally, Ellen went to her mother's bedroom and quietly opened the door. Her mother was curled up in a foetal position, her long hair spread over the pillow, the silver framed wedding photograph clutched in her hand, the soup on the bedside table cold and untouched. She slept fitfully, her breathing short and erratic. Ellen closed the door.

'I suppose we'd better go to bed,' she whispered to Amy, not daring, for unknown reasons, to raise her voice.

The two lonely girls slipped quickly into their long cotton nightgowns, and crept into the double bed they shared, and, for once united in their fear and confusion, they wrapped their arms tightly around each other, and prayed for sleep to remove them from the miserable present.

*

The following day black dyes were brought, and all the family's decent clothes were washed, dyed, and pressed ready for the memorial service which was to be held the following Sunday.

The Bishop spoke eloquently of the Lord's brave servant who died in the service of the Almighty, while bringing light to dark heathen places.

Grace couldn't help letting her attention wander long enough to worry about Henry, still struggling on by himself up there.

She had not heard from him, but knew his thoughts would be with them. She was the last to stand for the singing of the 23rd psalm; *The Lord is my shepherd, I shall not want.* The opening verse brought her mind to the cold reality of her position.

Would the church grant her a pension? Surely so! Samuel had died in its service, and there would be the insurance policies. Not a fortune, but it would be sufficient if she was very careful. Refusing to worry more, she set her mind on the rest of the service. When it ended, she stood beside the Bishop and the children lined up at her side as the congregation filed past, paying their respects.

As the last of the worshippers moved out of the church, Doctor Thomas drew Grace to one side and said, 'Dear lady, I don't want you to worry about your financial position. My clerk is sorting out the legalities and he should be in contact with you within a few days.'

Filled with misery, Grace and the children walked home.

*

'No pension? I don't understand.' Grace faced the Bishop's clerk a week later. 'Surely Samuel lost his life in the service of the church. They must take responsibility for his children.'

'I'm afraid the powers-that-be don't see it that way, Mrs Grimshaw. They feel that as the Reverend Grimshaw's venture was unauthorised, they cannot be held responsible.'

Stunned silence followed as Grace choked down the panic rising in her throat. 'Well, could you tell me how much the insurance policies raised?'

The clerk wished himself anywhere but where he was at that moment. He was a family man himself, and knew the blow his next words would strike. 'I'm sorry, Mrs Grimshaw, I really am, but there is no insurance.' He lowered his eyes so as not to see the cold fear now on the woman's face.

'Of course there is. There has to be. There must be some mistake. Samuel always told me of the policies. He took them out as a safeguard against just the situation I'm in now. Please Mr Watson, you'll have to check into it again. Maybe the policies weren't in the box. That's what must have happened.' So saying Grace leaped from her chair and started wildly pulling out drawers and tipping their contents onto the floor.

'It's no use, Mrs Grimshaw, please don't do that. I have checked. The policies were cashed in some six months ago.'

Grace stopped short and dropped the books she held in her hand. 'How could they have been?' she whispered.

'Well, it seems that there were no funds forthcoming from your husband's appeal. I'm afraid he cashed them in himself – to finance his expedition.'

Grace sank into the chair and covered her face with her hands. 'How could he? How could he? What in God's name am I going to do now?'

CHAPTER THREE

'There really is only one answer, Grace,' said Florence Payton-Smith as the two of them sat in the kitchen talking late into the evening. 'You'll have to go up to Henry. I can't see any other avenue open to you, my dear. As you say yourself, and I agree, it would be impossible for you to consider staying on here without a roof over your head and an income.'

Henry had written back immediately upon receiving his mother's frantic letter, and advised her to go to him, that somehow they would provide a home for the children.

'Yes, I suppose you're right, Florence, but I dread the idea. How on earth can I take the children to a wild and desolate place like north Queensland? What about all those diseases? We won't be near civilisation, let alone a doctor, and the living conditions! Lord knows we've been in some strange places, but never in the middle of a jungle. I don't feel I can do it to them.'

'But what is your alternative, Grace? I hate to say it, but there isn't one, is there?' Florence poured them both another cup of tea and began to speak again. 'Grace, I've been giving this a lot of thought and I don't want you to be offended or think I am interfering, but I have a suggestion to make. You know that I have lived by myself these last eight years, since my father died. I'm not wealthy, but I am comfortably provided for. I have a few investments Father made for me and that side of my life is taken care of. I didn't realise how lonely I was until Meg and little Sally came to stay with me during your tragic loss. Now they are back home with you the house seems so empty and quiet. They are such little darlings and we get along so well. I was wondering if you would consider leaving them with me? Not forever, I wouldn't expect that, but for a year or two perhaps. What do you think?'

Grace's first impulse was to say no. Leave her little girls behind? Of course not.

There was silence for a few moments before she spoke.

'For myself, I would say no. I can't bear the thought of leaving my children; but for their sake I feel I must say yes, no matter how much it will hurt. I trust you Florence. I know you are a good woman and will be a kind aunt to them. There is one stipulation I will make. You must try and teach them all you can, will you do that?'

'I'll do better than that, Grace. I'll have them enrolled in Miss Duncan's Academy before you leave, and pay for one year's tuition in advance. Will that help put your mind at rest?'

'You're a wonderful woman, Florence. God has sent me a true friend in my time of need.'

'It seems rather awful of me to be deriving so much joy out of your misfortune, but I promise I will love them as my own.'

Grace felt some of the huge burden lifting from her shoulders. Not only would her little girls be loved and well looked after, they would be getting a chance she would never be able to give them.

She felt at peace with her decision.

*

Next morning, Grace knew she must tell Amy and Ellen of

her decision. While Barney was having his morning nap, and the two little ones were in the yard playing, she called the older girls into the parlour.

Amy picked up the ladies journal, which was handed on to them each month, and started to thumb through the pages, admiring the fashions. 'Do you think you could make me a dress like this, Mother? Wouldn't it suit me? I could start to put my hair up too. I tried it the other day and it was most becoming, I think green would be a lovely colour for material, don't you?'

'Put the journal down Amy and both of you come and sit at the table. I have something very important to discuss with you.'

The girls looked at each other apprehensively and moved to a chair either side of their mother.

'We have to think about what is to become of us, now that Father has passed on. I have a little problem with money and, I'm afraid, we won't be able to stay in this house.'

'We could look for work, Mother. I'm sure I could get a position as a shop girl in Sydney,' blithely Amy chattered on. 'I would love to display hats and gowns and jewellery, or maybe I could sell perfume and powders, and lip rouge. I'd perhaps get to try some of them. Don't worry, Mother, we both could find work in a bigger town.'

Grace smiled and said, 'That's a very kind offer Amy, but not quite what I had in mind.'

Ellen looked at her mother and knew something was to happen that did not rest easy with her. 'Where are we to go, Mother?'

'We're going to live with Henry.' Grace could think of no easy way to say it.

'We can't,' blurted out Amy. 'Not in all that jungle, with those awful natives. Henry hasn't even got a house.'

'Then we will have to build one,' said Grace sharply. 'We have no choice.'

'I won't go. I won't!' screamed Amy. 'You can't do this to me. I'll run away. I like it here. I have some friends and things to do. Mother please, let's stay here. I promise I won't ask for anything ever again!'

Ellen turned from her mother to her sister. 'I think Mother means we can't stay here anyway.'

'That's right, I'm afraid, Amy. I said we have no choice and that is exactly what I mean. We have to go.'

'Will Henry have room for us all, Mother?' Ellen, always the strong minded, practical one of the pair, could see the futility of arguing against fate and was already considering the possible consequences of the move.

'No, dear, he won't but I've decided that we won't all be going. Meg and Sally are to stay with Miss PaytonSmith.'

Amy's eyes lit up as she grasped at a possible straw. 'Would she let me stay with her too, do you think?'

'No, she would not. Now let that be an end to it, Amy. I have made my decision. You are to come with the rest of us.'

Amy stormed out of the room, slamming the kitchen door. Ellen started up to go after her.

'Let her be, Ellen. She will be all right once she's had time to get used to the idea,' Grace said wearily.

Ellen wasn't too sure, she knew her sister much better than her mother did.

Passage was booked for them by Henry, who was still in receipt of his father's salary of two hundred pounds a year.

They were to sail from Sydney on the coastal run to Cairns

in two month's time. Once more they had to pack up their meagre possessions.

A farewell party was organised in the church hall, and most of the parishioners attended. The ladies brought huge plates filled with sandwiches, boiled fruitcake, pavlova and caramel tarts. There was beer for the men, and fruit punch for the ladies. The children ate until they were almost sick. Barney had great fun crawling under the trestle tables and heaving at the long white tablecloths.

Meg and little Sally joined in with the general racing and chasing of the younger children, not fully comprehending that they would be losing their mother and brother and sisters in a few days.

Grace had permitted them to stay every other night at Florence's house. Florence had given them a large bedroom and bought pretty curtains and bedcovers to match, which the little girls loved. She read them bedtime stories and cooked them special little breakfasts to eat on the veranda in the morning sun, always with flowers on the table.

Grace found it hard to overcome feeling possessive of the little ones, but encouraged their chatter and excitement after each visit.

The morning of their departure finally arrived and was made easier by Florence bringing the little girls over to say goodbye very early, and then taking them off to her sister's farm. She and Grace had agreed on this, and after quick kisses and hugs they went, with both women realising that the tears would start when they returned and saw the empty house. They had been told that their mother was going for a holiday to visit their brother, and had accepted this quite happily.

Amy was bursting with excitement at her first visit to

Sydney, and the long sea voyage. She seemed to have blanked from her mind the purpose of their journey, and chose to dwell only on the part that appealed to her.

Ellen on the other hand, had said little and thought a lot. She accepted the fact that they had to go, and had no real expectations of what they would find. The fact that their mother seemed easier of mind and spirit was enough to make her comply with the situation.

The coach journey to Sydney was long and uncomfortable. Barney was fretful and vomited twice. They arrived in Sydney on a hot humid day, their black mourning clothes absorbing the heat of the sun. They were tired and dirty by the time they had walked to the lodging house owned by Mrs Moore's sister, where they were to stay for two days before they sailed.

Those two days were spent, at Amy's insistence, visiting the shops, admiring the gowns and hats displayed in the huge windows on life-size models with flowers and ribbons floating everywhere.

Amy was enchanted, and Grace went along with the gazing and ahh'ing and the sighs of 'divine'. She knew it would be many years before either of the girls had another opportunity to see such sophistication and glamour, and though her feet ached and her back was nearly broken from carrying Barney, she didn't begrudge them their little pleasure.

The only money they had to spend was ten pounds Henry had sent her to buy lightweight materials for dresses, and a new set of cotton underwear each. Grace spent it very carefully as she knew Henry must have deprived himself greatly to send it.

The day they boarded the *Helena*, a brigantine of 126 tons, was overcast and rain threatened. They were shown to a little cabin, which all four were to share. It was pokey and cramped with its old polished wooden bunks, brass rails and dusty red curtains. They stacked their luggage as neatly as possible and went on deck to watch the hustle and bustle on the docks, as last minute cargo was put aboard and late passengers dashed up the gangplank.

Once the tide was right, the sails were set and the *Helena* made a very slow exit from Sydney harbour. As they watched the heads move slowly behind, Ellen gazed at the wake of the ship and knew that big changes were about to take place.

*

The voyage up the coast of Australia was steady and uneventful, except for ports of call where passengers disembarked and new cargo boarded. Grace and the girls didn't mix much with the other passengers, or join in the deck games and gossip, because they were still in mourning, despite Amy's efforts to persuade her mother to take their evening meal with the others in the dining room. Grace used the excuse of mourning to eat in the cabin, her secret reason being their lack of decent evening clothes.

As the sturdy ship approached the harbour of Townsville, the tropical sun was setting behind Castle Hill, throwing an amber glow over the little town nestled at its feet. They sailed quietly past the sleepy island named Magnetic by Captain Cook, where huge pine trees stood sentrylike guarding the massive boulders, which appeared to have been flung like giants' building blocks down to the soft sandy bays and inlets.

Members of the Townsville mission committee took the family in hand, and while the ship was taking on fresh water and stores, Grace was shown her husband's grave.

That night a quiet dinner and accommodation had been

arranged at the chairman's home. The family slept that night in comfortable beds in rooms overlooking Cleveland Bay. Soft night breezes flowed through open double doors that led onto a wide veranda.

Boarding the ship next day, they were accompanied by a few new passengers heading for Cairns. As Amy and Ellen passed along the deck heading for the gangway to their cabin, the ship lurched and Ellen was thrown against a stoutish man heading the opposite way.

'I beg your pardon, ladies,' he said as he steadied Ellen by the arm. 'Allow me to introduce myself. Edward Ryan at your service.'

Ellen moved quickly away, but Amy, putting on her coyest look replied, 'I'm afraid it's our fault Mr Ryan. We seem to be taking the whole journey to develop our sea legs. Do you sail frequently?'

'Yes, I make many trips up the coast in my capacity as agent for several cattle properties west of Townsville. With whom do I have the pleasure of making this journey?'

'I am Miss Amy Grimshaw and this is my younger sister, Ellen. We are the daughters of the late Reverend Samuel Grimshaw and are journeying north to visit our brother, also in the service of the church. He is at the moment superintending the erection of a Mission Station out of Cairns. We are travelling with our mother and having a great adventure. Mother feels that it is good for us to experience the undeveloped regions of the country to broaden our education. Of course, our permanent home is in Gildbourne where we have our holdings.'

Ellen stared at Amy in disbelief, and tried to hurry her towards the hatch.

'Will I have the pleasure of your family's company at dinner tonight?' Edward Ryan moved his solid body to prevent Ellen's escape.

'I'm afraid not, Mr Ryan, we are still in mourning as you can see by these drab dresses, but I will be walking the deck as usual tomorrow. Perhaps we will see you then.'

As the girls made their way to the cabin, Ellen hissed, 'How could you be so forward, Amy? Mother will kill you if she finds out, and telling Mr Ryan we had holdings in Gildbourne! Anyway he is too old to be interested in you.'

'I didn't tell lies. I only stretched the truth a bit. Anyway, it's been so dull up to now, at least I can flirt with him, and he's not too old.'

Next morning found Amy dressed, impatiently waiting for Ellen.

'Amy, why have you put up your hair?' Grace was trying to squeeze Barney into his clothes as she sat on the bunk.

'It's so hot, Mother, and I am developing a rash round my neck. I thought the air to my skin would help. And I have put on my white blouse because the cotton is cooler, I couldn't bear to wear my jacket.' Amy smoothed her long black skirt and tightened the cummerbund around her waist. The sun had bleached her mousey coloured hair and the tan created by the wind on her young face had given her a healthy sparkle. She looked her best and knew it. She pinned on her large straw hat and headed for the deck. 'Come on, Ellen. It will be too hot to walk if you don't hurry.'

The two girls circled the deck with the other passengers getting what exercise they could in the cramped conditions. Edward Ryan was speaking with an elderly couple when he spied the girls, he paused until they drew level.

'Good morning ladies. Glad to see you are up and about. We country people are always up with the larks, so to speak.'

'Do you always live in the country when you're not travelling Mr Ryan?' asked Amy, walking a little more quickly, leaving Ellen behind.

'I have a property south of Townsville, good grass country and a house in the town, but since my dear wife's death I usually choose to stay on the property where I can supervise the work. My wife never liked the isolation and preferred to live in the town, though even that, in the wet season, is hard on a lady used to English conditions. The humidity and heat can be very bad, you know.'

'I'm sorry your wife died, Mr Ryan. Was it recent?'

'Two years ago now. She died in childbirth, and sadly the child died too, so it's been rather lonely for a chap, but I shouldn't worry your pretty young head with my problems. Look, you can see some of the Great Barrier Reef at low tide over there. Further up the coast, the Captain usually sends out a boat so the passengers can have a viewing, if the weather is fine. Would your mother allow me to escort you and your sister, do you think?'

Amy jumped at the offer. 'I'm sure we'd love to see it, and as it's one of the wonders of the world, I think Mother may let us. She's very keen on our education.'

'Well, I will introduce myself to your mother, and as I have very good credentials with the Townsville church, I'm sure she won't have any objections.'

So it was that Ellen found herself the third, unwanted member, of many little meetings on and off the ship, as it called into the islands dotted up the coast to Cairns. Amy didn't seem to notice that Edward got rather red faced and out of breath as they climbed up hills to admire the magnificent scenery and sweeping vistas of the coast. Nor did she seem to mind the odd pat or sly stroke, cunningly covered as a helping hand or an accident.

Grace didn't seem to notice either. She was kept busy with Barney who had developed a vicious dose of prickly heat, and spent most of the time bathing him with cold water and kept him without clothes in the cabin.

One evening, just before their arrival in Cairns, Amy popped out of the cabin after dinner saying she had left a book on one of the deck chairs and would just be a minute. After Ellen had settled Barney and Grace had stripped to her petticoats to spongewash her sweating body, she asked Ellen to go and see what was keeping Amy.

Ellen wandered along the deck admiring the midnight blue sky that seemed to be bursting with stars. Everything was quiet with only the occasional soft swish of passing waves.

Reaching the stern of the ship, voices drifted from the galley where the crew were eating. Passing the lifeboat, Ellen heard a scraping of feet. Turning to the darkened corner she saw Amy, her hair loose down her half naked back, her blouse pushed from her shoulders, being held hard up to the planking by Edward who, breathing heavily, was mouthing her breasts and neck, pushing himself hard against her.

Ellen fled to the deck chairs and sat with eyes averted to the bow. She heard a muffled, 'No' and quick light feet approaching. She turned to see Amy walking quickly, pulling at her blouse buttons and trying to recoil her hair.

'Ellen!' Amy stopped in her tracks. 'Are you spying on me?'

'No. Mother sent me to find you. What have you been doing?' Ellen whispered anxiously.

'Mind your own business,' snapped Amy with a defiant toss of her head. 'You have no business creeping around after me. If you tell Mother I'll never forgive you or speak to you again. And anyway, it was nothing. Edward finds me very attractive and forgot himself for a moment.'

'I don't think what I saw was nothing. You'll have to marry him if Mother finds out.'

'Well, she won't find out, will she, if you keep your mouth shut. Anyway, I intend to marry him, although he doesn't know it yet.'

'How could you? He's old and creepy, and you're only young,' Ellen said, aghast.

'He's only forty-eight, and quite fit. I'm not going to spend the rest of my life buried in some jungle mission. Edward has money and position. He can give me the life I want and I'm going to get it.'

Arriving in Cairns Harbour some days later Grace was relieved and delighted to see Henry among the crowd on the quay, waving his handkerchief to attract their attention. He bounded up the gangway as soon as it was lowered and hugged his mother.

'I'm so relieved you had a safe journey. There can be very bad storms along this coastline. I've arranged for us all to stay at the Australia Hotel and we'll worry about the baggage and stores tomorrow. The boys will pick up your immediate luggage and carry it to the hotel.' Henry gave orders to a tall SouthSea Islander and a young Aboriginal lad.

As Ellen and Amy followed their mother off the boat, Edward Ryan, who was standing at the bottom of the gangway talking to the Captain, raised his hat to Grace and said, 'Goodbye Mrs Grimshaw. I do hope we see more of you and your family while you are on your visit here.'

'We don't leave for the mission for a couple of days yet, Mr Ryan,'interrupted Amy.'I'm looking forward to some time at the Australia Hotel. I'd like to do some shopping before we sail.'

'Really! I'm booked in at the Australia too. I hope Mrs Grimshaw, you will allow me to escort you around the town when I have attended to my business, which will only take a day.'

'Why thank you, Mr Ryan, but I think my son will be available to escort us.'

At that moment Henry returned and was introduced to Edward Ryan.

'I hear you are trying to tame our natives, Reverend Grimshaw. I think you have a merry chase in front of you,' said the older man. 'Tell me, what success have you achieved? How's your funding?'

Henry's ears pricked up at the mention of funds, his ever-constant worry.'Not too good I'm afraid sir, but I'm sure once people see what strides we are making they will be only too pleased to contribute.'

'Good! Good! Well, I will have to come and see for myself. Maybe I could then be of some assistance in that field. I'm not without some influence in these parts.' He let his eyes wander over Amy's young face and body.

'You'd would be more than welcome, Mr Ryan. We will have to arrange for your visit before we leave for the mission.'

Cairns was at her green tropical best as the family strolled after dinner along the tree-lined foreshore, past the harbour. The evening sky was glowing pink, turning the surrounding hills the colour of rich dark plums. Wading birds strutted importantly through the mad flats of the low tide as the calm sea ebbed with scarcely a ripple.

Henry carried Barney on his shoulders. Grace walked at his side. The two girls trailed behind, admiring the vivid orange and purple bougainvillea that draped the front fences of the sturdy timber cottages on their strange stilted legs.

'Do you think that Mr Ryan would be interested in contributing to the mission, Mother? We could really do with it just now. I didn't want to say anything in front of the girls, but to tell you the truth, things are in a bad way financially.' Henry looked down at his mother apologetically.

'Didn't your father receive any support from the Townsville Mission Society? They gave me to understand that they were providing all stores and equipment.'

'Well, yes, that's what I understood too, but in truth they are only sending what they have left over, or to spare, and when they feel like sending it. It would be so much better if they would allow me to make the purchases in Cairns. It seems ridiculous to send goods all the way from Townsville when we could buy what we really need on our own doorstep, so to speak.' He shrugged his shoulders in frustration. 'Word has gone around the tribes now and the blacks are starting to filter in. I need flour and tobacco to encourage them. There's a couple of small groups who have set up camp near the mission and I have taken in ten Aboriginal girls, mostly orphans, I believe. It's hard to tell but I'm responsible now for feeding them. I'm sorry, Mother, to bother you with all this as soon as you arrive, but you would have had to know the truth sooner or later.'

'You're still getting Father's salary though, aren't you? That should support the family at least.' Grace linked her arm into his, feeling safe at last, even if things were going to be a bit tight for a while.

Henry eased Barney into a more comfortable position on his shoulder as they turned the street corner to walk the back road to the hotel.

'Actually, Mother, that's something else I have to tell you about.' He cleared his throat nervously. 'You see the church has rescinded Father's salary. I'm to receive my old salary of four pounds a month plus ten pounds a month from the Sydney diocese, plus whatever food and equipment Townsville feel like sending us. I'm afraid that's the sum total.'

'But Henry, that's impossible! How many blacks are you feeding now?'

'Counting Billy and Beengoo, the ten girls, and the ones from the camp, I'd say most days about thirty, plus the family now, of course.'

Grace blew out a long breath between tight lips. 'How on earth they expect you to feed that lot and keep building is beyond me. It's certainly not going to be a picnic, is it?'

Henry shook his head sadly and they walked in thoughtful silence the rest of the way back.

Next day, Grace and Henry decided to sail straight away to the mission, instead of spending much needed money on hotel bills. Henry sent Billy and Beengoo off to load the family's baggage and household equipment onto the patched up little boat.

Amy sulked at having to leave so soon, she needed more time for Edward Ryan to press his attentions further. However, she was slightly appeased when, on bidding them goodbye, Edward promised to visit the mission on his next business trip up north.

The girls took their last look at civilisation, the little township, as the over-laden clipper sailed on the evening tide, each privately wondering what they were going to find at their journey's end.

CHAPTER FOUR

Even in the fast falling tropical twilight, the approach to the mission was easy to locate along the dense mangrove swamps. Fires gleamed like beacons on the headland as the native camp settled down for the night.

Once the boat had run aground on the soft sand, Billy Bambry went over the side and carried, first Ellen, and then Amy from the boat, over the wet surf, to dry land. Leaving a lantern with them he repeated the process, bringing in Grace, who carried a sleeping Barney. Henry tied the *Goodwill* to a log mooring intending to unload her in daylight. He left Beengoo to guard the boat and with the huge southsea islander leading the way, the weary party struggled up the track from the beach.

Stumbling over mangrove roots, getting their long skirts caught on the unseen prickle bushes, the girls made slow and frightened progress. Amy shrieked and grabbed hold of Ellen as a fruitbat skimmed the top of her head.

Finally they reached a small clearing where, by the light of a fire, they could see the outline of a tent, a small hut and a partly built slab cottage. Their hearts sank in silent dismay.

Henry, carrying the sleeping baby, came to the front of the little procession with the lamp held high. 'This is it, I'm afraid. It's not much but I'll soon have it fixed up. Mother, would you and the girls like to sleep in the hut tonight? I've rigged up some beds and a mosquito net. Tomorrow we will sort everything out after a good night's sleep.'

The girls and their mother wearily surveyed the makeshift beds. Three sacks stuffed with straw laid side by side, with a large mosquito net hung above to cover all three. As they struggled to undress in the confined space, they heard stifled giggling, at the door, four black faces with huge eyes and gleaming teeth, were grinning in at them from the darkness, pushing each other for a better view.

'What do you want?' snapped a tired Grace. 'Go away! Henry,' she called, 'take these children away.'

Henry crawled out of the tent and clapped his hands. 'Back to your beds immediately girls,' he ordered, shooing them away.

'Who white ladies Rev Farder?' asked the tallest offender.

'These are my family, Maisie, now off you all go. We will introduce everyone in the morning,' he explained as he bustled them off.

Ellen woke early next morning. Looking through the mosquito net and the open wooden slat window, she saw the early sunlight filtering through the tall trees and foliage, its rays illuminating the hut with narrow shafts of light. The cooing doves and the high-pitched shriek of parrots echoed through the still morning. She rose carefully and, easing back the mosquito net, quietly crept outside.

The fire surrounded by huge flat river stones still burned a glowing red under the remaining log. An Aboriginal boy was curled up asleep by the side of it, an old jacket over his legs.

The clearing was about as large as a small holding paddock. Stumps of trees lay chopped and raw waiting to be burned. The undergrowth had been slashed back to provide a weed filled lawn of sorts. The rainforest stood threateningly around the perimeter, as if waiting its chance to sneak back and reclaim the stolen ground.'

Ellen walked over to inspect the slab cottage, which was nearly completed. Only the roof needed bark shingles across the green timber trusses, which were already in place. Past the cottage was a small vegetable garden, struggling valiantly to produce tomatoes and silver beet. She heard, before she saw, a fast bubbling creek. Walking cautiously over mud and stepping from rock to rock, among long lush grass she bent and scooped up handfuls of the cool clear water, splashing her face.

She froze as a voice whispered close by. 'You keep 'im still. I dead 'im quick,' and as the last word was spoken a waddy flew past her ear with amazing speed. It made a sharp crack as it hit the large scaly reptile she could now see had been sunning itself on a rock, not four feet from her.

'Got 'im big fella,' came the delighted cry, turning, she saw the beaming face of the girl Henry had addressed as Maisie, the night before. Maisie reached past her and, expertly catching the half dead goanna by the tail, she twisted its neck and struck each leg with a flat edged stone.

'I didn't even see it,' gasped Ellen, shuddering as the girl dragged the slithering, four-foot long goanna past her.

''im good tucker,' said Maisie, examining the kill, 'good tucker, my people.'

'Really,' agreed Ellen politely feeling quite ill at the thought of eating such a thing. 'My name is Ellen, you must be Maisie.'

'Me Ulanga. Rev'and Farder say Maisie,' she shrugged her bare shoulders and wrinkled her round button nose, rolling her eyes upwards at the same time.

Ellen couldn't help laughing at the comical gesture and

Maisie laughed too.

'You come live along a white fella Rev'and?'

'Yes, he is my brother,' Ellen tried to explain, staring with embarrassment at the girl's dark naked body.

The girl rose, her small round breasts developing above a flat stomach and long lean thighs. 'You come in water swim?' she invited Ellen, quite unconcerned by the white girl's stare, she walked further up the creek to where a cool greenbrown pool rippled gently in the shade of overhanging trees. Vines hung low above the water, where pink water lilies bloomed beside the waving reeds.

'Is it safe?' asked Ellen cautiously. Maisie strode into the water, went under and cane up farther away, wiping water from her eyes, her brown softly curled wet hair clinging to her face. She beckoned to Ellen who lifted her nightgown and stepped gingerly into ankle deep water. It felt deliciously cool and clean.

Maisie swam towards her and pulled at her nightgown. 'Get white fella skin wet, no swim in 'im,' she chided.

Ellen quickly pulled the gown over her head and placed it on the bank before wading into the deep water, now as naked as her companion. As Ellen rubbed her dirty hair in the water, Maisie, understanding her need, swam further up stream with wattle leaves.

She rubbed the leaves together in the water until they foamed into a mild, soapy substance, which gave off a lovely musk perfume.

After washing, the girls floated idly on their backs for a while, watching rainbow winged dragonflies skimming and darting in and out among the water lilies. As they swam slowly in the pool they saw Amy and Grace heading for the creek with billycans in their hands.

'Ellen, is that you?' her mother called into the shaded undergrowth. 'What on earth are you doing?'

'Taking a bath, Mother. The water is lovely.'

'Without your clothes?' echoed Amy aghast.

'Well, I can hardly have a bath in them, can I? Maisie showed me the best place.'

'Good God Ellen! Get out immediately' her mother demanded, snatching up the abandoned nightgown and wrapping it around her dripping daughter as she emerged from the pool. 'What next? Swimming with the blacks, God help you if the men had come along!' she chastised, glaring at the ringleader, Maisie.

'This place belongawomen,' said Maisie in disgust as she swung her dead trophy over one shoulder and stomped off towards the Aboriginal camp, her bare buttocks swaying gracefully as she walked.

'She's stark naked!' exclaimed Grace flabbergasted. 'I really will have to speak to Henry about getting some dresses for these girls. How can they ever learn to be Christians walking around like that?' she shook her head in despair.

After breakfast, which consisted of damper and jam with black tea – there being no butter or milk available. Henry lined up his ten Aboriginal girls to meet the family. They stood naked and mute, while the little ones hid behind, too shy to look at the white ladies.

Their ages ranged from Maisie who Henry thought would be about fourteen to little Posie, her sister, who was approximately four. Henry disclosed privately to his mother, that most of the children were orphans whose mothers had been taken as virtual slaves by the Pearlers, who used them for diving and the sexual gratification of the crew.

Grace was horrified, and asked why the police allowed such a thing to happen. 'It's not that simple,' Henry explained, 'sometimes these women are given by the tribe, in return for leaving the rest of the women alone. Some are bribed away by the Chinese opium dealers who supply the goldfields with prostitutes. Or they are sold by the blacks to the Chinese, for pipe scrapings of opium, and opium ash balls, which the blacks are becoming addicted to. Either way, the police can't or won't do much to protect them. The women are usually used until they are so sick and diseased, or so heavily pregnant, that they can no longer work. Then they are dumped anywhere along the coast, usually to die.

'Oh Henry, that is horrible,' Grace shuddered. 'We must protect these poor girls here then, which brings me to another point dear, they simply can't be allowed to walk around naked. We must at least provide them with dresses. Perhaps the Townsville Committee could help us with some donations?'

Rising to the challenge, Grace began to organise the mission. First she inspected the cottage to see how quickly it could be made habitable.

'We're going to need a kitchen added on, Henry,' she decided, 'and an outhouse. I can't have a repeat performance of this morning with Ellen bathing with the natives. It just won't do, you will have to rig up a bathroom of sorts.'

So the work began.

The shingle roof was nailed on and flat river stones were brought from the creek to pave a floor in the kitchen. The back wall of the kitchen was built of stone and made into a huge fireplace with iron hooks to support large cooking pots. A bush shower was rigged up in the outhouse comprising of a kerosene tin with holes punched in the bottom, suspended over river rocks. A hole was dug and a wooden box with a seat was placed over it, providing a lavatory.

After the earth floor had been dampened and pounded until it was smooth and dust free, the family's belongings were moved into the primitive cottage.

Grace made curtains on her treadle sewing machine, which was her only possession of any sophistication in this wilderness. Rough wooden bed frames were built bunk style, in one room to serve as a bedroom with sisal ropes woven to make bedsprings.

The straw mattresses were given ticking covers and curtains made to draw across the beds, providing some element of privacy. The other room had a table and benches built out of logs embedded into the earth floor.

Shelves were placed around the walls for crockery and other utensils, and within a few weeks the family had settled to some kind of ordered existence.

Henry now put his energies to work, building the school house, and in the next delivery of mission society provisions were a number of slates and chalk and school books; plus a very odd assortment of dresses, ranging from silk party frocks to servant castoffs. Grace set to work to make the dresses fit the ten girls, determined that when the school was ready to open no pupils of hers was going to learn the word of God and receive an education sitting stark naked!

Henry's attempts to recruit the labour he needed from the Aboriginal camps met with little success, and he slaved from dawn till dusk using all the skills he had learned during his life as a station hand to finish off the rough but solid school house.

Henry administered the mission food supplies on a ratio of

work in exchange for flour and tobacco. It didn't take long for the Aboriginal men to develop a taste for damper and a smoke, and volunteers soon appeared, enabling Henry to get the schoolhouse underway, and sweet potatoes planted.

Under Grace's direction the women tended the garden and watered it, but the never ending battle with crickets, caterpillars and possums meant their crops didn't have time to develop before the tender green shoots were nibbled off at the stem and the whole process had to be started all over again.

Amy stayed close to her mother, and complained bitterly of the heat and mosquito bites that made her itch, and produced huge raised red swellings, which took days to subside. She cared for Barney and did some of the cooking but, unlike Ellen, gave a wide berth to the Aboriginal girls and the camps.

Ellen became quite fond of Maisie and would accompany her into the camps when she knew her mother was busy elsewhere. Grace had strictly forbidden the girls to go anywhere near the camps, and insisted they always wear their dress, shoes and hats. Ellen would slip out of her shoes and take off her hat, and follow Maisie into the group of bark humpies, which were built of bent saplings tied together with vines to form a frame, and then covered with sheets of paperbark peeled from the paperbark trees, which grew on the edge of the swamps.

The men ignored Ellen, as they did their own women, but the children and their mothers would laugh and beckon her to sit with them, as they pounded nuts and grains, collected in their dilly bags on their gathering walks each day, ready for the evening meal. They often had a baby at their breast as they worked, with other toddlers hanging around their neck, or picking at the food as they prepared it, but they never seemed to mind, and the children were never smacked or shouted at.

The fires always burned, dogs would wander around looking for scraps, or lie in the shade waiting for the cool of the evening. Maisie would show her all kinds of strange foods and fruit, and encourage her to taste them with a big grin and pantomime of eating. To Ellen's amazement, she found that the big fat witchery grubs they roasted tasted just like chicken, with a slight flavour of the tree where they had been found.

She spent some of her happiest times wandering with Maisie in the rainforest, with its dark mossy floor and towering trees full of stag horns and tree ferns. Beautifully coloured birds and butterflies flitted above with brilliant flashes of yellow, blue, red and green, the rainforest canopy allowing only broken rays of sun to spotlight a tree orchid or little fairy patches of fungus growing on rotting, moss covered logs. Their colours were an amazing range of soft pink to dusky black, with spots of brown and frills of startling yellow. Ellen half-expected gnomes and fairies to pop out from under them.

The schoolroom was finally finished and attended daily by the girls, each adorned in one of Grace's creations. With the frills and bows from the fancier dresses being sewn onto the plainer, more worn ones to balance out the favours.

Soon, aunts and cousins started to attend too. Henry found them very quick and eager to learn, at first some of the tribal elders refused to allow children under their control to attend the school, as they had been told by the *bechedemere* men that Missionaries would take their children away forever to another land. It took some time to convince them it wasn't true.

Trouble with the itinerant, scavenging whites began to occur at the mission, usually sexually deprived, isolated men looking for free labour. The blacks, began slowly to trust Henry, who didn't abuse or enslave their people, but offered flour and tobacco in exchange for their attending his story times of this new God who he loved to talk about at any occasion.

Being a polite race that loved a story, they were quite willing to oblige, even if they did leave later with a puzzled smile on their faces, and rations tucked under their arm.

*

One evening an Aboriginal elder dressed in full tribal regalia, tribal markings cut deep into his chest, who was obviously held in the greatest respect by the rest of the men, strode onto the mission site spear in hand. The rest of the men held positions behind him.

Henry, realising that this could be the acceptance or finish of the mission, walked nervously forward from the rough bench where he had been mixing flour for the following day's supply of bread. Wiping his hands down his shirt, he stood quietly while the chief surveyed the little collection of huts, symbols of the white man's lifestyle so out of place in the jungle clearing. Grace, who had seen the men approaching, beckoned the girls and, picking up Barney, moved quickly into the cottage, barring the door with a heavy timber beam.

'Welcome to our mission,' Henry said, extending his hand in friendship. 'My name is Grimshaw, Henry Grimshaw.' He smiled nervously and waited for the chief's reaction.

The old fellow stared curiously into Henry's face for a few seconds scrutinising his suntanned skin, black hair and trim beard. The spear came forward threateningly, and Henry closed his eyes and prayed. Suddenly a huge grin spread over the black man's face and he stepped forward to embrace the trembling young curate.

'You Undinda, you come back from Dreamtime. You my brudder,' sobbed the old man, beside himself with joy.

Henry was amazed, then remembered that Aboriginals believed in reincarnation. He had obviously been taken for the chief's dead brother. Recovering quickly from his surprise, he caught hold of the other man's hand and clasped his shoulder. 'I am every man's brother, so I am your brother,' he beamed and shook the gnarled old hand.

Thus the mission was accepted, and the black elder, who was given the title of King, spent many hours sitting by the camp fire with Henry, as they both struggled to make the other understand the differences and similarities of Christianity and Dreamtime. Henry developed a great respect for the old man who, in his wisdom, was trying to save his tribe from extinction by the white invaders of his land.

Henry now set to organising a schedule for the mission, holding morning service every day in the schoolhouse, and morning and evening service on Sundays. With the arrival of King, the men now started to attend some of the services. Henry never knew if this was on command of King or because they liked the singing and prayers, which they chanted to the accompaniment of their rhythmically clicking music sticks.

At Henry's suggestion, some of the young men now attended school, but great problems arose on the first day because the young men could not, by tribal law, look at the face of their motherinlaw.

Blankets were stretched down the centre of the schoolroom, men on one side, women on the other, and Henry thought the problem was solved. However, next day he found the men again outside.

They would not sit on a seat once occupied by a woman.

If they did, they believed, the female menstrual cycle would cause the young men to lose their strength.

So, the next job was to make rough log stools of two different shapes, one for the women and another for the men, and at last, all problems solved, the education could commence.

Ellen and Grace took quite a share of the work, teaching alphabet and simple mathematics, though the Aboriginal counting never really got past three unless indicated by fingers. 'Little mob' was anything up to ten; 'little big fella mob' worked out around twenty; and 'proper big fella mob' was anything over that.

Grace found this very frustrating. She believed in strict discipline, as had been her own basic education in a small Yorkshire village school, but Ellen laughed at the sayings and antics of the young children in her charge, and they looked forward to the times that she taught them.

Amy would not become involved in any way with Aboriginals. She dreaded the thought of any white seeing her reduced to these circumstances, and it became a fetish with her to always be properly dressed, gloved and hatted, as if this gave her some protection against the encroaching rainforest and native presence. She would only work within the cottage. Grace arranged for two of the native girls to do the cooking for the mission Aboriginals, although she insisted on cooking for the family herself, not trusting their liking for beetles and worms.

One day, Ellen and Maisie were down on the beach collecting the buds of the purple flowered vine creeper, which grew in profusion, its long runners binding the white sand dunes. The buds of the fallen flower, when stripped back, looked and tasted like Rosellas. Ellen had eaten her fair share when Maisie lifted her head towards the sea, smelling the air.

'Proper big fella rain come up soon, Miss Ellen,' she pointed towards the falling mist forming on the horizon.

Ellen, who never questioned Maisie's knowledge of the weather or the rainforest, asked 'How long will it take to come, Maisie?'

'Him be along tonight.'

'Well, I suppose we should get back and tell the others. We'll need to get some things into the store house.'

They set off down the beach, ducking through mangroves, and jumping pools of water caught around the high standing mangrove roots that always reminded Ellen of ladies trying to keep their skirts dry. It took them quite a while to reach the camp, and by this time huge spots of rain were pattering the leaves of the trees above them. The storm moved in with the swiftness only a tropical region can produce. In no time grey sheets of water were thrown from the sky, bending the trees and beating on the roof of the cottage, creating a noise that was hardly bearable.

Day after day the rains continued, soaking everything as water penetrated even the smallest cracks in the roughly built cottage. Buckets and kerosene tins were placed strategically to catch the constant drips and, with rain drumming on the roof combined with the constant plopplop into tins, the family imprisoned for days, felt nerves begin to fray.

Barney amused himself banging the buckets in time with the drips.

'Keep that child quiet, Ellen,' barked Henry. 'I'm trying to write these articles for the mission news. It's hard enough to try and hear oneself think in all this racket without him banging a tune out as well. Stop it Barney!'

'Leave him alone,' snapped back Amy. She had become very protective of her little brother, her only companion in her self-inflicted isolation. Her temper flared. 'He can't help it if we have to stay cooped up in this place. It's not his fault. You made us come here.'

'Henry didn't make us come here, Amy,' Grace interrupted firmly 'If you remember, we had nowhere else to go.'

'Well, I hate it here,' she blazed, throwing open the cottage door, only to take the full blast of rain onto her face.

'Shut that damned door,' Henry roared, grabbing his flying papers.

She stepped out and slammed it as hard as she could.

'Amy, get back inside! You'll be drenched,' called her mother, but ignoring her, she picked up her already soaked skirt and ran, mindless of the muddy ground sucking off her shoes, to the store shed. Flinging herself inside, she dropped onto a flour bag and sobbed her heart out. Tears turned to unreasonable anger, and she determined to escape this hell as fast as she could.

Hearing the sound of the rain easing to catch its breath for the next downpour, she opened the door and ran towards the beach, skirting the Aboriginal camp, following the swollen roaring creek down the track to where it emerged from the tangled dense mangroves and poured into the sea.

Having no clear idea of how she would escape, she headed into the shelter of a clump of mangroves at the mouth of the creek.

Her clothes steamed as the sun broke through the heavy cloud causing the atmosphere to become a stifling sauna. She stood dejected and exhausted after her outburst, hating everyone and everything. Suddenly, she heard the sound of breaking twigs and turned in fear to see brown legs appearing over the tangled mangrove roots. Maisie and her little sister, Posie, climbed into view, carrying a dilly-bag and a fine woven hair scoop net. Aware of their nakedness she focused all her anger and resentment on them. 'You horrible savages! You will never be anything else, and we have to be buried alive for you,' she exclaimed bitterly.

'You come catch little fella prawns too, missus?' enquired Maisie, holding up the dilly bag half filled with prawns, caught as they were washed out of the swollen creek by the torrential rain.

'No!' Amy snarled back, turning away, so they couldn't see her tear stained face. The two girls moved nearer. Little Posie, approaching Amy offered her a slimy grey prawn.

'Get away you dirty little savage.' She pushed the child viciously, causing her to stumble backwards over a slimy root and fall headlong into the creek. Posie's head surfaced above the water and she gave a gurgling laugh, thinking it was all a game, and began paddling to the bank. A loud splash made the two older girls look sharply across the creak horrified, they saw the primeval glitter of hunter's eyes as a crocodile slid down the opposite bank and headed with unbelievable speed towards the giggling girl. Both girls screamed her name in unison but poor Posie only had time to open her mouth, her eyes stark with amazement, before massive jaws clamped over her bobbing head and whipped her under the water in a death roll.

Maisie took a flying leap into the creek. Amy stood screaming, long, hysterical shrieks, as Maisie picked up a rock from the creek bed and beat frantically on the head of the crocodile, hacking, clawing at it's eyes, trying to tear the little blood spattered body of her sister from its jaws.

The crocodile's surprise turned to anger as it dropped the mangled flesh of Posie from its mouth, and turned its huge jaws, with one giant snap onto Maisie's flaying legs. She screamed, her screams joining in hideous duet with Amy's, who stood on the bank, hands covering her face, mindless hysteria her only weapon against the terrible carnage before her eyes.

The crocodile severed the leg of its second victim, planning no doubt, to retrieve the rest of the kill after its pain had subsided.

Posie's torn little body floated quietly with the current and was caught on an overhanging branch, the water changing from mossy green to brown red around her.

Maisie floated face down towards the bank. Amy's screams died in her throat as she looked at the torn stump where the girl's leg had been. It was still pumping blood. In a daze she reached down and caught the floating girl's arm, dragging her up on to the bank. Hysteria turned to panic and she took flight, running, stumbling, falling and dragging herself upright again, mindless in her terror, at last reaching the clearing.

Henry was bent over the soaked campfire, trying to relight it, while Grace and Ellen were emptying water cans and mopping the cottage floor, which was quickly turning to mud. Henry was the first to see Amy as she ran screaming into the clearing, she collapsed in his arms. Grace and Ellen rushed from the cottage stumbling through the mud.

'My God, what has happened?' Henry demanded, 'Tell me, Amy. Tell me! What is it?' He stared into the horror stricken face. Mouth agape, eyes glazed, she managed to say 'At the creek. The girls. Crocodile. I did it. I did it,' before collapsing in a dead faint.

Maisie was still alive when they reached the creek, but died as they carried her gently back to the mission.

Billy wept, as he scooped what was left of poor Posie out of the water.

Henry and the Aboriginal men took the carbine gun that had belonged to Samuel Grimshaw and searched the creek in their bark canoes, trying to flush out the killer. They dragged branches under the hanging mangrove roots on the banks and beat the water to no avail. The crocodile had disappeared, and no one knew when or where it would strike again.

The Christian funeral service for the girls was held in the schoolroom, attended by the family, the now eight mission girls, and all of the women and the men from the camp, including King.

While Henry read the service, the Aboriginal group remained strangely quiet. No mourning cries, just polite silence.

Ellen, heartbroken, sobbed quietly to herself, grieving for her only friend, and teacher in so many ways. She saw again in her mind's eye Maisie's infectious grin, sparkling eyes, easy grace, the quiet self-assurance, and her tears flowed freely.

After the service and hymn singing, the bodies were carried on bark slabs to the graveside. Dressed in their pathetic hand-me-down dresses and covered with white sheets. The shallow grave dug by the Aboriginals, didn't seem right to Henry, but he felt it unwise to comment. The blacks returned silently to their camps, leaving Ellen to cover the lonely mound with bush orchids and ferns. Later that evening, Grace and Henry puzzled over the attitude of the camp people.

'I expected there to be more noise and demonstration at

the funeral. Strange, they didn't insist on a tribal burial. Maybe we have made more inroads with the faith than we realised, Henry,' Grace reflected.

Two days later, just after sunset, Ellen wandered out to the grave. As she approached the gravesite, she saw the now dead orchids and ferns had been pushed to one side and the earth disturbed. Fearing animals had dug up the bodies; she looked closer and found the remains gone.

She hurried back to the mission, intent on telling Henry, but her attention was diverted when she heard the clackclackclack of music sticks coming from the tangled jungle close to the Aboriginal camp.

Curious, she crept through the bushes towards the sound. The bright glow of a large fire eerily lit the small clearing, silhouetting the surrounding trees into black waving monsters. On reaching the fringe of the clearing she crouched behind a rock, intrigued to see what was happening.

The fire lit up the faces of the women as they sat cross-legged and evenly spaced in a circle around it. Their voices rising in a synchronised spinechilling wail. While the men, beating the music sticks to the rhythm of their stamping feet, danced slowly round them, forming an outer circle, their long shadows writhing behind them, like attendant ghosts.

As Ellen's eyes grew accustomed to the gloom, she noticed a raised platform made from green saplings, erected over the hot orange embers of the fire. Near the platform, the tribe's medicine man crouched with his back to her, his parrot feather headdress flashed, brilliant green as it caught the light.

She watched fascinated, trying to see what he was doing. He seemed to be tearing something from a bundle on the ground. After a concentrated effort, he rose with a long parchment like sheet and laid it carefully on the platform. Next came what looked like joints of meat, each neatly butchered and reverently laid to cook.

Ellen turned away to brush off soldier ants that were tracking up onto her arm. As her glance came once again to the strange ritual, she shuddered in horror at the unmistakeable shapes of two heads arranged side by side on the trestle, clearly illuminated by the firelight. She curled over, dryretching, as she realised it was Maisie and Posie being carefully cooked!

She wanted to run, but her legs wouldn't move. She sat paralysed with morbid fascination as the human barbeque continued. 'Dear God, don't let them be eaten. Please God!' she prayed silently.

The cooking continued as the pulsing wail of the didgeridoos rose to join the clicking sticks, and the women's mournful keening, until it seemed that the very earth was trembling with grief.

Unable to drag her riveted eyes from the horrific ritual, Ellen stayed crouched in the darkness as the night wore on. The sickly sweet aroma of the roasting flesh rising to her nostrils as, at intervals, the women caught the bodies' juices in coconut shells. The juices were carried carefully to the girls' relatives and poured with great ceremony over their bent heads, as religiously as a baptism in a church. As the skin of the bodies dried it was lifted off and cut into strips, and presented to the women. Continuing her grieving chant, each woman placed a strip of skin into her dilly bag.

The Dreamtime music pulsed on and on, numbing Ellen's horrified brain. Her own world ceased to exist, and with it her body and soul, as she was drawn into this macabre pantomime being played out before her eyes.

She waited, without realising it, for the nauseating banquet to begin; but it did not. The human meat, crisped and dried leather hard, was also shared, and placed in the dilly bags to be taken by runners to far-flung relations, as a very personal memento of the loved one.

The climax of the ceremony came as the first streaks of grey dawn slid over the tops of the gently waving trees. The two hot, blackened skulls were now lifted down by the weary witchdoctor who reverently cleaned and polished them as if they were valuable antiques. The tribes' unearthly wailing and music rose to a final climax as the trophies were placed at the feet of the relatives of the two girls.

The drama ended suddenly. No curtain fell, no applause filled the air, the players took no bows. The cast disappeared as swiftly as black spirits into the shadows of the predawn, leaving Ellen staring dumbly at the empty space.

Stunned, Ellen remained blank and motionless, her mind unable to urge action. Slowly, painful cramps in her legs brought her back to reality. Stretching her stiff body, she looked at the sky to see the first rays of dawn filtering through the trees, casting shadow patterns on the ground. With a shock she realised she had been out all night. The family would be frantic! Jumping up, she ran through the bush as fast as she could go, and arrived, panting at the cottage just as her mother stepped from the door, heading for the outhouse.

'Ellen! You're up early. Still, I suppose you went to bed early too. When we came in, your bunk curtains were already drawn, so we didn't disturb you, though we could have done with your help last night. We sorted out the storeroom. What a mess! This rain has ruined half our stores. The tea is wet and the flour full of weevils. It's to be hoped the new stores arrive soon, or we will be in real trouble,' so saying she strode into the shanty bathroom.

Ellen breathed a sigh of relief. She had not been missed. That day, as she went about her work, she began to think of the night before as some weird nightmare, an experience so unreal in the bright light of day that it could not have happened.

Later, curiosity drove her to go back to the camp, but there was nothing to be seen. The camp had vanished like magic.

The rains continued, pausing only for a few hours at a time, when the beating sun appeared, causing the humidity level to soar.

Thousands of mosquitoes swarmed around everybody, sucking blood and leaving itching sores that became easily infected by the millions of flies that incubated in the ideal conditions.

Everyone was tired before they rose in the morning. Sleeping was impossible in the stifling heat and there seemed to be no end to their discomfort. No boat had called at the mission for months and the food supplies were critically low. The damp tea and tobacco were finished, and the small amount of flour that survived the rain, had to be sieved for weevils before it could be used. Everything that was edible was covered in mould. Ants rampaged through the last of the sugar.

The tinned meat had all been eaten, and the mission was now reduced to living on fish, which wasn't very plentiful during the storms, and sweet potato tops boiled as a green vegetable.

Everyone was hungry but Henry insisted that work go on as usual. School was held, and the religious services continued, with lengthy prayers said for clear skies and mission supplies, but as the weeks went by conditions steadily worsened.

*

Grace and Ellen were now running a sick bay of sorts, treating infected bites, which were especially bad among the babies. Although they had little medical knowledge, and no supplies, they did the best they could for each case.

Amy became more withdrawn and moody, seldom leaving the cottage and rarely speaking. She only went out to give Barney a romp around the clearing, but never let him out of her sight. His growth and health had become poor, as a result of a diet lacking milk and fats and eggs. He became pale and thin and not thriving as she knew he should. She tried to discuss this with Grace, but her mother was too busy and too distracted by the general food situation to listen to her worries until one morning he woke with a raging fever.

He whimpered and tossed, in obvious pain. Grace picked him up, suddenly realising how light he was. Her concern deepened when she saw how limply he lay against her shoulder, his little head burning against her cheek. Pangs of guilt assailed her as she became aware of how much she had neglected him of late, and how Amy had been trying to draw her attention to his problems.

She went to the door and called to Henry. 'Come over here and take a look at Barney. He's not well at all.'

Henry looked at the little chap and felt his head. 'He seems to have a fever. Better put him back to bed and sponge him. We'll have to get his temperature down or he will convulse.'

The baby refused to be put down, and clung to his mother crying hoarsely. Grace paced the floor trying to soothe him.

As she paced, she began to think of the effect this place was having on her children, and herself. Amy was sullen and unhappy, not leading the kind of life a young woman of her age should, and having no opportunity to meet eligible young men.

Ellen on the other hand, was running wild, becoming more at home with the Aboriginals than her own family. They both should really be sent to boarding school, but that was impossible. They were barely able to survive as it was, and the more success they had bringing the natives into the fold, the more it cost. Still, something had to be done. She couldn't work all hours assisting Henry and supervise her children as well. 'We'll have to get help,' she thought.

Grace sponged Barney down, and the baby settled eventually into a fitful sleep. She placed him near the open window to try and get some breeze and asked Amy to watch him. Then she hurried over to the schoolhouse where morning prayers were ending and the school pupils lining up to start the day.

Amy was left at the cottage, as they went about the day's activities. Grace popped in once to check on the sleeping toddler, but had to rush off again when a scream from the schoolhouse warned her that Bertie, the oldest of the Aboriginal boys, was up to his mischief again. He delighted, as did the other boys, in tormenting the girls, and always took advantage of her absence either by running away, or letting loose a snake or centipede, anything to create havoc.

Barney woke late in the afternoon, and lay for a while seeming not to focus his eyes. Amy sponged him and sang nursery rhymes but he didn't respond as he usually did, by laughing and, in his own way, singing the tune. As she anxiously watched, his colour got worse, and his eyes rolled up into his head. He began to shake his legs went rigid. When she touched them, he cried out in pain.

Panicking, she ran to Grace, who was instructing some of the women in cleaning their babies' eyes with salty water. 'Mother, come quickly! It's Barney! He's worse. He's shaking. I can't stop him!'

They both ran to the cottage, the Aboriginal women following, babies on their hips. They stood in the doorway watching as Grace picked up the sick child. 'Here, hold him, Amy, while I get Henry. We'll have to try to get him to Cairns. He'll die if we don't.'

Amy took the child, as Grace pushed through the women at the door, and ran down the track to the beach where Henry was trying to catch fish with the men.

Once Grace was out of sight, one of the native women, Nula, giving her baby to one of the others to hold, walked into the hut to Amy, who was holding the jerking baby and crying.

'Give 'im here, missus, I fix 'im good.'

'No, go away. He's too sick,' snapped the distracted girl.

''im proper dead finish! Prutty bloory soon,' Nula warned.

'No, no! Don't dare say that.' Amy hugged Barney closer, sobbing.

'Give 'im me!' The Aboriginal woman reached for Barney, and stared with such power and force that Amy became scared and handed him over.

Scooping the child to her breast, Nula strode swiftly out of the hut towards the stream, calling in her native tongue to one of the mission girls, who jumped up quickly, and ran into the rainforest.

Nula placed the baby on the ground, peeled off his clothes

and laid him in a shallow muddy pool. She smoothed the cool mud all over his little body and kept pouring handfuls of water over his head and face. She reached out for ferns growing near the water and rubbed the sticky sap from the stems into the red angry mosquito bites covering Barney's legs and arms.

Amy stood transfixed, not daring to snatch the baby back. Before long, the young mission girl loped into view carrying a bunch of vines. Nula looked up at Amy and said in a kind voice, 'You to put leaves in big hot water, we give strong fella medicine to baby.'

Grace and Henry came hurrying up from the beach. Grace stopped short. 'Oh, my God! What are they doing to him? Get him back, quickly Henry. Before they kill him.'

'No, leave them!' Amy interrupted. 'They know some things we don't, Mother. Look, he's stopped shaking and his eyes are better,' she whispered, with new respect in her voice.

Nula took Barney, over to where the vines were boiling. She scooped out some of the hot green liquid with an old tin mug and poured cold water into it. After testing the temperature with her lips, she tilted Barney's head back and expertly poured some of the liquid into his half open mouth. She then handed the mug to Amy and placed Barney into Grace's arms. 'You give little fella baby, big mob this tucker all day and night, 'im come good.'

'Thank you, Nula,' Amy said sincerely.

Nula smiled, reaching out and hitching her own child back on to her hip. She pointed to her healthy chubby baby and said, 'I grew him up good, heh?'

Grace, Amy and Ellen took it in turns to sit with Barney through the next few days and nights, administering the green medicine as Nula had directed. Soon he was back on his feet, although still pale and undernourished.

Henry knew he could wait no longer for the Townsville Mission Society to deliver provisions, and, although the weather was still unpredictable, he decided to risk the trip to Cairns to see what was causing the delay. Barney's illness, and his mother's constant fear that it would resume had forced him to look closely at their situation, and he didn't like what he saw. If he and his family were prepared to carry on this work, then he felt the least the church authorities could do was give him proper support. He was worried that he wasn't even ordained yet and had the lives and spiritual welfare of all these people as his sole responsibility. He resolved to get some assistance, and sort out his position at the same time.

The weather held off until he finally landed in Cairns. He went straight to the post office, to telegraph the Townsville Mission Society, demanding an immediate reply. He also posted his contribution to the mission news, in which he included an advertisement for an assistant, although he could think of no one who would be stupid enough to apply to work in the conditions he did. He said as much in the advertisement.

While awaiting return information he decided to drown his sorrows in the bar at the Australian Hotel. On entering the timber panelled public bar, with its high stools and towel runners along the marble top counter, he stopped to pass the time of day with a couple of old regulars.

'Bloody wet season's taking its time, eh Father,' one commented over his glass.

As Henry nodded in agreement the other grey-whiskered old chap began complaining bitterly. 'Things is getting right bad and no mistake. I 'ear tell that there's 'undreds out of work down south. There's talk of a big depression, but you couldn't get more depressed than us in this weather could you Father, eh?' he said dourly into his beer.

Henry moved further down the bar and ordered himself a beer. He sipped its foaming collar thinking of the remarks of the two men. The life he led kept him out of touch with public events, and it wasn't often he had the chance to read newspapers, or listen to informed opinion. He had heard many rumours lately though, that perhaps Australia's economy was in an unhealthy state. Still, that couldn't affect him very much. The mission economy was always on the verge of bankruptcy, and things couldn't get much worse if they tried! He smiled to himself at his own weak joke and took a long drink of the cold beer.

A voice called from the doorway, 'Good day, Mr Grimshaw. I thought it was you. I've been meaning to take you up on your offer of a visit to your mission, but last time I was up here, the weather was too bad. Are you staying long? Is your family with you, or have they departed to better climates?'

'Good to see you, Mr Ryan,' Henry replied as the man approached the bar. 'How's the cattle business?'

'Not too good, I'm afraid. Looks like a lot of my clients will be going to the wall if things don't pick up soon. It's getting bad, I can tell you.'

Edward ordered a beer, and another for Henry and sat his portly frame down on the next stool. 'How's your delightful sister, may I ask?'

'Which one?' Henry asked blankly.

'Oh Amy, and Ellen of course. I often think of our boat trip together. Are they still with you?' Ryan blustered.

'Yes, they will be making their home here now.'

'Really? I understood from Amy that this was to be a girlish adventure, a holiday of sorts.'

'No, that's not quite right. Mr Ryan. My mother fell on very hard circumstances on the death of my father, and had no option but to join me here,' explained Henry, staring morosely into his beer.

'I see. Well, how are they enjoying the mission life?'

'Mother, as usual, just gets on with things. Ellen is becoming quite tribal, but I'm afraid poor Amy is finding it very hard. She's just not cut out for roughing it, and since my little brother has been very ill, I am wondering if we can continue. I'm afraid it's all a big worry to us,' confided Henry, glad of an ear to pour his troubles into.

'I'm so sorry to hear that old chap, though of course, this country is no fit place for gentle women, as I found out with my dear wife. It's very hard on them you know.'

Henry felt he had said too much and tried to swing the conversation in another direction. 'When will we have the honour of a visit from you, Mr Ryan? My mother and the girls are starved for company and gossip from down south. We are very isolated, you know.'

Ryan thought for a moment. 'I could come back with you perhaps. When are you planning to leave? I've finished what I had to do here. I could spare a few days.'

'Champion! I hope to go tomorrow if things work out well. I would be delighted to have your company.' Henry wanted to ask if Edward had made any contacts regarding mission support, but thought it wiser to hold his tongue. He drained his beer, stood up and, picking up his hat, took his leave. 'Goodbye Mr Ryan, I'll call here in the morning. You are staying here, I trust? Good.' Well, see you in the morning, goodbye.'

He went straight back to the post office to see if a reply had come for him. It had. He walked outside into the stifling heat and opened the telegram.

HAVE BEEN ADVISED MISSION TO
CLOSE – STOP – NO MORE FUNDS
WILL BE FORTHCOMING – STOP – FOR
CONFIRMATION CONTACT PRIMATE
BISHOP SYDNEY – STOP – TOWNSVILLE
MISSION SOCIETY – STOP

Henry stood frozen to the spot, aghast at the news. How could they do this to him? They had sent him here, asked him to stay! They were responsible yet this was the repayment. Just close it. Just like that! My God! What about his people, his family, all their efforts? They could not do this to him, by God he would fight!

Fuming, he turned on his heel and stormed back into the post office, where he filled in another wire form to the Primate Bishop in Sydney.

PLEASE ADVISE POSITION OF BIBIRINGDA
MISSION BY RETURN – STOP

Henry angrily paced the streets of Cairns, then in disgust returned to the bar. Later in the afternoon he approached the post office yet again, this time rather the worse for a few beers.

His anger had simmered, and he was now frightened as to the reply he would receive. He knew that he had to keep the mission going somehow he could not let them all down. What would happen to his little girls, and King who now trusted him? No, he had to keep faith and hope.

There was no reply, so he sat and waited, numbly miserable, feeling very low and depressed. At last the postmaster called him over and handed him the cable.

MISSION TO CLOSE NO FUNDS BUT CAN
YOU MANAGE ON ONE POUND MONTH
PLUS FOUR POUNDS SALARY AND FEED
NO BLACKS – STOP

His heart fell to his boots. Were things not bad enough now? How could they manage with no support? A pound a month would be worse than useless, and no provisions from Townsville. It was impossible!

'Any reply sir? We're ready to close up,' asked the postmaster.

Miserably, Henry picked up the form and wrote one word on it.

YES

CHAPTER FIVE

Next morning, as he waited for Edward to arrive, Henry sat in the stern of the *Goodwill* watching nearby *beche-de-mere* fishermen unloading their catch. Impatient to be off, the white crew swore at the Aboriginal labourers who were doing all the work folding sails, hanging nets and swabbing down the decks. After months at sea they were impatient to reach the nearest joss house, shanty hovels stinking of incense and opium, which provided them with a few hours of drug induced escape and the bodies of the young, half-caste girls. Most of the girls had been bought as babies for as little as the price of a tin of jam and imprisoned by their Chinese owners. They were placed in the joss houses from the age of ten until they were riddled with venereal disease and totally addicted to opium. They were then discarded in favour of younger, healthier flesh.

Henry shuddered as he thought of his Aborigine girls. There was no way he could abandon them to such a fate. He resolved to fight to keep the mission going, but God only knew how he was going to do it.

The rapping of hooves, cursing, and angry bellowing snapped him out of his reverie. He looked up to see Edward, clad in moleskins, boots and a large stockman's hat, leading a very cantankerous brown jersey cow, its large udder swinging violently to and fro almost striking the little calf struggling to stay at it's mother's side.

'Sorry I'm late, but look what I scored!' Edward shouted down from the jetty. 'House cow for the folks. Chap I know is walking off. Can't make a go of it. He was going to shoot them, so I gave him five bob for the lot. Help me get them aboard, will you.'

They soon had the frightened beasts roped to the mast and they set sail.

*

As they neared their destination, Edward Ryan stood in the bow of the *Goodwill* and strained his eyes along the coastline, looking for the mission site, but he couldn't even find a break in the mangroves that lined the shore.

The view was magnificent, the sweeping coastline was edged with white sands, the emerald green of the low mangrove belt was backed by the tall ancient rainforest, some trees rising a hundred feet above the canopy of lush vegetation and waving palms.

The backdrop to this beautiful scene was the range of smoky mauve mountains, above which fluffy white clouds floated idly across the deep blue sky. This was beautiful country, deceiving in its gentleness. Everything looked so peaceful and timeless, but it did not do to lose respect for nature in these parts. Vicious cyclones could appear without warning, unleashing terror like hell itself, destroying everything, and anyone who dared to get in its path. Many a brave settler had fought the rainforest, hacked and chopped and burned for years, to expose the rich red soil in which to plant his crops, only to be wiped out in a few short hours by a howling, tearing wind, losing everything, sometimes even his life. Edward knew this country, and wasn't fooled.

Henry pulled in the sail, and used the old chugging motor to guide the little boat into the long flat shallows, towards the small break in the mangroves. Edward could now see the rough track leading up through the beach vegetation. The boat was tied up and planks put over the side. The cow was hauled up by its front legs and pushed unceremoniously onto the plank and into the water. It kicked and bellowed, complaining bitterly, as it swam and scrambled for the shore.

Edward waded at its side, shouting and striking it, as it tried to turn around to rescue its wailing calf. Henry heaved the calf over the side and helped it ashore.

Great shouts of surprise greeted them as they strode into the clearing. Grace rushed out of the schoolhouse, and clapped her hands in delight when she saw the cow. 'Fresh milk, butter and cheese, marvellous! Henry, where did you find them?'

'Courtesy of Mr Ryan, Mother. These will certainly solve some of our problems, especially for Barney.' He laughed and patted Edward on the back.

'Mr Ryan, wonderful to see you again, and with such a stupendous gift for us, Oh, thank you we are so grateful,' Grace enthused as she inspected the gifts.

Edward pulled his stocky figure to its greatest height and saluted. 'At your service, Madam.' Just then, his eyes caught the figure of Amy, standing in the doorway of the cottage, holding Barney by the hand.

'Miss Grimshaw. It's a great pleasure to see you again,' he called.

'Amy, come and look at the wonderful cow Mr Ryan has brought us. Isn't it fine?' Grace gestured to Amy who walked shyly across to the animal, her grey day dress clean and neat, her hair coiled at her neck. She held out a hand to Edward.

'It is indeed a wonderful gift, Mr Ryan, and so good of you to come. We had quite given up on you, you know.' Her face glowed, and she looked happy for the first time in months.

'I would have come earlier, but I had to go out west. Then the weather set in. Still, here I am. You must tell me all your news.'

'News Mr Ryan, here? I'm afraid there is nothing to tell, but I'm dying to hear about all the things that have been happening in the real world,' she said bitterly.

Just then Ellen came wandering out of the rainforest with a cluster of little Aboriginal children, pot bellied, bare and happy, all singing 'Nick, knack paddy whack' as they trouped into the clearing. The children had feathers and flowers in their hair and Ellen had a huge white orchid behind one ear. Her hair was loose, her dress had clumps of burrs sticking to the hem, and her naked feet were covered in mud.

'Hello there, Mr Ryan,' she called. 'Amy thought you'd never come.'

Amy blushed scarlet and turned her back on her sister.

'Just look at that girl,' Grace muttered, 'Way past her sixteenth birthday and still she can't act her age. I don't know what I'm going to do with her.'

She turned with relief to her more acceptable daughter. 'Amy, my dear, go and make some tea. Henry did you get the stores? We only have a handful of tea left.'

'Err, well not quite, Mother, but I did bring you a packet of your favourite brand.' He pulled the packet from his pocket and gave it to Amy. 'There you go. Make it strong and I'll see if I can't get some milk out of our friend here.'

Henry avoided Grace's puzzled look, and led the cow and calf away to tether them.

That evening they had a celebration meal of fish, roast sweet potato, with the tops cooked as a green vegetable, and to follow a rice pudding (courtesy of the cow) in which not too many weevils floated. Later, the family plied Edward with questions about the great wide world outside their isolated settlement.

'This depression seems to be worldwide. There's talk of hundreds of men without work becoming nasty in Sydney and Brisbane. Food kitchens have been set up in the streets to try and ease the unrest. I think it will be a long time before the country is on its feet again.'

Henry quietly quaked at the thought of his princely sum of one pound being withdrawn.

'The politicians are talking about Federation, but I can't see it happening for years yet, maybe not in Queen Victoria's life time, she looks set to reign forever. The gossip has it Prince Edward is running quite wild, gambling freely, with mistresses by the score, begging your pardon ladies.'

'Well, the poor man is quite middle aged, and has no real position until his mother dies.' Ellen gave her opinion. 'He must be about as old as you, isn't he, Mr Ryan?'

'Quite,' coughed Edward, and quickly changed the subject. 'You will have to show me around the mission tomorrow, Miss Grimshaw. I can see you have all worked tremendously hard to bring about all these improvements.' He looked around the squalid cottage with his disgust barely disguised. It was beyond him why anyone would commit themselves to this kind of life, just to minister to a few blacks, who would likely as not steal the coat from your back, or slit your throat, given half the chance. Not that he hadn't started out in the very same way, living rough, being deprived of all creature comforts, but he had had a goal in mind; land, money, some reward at the end of it. Little wonder a sensitive girl like Amy was so obviously miserable, and out of place. She wouldn't take much persuading to leave, and he had to admit that he had quite taken a fancy to her. It made him feel young again, having a girl blush at his look and obviously admire him. After all, he wasn't in his dotage yet. He would be able to give her a run around the bedroom given the chance. It would mean marriage. No doubt about that, with this religious lot. Still, that wouldn't do him any harm either, always good to have a leg in with the church, very respectable.

'Oh Edward, do tell us about the ladies' fashions. What are the latest styles down south?' Amy gushed.

'Good Lord, dear girl, it's no good asking an old bushie like me about such things. You'll have to come to Townsville and see for yourself.'

'That would be wonderful. Could we, Mother?'

'I'm not sure dear, we would have to think about it later.'

Henry rose. 'Well, it's about time to turn in, I think. It's been a long day, and I will have to be up early tomorrow to build a pen of sorts for the cow. Will you be happy to bunk down in the store Edward? Come on, I'll show you.'

Amy lay in her bunk and waited until the others were asleep, then quietly let herself out of the cottage. She crossed the ground silently and tapped gently on the store door. 'Edward, are you awake? It's me, Amy.' She waited in the darkness, and then tapped again. 'Edward, it's me, let me in.'

The door creaked open and Edward peered blearily out from behind the door. 'Oh goodness me, just give me a minute to pull on my pants,' he said, half awake, but Amy slipped into the shed and closed the door.

'I can't wait out there, Edward, someone will see me,' she said as she groped her way in the darkness. Edward fumbled for his matches and lit the candle. Amy tried not to look at him as he stood, half asleep and slightly bewildered, in his long flannel combinations, which pulled tightly round his paunch. She eased past the few half empty sacks and wooden crates and sat on his straw mattress, pushing aside the rumpled sheets.

'I had to come and see you. I couldn't talk to you in front of the others. I really have missed you, Edward,' she looked coyly up at him.

'Err, well. Yes, I have missed you too, my dear, but I don't think your mother would be pleased if she knew you were here with me in my, err, underwear.' He blushed scarlet as he rubbed his greying sidewhiskers.

'I know, but I really had to see you. I've been so lonely,' she pouted, and patted the mattress beside her. 'Come and sit down and talk to me.'

He lowered his portly frame and sat, pulling the sheet over his knees.

Amy let her hair waft against his face as she leaned forward to take his hand. 'I thought you were never coming back, that you'd forgotten all about me,' she gazed into his eyes, still holding his now trembling hand. Her soft white skin gleamed in the candlelight as he brought his weather beaten face down to kiss her. Her arm slipped around his neck and she clung to him passionately.

Thoroughly aroused now, he ran his hands through her long hair, her breasts pushed against his flannelled chest. He felt his thighs throbbing powerfully. He eased her back onto the bed, as she still clung to him. Releasing her hands he fumbled under the sheet.

Looking up he saw her eyes wide with fear. She quickly drew herself up into a tight ball.

'Oh no, Edward! Stop it. You mustn't. We're not married!' She put her hand over her mouth and stared at him in horror. He stared back in bewildered amazement. He felt his magnificent erection wither and droop. Angrily he stumbled off the mattress and pulled on his moleskins, snapping the elastic braces sharply as he pulled them over his shoulders.

Amy sat, hugging her nightgown tightly round her, tears rolling down her cheeks. 'I'm sorry,' she sobbed. 'I didn't know – I shouldn't have come. Edward, don't be angry with me. I only came bbecause I wanted to see you,' she wailed.

Resignedly he handed her his handkerchief, and said gruffly, 'Come along, pull yourself together. No harm done, but you really can't expect to creep into a man's bed in your nightdress and not have him think you want seducing!' He took her hand and pulled her to her feet.

'You're not angry with me are you?' she wheedled, in full control of herself once more. 'It's not that I didn't want to, but I really couldn't. It will be different when we're married, Edward, I promise.' She stood like a little girl before him, with her loose hair and long white gown, imploring his forgiveness.

His anger faded and he placed his hands on her shoulders. 'You'd better go back to bed now, and don't tell anyone this happened, there's a good girl.' He kissed the top of her head and eased her out of the shed. Returning to his bed, he blew out the candle, and spent the rest of the night tossing restlessly.

The next day, Amy and Edward strolled sedately around the mission as if nothing had happened, Edward politely admiring everything.

Grace watched them, as she walked over to where Henry

was putting the last nails into the rough sapling holding pen.

'Lucky we had these nails left over,' he commented as she approached 'Shouldn't twist too much. This cow is a real Godsend, Mother, and the calf's a bull, so we can either breed from him later or use him for meat.'

'Speaking of Godsends, Henry, what has happened to our supplies?' Grace demanded firmly.

'I couldn't mention it in front of Edward, Mother, but I'm afraid it's bad news. They want to close the mission! Can you believe that? I wired Sydney immediately, and told them just what I thought of the idea! The outcome is, we've been cut back a bit that's all,' he added apologetically.

'Cut back? By how much?' Grace's brow furrowed.

'Well, we're still to receive my salary and a bit extra,' Edward hedged.

'How much?' she demanded, glaring at him.

'A pound a month, and feed no blacks,' he blurted out, hanging his head.

'What? We cannot manage on that.' What about the Townsville Mission Society? Are they sending us extra?' Grace asked hopefully.

'I don't think so, Mother. In fact they have stopped sending anything. They have closed their doors on us.'

Grace flushed scarlet, her hands went to her hips. 'It's impossible, Henry. We will just have to close the mission,' she shouted.

'No I can never do that. We are needed here. We can't just walk away from these people now. God sent me here Mother, and here I will stay until He tells me otherwise. Have faith, Mother, we must have that or we are nothing.'

'Faith won't feed empty bellies, Henry. You sound just like

your father,' she accused him coldly, as she turned and stormed off.

Grace seethed. Her Yorkshire common sense told her that five pounds a month was not going to feed all these mouths, and things were going to get much, much worse. She marched angrily back to the house passing the Aboriginal girls doing the laundry at the creek. They were laughing hilariously as one of the older girls displayed a pair of Grace's best white bloomers. Her anger boiled over, and she took her mood out on the feckless laundresses. 'Stop wasting that soap. It all costs money, you know, and when you've finished there the vegetable garden has to be watered. We will have to plant extra as it is, or we will all starve. And you can tell those camp blacks that if I find any more vegetables missing, I'll be down that camp with the carbine, so they'd better look out!'

The girls put their heads down in silence. They were learning not to cross Grace these days.

Still fuming, she walked back to the house, where Amy and Edward sat talking heads close together. Maybe it wouldn't be a bad idea if Edward proposed, Grace mused. He seemed interested enough. Of course, he was older. When Grace thought about it, he must be about her own age, older maybe, but he was comfortably off, and seemed of solid character. Amy could do worse; perhaps he could exert some influence on their behalf with the business people in Townsville and Cairns. They were certainly going to need all the help they could get. Yes, it would be worthwhile encouraging the match, but very discreetly, of course.

As she reached the cottage, Henry caught up with her and handed her a key. 'I think we had better start locking the store. I've put a padlock on the door. Oh, and I placed the advertisement for an assistant with my articles. It should be in the Mission News this month.'

'If someone is crazy enough to reply to it, I'll eat my hat,' snapped Grace as she attached the key to her belt.

The last evening of Edward's visit brought things to a head. They were discussing their proposed visit to Townsville, Amy pushing the conversation in that direction for all she was worth. 'Really, Mother, it would do you good, and Barney, the sea air on the boat, and just think of being able to be in a town and live in a house even for a short time. I'm sure you would enjoy it.'

'Yes dear, I'm sure you're right, but one simply doesn't sail off without some preparation. You know how hard it would be for Henry if we went; and besides that, Edward isn't a relation of ours, not someone we can expect to allow us to spend weeks under his roof.'

Edward saw his opening, coughed and cleared his throat. 'I was waiting to talk to you about that, Mrs Grimshaw. Err, as you must have noticed, I have become fond of Amy, and I do believe she holds me in some esteem. I haven't spoken to Amy about my feelings as yet. I felt I should approach Henry here first, but since you have raised the subject, I'd be honoured if you would consider me as a future husband for your daughter.'

Amy looked swiftly to her mother's face. It was blank and expressionless, giving away nothing. She glanced at Edward, his face flushed with embarrassment. She would have preferred a romantic proposal in the moonlight on some far distant terrace, but at least here was her chance, and she wasn't prepared to lose it.

'Really Edward, this is such a surprise to me! I am quite breathless,' she simpered.

Ellen raised her eyebrows in amazement; there really was no end to her sister's guile.

'I am surprised too, I must say, Edward,' Grace said primly. 'I had no idea you were planning on stealing our girl away. We would have to give this serious thought, Henry and I. I could not give you an answer immediately. We would have to discuss it.'

'I fully understand, Mrs Grimshaw. I only made so bold, this being my last night with you. It will be some time before I will be able to come back again. I felt I had to broach the subject before my departure. I hope you understand,' Edward rose, 'I will retire early to give you a chance to discuss the matter.

'Maybe you will be able to give me an answer in the morning before I leave. Goodnight dearest Amy. Goodnight all.' So saying, he beat a hasty retreat to the storehouse, and pulled out a bottle of rum from his pack. After a couple of good swigs he felt calmer, and undressing settled down for the night.

They wouldn't refuse him, he felt sure, but they had to play their little games of breeding and etiquette. 'My God, I feel tired, getting too old for these silly games,' he mumbled to himself as he undressed.

As soon as he had left the house, Ellen was ordered to bed.

The three remaining sat at the table, Henry broke the silence. 'Amy, I'm sure you must realise that Edward has paid you a great compliment tonight, by asking for your hand in marriage. It is my duty in place of Father, to decide what is best for you. Mother and I pride ourselves, on being modern and liberal in our outlook when it concerns you girls and your wishes must be considered.'

'Amy dear,' interrupted her mother, 'do you wish to marry, Edward? '

Amy hesitated, now the decision had to be made, and made for life. All her play acting and flirting would no longer suffice; this was reality. Suddenly, Amy felt very frightened, and very young, and not too sure at all. 'I don't really know, Mother. I'm flattered as Henry said, but if you think I shouldn't.' She looked hopefully into her mother's eyes.

'I didn't say that, child. I think Edward is an admirable man, slightly more mature than you, well, quite a bit in fact, but he would be a steadying influence on you, and provide you with a good home for the rest of your life. That's a very important point to consider. Romantic nonsense doesn't provide security. I feel you have made a wise choice.'

'But, Mother, I haven't really and truly decided for sure, yet,' Amy felt things moving much too fast for her to cope with.

'Well, dear, you can't keep a man like Edward dangling on a string. He will expect a reply in the morning.'

'Perhaps we should demand a long engagement,' suggested Henry, 'that would give you time to get used to the idea.'

'Oh, it is not that. I do want to get out... I mean marry Edward. It's just, oh. Yes. An engagement of six months won't be too long to keep him waiting, will it? And I have to get my trousseau together and order my wedding dress.'

Henry and Grace winced at the mention of more money to be outlaid, but they knew it would have to be found somehow.

Edward was informed of the family's decision as he packed ready to depart on the following morning. He acted suitably surprised, and joked that he would be sailing back in six months time to claim his prize. He kissed Amy lightly on the forehead, in front of the family, and Ellen, remembering the passionate clinch aboard the boat, was the only one not deceived by the hypocrisy. Henry took Edward back to Cairns on the early tide.

Amy now positively sparkled, the fear of her commitment being overcome by her excitement, at the prospect of being star performer at a wedding, her wedding, and the lady of the house in Townsville. A backwater for sure, isolated from the capital by eight hundred odd miles, but high society indeed after nearly a year of being buried alive.

Amy received a letter from Edward, asking that Henry take her to a jewellers shop in Cairns, where arrangements had been made for the fitting of her engagement ring. She was beside herself with excitement, and nagged Henry unmercifully, until they sailed into Cairns, where the jeweller displayed on a black velvet cushion the ring Edward had chosen for her.

It was a huge sapphire with a diamond each side, and studded with tiny seed pearls. After the ring was adjusted in size, Amy wore it back to the mission in triumph. Grace cooed over it, but Ellen privately thought it ostentatious and just another example of Edward's bad taste.

The weeks passed steadily as Christmas approached. On Christmas Eve, Henry held midnight service, which was especially beautiful, the schoolroom being decked out with palms and flowers. The midnight sky was studded with diamondlike stars on a deep purpleblack velvet cloth, and it was easy to imagine the three wise men and the star of Bethlehem. The Aboriginals attended the *Rev'and Farder's* corroboree in great style.

Dressed in their best outfits, which ranged from Grace's home sewn dresses to old moleskins chopped off at the knees;

sailors' jackets pilfered from the town and an amazing array of hats, from maid's dust caps to a pith helmet, all worn by the men. One young fellow sported a lady's camisole, which Grace eyed with suspicious recognition, but the prize for originality had to go to the small dapper black, who was naked, except for an illuminated religious text threaded onto his lap-lap, which glistened as he walked, flashing the message, 'The Lord will Provide,' for all who cared to look.

Ellen's Christmas presents to the family were a bouquet of beautiful purple bush orchids for her mother; a spear, crafted for her by one of the old men in the camp, for Henry's artefact collection; and a beautiful fine hair belt for Amy, that had been given to her by Maisie's Aunt. She would have loved to keep it herself, but desperately wanted to give each a present. She had made Barney a toy boomerang, which he loved waving over his head, attacking any poor creature that dared creep into the camp.

The Christmas carols were sung with great gusto, Henry having spent weeks organising a choir of sorts. 'Away in a Manger' and 'Silent Night' rose with beautiful simplicity from the jungle clearing, bringing tears to Ellen's eyes.

The feast next day was pretty poor, with Henry cooking a damper from the flour he had bought with his measly funds. Even this was a real treat nowadays. In addition, each man received a twist of tobacco.

Suddenly, and unannounced, the wives of King came swaying into the mission clearing, carrying wooden platters, on which rested huge bush turkeys, roasted to perfection in a fire pit. The children ran in front, laughing and pushing, to be at the front of the queue.

The roast was accompanied by woven baskets full of

granadillas, sour-sops, and baked yams. Even Grace had to admit that it was delicious.

*

After Christmas the family settled down to 1894, which was to be an even harder struggle than 1893. The cow did not thrive and the calf caused Henry much concern as it became listless and poor. Cattle didn't fare well in the tropical humidity.

January brought more rain. Wild storms ripped along the coast, felling trees, and lifting some of the shingles from the schoolhouse, but luckily no cyclone headed their way. Rain soaked the ground and the vegetables died where they stood, roots rotting in the mud. As food supplies dropped even lower, Grace had no choice but to overcome her revulsion of the 'heathen' food. Henry kept them in meat by shooting kangaroos; they roasted the legs and made soup from the tail, which resembled ox tail.

The blacks, came with dugong which they caught hunting in their twoman ironbark canoes. The dugong was butchered and the steaks divided between the clans, enough for the whole camp. The fat was rendered into oil and used for cooking; it was also greatly prized as a hair and skin treatment. Nothing whatsoever was wasted. Henry's salary was stretched to buy only the barest essentials from the general store in Cairns, where his credit account was always in the red, as he took what little money he had to pay the backlog only to fall into debt again with the order for the next month's supplies.

Grace painstakingly unpicked her own wedding gown, which she had taken with her on all her many moves, never being able to bear to part with the loveliest dress she had ever owned.

It was a crinoline, with yards of self-spotted muslin, over heavy silk. She had had to discard many yards, which had become mildewed from being stored. Every night she patiently cut, tacked and sewed, straining her eyes, having only the light of the oil lamp to work by. She created a simple, elegant gown, styled in the high busted Empire fashion, using the silk to line the bodice and form an underskirt, while the soft muslin was draped into an interesting overskirt, and a flowing train.

Using all the skills she had learned from her mother, an expert needlewoman, she cut and appliquéd a spray of silk orchids onto a shoulder and down one breast. The material, slightly yellowed and mellow with age, took on an antique look that blended perfectly with Amy's sun-streaked hair and tanned complexion. It was a dress to be proud of, and even Amy, who was dismayed when she realised her wedding dress was to be made from second hand material, was delighted with the result.

Grace had to forbid her from trying it on anymore, as she feared it would be dirty before the event. It was carefully covered with sheets and hung in the bedroom. Camphor balls placed in little cloth bags were hung with it to keep any moths or other pests at bay.

*

The weather started to cool off with the approach of the tropical winter, and the climate turned to perfection. Nippy mornings developed into warm days, with fresh breezes blowing pleasantly from the sea.

The mosquitoes faded as the muddy ground dried up, and

living conditions became pleasant. It was a delight to curl up under a blanket at night, and feel the tip of one's nose get slightly cold, in the early mornings.

The weather brought new demands on the family, as the Aboriginal girls needed blankets and warmer dresses. Henry was pondering this problem as he planted vegetable seeds for the coming season when he heard a voice calling from the beach track.

'I say! Anyone there?' the voice called again, and a tall thin young man came into view. He wore a dark suit, waistcoat, and white shirt, tie neatly knotted under the starched collar.

Henry aware of his own patched, mud stained moleskins, and his collarless clerical shirt, groaned, 'What a time for visitors.'

'Hello,' the visitor greeted him, as he climbed across the rows of vegetables. 'I think the boat has dropped me off at the wrong place. Could you tell me if there is a mission in this area?'

Henry smiled and replied, 'This is it. You're standing in its vegetable patch.'

Placing his Gladstone bag on the ground, the new arrival looked around, taking in the rough buildings and primitive conditions. 'Is it really? Gosh, what a challenge. I'm looking for a Mr Grimshaw. I've come in answer to his advertisement for an assistant. Do you know where I might find him?'

Henry gaped, open mouthed, unable to answer, his eyes absorbing in dismay, the young man's frail build, and pale sickly complexion. He hadn't expected a miracle, but surely the Lord could have found him a stronger, healthier looking specimen!

'I'm Henry Grimshaw. Have you really come to offer your

services?' he asked doubtfully.

'Oh yes, definitely. As soon as I read the advertisement, I knew it was just what I was looking for. The position hasn't been filled, has it?' the man asked anxiously.

Henry shook his head in disbelief. 'You do realise we can't pay you, and the conditions, as you can see, are far from ideal. To tell the truth, you don't look strong enough to stand the life here. It's very physical work, and poor food; the climate in summer is a killer. Are you sure you could tolerate it?'

'It will certainly be different. I worked in a bank in Sydney and I hated it, the same thing day after day. I saw your advertisement in the church news and I knew immediately it was what I wanted. To give some purpose to my life, do something to help these poor devils. I lived with my widowed mother until she died. Then I lived alone in that big old house so I sold it and used the money to finance my trip here and purchase stores.'

'I promise I will give it my best try. I have been ill, but the fresh air and physical work may be just what I need. I understood from the advertisement that there would be no remuneration, and I came quite prepared for that. The stores I purchased in Cairns are sitting on the beach now. Do you think someone could give me a hand up with them?'

Henry strode out down the track, with the young man trotting nervously behind. 'I say, my name is Reid, Laurence Reid. Is it going to be convenient for me to stay?'

Henry stopped so abruptly that Reid walked into him. 'I'm so sorry. I must appear rude, it's just that you have come as quite a shock, and I think my mother will be duty bound to eat her hat.'

On the beach stood a mountain of drums, crates and canvas

sewn bundles. Henry called to the boys who were examining the treasure dumped on their shores. 'Hey you boys start carrying Mr Reid's luggage up to the mission. I think you must have arrived in Noah's Ark, Mr Reeves.'

'I'm sorry if it's too much but I didn't know what to bring, and I couldn't leave my books behind. I brought my tools, too, thought they would come in useful. Do you think a year's supply of foodstuffs will be enough? I wasn't sure, so I bought six drums each, of flour, sugar, rice, tea, a side of smoked ham, and two crates of bully beef. Does that sound adequate?'

'That, Mr Reid sounds marvellous.' Henry slapped the mild mannered man heartily on the back. 'You are indeed a Godsend! Come and meet my family. I'm sure you are just what they need.'

Thus Laurence Reid started his life as a missionary's assistant. He was so eager to please, he jumped at Henry's every command. He would not be spared the heaviest, hardest or dirtiest task. His natural gentleness soon won him the hearts of the Aboriginal women, and, in time, the respect of the men. To him, they were little lost children, to be guided, and gently admonished when they did wrong.

Henry, who was made of much sterner stuff, determined to speak to Reid later, as to the cunning and manipulation the Aboriginals were capable of.

With enough food in the storeroom now, and less work on her shoulders, Grace began to relax a little, and take a happy interest in Amy's coming wedding.

Edward had written to suggest that the ceremony be held in Townsville and Grace agreed with relief. The date was fixed for September, before the hot weather was in full swing, or the rainy cyclone season could put a stop to their departure from the mission.

Ellen ignored her sister's performances, and point blank refused to be a bridesmaid, no matter how her mother bullied and bribed her. She ignored the fuss, and carried on teaching the little ones at the school, and undertook most of the clinic roster. She found that most of the Aboriginal children suffered from ear infections and gastric troubles. The ear she treated with warm olive oil, and the gastric with a corn flour and water mixture, which surprisingly, met with some success.

She treated the children's ringworms, that blossomed in profusion in the humidity, with a plant that Maisie had shown her. She would scratch the circle of the infection and squeeze the white sap from the special bush onto it. The poor little souls would jump up and down as it stung them, but after a couple of treatments the ringworms would disappear. She even learned from Henry how to stitch up a wound using cotton twine and bag needle. The camp men preferred to pack their wounds with charcoal ashes from the fire, much to her mother's disgust; but she had to admit, they healed up just as well.

Laurence soon settled in. Grace regarded him as a gentleman and went out of her way to be pleasant to him. Barney adored him as he was allowed to climb onto Laurence's knee and listen to the ticking of his pocket watch. He would draw pictures for the boy, and became a father figure in his small life; a position Henry could never have filled, with his impatience and driving vocation. Everything else had to take second place to that.

Ellen found Laurence pleasant enough. He listened eagerly as she explained the Aboriginal way of life and told him the Dreamtime stories she had heard in the camps. He concurred with her that if ever any good was to come from their work, it would have to be through mutual understanding, not forcing an alien culture upon the Aboriginals.'

It was to Henry that Laurence was the greatest boon though, as over the months he became his friend, workmate, confidant, and brother; listening, learning, never lagging behind, even if it took him twice the effort to keep up. In Laurence, Henry had found someone with whom he could share his hopes and dreams, a quiet and steadfast companion, something he had never had before.

Henry and Laurence now spent hours each night planning the building of their most ambitious project yet, the church. They drew dozens of plans, each one being more elaborate than the one before. Henry's eyes had gleamed when Laurence had unpacked his toolbox: hammers, planes, set squares, finely sharpened saws, even chisels, clamps and mortars.

When Ellen's seventeenth birthday arrived it was Laurence who arranged a surprise party. Grace had used the spare material from the crinoline to make Ellen a simple muslin dress, as a birthday present. It had a fitted bodice with puff sleeves and gathered skirt. Henry had spent money from his little hoard to buy a blue satin sash and Amy rethreaded her old blue beads to make a dainty choker.

Laurence went to Cairns and bought her a tiny bible, backed in mother of pearl.

They all insisted that Ellen change into the new dress immediately, and when she walked into the evening light, everyone stopped talking, and stared at her transformation. The dress fitted perfectly, her small breasts filling the bodice and showing a little cleavage. The blue sash round her slim waist pinched in the gathered skirt, which flowed to the floor in a cloud of softly floating cream. The little choker matched the colour of her vivid blue eyes. She had piled her hair up and pinned it in place with her grandmother's jet combs. Soft curls fell onto her forehead, and long tendrils hung down her neck. No one had ever realised before that Ellen was quite beautiful. Even she herself was unaware of the fact as she walked shyly towards the group.

Henry spoke first. 'Ellen, you look lovely. Who would have thought our wild little duckling would turn into a beautiful swan?'

'Oh Henry, stop teasing me. I feel fool enough, all trimmed up like this but I'd like to thank you all for my dress and everything, and the bible, Laurence. It was very kind of you all.'

Laurence couldn't take his eyes off her, and as he followed her around, helping fill her plate, holding the little wooden seat out while she sat, he felt he had never known a girl so unspoiled, honest and lovely.

He fell deeply in love with her that night, and was to remain so, for the rest of his life.

*

After that evening, Laurence made excuses to spend more time with Ellen. He would accompany her at any chance he could, be it in the schoolroom or weeding the garden, as long as she was there.

Ellen, blissfully unaware of the turmoil she was causing her brother's friend, for that was how she thought of him, accepted his company easily enough, although at times, she would have preferred not to have to share the solitude of the rainforest with anyone, but as Laurence was quite happy to walk silently by her side, she didn't feel she could refuse his company.

The ever-watchful Grace could see which way the wind was blowing, and was content to let nature take its course. She decided if anything did come of the friendship in time she would be quite pleased. For the moment there was no hurry, and to push Ellen into anything would only make her back up, and run in the opposite direction.

*

As the date of the wedding approached, it was arranged that Laurence would hold the fort at the mission while the family journeyed to Townsville to attend the wedding, and spend a few days settling Amy into her new home, before the bride and groom left for their honeymoon in Brisbane. The family would then return to the mission.

The arrangements sat happily with everyone, until a cable arrived instructing Henry to go forthwith to Sydney, to be ordained. Grace was very upset. She wouldn't be able to attend the most important ceremony in her son's life. His efforts had finally been recognised.

A letter from the Bishop followed the cable asking Henry to break his journey south at the Aboriginal settlement, on Kalangari, an island north of Brisbane, where there were administrative troubles. The government had approached the Anglican Church, with the suggestion that they form a mission there. Henry was to investigate.

Flattered that such eminent people had sought his advice, Henry replied, that as he already had plans to visit Townsville to attend his sister's wedding, he would carry on down the coast, and inspect the settlement on the way to Sydney for his ordination. He would be in the company of his mother, who would be able to give valuable advice as to the situation of the women, following her experiences at the Bibiringda mission. He also advised that his sister would be travelling too and he would expect the church to meet their travelling expenses.

He was overjoyed when he received a telegram confirming his proposal, enabling him to offer his mother the first real break she had had for years, and with all expenses paid.

In great holiday spirit, the family embarked on the voyage to Townsville, with wedding dress and trousseau box, filled with new nightgowns and hand made linen, not in great abundance, but well made and elegant.

As he watched the boat sail, Laurence secretly missed Ellen already.

*

The wedding was a great success. Carriages were hired to take the guests to the new church built high on the hill overlooking the sea and Magnetic Island.

On the family's arrival in Townsville Barney had been handed over to Nellie, one of Edward's servants who would act as his nursemaid for the duration of their stay in Townsville. Giving Grace a real holiday and welcome rest from the demands of a small child and she was free to enjoy the wedding unhindered.

Most of the town's influential citizens attended, dressed in their best finery. After the service, as the bride and groom posed for photographs and the assembled guests chatted, the officiating Minister took the opportunity to introduce Grace and Henry to the variety of guests who stood waiting. One young girl simpering for Henry's attention, asked 'How many niggers do you have on your mission, Reverend Grimshaw?'

'About sixty or so, it's hard to say. They come and go, but we have many children attending the school, and my mother here does great work with the women, teaching domestic duties and sewing,' Henry answered, embarrassed by her adoring gaze.

'You're wasting your time, if you ask me, Reverend,' said the young girl's father, and a murmur of agreement went around the group.

'They'll never be any different. It's the brain you know. It's too small. You can train them all you like but they'll never be any good.'

'That's right,' agreed another. 'You can't trust 'em, always turn in the end, or go bloody walkabout. If you ask me we should shoot the bastards out, excusing the language ladies.'

'Well, I know I will, if I lose any more cattle.' A third grazier joined in, pushing back his large hat. 'Worse than dingoes they are.'

Henry's face blanched with barely controlled anger. He realised he would receive no financial help from this quarter. 'I'm sorry, gentlemen, I cannot agree with you. We have some fine men at our mission, honest and hard working. I think it depends upon the way they are treated. They are just like children, you know, and you have to be very firm with them. I don't stand nonsense, I can tell you. But I do believe that if we can get them young enough and train them properly, they will become very good stockmen, and domestic servants for you people in the future.

'Of course, they should never have strong drink available to them it destroys them. And they should be paid for their labour in provisions, they could never be expected to handle money.' He stopped, knowing he had failed to convince them, and added, 'Come on Mother, I think we are needed for the photographs.' Taking his mother's arm, he steered her away from the group.

The wedding breakfast was held at Edward's house, which stood on a rocky outcrop high on Castle Hill, and offered views of both the bay and the harbour. Its rambling colonial style was just right for the climate, catching the breezes that swept in from the sea, under its spreading verandas, where the food was spread out on snowy lace covered tables.

Grace and Ellen gorged themselves on: chicken, pastries, pies, fresh strawberries and cream, and huge slices of chocolate cake. It was so marvellous to see a table laden with all the good foods they missed so much that it took all of their will power to walk away, and not make a vulgar spectacle of themselves.

After the toasts were drunk and the cake cut, Ellen found herself very much in demand for the dancing that followed, out on the cool verandas.

Beaming, Edward steered his new wife over to where Grace and Henry were sitting. He looked plumper than ever in his morning suit and grey waistcoat. 'I hope you are enjoying yourselves, my dear Grace, and that everything meets with your approval,' he asked, his ruddy face already aglow with the wine he had drunk.

'It certainly does, Edward, you have done a magnificent job, arranging all this for my daughter.'

'Ah! She's my wife now, aren't you sweetheart?' he said, giving her a big hug and leering grin.

'Really, Edward. Please,' she pulled away in disgust, 'Not in front of all these people. What will they say? I think you've had enough to drink, don't you?'

'Not on your life, darling,' He slurred, 'I've only just begun, come on let's fill your glass. Tonight's the night!' he giggled as he wobbled off, pulling Amy along behind him.

Amy, Ellen, Grace and Henry retired early, as the hard-core drinkers took over the party. The rowdy group got louder, and screams of laughter floated up to the bedrooms.

Some time later Amy heard a stumbling on the stairs as Edward wove his way to his marriage bed. Amy laid waiting in the darkness, the sheet pulled up to her chin. The teasing was over; tonight she would become a woman. She had only the vaguest idea of what to expect, and shook with fear. The money, the clothes, big house and servants didn't look as attractive as they once had. Edward lurched into the room, belching and stripping off his clothes as he went. Amy quaked in terror and hot tears slid down her cheeks.

She felt as though an absolute stranger had rolled into her bed as he reached over and kissed her, his heavy breath reeking of whiskey.

'Come on, take that thing off,' he mumbled, pulling at her nightgown. 'I remember those juicy plump breasts. I've felt them before, haven't I? No need to hold back now, Amy. We're married.'

Expertly he pulled the nightgown over her head, and she lay naked, her face averted as he fondled her. She stiffened, rigid, as his hands went down her stomach and parted her legs. 'Come on, girl. Give me a cuddle. A man likes to feel wanted,' he complained irritably.

Amy lay frozen with humiliation. No one had ever touched her there before. She felt she would die of shame.

Edward grew impatient. 'Oh well, if that's how you feel. Hold still. It won't take long,' he said, as he heaved his massive weight on top of her, knocking the breath from her lungs, he pounded and pushed, grunting all the while ignoring her cries of pain. He gave one final heave of his massive quivering body then rolled away. Mumbling to himself, he settled himself onto his back, and commenced to snore loudly.

Amy lay stricken. A disgusting warm stickiness flowed down her legs. She reached out for the sheet and cleaned away as much as she could, then just lay, not daring to move, as the monotonous snoring droned on and on in her ear.

When she awoke next morning, Edward was gone. Amy crept down the stairs and slipped stealthily into the kitchen, only to come face to face with the plump middle-aged cook.

'Well, if it isn't the little bridey finally come down,' she sniggered to the housekeeper. 'Our Mr Ryan's a right one and no mistake, isn't he?'

Cringing, Amy turned to make a quick exit, when the housekeeper asked, 'Did you want something Miss, I mean Mrs Ryan?'

'Oh! Only a cup of tea, if it wouldn't be too much trouble, please,' Amy answered meekly.

'Righto, I'll bring it in a jiffy. Your sister is out on the veranda.'

'Hello Amy,' Ellen said so normally, that Amy could have kissed her. 'Come and look at the harbour. They are loading cattle over there. Is that where Edward's gone?'

'I don't know. Would you like some tea? I've ordered some.'

'Yes, fine,' Ellen walked over to where Amy was sitting, a ball of misery. 'You don't look too good. Must have been all the excitement of yesterday?'

'Oh, I suppose so,' and before she could control herself she was sobbing bitterly.

'Whatever's the matter, Amy?' asked Ellen, genuinely concerned.

'You wouldn't understand. But it's awful, what happens to you, when you get married.'

'What is?'

'I can't tell you, but never get married, Ellen, men are horrible.' She sobbed hiding her face in her hands.

'You mean when they want to make babies?'

Amy stared at her in horror.

'Oh, it's all right,' Ellen informed her cheerfully. 'I once saw an Aboriginal couple on the beach. I don't suppose it's much different to us. I thought it looked rather lovely really, all that touching and stroking, and they laughed a lot too.'

Amy leaped to her feet with another loud sob and, careering past the housekeeper, nearly knocked the tea tray out of her hands as she ran back to her room.

Ellen sat with a very puzzled expression on her face, then, shrugging her shoulders, leisurely drank both cups of tea.

Edward arrived home, bade a sheepish hello to the family, and enquired about Amy.

'She's up in her room. She's not very well,' Ellen informed him.

'Oh Lord, I'd better go up.' He knocked on the bedroom door and entered quietly. Amy was sitting at the window, and didn't turn as he entered.

'How are you, my dear?' he asked solicitously, as he approached her.

'Go away,' she snarled.

'Forgive me, Amy. I wasn't at my best last night. I shouldn't have had so much to drink.'

'I hate you,' she spat back.

'Please, Amy, let's try to start again, eh?' he wheedled over and knelt beside her.

'You're nothing but a beast. I should never have married you.' She swept her hair away from her face in an angry gesture.

'Try to forget it ever happened, darling, please. I promise I'll never be like that again. Look, I brought you something to say how sorry I am. Here, take it.'

His legs were getting stiff from kneeling, and he rose awkwardly, reaching over to place a cream coloured leather box in her lap.

She ignored it for a while, then, curiosity getting the better of her, opened it. A beautiful opal necklace lay on the red padding. She picked it up, and held it to the sunlight. Vivid flashes of green and red winked at her from the pale stones, held in a heavy antique silver setting.

Edward reached out and fastened it round her neck. 'There, you should only ever have beautiful things, and I will always give you all you ever want,' he promised.

Amy spent the rest of the afternoon wandering through the house; she noted the rich carpets, velvet curtains, beautiful antique furniture and gleaming silver. As she moved from room to room she realised the price she would have to pay to own these beautiful possessions.

At dinner that night, Amy had a new air of confidence, she directing the maids, and smiled charmingly, as the guests admired her opals. She may have faltered on the first round, but she knew now the power was hers. She had learned how to play Edward's game.

Discussion began about Henry's forthcoming ordination.

'We will be leaving tomorrow, Edward,' said Henry. 'I only just managed to get two cabins as it was. There's a lot of people leaving the north just now.'

Henry, Grace and Ellen boarded the steamer for their journey south. Their accommodations were comfortable and Grace was quite happy to put her feet up on a deck chair, be waited on hand and foot, Barney having been taken in hand by one of the stewards.

Henry spent long periods in his cabin, writing reports on the mission's progress, and detailing the programmes he had initiated, to present to the Ecclesiastical Council in Sydney.

Ellen wandered the ship and chatted to the other passengers. She talked with more than one battler family, who had walked off their land, after having suffered a miserable existence for years. They had struggled to clear and stock the grants they had taken up with such high hopes, only to find that the land and the climate were destroying them. In the end they were forced to leave, with only their clothes and a few sticks of furniture to show for all their years of backbreaking work. The women also left behind many tiny graves.

Ellen began to realise that the mission had not seen the only deprivation in this vast untamed area and the plight of some of these poor folk was little different to that of her family's. There seemed to her to be three levels in Australian society; the Aboriginal, the poor whites, and the rich; and strangely her life seemed in limbo between the three. She lived with the Aboriginals, her family were indeed poor whites, and yet socially, they mixed with the rich. Where did she belong? It all seemed so very confusing.

Her first sight of Kalangari Island came just after daybreak one morning as she leaned on the ship's rail. She had risen early, unable to sleep, strung up by the tension that had built up in her throughout the journey, a tension she was at a loss to explain.

As she leaned over the side of the boat, she saw the island in the distance rising high from the water, stretching into the mist on the horizon, its rippled cliffs glinting in the morning sun. The strong wind lashed the turquoise water into swirling, foaming breakers that crashed along miles of white sandy beaches.

The Island, seemed to have an existence of its own, a piece of land which disdained clinging to the rest of the earth, and had chosen to stand alone, self-sufficient, arrogant but beautiful.

It beckoned her, as though it was her destiny, and she was powerless against it. It almost seemed as if all her life had been a path leading her here. The feeling was so powerful that she closed her eyes and turned her back on it. 'How stupid,' she muttered to herself as she walked away.

CHAPTER SIX

The boat skirted the tip of the island, sailed through Broad Bay and into the estuary of the Mariette River, the water turned cloudy brown as sprawling mud flats and mangroves gave way to the river proper. The winding course of the river narrowed as the first houses of Bracefield town came into view.

These elegant residences set on acres of land, with rolling lawns sweeping to the water's edge, were the homes of the wealthy timber merchants. Ellen could see babies, attended by white-aproned nannies, playing on rugs spread beneath shady trees. Boys in sailor suits propelled toy boats between the weeping peppermint trees, which trailed their soft green leaves into the cool water's edge.

The depression had also taken its toll on Bracefield. Timber mills stood idle, their huge steam driven saws silent. Vast rafts of logs floated abandoned, and moss covered the sides of the once busy steamships and barges moored at the timber jetties, their only function now, providing nesting places for the soaring seagulls.

A hired carriage took the family from the wide timber wharf, into the pleasant broad streets of the town. Fine hotels, imposing stone facade banks, and gracefully spired churches, indicated the prosperity the town had once enjoyed.

Men stood in idle groups, smoking and talking, at a loose end without work to give purpose to their day. Grace noticed the women still walked briskly about their business, stopping to admire the tempting goods displayed in specialty shop windows, but few entered to buy and it was only the food shops that were patronised.

To the delight of Grace and Ellen, their hotel was large and stylish, situated conveniently in the main street. After having to make a sea journey to buy whatever they needed, this was indeed civilisation.

Henry immediately contacted the Bracefield Mission authorities, to arrange for his inspection of the failing Barragan Mission station on Kalangari Island, impatient to see the problems for himself, and collate an accurate report to take with him to Sydney.

Grace and Ellen relaxed and made the most of their holiday. They examined the town's shops with keen delight, surprised by the wide range of goods on the shelves after the privations of the mission. They wallowed in the pampering of the hotel dining room where they had a choice of menu, and well-cooked meals placed in front of them by crisp aproned waitresses, happy to indulge their every whim.

After a day or two of this self-indulgence, they began to feel guilty, so took to walking along the riverbank each morning, admiring the riverfront mansions as they went.

It was to one such home the Grimshaws were invited two days later, accompanied by the Rector of the Bracefield church. An afternoon tea was organised by the "Mistress of Springfield", Mrs James McGuffick, who had also invited the prominent ladies of the town to meet the family.

The grey haired, stout matron greeted them warmly, 'Welcome, Mrs Grimshaw, how good of you to spare us some of your valuable time. I'm so looking forward to hearing of your experiences with the Aboriginals up north.'

'I didn't realise that people knew of our work?' Grace replied, surprise.

'Oh yes, we have lectures at the Ladies Circle, and I have read your son's reports in the Mission News. But please come into the garden. The other ladies are anxious to meet you. Such a shame your son could not be with us, but I do realise he must be a very busy man. I'm glad to see we have your daughter's company though. Come with me dear and I'll introduce you to my girls. I'm sure you must have exciting adventures to relate.'

Grace stared at Ellen, and the message was quite clear. 'Don't you dare.' That girl had seen and heard too much, much more than was good for her. Poor Grace never knew what amazing but definitely unladylike stories about the blacks Ellen would relate.

Ellen was introduced to the two Miss McGufficks, Laura and Olivia. Laura, Ellen's own age, was cheerfully solid, with a freckled face, light wavy auburn hair caught up in a green ribbon to match the green sprigs on her summer muslin dress.

She took Ellen's arm and led her down the garden, towards the river. Olivia followed. Slightly older, she was tall and thin, looking grossly overdressed in her pink satin dress, with its huge leg-of-mutton sleeves and a bustle, her manner was affected and snobbish. She complained of the deathly boredom of Bracefield compared with Sydney.

The two younger girls managed to detach themselves from her company and moved away to the shade of the weeping tee tree at the river's edge, where they sat talking and trailing their bare feet in the water.

'What's it like, living on a mission, Ellen?' Laura asked curiously.

'It's not too bad, really. I don't mind it.'

'I bet it's frightening, living with all those natives.'

'No, not at all, I like them. You just have to understand them.'

'Mother says your brother is here to advise on the Barragan Mission settlement. Will you be living there?'

'I shouldn't think so. Henry is on his way to Sydney to be ordained. Then I suppose we will go back north.'

'Do you think I would be able to come and visit you sometime while you're over on the island? I'd love to see a mission. I think you're all wonderful, dedicating your lives to saving the poor Aboriginals. Mother sometimes lets us give the little ones a penny, but not too often. She says it will make them idle.'

'I'm sure my mother wouldn't mind you coming to the island, but it wouldn't be like here you know, no fancy house, or anything.'

'I wouldn't mind that. It would be fun.'

The girls chatted on all afternoon, and arranged to meet the next day.

That morning, Henry had boarded the steamer in the company of George White, Inspector for Police for Bracefield, and John Melville the Brisbane Mission Board's representative.

White was exmilitary, square shouldered and barrel-chested, with a profusion of immaculately groomed whiskers. He wore his navy blue uniform with such pride and bearing, that Henry felt more inclined to salute than shake his hand.

Melville, on the other hand, was frail, and rather stooped, in his shabby dark suit and bald under the un-brushed bowler.

He carried a briefcase and rolled umbrella, which gave the impression that he had just stepped off the 8:35 from Brixton.

They stood by the rails, as the boat made its way out of the river estuary and into the wide expanse of Hervey Bay. The weather was squally causing the steamer to buck and wallow.

Melville whispered confidentially, 'Oh, dear me, it's rather rough, isn't it? I'm not at all used to this sort of thing. I think I might find some shelter, if you gentlemen don't mind. Tummy a bit off, you know.' Henry looked at his greentinged face and had to struggle to keep the smile from his own.

'Yes, of course, Mr Melville. You move inside. The Inspector here can fill me in on a few details about the settlement.'

George White, who still appeared to be standing at attention, flicked sea-foam from his gleaming brass buttons. 'Delighted to, I'm sure, Reverend,' he replied, clicking his heels.

'Tell me, how did the settlement start on the island?' Henry enquired.

'Well, the very first was started quite a few years back, by a Reverend Fallon. He came alone and worked for a while with the Kalangari Island Aboriginals, all out of his own pocket too, so they say.

Henry thought of his father and nodded.

'Didn't last too long of course, same old trouble. The whites wouldn't leave him alone, always after the gins and the young bucks for the boats. Old Fallon did his best, but he was no match for the grog and opium, so he left in the end.'

'Who started the current one then?' Henry queried.

'Anthropologist chap called Marsden, Algernon Marsden. He's still around, but had to give up his position after the Aboriginal Protection Act was passed. Has some strange ideas that fellow! Wanted to take 'em all back to the past, set 'em up in their old tribal ways. Did too; but of course he had the same trouble as Fallon, and once the act was passed well, the Aboriginals were shipped in from all over the state. Ex-criminals mostly, real shifty lot, sent here because they caused too much trouble with their own tribes. If you ask me they should have just shot the lot, nothing but trouble.' White took out his snuff and sniffed a good pinch up each nostril.

'How many are there on the settlement now?'

'Oh, about a hundred and fifty, so Marsden claims, though it's hard to say. Been a few escapes that I know of, but Marsden won't have it. He's very bitter about the changeover, reckons the Aboriginals should be left alone, doesn't believe in schooling or religion for 'em, doesn't want anyone interfering.'

'If you ask me he had set up his own little kingdom over there, and didn't like being ousted. Mind you, kept 'em in line; wasn't averse to using his Snider carbine on them. Still, you'll see for yourself. You'll most likely meet him. He is usually sticking his nose in, and if he's heard of your visit, you can expect him. We should be there in a couple of hours. Fancy a turn round the deck?'

The two men strolled around the cramped ship as it passed Rocky Island lighthouse, and the little settlement of Picerton, where they picked up stores for the island from the five-mile long sandbank, that jutted out into the bay. Buggies and carts were assembled on the end of the bar, to pick up deliveries, or passengers alighting, this being as near as the boat could get to the small town. The steamer then made good headway to the island, and they disembarked three hours later, to be rowed over the mud flats to the settlement.

The three men trudged up the sandy track, the police inspector keeping up a lively narrative, while the wan-looking

Melville struggled on behind.

'How far is it?' Henry asked.

'About a quarter of a mile,' answered the inspector, stopping to mop his brow. 'Starting to get hot again. Still, I suppose you're used to it, living up there.'

'Well, I wouldn't say used to it, but I'm learning to cope.' Henry stopped too, as they waited for their companion to catch up.

At the superintendent's house two constables and a platoon of uniformed native police, all smartly drawn to attention, greeted them.

'Right constable, these gentlemen are here to inspect the settlement. You will assist them in any way you can. Is everything in order?' enquired the red-faced inspector.

'Yes, sir, not much trouble today, eh, Mr Marsden arrived earlier though sir. He said he wished to speak with the Reverend gentlemen when he arrived. I think he's down at the Aboriginal camp now.'

'Oh Lord, is he? Well, send a runner down to tell him we have arrived,' George White turned to his two companions. 'You'll have to meet him I'm afraid. Have a look around, while I check the inventories, would you gentlemen?'

Henry scrutinised the veranda of the residence and the small red building close to it. 'What's that small building, Mr Melville?'

'That must be the punishment cell, I think. The camp is over the other side of the compound.'

'How much land is there?'

'Something like 1200 acres by the survey map, but not much of it is cleared.'

The two men strolled across the sandy, sparsely grassed

compound. No Aboriginals were in sight, but they could hear the distant chatter of children, and the barking of dogs. They headed towards some larger buildings on the edge of the clearing close to where the timbered bush perimeter. Henry made careful note of a good creek that ran beside their path. The noise increased as they approached the camp area, which was surrounded on all sides by squalid humpies. Men sat in sullen groups, smoking clay pipes, watching suspiciously at the visitors approached.

Campfires burned outside every humpy; raggedy children ran in and out; women gossiped in groups, or attended the cooking pots; camp dogs roamed in packs, unchecked.

'Oh my goodness, what a shabby looking place,' Melville whispered nervously, to Henry, who stood surveying the scene. He watched the nearest group of Aboriginals, dressed in dirty oddments of clothing, gathered in a rubbish littered circle, gambling with home made dice. Empty bottles lay tossed aside as they argued drunkenly.

Moving further along, he stopped to talk to a group of women sitting around a fire, one was breastfeeding a baby; another had a small puppy curled up on her lap.

'My name is Grimshaw, Reverend Grimshaw, and this is Mr Melville. We have come to see if we can improve your camp here, and perhaps have a school for your children. Do you think that would be good?'

The women looked at each other; some giggled into their hands, they dropped their gaze and didn't answer.

Henry tried again. 'Would you like a school for your children?' he repeated, not sure if they understood English.'

'Yes Boss,' a middle-aged gin answered. She was cleaner than the rest, and her hair was pulled back into a neat coil.

'Who are you?' Henry asked.

'Bella, Boss.'

'Where are you from, Bella?'

'Brisbane, Boss,' she answered his questions warily.

'What are you doing here, Bella?' Henry crouched in front of her.

'Policeman made me come, but I want to go back my 'usband. He still in Brisbane.'

Henry realised she must have been one of those rounded up off the streets, and sent to this reserve little better than cattle.

'Do you women have trouble here, Bella?' he asked gently.

The other women glared at her warningly, but determined to say her piece, she continued. 'Black police take all tucka Boss, make women sleep alonga 'im if they want food for their children, take any girl they want, even young ones. Mr Marsden give 'em big punishment if they complain.'

Now the others were really frightened, and moved away quickly, not wanting to be involved with this dangerous talk.

'What kind of punishments?'

'Black police tie women to boat, out in water all night with sharks, or beat us with big sticks, tie us in cemetery all night with bad spirits. Mr Marsden, he says men get whipped, locked up in punishment cell lot of days, with no food or water, sometimes they shot with carbine gun.'

'What bad things have they done to deserve this punishment?'

Henry was beginning to see what he was about to get involved in, and didn't like the sound of it.

'Get grog from boats, opium from Chinese, try to escape island. They don't like it 'ere, Boss. They want to go back to own people. I want to go back too, Boss. I work for lady in Brisbane, do good housework, but they make me come here Boss 'cause of new white man's law that all blacks live on settlement stations. Can I go back, Boss?' she asked, tears filling her eyes.

Just then a voice boomed behind him. 'Mr Grimshaw, I presume! Having a little chat with our Bella, are we? Don't believe a word she says. They know only too well how to manipulate newcomers.'

Henry turned to see the striking figure of a man, broad-shouldered, slim-hipped, at least six foot two or three, dressed immaculately in a dark tailored suit, flamboyant shirt, and high heeled riding boots.

'Marsden's the name, Algernon Marsden, late administrator of this dumping ground,' he announced arrogantly.

Henry held his temper, 'This is Mr Melville, he is here to represent the Brisbane Mission Board in our investigation on the feasibility of starting a mission here. You already know my name obviously.'

Marsden scoffed, 'You're wasting your time sir! I have spent three years trying to regenerate the tribal system in this area. I am an anthropologist, with years of experience behind me, but the task is impossible. Once the scum of the white race has tainted these Aboriginals, they are no longer fit for this planet.

'Once he stops speaking his own language, and making his own weapons, he is no longer of interest to anyone,' Marsden declared, turning on his heels and walking off. Henry and Melville followed, while Bella scurried into her humpy.

Henry disliked Marsden on sight, and was hard pressed to keep his voice civil 'I beg to differ, Mr Marsden,' he said as he drew level with the man, 'I have had great success in my work with the Aboriginals in the north'

'Poppycock!' Marsden exclaimed. 'My dear young man, I am talking of twenty years experience, and a lifetime of studying this race.

'They are stone-age people, who have had the modern world thrust upon them, by the very worst of the white race. You religious fanatics come out here, with nothing but your bible and your ignorance, and think you can turn them into upright little Christian's overnight. The only way to save these people is to take them backward, not forward!'

Henry's temper boiled. 'Well, I see very little evidence of your success "sir", even with all your years of socalled experience, unless, that is, you measure success by starvation, imprisonment, brutality, and fornication! That is all I have seen worthy of note so far. Good day to you!'

Grabbing the bewildered Melville by the arm, Henry stormed off towards the superintendent's house, determined now to establish the mission immediately.

'Ah, back already Mr Grimshaw. Seen all you need to?' George White met them on the veranda steps.

'Indeed I have, and seen enough of your good Mr Marsden too! What an insufferably arrogant man he is, telling me I have no experience with the Aboriginals, the cheek of it, especially after the mess he seems to have made of it. I wish to start immediately, Mr White, and I shall need some help from you and your men. And from your committee too, Mr Melville.'

He turned to the now completely confused little man. 'I want you to organise some immediate emergency funds. I plan to place my mother here, in charge of the women and children until I can return and put things in order. That's where you come in Inspector. She will need police protection.'

On his return to Bracefield, Henry related his experiences to his mother and informed her of his intention to begin a new mission immediately. His plan was to protect the women and children first.

'There's quite a nice house for you to use, Mother, solid timber with two bedrooms and a big kitchen. It even has a full-length veranda,' he bribed.

Grace laughed. 'Well, that's luxury indeed, Henry. All right, what do you want me to do?'

'I thought that I would make you matron of the women and children, and leave them in your care until I return from Sydney.

'Ellen could help you. I want you to control the rations. The men are not to receive anything, only the women. Then at least we will know the children are being fed. The men can do without for now, and they may be more ready to listen when I return. If you can hold the fort, I will be able to set up a similar system to the one we have at Bibiringda when I return. What do you think, Mother? Can you manage?'

'I suppose so, but they sound a real mishmash to me. Do they speak English?'

'Yes, quite well fortunately, the ones I have seen. Most of them came from far flung tribes with different dialects, so the only way they can communicate is in English.'

'Would there be any white authority over there I could turn to, in case of trouble?'

'Yes, the Inspector has guaranteed me two constables. It will only be a few weeks, I promise.'

'All right, dear, if it will help. I do like this town, and Ellen seems to have made a friend already in Laura McGuffick.

They have been together every day since they met. I only hope some of Laura's refinement rubs off on Ellen.'

'Yes, we should encourage the friendship,' Henry agreed. 'It will do her good to mix with some of the families here. She's been too isolated.'

*

Ellen again felt strangely drawn by the island as they slowly approached it in the lighter boat. To the left were the towering white cliffs that had been the settlement's first home, but the new site was on Barragan Creek, and only accessible most of the time from the beach.

One of the constables carried her ashore, and while the boat was being unloaded, they walked over the shallow mud flats, to the wide sandy track through the mangroves that led up the hill.

'Goodness, it's like being home,' puffed Grace as she struggled with her long skirts through the deep drifts of white sand. 'Henry can't we find anywhere that hasn't got mangroves?'

He laughed, and took her hand to help. 'Sorry, Mother, they do seem to follow us around, don't they?' He stopped at the top of the track and looked around. 'I think the mission has been dumped here because it's the worst place on the island, though the creek will give us a very good water supply. I don't like the look of this sandy soil, I fear it will give us problems, not like our good rich earth at Bibiringda,' he said running the arid sand through his fingers.

They walked along a lightly timbered track, bordered with sparse bushland, until they came to a large clearing, dry grass sprouting from the sandy ground, and in the centre stood a solid looking timber building, obviously the house Henry had described. The corrugated iron roof looked reasonably sound, with only a few patches of rust.

Grace delighted at the wide veranda, as they walked along it to the front door. The sitting room was quite large, with a kitchen off one end, and a passageway leading to two spacious bedrooms. All the walls were unlined timber and the wooden floors had no covering. Still, this was comfort indeed after the little sapling cottage at Bibiringda.

'We could make this quite comfortable, Henry, if we were staying,' Grace commented cheerfully.

'Yes, I suppose so Mother, but I can't stay away from Bibiringda for too long. Laurence can't manage on his own indefinitely. I do hope he's coping. I must check at the post office when I go over to the mainland. We should have some letters from him by now.'

Ellen was looking out of the sitting room window. 'What are those buildings over there, Henry?' she asked curiously.

'One is the store and tool shed the other is empty. I plan to put the women and children in it, for the time being, until I can arrange something different. It will do nicely as a school when we get organised, but for now it will be the dormitory.'

'Where's the black's camp?'

'Over the other side, well away from the house. You can just see the humpies from the back door if you look.' He pointed them out.

'Now don't you start hanging around there, Ellen. I want you to stay away from the camp. Some of those men are criminals, remember, not innocent natives like our own people. Do you hear me?' Grace warned.

'Yes, Mother.' Ellen sighed, still gazing out of the window.

'What's the small red building at the back for?' she enquired again of Henry.

'That's the punishment cell.'

'Why do you need a punishment cell?'

'Mother's just told you, these people aren't free, Ellen, they can't just leave the mission without permission and a pass; some are dangerous criminals and need punishing sometimes.'

'But surely they are not all criminals.'

'Well no, we have the island tribes as well, what's left of them.'

'Surely they can come and go as they please?'

'No!'

'Why not?'

Henry, tiring of the difficult questions, answered, 'Because this is a reserve especially for them! The Aboriginal Protection Act has placed them here, and here they stay.'

'All of them?'

'Yes, for goodness sake.'

'But that's not fair!' Ellen exclaimed at the injustice of it.

'They're better off here, than hanging around the towns. The mission will be here to educate them and teach them white ways.' Henry said, trying to justify his point of view.

'Then they're prisoners, all of them!' Ellen declared hotly.

Grace interrupted. 'For goodness sake, Ellen, stop carrying on! You heard what Henry said, it's for their own good.' She walked to the door where their boxes were stacked. 'Stop being so annoying and help me unpack.'

The following evening, the constables rounded up the sullen uncooperative women, who had tried to hide to avoid the hated police. Finally, they were shuffled into line, frightened children hanging to their hands or legs, or to the dirty ragged skirts of those women who were clothed. The group consisted of about forty women and twenty children, ranging from tiny babies to teenage girls.

They were marched to a halt outside the new dormitory hut, where Henry stood waiting. They looked at him with distrusting, sideward glances, from under half lowered eyelids, as he addressed them sternly.

'I have brought you here to protect you from the native police, and from the men who are molesting you. You will live in this dormitory and Mrs Grimshaw here will be in charge. You will address her as Matron, and obey her orders. Anyone who refuses to do so will be brought before the constable and punished. You will be given rations daily, enough for each woman and child. *Provided* you carry out the work allotted to you by Matron. Are there any questions?' he waited impatiently.

Nobody spoke. The women shuffled their feet in the sand, and stared miserably over the mission grounds towards the humpies. Ellen, standing next to her mother, felt as embarrassed, and as humiliated as the women.

Henry searched among the dejected group for Bella, believing she would be an ally, but she was nowhere to be seen. 'Where is the Aboriginal woman, Bella?' he enquired.

The women glanced anxiously at each other, but said nothing. Henry singled out one young girl and demanded of her, 'Where is Bella?'

Shaking with fear the young girl mumbled, 'Mister Marsden take her to 'ospital, Boss.'

'What for? Was she sick?'

''e bash her, Boss, broke 'er arms.'

'The bastard!' Henry breathed to himself, turning away in fury as the dejected group filed towards the hut door.

Ellen noticed one girl standing tall beside the others her hair and skin lighter than the rest of the group.

Her arms were folded over the torn man's shirt she was wearing, tucked into a skirt made from old sacking tied at the waist with string. She turned her head as she felt Ellen's eyes upon her, and threw her a look of pure hatred. Ellen quickly dropped her gaze, feeling fearful.

Henry again took control. 'Right, move inside and find yourselves a pallet, small children will sleep with their mothers. Take all your belongings with you, as the door will be locked until six o'clock in the morning. Slop buckets have been provided for your ablutions. Will you take over, please Matron?'

Grace shooed the children after their mothers to the allotted beds, which consisted of coarse sacks filled with straw, set side by side in long lines down the hut. When everyone was standing beside their beds, Grace gave her orders. 'In the morning, I expect you to empty your slop buckets before you line up at the trough outside. You will wash yourselves, and each child will be bathed. You will then be given breakfast. Goodnight girls.' She closed the heavy door and turned the key in the lock. No light was left in the silent shed and a frightened baby began to cry.

Next morning, Henry left for Sydney. Grace was soon busy supervising the washing of the women's hair and that of the children with kerosene to kill all head lice.

The little ones cried as the liquid stung their heads and made their eyes water. Some tried to escape, but the constable was too quick for them, and dragged them back by the ear.

All clothing was taken from the group, and, as the women wandered round naked, Grace supervised the boiling of every article. The sullen mood of the Aboriginal women deepened as they began to realise they had exchanged one jailer for another. This prison was cleaner and the rations more plentiful but it was still a prison.

Ellen walked among them, smiling at a baby, rubbing a child's hair, nodding to an old woman, but they all responded in the same way, shrinking from her and lowering their eyes.

Embarrassed, she walked around, uncertain of what to do next. As she passed a group, the girl with the light hair stuck out her foot and tripped Ellen, sending her sprawling to the ground. There was an audible gasp from the women; this meant trouble.

Ellen picked herself up with as much dignity as she could muster. She knew she had been challenged, and that her position with the Aboriginals would depend on how she reacted. If she caused a scene, the constables would be obliged to order a beating. If she did nothing she would appear weak.

Drawing herself to her greatest height, she faced the girl. 'Seeing as you've got nothing better to do than sit around here getting your feet in everyone's way, I think you should make yourself useful by scrubbing out the slop buckets.' She waited for the groups' reaction.

A titter rose from the women, and she knew she had called the girl's bluff. 'What's your name?' she asked the glaring girl.

'Kalinga,' she replied, looking at the other women for support, but they simply shrugged their shoulders and moved away.

'Well, Kalinga, off you go.' Ellen was determined not to back down.

The women now eyed Ellen with a little less distrust. They knew she had saved Kalinga from a vicious beating at the hands of the black police by not reporting the girl's foolish gesture.

Deloused and wearing dry clothing, the women lined up for the evening meal, which consisted of gluey maize meal porridge, made with water and slopped into tin pannikins.

It looked revolting, but the women did not complain, as they spooned the vile substance into their children's mouths, before eating what little was left themselves.

The sun had hardly set when they were herded back into the stifling heat of the shed, and the door slammed shut and locked. This became the pattern of the first weeks of their "protection".

The men kept away from the dormitory, they knew the two constables had guns, and orders to shoot the first intruder.

At night Ellen would watch the black's campfires, from the back window of her bedroom, the ancient tribal music pulsing into her darkened room. Ellen suspected the music was being played loudly to comfort the imprisoned women. Some evening's fights developed. She suspected these were the nights the sly grog was smuggled in, but the trouble was confined to the camp, and life settled down to a humdrum routine.

As the weeks went by, Ellen grew tired of walks down the track to the beach, and one day her curiosity drew her towards the forbidden Aboriginals' camp. She had not gone far when a dog barked and, afraid of discovery, she turned back.

Without warning, a powerfully built Aboriginal stepped into her path. He wore a neat tracker's uniform, buttoned up to the neck; his grey wavy hair was cropped short. He stood blocking her way, pointing towards the house. She froze, terrified.

'Go!' he ordered in a booming voice.

'I'm sorry. I didn't mean to intrude. I only came to have a look at your camp,' Ellen apologised, stepping back.

'You go, pretty quick. You get big trouble down here!' he barked again. This man was obviously used to being obeyed.

As she turned and stumbled off he called after her, 'You don't come back no time.'

Ellen felt rather foolish. She had been warned to keep away. She walked back home passing one of the constables, sitting in the shade of the punishment hut. 'Hello,' she called out.

'Morning miss, going to be another 'ot one today.'

'Yes, it looks like it. I would love to have a swim.'

'I wouldn't advise that, miss, until the Rev'and gets back, and things is more orderly, then we'll know where they all are, and keep 'em busy. There's some real mean ones amongst this lot.'

'Do you know one of them who wears a tracker's uniform? A fine looking fellow, who seems to be a leader of sorts, do you know who I mean?'

'That'd be Currie Munyabra, miss, there's a few of 'em trackers round 'ere. They got noses like bloodhounds, and eyes like eagles. But there'd only be one of 'em like old Currie. It's 'im was taken down to track Ned Kelly, you know, quite famous 'e was, at the time, so they say.'

'Then why does he live here?' Ellen asked curiously.

'Oh, 'e don't really 'ave to, being a tracker, but some of these people is 'is people? 'e's head of the Tumbula tribe, 'e is.'

'Well, he tracked me all right, frightened me half to death. I didn't even hear him.'

'Did 'e now? Well, I'll 'ave to see 'bout that,' said the constable rising to his feet.

'No! Really! It was my fault. I shouldn't have been near the camp. He was only warning me off.'

'And right he was too, if you went down there; there's some desperate types in that lot, miss. They don't want to be 'ere, you know, will try most anything to get away. If you ask me it ain't right. They served their time, in chains mostly, then they gets sent 'ere for life 'cos some boss cocky don't want 'em stirring up trouble back on 'is land. Still, I suppose these 'ere are the lucky ones, most of 'em gets hung straight off. I've seen it! One cow gets butchered, and they 'auls off arf a dozen of 'em in chains and 'angs the lot, just to make sure they gets the right 'un. I'm no nigger lover, miss, but I reckon you can't blame 'em for some of what they do, best you keep right away miss, really it is.'

'Yes, I see what you mean. I won't go there again.'

'That's the ticket, miss, no good looking for trouble,' he nodded as he settled down in the shade again.

Later that morning one of the timber workers rode over with a bundle of mail for the family, there was a letter from Henry, one from Amy, and one from Laurence. The mail always came like that to people in the bush – a feast or a famine. Grace chose to open Henry's letter first. Ellen listened as she read aloud.

'Dear Mother,

Hope you are managing to hold the fort for me without too much trouble to yourselves. My ordination was a most moving experience, and one I shall remember for the rest of my life. I have had meetings with the Sydney Mission Committee, and we are in agreement as to the methods to be used in establishing some law and order among our new black friends. I am empowered to instigate my mission programme as soon as I return and I have also, Mother, what I hope will be good news for you.

As you know I will not be staying on at Barragan, once I have it running efficiently. One, Reverand Featherstone, will be taking over. There is talk of me being sent to explore the Gulf of Carpentaria in search of mission sites. The Bishop has heard that the Catholics are moving into this area, and he feels we should be represented there also. Anyway, enough of that for now.

I have suggested, Mother, that you remain at Barragan for a while, in the paid position of Matron, and as my representative, to inform me of the progress made, and any difficulties arising that will need my attention. I feel certain you will do admirably in this position, and I know you would appreciate living at least within easy distance of decent social contact, especially for Ellen's benefit. I have accepted this position on your behalf, and hope it meets with your approval.

I have news of Laurence who is keeping quite well (although he wouldn't tell me if he wasn't) handling Bibiringda with his usual enthusiasm and dedication. I will be glad to get back there after the noise and dirt of Sydney. I feel it is my country now, and where I belong.

I will be returning in two weeks from the date of this letter, and will bring the material you wanted for the women's dresses. Are you destined to clothe the whole of the Aboriginal race, do you think?

Your affectionate Son,

Henry

'What do you think of that, Mother, are you pleased?'

'I don't know, Ellen. It will be a change to have a town like Bracefield on our doorstep, and the opportunity for you to be able to mix with girls of your own age. I do like living here, in this house, but I feel we will have our work cut out, taming these natives; they are definitely not the gentle people of Bibiringda.

'You know in these weeks I have made scarcely any headway with those women. They are still sullen and disrespectful.

'They seem to have no appreciation at all for what we are trying to do for them. That girl, Kalinga, is the worst; dumb insolence I call it. I will have to come down heavily on her, I can see. I suppose we can only try it for a while.'

'Open Amy's letter and card, Mother. Let's see how she is enjoying Brisbane.'

The folded picture postcards of Brisbane tumbled out and Grace read:

Dear Family,

Brisbane is very exciting, we have attended the theatre and dined out numerous times and I'm quite dizzy shopping for my new wardrobe, and new additions to the house. Edward is sweet, and bears tolerably well with my spendthrift ways. He spends a lot of time at business and says that as long as I am happily occupied, he is happy too, so no complaints.

We will be returning to Townsville in two months, for the opening of the meat work season. Edward has been very clever buying cattle from the drought stricken areas out west, and agisting them on his good Townsville grassland. He expects to get a very good price for them. I hope you are all well too, and the new mission is not too exacting for you.

Rather you that me, I'm afraid.

Love and kisses to all,

Amy

'Just what I expected,' Ellen laughed. 'She will have bought half of Brisbane if he doesn't get her out of there soon. Poor Edward, he really is a silly old fool.'

'Ellen, really, when will you ever learn to be a little less blunt? I'm afraid you will always call a spade a spade, won't you? It's your Yorkshire heritage, I suppose, just like your grandfather, but it will get you into trouble one day. Mark my words! Now, let's see how Laurence is faring, all on his own, poor man. He will be missing you, Ellen.'

'Missing me? What on earth for? Missing Henry more likely. He's like a lap dog with his master.'

'There you go again, stop being so critical. He respects your brother, for his knowledge and experience. Laurence is a very earnest young man, and is invaluable to your brother.'

Opening the letter, Grace found another envelope inside. 'Look, here's a letter for you. Isn't that nice of Laurence?'

'I suppose so, but I could have read yours.' Taking the letter Ellen ripped open the envelope.

'My Dear Miss Grimshaw,

I hope I have your permission to correspond with you, as I miss our discussions about our black brothers, and your advice, which I hold in such high esteem, and practice daily.

We at the mission here are surviving quite well, and I have taken it upon myself to introduce a few small changes, of which I am sure your brother would heartily approve of.

I must also tell you of my surprise I have prepared for him, on his return. I have had some of the boys clear the site for our new church, and we have already started on the foundations. I'm sure he will be delighted.

I must say I miss all my adopted family very much. How is my little friend, Barney? Enjoying his trip? What a dear little fellow he is, to be sure. Tell him his Uncle Laurence is thinking of him.

And how are you keeping, Miss Grimshaw? I hope the more temperate climate is giving you a refreshing rest, and you will return to us, in the bloom of good health. All our brothers and sisters here ask of you, and your return, I do pray it will be soon.

I remain your obedient servant,
Laurence Reid

'What does Laurence have to say to you, Ellen?' Grace asked knowingly.

'Nothing much. I think he must have a touch of the sun!' Ellen replied, dismissing the letter and carelessly putting it into her apron pocket.

'I'm going to see if the women will trust me to play games with their little ones. I think they still believe I intend to eat them,' and off she strode across the compound whistling.

'A whistling woman, a crowing hen, fetches the devil out of his den! Ellen, it's not ladylike!' the exasperated Grace called after her.

'Amen,' Ellen muttered to herself.

*

Upon Henry's return, he began at once to apply his mission rules. All the Aboriginals were rounded up, men, women, children, the elders, the halfcastes, the native police, the trackers, who by the nature of their skills had a higher social standing than a mission black, but no exception was made; all were assembled in the compound outside Grace's house.

Henry stood on the veranda, Grace and Ellen at either side of him, flanked by the two constables. The native police, in uniform, formed a platoon, and stood so rigid and straight they would have done justice to the Grenadier Guards. Theirs too, was a sought after position, but it was policy to choose them from far away places, even another state, so they would have no bonds of kinship with the local tribes, and no qualms about bullying their fellow blacks.

Before speaking Henry looked around at the miserable group of humanity assembled before him. The men stood grouped at the rear, listless and ragged. Anything that could be used as clothing was draped or buttoned on to keep out the cold wind. Some stood in small groups, maybe clans, maybe friends, or maybe for protection.

Others squatted on the ground, backs hunched, picking

at blades of dry grass or running sand through their fingers. All eyed the guns of the constables. When they were herded together it always meant trouble, and they waited warily.

The women squatted on the sandy earth in the front, children hugged close, trying to keep them warm.

Henry cleared his throat and began to speak, 'Everybody stand up, get up! Come on!'

The ragged shuffling group of people rose unwillingly, and once everyone was on their feet he continued, 'From this day on, this beautiful land here at Barragan is for you. It is now a mission of the Anglican Church. This means that his Grace the Bishop, who is a big boss man with God, will look after you all, like his own brothers and sisters. Some of you have done great wrongs, been very bad fellas, but God is good and forgiving. He sent me to save you and help you. Things have been bad here, very bad, and wicked, but no more. All bad things to stop. No more after today. If you do good, you will get plenty of tobacco and tucker. You have to work hard for these good things. If you do bad: gambling, drinking, opium, or are lazy and won't work, you will be punished. Do you understand?' he paused, looking down at the sea of bewildered black faces staring back up at him.

No one spoke.

'No black can leave the mission. Not go away, never, unless I give you a paper to say so. If you do try to go away, over water, the policeman will get you, punish you, very bad. I want some of you people to come and help me make this good place, to be my assistants. Come out here to me anyone who can read and write.'

The captive audience looked from one to the other, no one moved, until a young black of about twenty, glanced at an old man near him, who nodded, almost imperceptibly. The young man then came slowly forward.

'What's your name?'

'Charlie, Boss.'

Henry smiled. 'What can you do?'

'I can write good blurry name on paper, Boss.'

'Who showed you how to do that?'

'Old Boss and missus did.'

'Did you work for them?'

'Work blurry good, Boss.'

'Why are you here?'

'Don't know, Boss.'

'Were you bad?'

'Yes, Boss.'

'What did you do bad?'

'I 'it Boss's brudder. I 'it 'im good.'

'Why did you hit him?'

Charlie hung his head and shuffled his feet. 'Don't know Boss.'

'Of course you do. Tell me.'

''im very bad, Boss. 'im take my woman. 'im break blackfella law, Boss,' he mumbled into his dirty old collar.

Henry cleared his throat, 'Ah, well, yes. It is very bad to hit anyone, Charlie, but if you can write I will make you my assistant.' Henry dismissed the black quickly to cover his embarrassment.

'Anymore?' A couple more young boys shuffled forward.

'You first. What's your name?'

'Tom, Boss.'

'Where did you learn to read and write?'

'White lady take me when I little fella picaninny, Boss. She very good, Boss. I learn good.' The boy grinned proudly.

'Why did you leave?'

'Didn't, Boss. She go Dreamtime, all gone.'

'Why are you here?'

'Police bring all blackfellas from town Boss, said I had to come.'

'All right, you can be my assistant too.'

And so it went on, until four had been chosen, but not the types Henry really wanted. He needed some elders or some who had power over the Aboriginals. 'I now want anyone who is an elder in the camp, boss fella for you people, to come out.'

No one moved. The elders' faces were stony and blank.

They totally ignored his request, and Henry knew better than to force the issue. 'All right, any trackers here, come out,' he knew that they had the respect of their people. One young fellow came forward.

'Good, you will help me too.'

One of the constables leaned over to Henry, and whispered in his ear. Henry nodded, saying loudly, 'Currie Munyabra, come forward.' Nobody moved.

'Where is he?' Henry asked the constable.

Ellen scanned the crowd, and picked out the neat uniform and trim grey hair, above the heads of most of the other men, his face blank as he stared straight ahead.

'You, Currie Munyabra! Come here, I say,' demanded the constable stepping forward.

The older Aboriginal had started to move when the tall young man at his side placed a protective hand on his arm.

Currie stopped for a second, and gently removed the hand, smiling at the young man's obvious concern. Marching straight ahead to the front of the crowd, he stood at attention, stiffly erect, his eyes looking over the head of Henry. Ellen gave him a tiny smile of recognition, which he did not acknowledge.

'I asked you to come out front, Currie Munyabra, because I want you to be my assistant. Don't you want to be?' Henry challenged him.

'No, Boss.' Currie replied shortly.

'But I hear that you have great skills, and have been as far as Victoria, where your name is respected. Don't you want to help your people, Munyabra?'

'Yes, Boss.'

'Then you will be one of my assistants?'

'No, Boss, my son, he be one of your assistants.'

'Which one is he?' Henry enquired, not pleased by the man's insolence.

Currie stared ahead, as he called out in a calm voice, 'Come up along a me, boy.'

Ellen watched the tall young Aboriginal, who had been beside Currie in the crowd, ease his broad shoulders through the men and step carefully between the women and children. As he passed Kalinga, she smiled up at him quickly touching his leg. The gesture was executed with such secrecy and speed that Ellen felt she must have been the only one to notice.

The young man made it clear to all, by his arrogant stance, that he had come to stand beside his father, not to grovel in front of Henry.

'What is your name?'

'Munyabra,'

'Your English name?'

'Cob, Jacob.'

'Can you read and write, Jacob?'

His eyes narrowed slightly and he looked disdainfully at Henry. 'Yes, I can read and write.'

'You speak very good English. Where did you learn?'

'I've travelled with my father since I was very young. When he was tracking I lived mostly with the white police.'

Henry nodded. 'I see. Yes, that would explain it. You will do very well as an assistant. Does that suit you?'

'I care about my tribe; I will help them.'

Henry knew this was not the answer to his question, but the answer Cob chose to give, and wondered if this man would be trouble. He was obviously intelligent, and his father had power with the tribe. He would toe the line. Like the others, he had no choice.

'Good,' Henry raised his hand and pointed to the recruits. 'These men you see out here are now assistant boss men. They will help you to keep my new rules. I will now tell you what they are.

'6:00 am, bell will ring, you all come here.

6:30 am, morning service, we say prayers to God.

7:00 am, your women will be given your ration for the day. From that time on, all women will return to Aboriginal camp.'

A murmur of hope spread like fire from one to the other.

'But,' said Henry, looking at the women, 'all children will live in dormitory after they are two years of age until they are fifteen.'

The women gasped, and looked frantically to the men for help, pulling their children closer.

Henry went on quickly, not giving them time to gather their thoughts.

'7:30 am, will be staff breakfast.

8:00 am, dormitory breakfast, that is the children.

8:30 am, tobacco serving, for those who have worked hard and deserve it.

9:00 am, the men will work at labouring. The women will work at domestic duties, and Matron here is going to teach you all how to sew your own clothing, the same for the girls who may be lucky and gain a position in domestic service, with a good Christian family.

12:00 pm, you will cease work.

12:15 pm, you will eat dinner.

1:00 pm, staff dinner.

2:00 pm, school for the women and children.

4:00 pm, men's school.

5:00 pm, tea will be served.

7:00 pm, evening classes.

8:00 pm, we will have drill, you will learn how to march, and take orders, salute and have the bearing of a soldier. This is very good exercise and discipline.

'So you will all know when to do these things, a bell will ring, and you will all attend. It will be the first duty of the assistants to see everyone is there. I'm sure you will all enjoy this new way of life, and see yourselves and your children become happy healthy people because of it. Right now, Dismissed!'

The inmates turned to each other with puzzled expressions and a buzz of muttering rose, as they complained bitterly to each other. Ellen glanced at Currie Munyabra, who was watching his son, waiting for trouble.

Henry was chatting with one of the constables, who was nodding his head in vigorous agreement. Currie clamped Cob's arm in an iron grip. The son turned to the father, outrage stark on his face, but he turned with the older man and was led away.

Ellen jumped down from the veranda and called out, 'Mr Munyabra, may I speak to you?'

They both turned.

'Oh, I meant Mr Munyabra senior.' Ellen faltered.

'What do you want, Miss?' Cob growled sarcastically, his arresting brown eyes blazed angrily from his dark face.

'I was wondering, well, I would really like to talk with your father sometime. I'm extremely interested in your culture and have spent a lot of time at Bibiringda learning your customs and stories. I wondered if he would answer same questions for me on the Tumbula tribe?' she lowered her eyes acutely embarrassed under their accusing stare.

'Want to know what makes the abo black, do you?' Cob lashed out. 'Go ask your brother. He has the timetable, just copy that!'

Ellen flinched as the words were thrown into her face.

'Enough.' Currie turned on his son.

At that moment Grace spied Ellen from the veranda. 'Ellen, come up here immediately! Immediately, I say!'

'I will speak words with you another day, miss,' Currie raised his hand in mock salute to her mother and walked away pushing Cob before him.

As Ellen watched them go, she saw Kalinga attach herself to Cob. Turning her head to look over her shoulder, she threw Ellen a venomous look.

The family moved inside for breakfast and Henry sat down with a sigh of relief. 'Thank goodness that's over. I didn't know how they would take it. I was quite prepared for trouble,' he said, pulling a pistol from out of his belt and placing it on the table.

'Henry, you wouldn't have used it?' Ellen stared in horror at the gun.

'Might have had to, there's no point in being sitting ducks,' he answered calmly.

'I didn't like the way those Munyabras spoke, Henry,' said Grace, putting a plate of chops and eggs before him. 'I think you should have been firmer. They were bordering on insolence! You can't afford to let even one get away with such behaviour, or your authority will be lost. Did you notice that Kalinga girl go off with them? She's trouble, that one.'

'Yes, I thought the young man was going to refuse the position when he gave me his tribal name. Munyabra indeed! And he speaks English as well as you or I.'

'Yes, and you my lady!' Grace challenged. 'Just what were you talking to them about? I heard you. Mr Munyabra indeed. They're only blacks.' Her mother slammed a plate down in front of her. 'Come on, tell me.'

'I only asked if I could speak with the elder some time about Aboriginal history. There's nothing wrong with that, is there?'

'Honestly, You'll be the death of me, really you will. Of course, there is, stupid girl! We are in charge here. We do not ask favours of these people. Familiarity breeds contempt, you know.'

'Well, Henry used to talk to King for hours,' Ellen pouted.

'That's different, Ellen. I'm a man and a missionary. It's my place, certainly not yours. Now, I will not tolerate anymore of this. When I go back to Bibiringda you and mother will be here with Reverend Featherstone. What will he think of my family, if you keep up this stupid and dangerous behaviour? I forbid it, do you understand, for the very last time?'

Henry's face was white with anger. 'Do you?'

'I suppose so, but I don't think it's fair.'

'Go to your room, immediately, and don't come out until you can see the error of your ways.'

Ellen rose from the table. 'I could be there a long time,' she mumbled in defiance, as she left the room.

*

Henry sailed for Bibiringda two months later, leaving his programme at Barragan in full swing, supervised by old Reverend Featherstone, who was feeling more than ready for his retirement and a quiet bachelor life, with help from his assistants, and the black troopers. The mission population appeared to be bending to Henry's will, and on the surface, to be running smoothly.

Ellen's social life began to flourish. She was taken under the wing of the McGuffick family. She spent most weekends in Bracefield at their 'Springfield' home. Musical evenings were the vogue, and Ellen found, to her surprise, her strong mezzo soprano voice was much in demand.

She joked that it must have developed through having to sing so loudly to make herself heard over the Aboriginals at the church services at Bibiringda, as she was the only one who knew the words. Her partner at these evenings was an English boy called Andrew Ramford, who was in Australia to study timber, and was heir to a small estate in southern England. He had a wit, and a sense of humour to match Ellen, and they performed comic songs together, which had the other guests in tears of laughter.

Her friendship with Laura blossomed into a deep affection,

but this was not the case with Olivia, who had an eye for the pleasant young Englishman.

Olivia constantly tried to belittle Ellen, with sly remarks about her black brothers on the island, and her home made clothes that poor Grace spent hours making and which put some of Olivia's Sydney models to shame. In all her frills and ribbons, Olivia, could not disguise her rod thin figure and sallow complexion, which was not aided by her acid personality. Set beside Ellen with her simple classic dresses, and her thick dark hair, vivid blue eyes and her fun-loving, caring nature, Olivia was decidedly second best, and she knew it.

The Christmas Ball was approaching and Mrs McGuffick was preparing the guest list.

'Must we really invite the church mouse and her matron mother?' asked Olivia.

Laura exploded. 'How can you be so horrible? You're jealous because Andrew prefers to spend his time with Ellen, and I don't blame him. I hope he marries her! It would serve you right.'

'Girls, girls! Stop bickering. Of course, Ellen and her mother will come, and Olivia, I think you should stop and remember where you come from. Your grandfather was a penniless migrant, don't forget, who sold possum skins and firewood to provide food for your father. You should also look around this town and see how many families, who were our neighbours, have had the misfortune to lose everything in this depression. How do you think they are living now? And don't think it couldn't happen to you. It could, very easily, so be careful what you say.'

Olivia privately vowed that if she could ever do Ellen a disservice, she gladly would.

Grace was delighted that Ellen had been accepted so readily into the town's young social set, and kept her free of duties on the mission, encouraging her to go to Bracefield at every opportunity.

Grace had organised the Aboriginal girls to do the domestic work and had chosen a quiet, biddable girl to look after Barney, who roamed at will. He was healthy and happy under the hawk-like gaze of nanny Rosie.

Laura was invited to the island to stay for a few days. When she arrived, Ellen was delighted to see Andrew was accompanying her, equipped with tent and rifle, obviously intent on camping on the island.

'I say, it will be all right with your mother that I came, won't it? I suppose I should have asked permission first.'

'Of course it will. I'm sure she will want you to come to dinner too, before you go back to the mainland.'

Agreeing to call back later, on Ellen's advice, the boy strode off towards the timber settlement, where one of the island's most beautiful lakes gleamed brilliant blue, the sky reflecting into the clear water causing a mirror effect. It was one of Ellen's favourite places, but she was only allowed to go there, or anywhere else on the island, escorted by her mother or a constable.

Laura immediately settled in, sharing Ellen's bedroom and helping her with some of the small Aboriginal children, who she loved to play games with and take for walks. Not having any work to do these days, Ellen and Laura were free and had the whole afternoon to do as they pleased. Laura wanted desperately to visit the Aboriginal camp.

'We shouldn't really, you know,' said Ellen, remembering the last time, but not wanting to disappoint her friend. 'If

Mother finds out, I'm in for it… come on anyway, may as well be hung for a sheep as a lamb.'

They giggled and crept away, stopping at the creek to watch the camp inmates building a bridge, their muscles straining as they hauled massive slabs of timber and shored them into place.

'Do you know any of them, Ellen?' whispered Laura.

'No, not really. I'm not allowed to mix like I did at Bibiringda.'

'Look at that handsome fellow giving the orders. Isn't he strong! See how he is shifting that log!'

'That's Cob. He's the son of one of the Kalangari Island elders.'

'Isn't he divine?' Laura sighed, pretending to swoon. Ellen laughed, 'Come on, stupid.'

The girls crept quietly away further down the creek, and lay under the trees.

'Gosh, it's getting hot. Let's go for a swim,' suggested Ellen. 'Dare you to skinny dip.'

'What? Here?' asked Laura, taken aback.

'Yes, why not?'

'Well, those natives are just at the bridge.'

'That's all right. They aren't allowed any further than the bridge, and they go the other way back to camp.'

Laura shrieked and flung off her clothes, leaping into the creek. Ellen followed, and they swam lazily up and down for a while.

'Where does this creek go?'

'Into the sea, further up from the mission. You can't see it from there for the point.'

'Shall we follow it out?'

'All right, but it gets a little rough, plenty of mangroves and mosquitoes. Are you worried?'

'Suppose I'd better take my clothes, I'll be eaten alive,' said Laura, mindful of her white skin.

They bundled up their clothes, and waded in waist deep water down the creek, half hidden by overhanging trees and grass. It took them half an hour or so to reach the sea. Pushing through the mangroves was extremely difficult, and they were exhausted when they finally climbed from the water. Bodies wet and long hair soaked, they sat to dry off on the bank before dressing.

'It's really peaceful here, Ellen, this island is like another world.'

'Wait till you see the rest of it, the rainforest and the lakes. There are lakes everywhere. I haven't seen half of the place yet.'

'We'd better get dressed.'

They crept into the dense thicket and sat sorting out their clothes.

'They're a bit crumpled I hope mother doesn't notice. She'd have a fit and never recover if she knew.'

'Can you imagine Olivia's face if she saw us now?' Laura giggled, and they both laughed helplessly. 'I can't get my drawers on. I'm still wet!'

'Well, put them on your head. I've seen Aboriginals wearing them like that!'

'Really? What a lark! Like this?' Laura posed with her drawers pulled down over her auburn curls.

'Silly fool,' laughed Ellen, 'Get dressed. We'll be late.'

Silence fell as each concentrated on buttons, underskirts and stockings.

Suddenly, close by, something splashed into the water. Ellen froze, her mind springing back to the horror of Maisie's death. There was another splash, followed by a scraping noise, and a subdued murmur of voices. The girls stared at each other in terror. Ellen slowly eased herself into a kneeling position, and peered through a telescope like tunnel of undergrowth. She could see a small section of the creek leading out across the flats to the sea.

Two Aboriginals were pushing a bark canoe, very cleverly disguised with branches of green foliage, across the soft mud. They were using it for cover, keeping low, almost crawling, until they reached deeper water.

'Look, they're escaping,' she whispered to Laura, grabbing her hand and drawing her to her feet, 'come on we must get out of here.' She led the way under the bush, and out into the bank, coming face to face with Cob Munyabra!

He and Ellen stared at each other in absolute amazement; she, wet haired, crumpled and covered in dry leaves; he, gleaming naked, except for a small laplap. Their eyes locked in mutual panic until Laura, struggling out from the bush, saw Cob and gave a loud scream.

In an instant, Cob leapt across the creek, and disappeared into the undergrowth.

'Why on earth did you scream?' Ellen demanded.

'I thought he would kill us. Let's get out of here quickly.'

Dusk was rapidly falling as they arrived home, and the 7 pm roll call bell was sounding, as they hastily washed in the bedroom basin, and changed for dinner.

A commotion outside drew Ellen's attention to the window. Native police were running about shouting.

'What's the commotion, Ellen?' asked Laura as she pulled a

clean dress over her head.

'Don't know. Let's go out front and see.'

All the Aboriginals were being lined up in the compound. Reverend Featherstone was pacing up and down, counting and checking names.

Grace came up onto the veranda. 'You girls stay in the house, where did Andrew say he was going?'

'I don't know, why? What's happened, Mother?' Ellen asked anxiously.

'We're not sure yet, stay there,' she insisted, as she hurried off to shoo the children into the dormitory.

The assistants were lined up just below the veranda. The constables jumped down from their horses and held guns at the ready.

'Where have those two blacks gone?' one shouted at the lined up men. 'Did any of you see them escape?'

Ellen looked over the veranda and could see Cob Munyabra dressed in a mission shirt and dungarees, standing in line, his eyes staring up at her, silently pleading. So that was it, she thought. He was helping them escape. Now she understood his unwillingness to be an assistant.

'Escapees! Goodness Ellen, that could have been what we…'

Ellen squeezed Laura's arm so hard she nearly cried out in pain, but the move silenced her. With an imperceptible nod, Cob turned his eyes back to the front. He stood blank faced as the constables ranted and beat him, and other men, around the head and legs with sticks, to no avail. They all remained silent.

Ellen could not bear to watch and turned her face away.

The constables headed off to search the island followed

by the native troopers. All mission inmates were confined to quarters.

*

Reverend Featherstone sat at the table with the three women, Kalinga served dinner silently, all the while alert to the conversation.

'I hope they catch them tonight, Mrs Grimshaw,' Reverend Featherstone quavered, 'but I don't fancy their chances if those blacks have a whole night to get away. I'll sleep on the couch here tonight, just to be on the safe side. You ladies must be protected. They could still be around, though I doubt it.'

'I'm sure we are grateful, Reverend Featherstone, it will make us feel much safer, until they are caught. That's the fourth escape this month! Something will have to be done. We could all be murdered in our beds.'

'Were they criminals, Mr Featherstone?' Ellen enquired innocently.

'I don't think so my dear, but it makes no difference. They must be caught and made an example of.'

The girls retired early, wanting to share their secret.

'He is helping them escape, isn't he?' Laura whispered. 'Why didn't you tell?'

'I don't know really, except they haven't done anything wrong, they simply wanted to escape from this place, I can't blame them for that, and he seemed to sort of trust me not to. I can't really explain. Perhaps it was the look on his face.'

Despite an intensive search of the island, there was no sign of the escapees. After a few days, the tension relaxed, and everything returned to normal. Andrew arrived one morning, with three horses, and asked Grace's permission for the girls to spend the day with him, exploring the island. Grace was more than pleased, and had one of the domestics pack a picnic hamper.

'We'll ride to Happy Valley through the rainforest, shall we, and on to the back beach?' Andrew suggested.

The three rode along the deep white sandy track in single file, through the cool shady rainforest. As she rode, Ellen thought of how her life was changing, here she was, with a new best friend, living the social life of a lady, and with a soon-to-be lord as an attentive beau. How Amy would approve, she smiled to herself.

By lunchtime, they had arrived in an isolated valley, and decided to eat lunch in the shade of the trees, before going down to the beach.

Grace had done them proud with a couple of chickens, tomatoes, crisp green cucumber, thick chunks of bread thickly spread with butter, hard boiled eggs and a big boiled fruit cake. They stood bottles of Lemon Barley water in a fresh creek to cool, then ate until they nearly burst.

'Your mother certainly knows how to feed a man Ellen. That's my idea of a motherinlaw. I'll have to marry you, just for her cooking,' Andrew laughed and rolled lazily onto his back. 'You know, I really love this island. It's different from anywhere else I've been. I might just stay here for ever.'

'What, and have your English castle floated over on a timber barge?' Ellen laughed.

'Oh, that draughty old place. Do you know it's as miserable as sin, all cold stone and dark corners, and the dry rot! The bally place is falling down around our ears. Give me this tropical paradise any day.'

Ellen gazed at the peaceful beauty around her. 'That's how

the Aboriginals must have felt, but now look at what they have – a few acres for a prison. They can't fish or hunt, and it is their island. We just came and took it from them.'

'Mmm! I see what you mean. I heard two escaped the other day. Were they caught?'

'No, no sign of them.' The girls exchanged nervous glances. Ellen jumped up, quickly changing the subject. 'Race you along the beach!' she challenged. They galloped the horses along the wet tideline, which stretched as far as the eye could see, finally disappearing into a surf spray mist. The wind lashed their hair and the sea spray stung their faces. It felt good to be alive.

Ahead, a crystal clear creek flowed out from the cliffs, and they stopped to give the horses a drink.

'This is beautiful,' said Laura, splashing her face and arms with icy fresh water. 'I'm pooped, let's have a rest?

They lay down on the warm white sand, and in no time Andrew and Laura were both asleep. Ellen sat for a time watching the turquoise waves crashing in and out, soothed by the constant movement. Soon, she rose and wandered along the bottom of the wind eroded cliffs, which rose like pinnacles in layers of coloured sand, ochres, browns, pinks, yellows, reds, and even black. They reminded her of a giant rainbow cake.

Suddenly a black apparition dropped from the sky and landed with a thud at her side. Losing her balance, she slid down to the sand, landing ungracefully on her behind.

'Oh Lord, not you again,' she gasped, looking up into the grinning, black face.

Above her Cob Munyabra dropped the sacks he was carrying and held out a hand to help her up. 'Sorry to frighten you, you here by yourself?' he asked her warily.

'Goodness no. I wouldn't get away with that. I'm with my friends. They're both asleep down on the beach.' she replied, taking the offered hand and pulling herself upright.

'Thank you for your silence the other day. You could have had me shot.' He smiled gratefully.

'You are helping the others to escape, aren't you?' she asked him directly.

'Yes,' he answered simply, holding her gaze.

'Why do you stay?'

'This is our island; these are my people. We have to stay for the old people.'

'But you are young. The old people will die soon!'

He shook his head. 'They're already dead, but they still tell us to stay on our land.'

'You mean spirits?'

'If you like.'

'But you have been away for so long. Why would a superstition like that bother you, or your father?'

'It's not a superstition. We always come back to the island, no matter where we go. All of the Tumbula people. We travel with our bodies, but our spirit stays here, so we have to come back for it. What's a man without his spirit? That's what your brother preaches, isn't it? Your white spirits go home to your god, don't they?'

'I suppose you're right, she mused.

He began to gather his sacks together, making ready to leave.

'What's in those?' she asked curiously.

He smiled and opened the bags, displaying the different coloured sands.

'How do you use these sands?'

'I make the sand bottles, you know, ships and castles and horses and the like, and sell them to the travelling show people. The money gives the boys who get away a start on the mainland.'

'What happens to them if they get caught?' she asked seriously.

'Depends who rounds them up, or if they have been in trouble before.' He shrugged off the question and changed the subject abruptly. 'My father says he will speak to you now, if you want to.'

'Will he? Oh, that's fine. There are things I'd like to know about your tribe and the island.'

'He will be able to tell you, he knows everything.'

She smiled at his pride in his father and held out her hand. 'Well, goodbye. I must be going now.'

He almost reached for her hand then drew back abruptly. 'G'day,' he mumbled, settled the sacks on his broad back, and walked away. She stared after his retreating figure before turning and walking back to the beach to wake the others.

CHAPTER SEVEN

'Springfield' vibrated with activity as the household prepared for the Christmas Ball. Screens dividing the two main reception rooms had been removed to create a ballroom; the parquetry floor had been polished with milk until it shone. Crystal chandeliers had been washed and filled with shining candles, which reflected hundreds of sparkling, tinkling, crystal tear drops.

The mill foreman had especially picked the enormous pine tree, which stood in the bay window overlooking the river, winking a Merry Christmas message to the guests as they arrived.

Every chair in the house had been commandeered, and placed around the dance floor and garlands of vines and mistletoe hung on the walls. The morning room had been transformed into a buffet. Tables groaned with food: glazed hams decorated with cloves, crisp skinned turkeys, legs of pork covered in golden crackling, capacious glass cut bowls held sherry trifles inches thick with whipped cream and decorated with cherries and angelica. A chocolate yuletide log complete with robins and holly stood next to the cook's triumph, the Christmas cake. The punch bowl had pride of place on it's own table, where it glowed amber and effervescent with a mixture of brandy, liquors and champagne, floating slices of orange and lemon; guaranteed to lighten the hearts and feet of the would-be dancers.

All the young girls shared Laura's room to dress. They fussed and preened and despaired, as a frill wouldn't sit right, a curl fell down, a hole had appeared in a stocking. Giggling and chattering, they pinched cheeks, bit lips, smoothed brows and lashes with tongue wetted fingers, while some daring ones even used a little powder!

Laura's gown was of cream coloured taffeta, threaded at the sleeves and hem with apricot coloured lace. She wore her mother's amber necklace and bracelet, her golden hair was piled high, held in place with tiny ribbon bows. As she pulled on elbow length, cream gloves she let out a wail, 'I've broken a fingernail, oh, dash!'

Ellen frowned as she stood in front of the mirror straightening the skirt of her dress, and trying in vain to fasten all the tiny buttons up the back. 'Honestly, Mother must think I am a contortionist, expecting me to get into this. How am I going to sit down with this thing on the back?' she complained, pulling at the slight bustle effect created by a softly draped bow.

'Oh, come here. Let me help you. You're hopeless,' Laura chided her, deftly slipping the buttons into the silky loops and arranging the bustle. 'There you are,' she said, looking over Ellen's shoulder into the mirror. 'That dress is absolutely gorgeous, and the colour is just the same shade as your eyes. Gosh! Your mother's clever. She always seems to know just what suits you.'

The orchestra downstairs started to play and the girls grabbed their last minute accessories and rushed for the door, not wanting to miss a minute of the fun. Ellen waited while Laura pinned Ellen's spray of dark red roses to the bodice of her gown.

'Would you like to borrow some jewellery?' Laura asked, knowing Ellen had none of her own.

'No thanks, this is quite enough. I'll compete with the Christmas tree if I wear anything else.'

'Silly thing. You look lovely,' Laura said as she sneaked some powder, left open on the dressing table. 'Darned freckles,' she groaned.

Together, they walked down the curved staircase; their dancing shoes making no sound on the thick crimson patterned carpet. People were crowding every room, and the dancers were already swirling and bobbing to the music. The chairs were filling up with shy young girls and their protective dowager mothers, while old grey haired gentlemen, immaculate in bow ties and tails, stood in groups talking and sipping good whisky.

'There you are, dear,' said Grace as she approached here daughter, eyes checking the hang of the dress, and the sit of the shoulders.

She was satisfied that she had done a good job. Ellen looked lovely, and a credit to the Grimshaw family. 'Where's that nice young man of yours?' she asked. 'You should be dancing.'

'I'm here,' said a voice behind her, and the blonde haired, very English Andrew appeared. 'I've been trying to fight my way through the crowds. You're looking very charming tonight Mrs Grimshaw. I hope I will have the honour of a dance later.'

'How gallant of you Mr Ramford. I would be delighted, but later, dear. Now off you go, you young ones, and enjoy yourselves.'

Andrew swept Ellen into the happy crowd of dancers and they laughed and joked as they danced around the floor.

'You look lovely tonight,' Andrew smiled down at her. 'All you need is a tiara and you'd make a first class princess.'

'Silly idiot,' she gave him a gentle push.

'I'm going home in the New Year. Will you miss me a little?' he asked hopefully.

She stopped smiling and said seriously, 'You're not, are you? I certainly will. You're my best friend, along with Laura.'

'I am, am I? I hoped I'd be your favourite beau.'

'You're my favourite English gentleman. Does that help?' she joked.

'Wouldn't you like to come live in my draughty old castle?' he invited with a grin.

'I'd most likely get rheumatism, or is it gout you rich people get?'

'I am serious, Ellen. Come outside into the garden. We can't talk here. It'll be quieter there.'

They pushed their way past the waltzing couples and through the French doors, which were thrown open to catch the breeze on this hot summer night, and walked down onto the lawn. The night was silky smooth, the river barely rippled, the huge full moon looked as if it would drop from the sky at any moment. They walked silently towards the weeping peppermint trees. She wandered a little away from him, looking back towards the house to see the Christmas tree illuminating the window with a friendly welcoming glow.

'Ellen, would you consider getting engaged to me before I leave for England?' Andrew asked softly.

Ellen turned, startled. 'You're not serious?'

'I definitely am!' he declared, moving to her side.

'You have really taken me by surprise, Andrew. I don't know what to say,' she answered in confusion.

'Well, it makes sense. We get on so well together, and enjoy the same things, don't we?' he reasoned, reaching out to her.

'Well, I suppose we do, but aren't we supposed to be madly in love, or something?'

'I don't know too much about that, to tell you the truth, but I do know you're the nicest girl I've ever met, and I feel comfortable with you.'

Ellen looked at his fine-boned, serious, pale face and knew what her answer would be. 'I'm very fond of you, Andrew,' she said honestly, 'but we come from different backgrounds. I don't think it would work.'

'Why?'

'Well, what about your parents? How would they feel about you choosing a church mouse? That's what Olivia calls me.'

'Oh her, she's just jealous of you. She does nothing with her life. My parents? I honestly don't know; but I don't think we need an heiress to prop up the family finances. We do quite well. If they don't like it I'll come and live in Australia. Will you think about it?'

'All right. I'll think about it,' she smiled. 'Come on, let's go back and join the others,' and she gently led him back inside. As the evening wore on, and the punch began to release inhibitions, there were plenty of volunteers to recite and sing songs, many eagerly remembered from the old country. Kilts were swinging as the expatriate Scots danced over their crossed swords to the stirring battle call of the piper.

Tears filled homesick eyes when the tune changed to the haunting laments of the Highlands. Old men sniffled and drank deep drams of their whisky as memories of loved ones and far-away places came creeping unbidden into their minds. Christmas was the loneliest time of all for these strong, self-sufficient migrant people. The evening ended with carols, and presents from under the Christmas tree.

*

Boxing day was well under way before most of the guests awoke, some still feeling the effects of the night before. A picnic on the island had been organised for the day's entertainment, and hampers were ready packed and loaded onto one of the timber mill boats before the guests embarked. It was a cool breezy day, and the fresh sea air helped to revive flagging spirits. The guests disembarked in holiday mood, laughing and joking as they trooped up the sandy track to the mission, where logging carts waited to take them to their destination at the blue lake.

As the strolling groups crossed the mission grounds, Aboriginal women and children stood shyly under the trees watching the column of picnickers swinging past. The ladies light summer dresses billowing in the breeze, parasols twirled in gay pinks, blues, lavender and yellows, looking like a field of spring flowers. The men followed, dressed in Sunday suits and polished boots, their wide-brimmed hats set at jaunty angles. Between them they carried picnic hampers, and iceboxes filled with food, cold beer and chilled wines.

As she walked past the ragged hungry children, Ellen's happy day soured in her throat. Not for them parties and presents, and scrumptious food. She thought of the miserable hominy, the water based gruel, the mission's staple diet, and felt ashamed. She hurried past, pretending not to see them, and joined the jostling crowd waiting at the wagon. As she hitched her skirt and climbed to take her place, a black hand reached out to steady her. She looked down to see the striking dark face of Cob Munyabra. He smiled a shy, half smile, and helped her into the cart. 'Merry Christmas, Miss Grimshaw,' he said, inclining his head slightly.

'Merry Christmas, Cob,' she replied, feeling herself blush. 'Are you coming to the picnic?'

'I'm driving the horses, Miss, taking your party to the lake,' he answered politely, reminding her of his status.

'Oh, I see,' she said weakly, and hurried to her seat next to Laura.

'I see your favourite black is coming too,' Laura whispered teasingly.

'He is not!' Ellen denied hotly. 'I hardly know the fellow.'

'Well, we always seem to be bumping into him, don't we?' Laura laughed at her friend's obvious embarrassment.

'Righto! Is everyone aboard?' called one of the timber merchant's sons. 'Good!' Leaning forward, he tapped Cob on the shoulder. 'Drive on, boy!'

Cob snaked out the stock whip and cracked it down hard on the backs of the big old draught horses. They leaped forward in fright, causing the cart to jolt heavily, throwing the timber merchant's son onto his back into the crowded wagon.

'Hey steady on,' he called, picking himself out of a mass of tangled legs and hampers.

'Sorry Boss,' Cob called back in an innocent voice. Ellen couldn't resist a smile.

As they entered the rainforest, everyone gazed up in wonder at the towering trees, completely overawed by the beauty and grandeur of nature. The filtering sunlight sent leaf-patterned shadows down upon their upturned faces. Someone started to sing a sweet old love song, and they all listened happily in silence as the wagon rolled on.

Arriving at the lake everyone tumbled out, the young men to one side into the bushes, and the young ladies to the other, to change into their bathing suits. The older women unpacked the hampers while their husbands relaxed, removing their jackets and settling back to enjoy an ice-cold beer.

Cob unhitched the horses and tethered them out to graze. Then, from a respectful distance, he sat alone on the back of the cart watching the swimmers from a distance. He sighted Ellen and Laura, swathed in long pantaloons and frilly caps, giggling and splashing in the water. He smiled to himself as he thought how stupid they looked; these whites had a funny way of enjoying themselves. Left to himself, he would have stripped off naked and dived into the glistening blue water, to swim out across the lake as he always did. *What a commotion that would have caused*, he thought wryly.

He found himself watching Ellen again, as she waded back into the shallows, pulling her cap from her head and shaking out her long black hair. There was something about that white girl... he wanted to seek her out, talk to her, look at her, and that was bloody dangerous ground to be on. *They were all the same, talk to you nicely but think of you as some kind of performing animal.* He had seen the white women eyeing him off when they thought no one was looking. They were no different to the white bosses with their gins. To hell with them all he thought...

*

A week later, Andrew sailed for England. But before he left he presented Ellen with his beautiful bay mare and saddle. 'I want you to have her, she's a lovely old thing and I wouldn't trust anyone else with her. Please take her.'

Tears welled in Ellen's eyes as she stroked the horse's muzzle close to her face. 'Thank you, Andrew. I'll always keep her and remember you when I ride her.' She turned and kissed him gently on the cheek. 'Goodbye dearest friend, and thank you.'

It was the custom of the wealthy northern families to travel south after Christmas to visit scattered relations and to avoid the sweltering heat of summer. So it was that Ellen found herself without the company of her friends and spending more time at the mission.

Instead of the lot of the Aboriginals improving with the introduction of the missionaries, things began to get steadily worse. Reverend Featherstone, not having Henry's flair for stretching the inadequate funding to its very limits, had cut the inmates' rations to the barest minimum. Fear of rebellion made discipline overbearingly strict and the place began to resemble more a prison camp than a place of Christian charity. Hunger brought weakness, which in turn was an open invitation to disease, and they began to die at an alarming rate. Their ration of maize meal and dry bread was only enough to keep the strongest alive. The very old and the youngest were the first to succumb.

Ellen wept in despair as yet another child died. 'We've got to do something, Mother,' she sobbed. 'Let the men fish. We used to survive on fish at Bibiringda, remember?'

'It can't be allowed, Ellen, you know that. Give them half a chance and they'll escape,' snapped the distracted Grace, who was slowly being overwhelmed by the mission's problems.

'Isn't that better than keeping them here to die?' Ellen argued.

'It's their own fault. They're dying because of that confounded white clay they insist on drinking. Reverend

Featherstone has forbidden the practice, and the assistants are supposed to confiscate any they find. Somehow they still manage to smuggle it in. These blacks are hopeless! You can't teach them anything. They simply refuse to listen.' Grace was ready to wash her hands of the whole place.

'But Currie Munyabra says it's good for them,' Ellen blurted out before she could stop herself.

'Have you been talking to that old devil again? What have you been told?' Grace shouted, thumping the table angrily.

'I just asked him why they insisted on drinking the clay, that's all.'

'Well, how would he know?' Grace raged. 'He's as big a savage as the rest of them, drinking clay, to do you good! What next?'

'He says it has minerals in it, and that the food we provide is useless to his people,' Ellen explained.

Grace exploded. 'My God! Now they want a daily menu! Aren't they ever satisfied? We clothe them, feed them, educate them, and all the thanks we get is a sullen ingratitude, disobedience and escapes. This place is nothing but trouble. Something has to be done.' She stormed out of the room determined to wire Henry.

That afternoon, Ellen was sitting alone in the schoolroom, marking some of the children's slates, when the door eased open and Cob crept furtively in.

'Shh, don't yell or I'm in trouble,' he said placing a bundle wrapped in leaves down in front of her. 'I want you to see that the children get these.'

Puzzled, she pulled back the leaves to see dozens of small cooked fish.

'You're breaking the rules, fishing, you know that Cob.

How on earth can I give them out without being seen?' she looked worriedly at the fish.

'You'll think of something,' he whispered as he headed out the door. 'I'll be back later if I find anything else for them. Do your best,' he added and was gone.

Ellen stared at the pile of fish, and suddenly an idea formed in her mind. She hurried over to the dormitory, hiding the bundle of fish under her skirts.

Once inside, she hurried round pallets and placed a couple of fish under each threadbare blanket. Before slipping out again, throwing the leaves into the bushes.

Next morning the children trooped innocently out of the dormitory to wash their faces in the trough, before marching off for morning prayers. Ellen slipped quietly into the hut to remove any tell tale evidence. To her amazement, not a scale or a bone was visible. They had eaten the lot, head, bones, tail and all!

Her next encounter with Cob was on the mission beach a few days later. She had just finished telling the wide-eyed little ones the Aboriginal tale of the naughty boy who disobeyed his elders and left the camp without permission, only to be turned into a rock at the water's edge, by the god of the sea, for his disobedience. The children were eyeing the rocks suspiciously. She laughed and let them wander off down the beach to play. She was gazing at a large rock herself, thinking how clever the legend was, keeping the little ones away from dangerous places when a head popped up from behind it.

She shrieked in fright.

'Hey, it's only me.' Cob said laughing softly.

She sank on the rock, her hand on her heart. 'Will you stop creeping up on me!'

He swung his legs easily over the rock and sat beside her. 'I followed you down here to give you some eggs for the little ones. I couldn't resist it when you started telling the legend. 'Your face was a picture,' he grinned widely. 'Anyway, what are you doing telling them Aboriginal legends? You're supposed to be whitewashing them. How did you know it anyway?'

'Your father told me, and I didn't want them coming down here by themselves. He says there's a lot of sharks in the bay.'

'There are,' Cob agreed, handing her a woven basket.

'Look, here's some boiled turtle eggs. You can feed them to the children before they go back to the mission. Then you won't have to smuggle them under your skirt!' he looked at her cheekily.

'How did you know?' she blushed.

'I watched you. Twenty-four fish under your skirt, not a bad effort, Miss Grimshaw,' he chuckled.

'You just stop laughing at me or I'll turn you in,' she threatened half-heartedly.

'You wouldn't, would you?' he asked, not looking at her but dragging his big toe through the sand and watching the pattern.

'No. You know I wouldn't, but the Lord knows why,' she answered, standing to brush the sand from her dress.

'Maybe it's because I'm such a likeable black fella eh,' he suggested, still concentrating on his sand design.

'You're an incorrigible rogue with a high opinion of yourself,' she answered tartly.

He rose and stood tensely, as if about to say something. Changing his mind abruptly, he furiously stamped on his design in the sand, obliterating it and stalked off.

Ellen started after him. 'Where are you going, Cob?'

He turned, holding up his hand to stop her from following, 'My fault, Miss Grimshaw. Some damn blacks just never learn their place, do they?' He walked off not looking round again.

Ellen felt confused. She wanted to run after him but instead stood dumbly, watching his footprints receding across the sand.

Cob did not approach her again, but the food supply kept coming. He left it where she would find it: cooked 'roo meat, strips of dugong, anything edible. She shared it out among the children and said nothing about it to anyone.

*

Grace was puzzled and alarmed when she saw Laurence Reid disembarking from the mission lighter. Had something happened to Henry? She ran down to meet him. He smiled in genuine delight when he saw her coming. 'Mrs Grimshaw! How good to see you after all this time,' he shouted and hurried to meet her.

'Is something wrong with Henry?' Grace gasped, out of breath.

'No! No, he's fine. He is just so busy preparing for his expedition to the Gulf he sent me instead. I'm sorry if I frightened you.' He patted her arm as she linked his and they walked back to the mission.

'How's Ellen?' he asked as they walked. 'Is she here?'

'Oh yes, she's around somewhere. I'll send someone to look for her straight away. I'm sure she will be delighted to know you are here.'

Laurence sat uneasily in the parlour making polite conversation with Grace, waiting anxiously for Ellen to appear. He hadn't seen her for nearly a year, and though he had written to her regularly, he had not received much in the way of replies.

'I suppose Ellen has been enjoying herself down here?' he ventured afraid she may already be involved with someone else.

'She has, Laurence. She's quite a changed girl, you know, and very popular too, always being invited to parties and such like. You'll see quite a difference in her, I'm sure.'

His heart sank to his boots. 'I don't suppose she'll have much time for a chap like me then, will she?'

'Come now, Laurence, she's always been very fond of you. I believe you are fond of her as well, aren't you?'

'Yes, Mrs Grimshaw, to tell you the truth, she means the world to me. I think that is partly why Henry allowed me to come in his place. He knows of my deep regard for her. Could you tell me, well, what I mean is, has she become fond of anyone else down here?'

'Well, she was seeing a great deal of a young English boy who seemed quite smitten with her, he was very well connected too. But he has returned to England now, so I don't think anything will come of that relationship.'

Laurence breathed a sigh of relief. A bout of coughing suddenly shook his frail body. He tried to muffle the sound in his handkerchief.

'That's an awful cough, Laurence. You should do something about it,' commented Grace with concern.

'It's just a dratted nuisance,' he choked in reply, trying to catch his breath. 'A hang over from my illness, that's all.'

'Maybe the air down here will do you good. How long can you stay?'

'It depends on what's wrong here. Henry was very

distressed by your cable. Can you give me some idea of what is happening, before I see Reverend Featherstone?'

'Everything Laurence, absolutely everything! You've no idea what it's like here working with these blacks, not a bit like our dear people at Bibiringda, I can tell you. It's impossible to control them, not that the Reverend Featherstone has the same command of respect that dear Henry has, but even I am finding it very difficult with the women. Oh, they learn quickly enough! I have quite a few now making the mission dresses and shirts, but it's their attitude that makes them quite impossible. Ellen was telling me the other day that they even have the nerve to complain about the food! Well of course, I realise it's not the best, but what else can we do with the money we receive? Health here is poor too. We're having a lot of deaths, but they insist on drinking the confounded clay.

'Clay would you believe? They say it contains minerals or some such rubbish. That came from Ellen of course. She's still hanging around them, you know. She won't listen to a word I say. It really worries me, Laurence. Thieves, murderers, down-and-out criminals! There's one clan, or whatever you like to call them, the Munyabras, they are trouble. Up to no good most of the time, if you ask me. I blame the whites! The father was a tracker of some fame with the Bush Police and as usual, give an inch, and they take a mile. Ha! The arrogance of this black, you've seen nothing like it! Thinks he owns the place he does, and his son is just as bad. He's one of the assistants, but I have my doubts about who he is assisting, I can tell you! What we need here is stronger discipline and more work, they won't have the time or the energy to get into trouble then. Something will have to be done Laurence, really it will. I can't keep going like this.' Having vented her anger, Grace paused for breath. As she did, Ellen walked in.

'Hello Laurence! Where is Henry? Isn't he coming?'

Laurence jumped to his feet in delight. 'Miss Grimshaw, how wonderful to see you again, and looking so well. It's been such a long time. We've all missed you.' Laurence would have dearly loved to pick Ellen up and squeeze her tightly, but instead he shook her hand gravely. 'Henry, I'm afraid is too busy. He is too busy. He has sent me in his place. I hope you're not too disappointed?' He looked hopefully into her eyes for some sign of affection.

She smiled openly at him. 'We'll just have to be satisfied with you then, won't we Laurence?' she laughed. He joined in her laughter half-heartedly.

'Ellen stop teasing. You know you're as pleased as I am to see Laurence. Wait until Barney sees you, he will be overjoyed. He still talks about you.'

'Does he really, after all this time?' asked Laurence, pleased that he had at least the child's affection. 'Where is he?'

'We have one of the girls trained as nanny for him now as I am too busy with the women and children, he always comes to say goodnight to me after dinner. You'll be able to see him then. The climate down here is much better for him but he's never been really strong since his illness at Bibiringda.'

After dinner was served Barney was brought in to say goodnight by his Nanny Rosie. His little face lit into a huge smile as he recognised Laurence. He proceeded to climb, uninvited, onto Laurence's knee and tug at his watch chain.

'You don't forget much, do you, little fellow?' Laurence said as he placed the ticking watch against the little boy's ear. 'You're getting to be such a tall young man, aren't you?'

Laurence affectionately ruffled his blond hair. 'Can you say your prayers yet like a big boy?'

Rosie's face beamed with pride as she lifted Barney down and whispered in his ear. He gazed back into her smiling face, then turned to his waiting audience and said loudly:

'*Gentle Jesus milk and mild*
Look upon this little child
Pity my simplicity
And suffer me to come to tea!'

He proudly waited for the applause, Laurence laughed uproariously. 'You got it a bit wrong, old chap, it's "suffer me to come to thee" not to tea! But it was very good all the same.' He chuckled.

Embarrassed, Barney ran and hid his face in his nanny's skirt. Gently Rosie lifted him into her arms and cuddled him.

'It's bedtime now, Barney. Give me a kiss then off you go,' said Grace, kissing him absently on the forehead before sending him off with Rosie.

'The girl seems to look after him very well Grace,' Laurence said.

'Oh yes, she does, but I still like to keep an eye on him. One can't trust these blacks.'

Laurence spent the day with Reverend Featherstone and came back after drill, looking tired and worried. 'How did you find things, Laurence?' Ellen asked as he sat down beside her on the veranda.

'It's a bit of a mess, isn't it?' he answered with deep concern. 'Some of the women and girls should be placed in service now, I believe. They seem quite capable of domestic duties, and that would relieve the food situation a bit.'

'Yes, I agree,' Ellen nodded. 'but it's the children who

concern me most. They are dying. The mosquitoes are spreading malaria and they seem to get a stomach upset that I can't cure,' she said helplessly.

'I've talked to Reverend Featherstone about putting in more gardens,' Laurence said. 'They could even grow surplus crops which could be sold in the town to provide more funds. Cattle could be bred. Some of the men here have worked with cattle before. They should be able to do it.' He wracked his brain for answers.

'The problem is no one asks the Aboriginals what they need. Would you come with me and talk with Currie Munyabra, Laurence? He could tell you, really he could,' Ellen pleaded.

He smiled fondly at her. 'I thought you weren't allowed down at the camp, Ellen.'

'Please don't tell Mother, Laurence. She wouldn't understand; but will you come? Old Reverend Featherstone just can't see what's happening, or won't. He pretends everything is fine and writes as much in his reports. He won't listen to me, and Mother is as bad. She seems to hate the blacks here.'

He patted her hand. 'Of course, I will. You know, I've really missed you, Ellen.'

She smiled and gently withdrew her hand. 'We'll go tomorrow then, shall we?' she suggested purposefully, avoiding his remarks.

Ellen waited until morning prayers were over and everyone was busy with the tasks of the day before seeking out Laurence. At the camp they found Currie seated by the fire polishing his boots with a tin of nugget polish and an old rag. As they approached, he rose and pulled on his uniform jacket.

Ellen introduced the men, giving Currie the respect of his position. 'Currie, I'd like you to meet a friend of mine, Mr

Reid. He would like to talk to you about the problems at the mission.'

Laurence held out his hand and the old man shook it gravely. They all sat on a log.

'Tell me, Currie, what do you see as the answer to this problem?' Laurence asked politely.

Currie thought for a while, before answering, 'This place is like a jail Boss, people get very sick. Children dying. Let 'em go, Boss. Let 'em fish. Get good tucker from island. Everyone gunna die pretty soon Boss. This Mission no good place,' he warned. Picking up a boot, he spat on the toe and began to polish it rhythmically.

'We can't do that, Currie,' Laurence replied watching the rag go 'round and 'round, 'but we can improve the place. I thought we could grow more vegetables, get some cattle and sell them to buy more food,' he said hoping for the old man's approval.

Currie condemned the idea. 'We need our tucker, Boss, not white man's. White man's no good black fella.'

'We could send some of the women away to work, and have fewer mouths to feed. What do you think of that Currie?'

'Let lubras go; gins stay with children.' Currie decided firmly.

'Yes. Yes, I see your point. The women wouldn't want to leave their children,' agreed Laurence, happy to have reached some common ground with the black leader.

'Give children back to the camp gins; they feed 'em up good and teach 'em good too,' Currie ordered.

'No, Currie, we can't do that either. The children must stay in the dormitories. They have to forget the bad old ways and learn the white man's new ways so they can find work when they grow up,' Laurence explained patiently.

Currie shook his head angrily. 'You take away white fella. Make 'im good! Then you can come back, make black fella good? Eh Boss?' He looked at Laurence accusingly. 'Black fella need old people and Dreamtime. Children should learn to hunt kangaroo and spear fish, read tracks, go walkabout and get bush tucker. Go big walk to mountains at Bunya time, make spears, boomerangs, canoe from canoe tree, learn to be man in the Bora ring. This Jesus fella not much good. Only gives us bloody maize meal tucker. Jesus God, locks black man up, makes 'im die! Poor bloody black fella. Let us go, Boss!' demanded Currie fiercely.

'But we can't, Currie. It's a law. The Aboriginal Protection Act,' Laurence almost shouted in exasperation. He turned to Ellen. 'Can't you explain it to him?'

At that moment Cob arrived. At the sight of the powerful black, Laurence rose and placed a protective arm around Ellen. He stood thin and frail before the towering, muscular Aboriginal man. Ellen felt flustered by Cob's accusing stare and jumped up from the log, blushing. 'Laurence, this is Currie's son, Cob. He is one of the assistants.'

Laurence offered his hand. Cob, ignoring it, placed the sack he was carrying on the ground. There was a clinking of glass. 'What do you want with my father?' he enquired rudely.

Currie put down the boot he was polishing and said, 'He works along Rev'and Grimshaw, and has come to talk with me about helping our people.'

'It's true, Cob. Mr Reid wants to help,' Ellen interrupted nervously.

Cob moved around the fire to his father's side. 'Too many white bosses come to help, not enough do anything. Talk won't keep the children alive,' he said scornfully.

Laurence was amazed at his attitude and decided to assert his authority. 'What have you in that sack? Not strong drink, I hope?'

Ellen pushed nervously between the two men. 'No, it isn't, Laurence. Cob makes sand bottles. He's very clever. He collects the coloured sands from the island. Here, show him, Cob.' She turned imploringly to Cob, who looked at her with disdain.

Cob shrugged his shoulders and walked inside the humpy. He reappeared carrying two bottles. Laurence was greatly impressed by the ship in full sail that rose on waves of red and brown sand, before a background of white clouds.

'This is very good, Cob,' he said.

Cob brushed off the compliment.

'What do you do with them, once they are finished?' Laurence enquired.

Ellen glanced sharply at Cob knowing he couldn't admit to selling them.

'Just give them around. Would you like that one?' he answered evasively.

'I certainly would. It's beautiful. Maybe you could teach some of the others to do this work, and we could sell them to help the mission. What do you say, Cob?'

Ellen choked. 'We really should be getting back, Laurence,' she said, hurriedly taking his arm.

'Yes, Ellen, but I think I've hit on a good idea. I'm sure people would buy these.' As he spoke, he pulled her hand through his arm and gently patted it.

Cob stared at the linked arms and lifted his eyes directly into Ellen's face. As their eyes locked, he silently challenged her. She stood, as helpless as a cornered rabbit, wanting to deny any relationship with Laurence. The searching, dark eyes continued to interrogate her, and her knees trembled. Hurriedly, she pulled her hand from Laurence's grasp. Panic began to rise in her stomach and it took all her self-control to stop from running away.

'Please, Laurence, let's go,' she begged. 'Mother will be needing me at the school.' Her voice sounded so uneven that Laurence turned to her with concern.

'Are you all right, Ellen? Why, you've gone quite pale. Yes, of course, we must go; you don't look well.' He put an arm around her shoulders feeling her trembling body, 'I hope you're not in for a dose of malaria. You'd better go straight to bed. You look quite faint.'

Instinctively, Cob moved forward and gripped her other arm. His strong black fingers burnt like fire. 'I'll go and bring your horse, Miss Grimshaw, to save you the walk back,' he offered, his grip tightening. The two men stood, one on either side of her, making silent claim.

Laurence angrily brushed Cob's hand away. 'That won't be necessary thank you, Cob. I will take Miss Grimshaw home. Come Ellen dear, let me help you.' He placed a protective arm around her.

Ellen glanced helplessly at Cob who had stepped back stiffly, his body rigid, his jealously now under control, except for a tightening of his lips and an angry glint in his eye.

'Thank you Cob, it's nothing. I'll go home,' she called helplessly as she was lead away by Laurence.

Frustrated, Cob stood and watched them leave, every instinct made him want to knock the skinny, weak-looking, white man to the ground. Shock ran through his body as he realised why Ellen had become sick and faint. That look she had given him! She felt as caught up with him as he did with her! He was sure. She wanted him, a black man! Fear now churned his innards. What could he ever be to her? Or she to him? He jumped, startled as his father's voice broke into his dangerous thoughts.

'Keep away from that one, son,' his father warned, reading his son's face. 'She big bloody trouble for you. I've seen men think like you on my great walk. The white gets him good. He dies fast. Black fellas can never touch white women and live. Go away, son. Get out, pretty bloody quick,' he advised sadly.

Cob swung on his father, who still sat on the log looking at him worriedly. 'Your mind's going, old man,' he snarled defensively. 'You don't know what you're talking about. I wouldn't touch a bloody white woman. Never!'

He picked up the remaining sand bottle and stood looking at it, shaking in anger and confusion. 'That to bloody white women!' he spat, and smashed the bottle on to the log where it shattered into a thousand pieces. Then he stormed off into the bush.

Kalinga, sitting in one of the humpies near by, had seen the whole incident and, although she was not near enough to hear the conversation, no words were needed to explain the rivalry displayed by the two men. Her instincts screamed – she was losing her man to another woman! No matter if she was one of the white untouchables. It was happening, she felt sure. Hugging her knees, she curled her body into a miserable ball. She was Cob Munyabra's woman, not that white bitch. She had always saved herself for him alone, and since his return to the island he had always come to her.

Aboriginal men took their women for granted, she did

not expect a show of great emotion or affection, but this was different. She had seen with her own eyes the possessive way he held the white girl's arm against the skinny white missionary. His anger at his own black impotency displayed in the harsh words he had used with his father, and destroying his art.

Cob was strong-willed and self-sufficient, and begged nothing of any woman, but since this white bitch had come to the island, he had behaved differently. He followed the girl and her friends, even over to Bracefield, when she was staying with the bosses at the big house. He had volunteered to drive their Christmas party to the lake. That had been the night he had come to her, and told her how stupid the white girls looked, slopping around at the edge of the water in silly long pants with frills. They had both laughed uproariously at his descriptions but that night when he made love to her she wondered why he seemed so angry.

She had thought it had been his hatred for the whites, and the virtual imprisonment of his people. Well, she would fight for him. She had all the advantages. She was his kind. She was available, and she knew what was happening to him, even if he didn't. If only she could escape from the dormitory, so she could be with him more, make him forget his fantasy of the white girl.

That thought reminded her that she must get back to the laundry before she was missed, or she would be the victim of the old nagging white woman as well. Wiping her tears on the front of her calico skirt, she slipped quietly out of the camp.

At the house, Ellen thankfully took to her bed to hide, and try to unravel her wild emotions. Why did she always react so violently when that nigger was near her? She deliberately thought of him as a 'Nigger' in an attempt to put him in his rightful place, but it didn't seem to demean her feelings for him at all.

He was rude to her almost every time they met, so why did she feel so happy when she saw him? He was arrogant and conceited. He was breaking all the rules, and had her covering for him. The more she thought, the more confused and defensive she became. Perhaps he stole to supply the children with food, but he hadn't forced her to help him, had he? No! And he had never spoken out of turn, or given an indication that he would harm her, even when they were alone on the beach. He had even been too shy to shake her hand! Then why was she so afraid? Her head ached, and she began to wonder if she really was ill, and all these thoughts simply an illusion brought on by fever. If only they were!

Why did he look at her like that? What did he want of her? What did she want of him? My God, if her mother knew she was even thinking these thoughts she would strike her dead. Perhaps her mother was right. Perhaps she spent too much time with the blacks. If only she could spend some more time with him, just talk, surely there was nothing wrong with that? But she knew that there was, even as she thought it. Finally, mentally exhausted, she fell into a troubled sleep.

*

Grace was disgruntled. How was she supposed to run the children's school, supervise the dressmaking, and keep an eye on the laundry all on her own? With Ellen sick, it was impossible to be in two places at once, and where was that dratted Kalinga? Over at the camp once again, no doubt! She hurried across the compound to where nanny Rosie was sitting under a shady tree, watching Barney playing in the dirt with his old wooden train.

'Rosie, come here,' Grace barked harshly. 'Go down to the camp and see if you can find that Kalinga. I will not tolerate her skipping off any longer, and don't you be too long either,' she warned.

Rosie hesitated, looking from Barney to Grace.

'Well, go along! I can look after my own son for a few minutes, you know,' Grace snapped unkindly.

Laurence looked from the window of Reverend Featherstone's house, 'Any problem, Grace?' he called.

'No dear, not really, but I'm terribly busy, and that Kalinga has gone missing again. She won't get away with it this time! It's every minute my back's turned. I'm sending Rosie to find her but I must get back to the school.'

'I'll watch Barney, if you like. Come on old chap. You can come with your uncle Laurence.'

Barney trotted over to Laurence quite happily, dragging his toy train behind him. He sat playing outside the door while Laurence continued to make sense of the mission books. Fifteen minutes later he remembered Barney and went to speak to him. His toy train was at the doorstep but Barney was gone.

Laurence, supposing that Rosie must have taken him for his nap, returned to his books. Grace popped in a few minutes later almost tripping over the train and asked where Barney was.

'Oh, Rosie took him for his nap I think,' Laurence called absently from his desk. Grace picked up the slates she needed and rushed back to the school.

Kalinga wandering slowly back to the mission, stopped at

the creek and bathed her face and hands. She wouldn't let those whites see that she had been crying. Dipping her feet into the stream to wash off the dust, she wiped them on some dry grass. As she reached for another handful of grass, she caught sight of a small white object poking out from behind a bush, further up the track. Puzzled, she rose and walked slowly towards it.

As she rounded the bush she realised it was a small hand and arm! Running forward she pushing back the lower branches only to see Barney lying face down in the dirt, still and silent. Quickly she turned him over, one look at the blue stain around his lips and down his shirt told her what had happened. He had eaten the berries from the bush… and they were deadly poisonous.

Hurriedly scooping the little boy up into her arms, she ran to the mission as fast as she could, knowing Grace would be there. Panting under the load of the limp little body she tried to protect his lolling head from overhanging bushes that slashed her arms as she ran down the track.

She burst into the school screaming, 'Missus, missus, come quick, little fella been alonga track, eat berries, 'im big poison, quick, Missus, quick!' she gasped as she lay Barney on the table.

For a few seconds Grace sat frozen to the chair in front of the class as the children turned and stared in fear at Barney's limp body.

Suddenly, Grace sprang to her feet, tipping over her chair as she ran to her son. She took him in her arms, shaking him and calling his name hysterically. 'Barney, wake up, Barney, wake up!' She shook his little body as if to command him back to life. 'Barney, you naughty boy, wake up when your mother tells you. Do you hear?' In dazed bewilderment, she shouted at the blue-lipped lifeless child, in turn threatening and cajoling.

Kalinga, seeing a trace of madness in the older woman's face, hurriedly backed out of the door with the last of the scampering children. She ran to Reverend Featherstone's house and bumped into Laurence, who was coming over to see what the commotion was all about.

'Kalinga, where have you been? Matron has been looking for you. So has Rosie. You're in trouble, girl' He stopped short as he read the fear on her face.

'Come quick, Mr Reid! Matron has the little fella, he's dead, Mr Reid.'

'What! What are you talking about, girl?' he thundered, but she was gone, heading back to the school.

Laurence ran after her. He was gasping for breath and coughing with exertion by the time he jumped the school steps and barged into the classroom. Grace stood rocking Barney's body to and fro making whimpering noises.

'Oh My God! No!' was all Laurence could repeat, over and over.

Finally, he prised the small body from Grace's arms, and placed it gently on the table. Wrapping his arms tightly around her, he led her away. 'Come Grace, come away, that's right. Let's go back to the house. Come along dear.' He steered her gently onto the veranda and into the sitting room. Rosie, who was peeling vegetables, came to the kitchen door and stopped in her tracks, as she saw them come in.

'Dear God Rosie, I thought you had Barney with you,' Laurence accused the girl.

'Couldn't find Kalinga so I came back to work, Boss. Missus

had Barney, Boss,' she replied with a puzzled look on her face.

At the sound of Rosie's voice Grace's head jerked up, her lips curled viciously as she screamed hysterically, 'It's her fault! She should have watched him. I'll kill her the dirty black bitch.' Her voice rose to a howl as she broke from Laurence's grasp and launched herself at Rosie. The girl recoiled in terror, backing into the kitchen. Grace sprang after her, snatching the old buggy whip and slamming the kitchen door shut, trapping Rosie inside.

Rosie screamed as the lash fell, again and again, ripping open the flesh on her arms as she tried to protect her head. Blood oozed through the back of her thin cotton dress, as it was torn open by the dried leather hide.

Laurence tried frantically to push open the kitchen door but Rosie's body lay heavily against it. Wakened by the screams, Ellen, dazed and terrified, ran into the room, her white nightgown billowing around her. 'Mother. Laurence! What's happening?'

Seeing Laurence trying in vain to heave the door open she implored, 'Laurence who is in there, what's happening?'

Ignoring her, Laurence continued to beat on the door. 'Grace, stop. For the love of God, stop! It was my fault, not hers. Do you hear me? My fault!' he sobbed, gasping for breath.

Without fully understanding his urgency, Ellen added her weight to the door and between them they managed to wedge it slightly open. Rosie's screams mingled with Grace's curses.

'Damnation to you and your like, you lazy black bitch! You let my boy die! It's your fault.' The lash cracked emphasising every syllable. Laurence heaved again on the door and as it swung back, the stock whip came flaying down lashing him across the face. His head jolted back in pain and he stumbled and fell onto the kitchen floor, Ellen fell after him.

Grace stepped back, her eyes glazed and her face scarlet. Saliva dribbled from her open mouth. The whip was raised above her head ready to strike again.

'No! Mother, for God's sake. Stop it!' Ellen screamed, staggering up and snatching the whip from her mother's hand. For a moment Grace stared open mouthed into Ellen's face, then slid unconscious to the floor. Gasping for breath, Laurence crawled to where she lay. He wiped her face with his shirtsleeve before pulling himself up to the sink to get water. 'See to Rosie, Ellen,' he croaked.

Ellen turned to the bloodied huddled heap wedged behind the door. She recoiled in horror as she gently turned Rosie over. A huge red welt had closed one eye and split open the girl's lip.

Blood poured from her nose. Her arms and back were a mass of bleeding cuts. She clawed frantically at Ellen's nightdress as she spluttered. 'I didn't do nuthin' Miss Ellen,' she sobbed. 'I didn't kill little Barney, he like my own baby, poor baby, poor baby,' and she fell sobbing into Ellen's arms.

'Hush, Rosie, hush. It's all right,' Ellen crooned as she rocked her gently, oblivious to the spreading bloodstains on her white nightgown.

CHAPTER EIGHT

Heavily sedated with laudanum, Grace was unable to attend Barney's funeral in the small Anglican churchyard in Bracefield. Few people other than Laurence and Ellen were there as most of their friends were still down south escaping the summer heat. Amy was unable to book passage on a ship that would arrive in time and sent a funeral card to her mother, apologising for her absence.

Rosie had been removed from the mission under cover of night. Her wounds were hidden by one of Ellen's long sleeved nightgowns and a large hat with a veil covering her mangled face. She was placed in one of the backroom Aboriginal wards of Bracefield hospital, and the official story given was that her husband had beaten her. It took weeks for the cuts and bruises to heal, after which she was placed safely into domestic service on a property two hundred miles inland.

It was decided that Grace should leave the mission for a while and go back to Gildbourne, to visit Florence and the girls. Although she had kept regular contact with her daughters all through her confinement in the north, over time their letters had become fewer and less involved. The young girls had grown used to their surrogate mother, and had happily adapted to their new life. Florence had grown to love the girls, and look upon them as her daughters. She spent time and money making sure they enjoyed life to the fullest and were trained in all the accomplishments becoming young ladies of good breeding. Afraid that Grace's latest bereavement would induce her to remove the girls from her care, Florence waited anxiously, dreading Grace's arrival.

Grace received a letter from Henry in reply to the wire telling him of Barney's death.

My Dearest Mother and Sister,

I am devastated by the news of my dear little brother's death. I feel so deeply for you at this time, Mother, and I only wish I could be with you. My only consolation being that my dear friend, Laurence, is by your side to support you.

It is impossible for me to leave Bibiringda at the moment as I am in the final stages of organising my expedition to the Gulf. I will head the expedition of two white constables and a platoon of black police into the interior, following the telegraph wires as far as possible, then branching out into the Gulf region to assess conditions and survey for suitable mission sites. The going will be tough indeed, mostly uncharted. We are arranging for a ship to pick up our party six months hence, on the coast at a rendezvous yet to be decided, probably around Mornington.

Great planning is needed if we are to survive this mission, and nothing can be left to chance. The horses I choose must be sturdy and able to survive the heat and tough terrain. I am sure that inland stock horses will be our best mounts. Provisions must be non-perishable and not too bulky, or that could be our downfall, but also must be enough to see us through any eventuality. I am planning to avoid the cyclone season, which could affect our rendezvous with the ship and cut us off by flooded rivers, but by doing so we could diminish our supply of water! At least in the winter months the temperatures should lower. It is said that the heat can be as high as 130°F at times out there, not a very happy thought.

We have little idea of the hostility of the natives in this region, though reports from the brave Catholic Friars further into the Northern Territory, seem to indicate that the elements are the main adversary, and pitiful tales of their deprivation and suffering are coming through. I pray that the good Lord will look kindly upon us and preserve us through our adventure. 'Unto the valley of death,' for this is as it appears to be.

I hope to have all preparations concluded and set out in about five months time. Until then, I must also commit myself fully to organising the mission here ready for Laurence to take over. Most of the buildings are now completed, and Ellen, you will be pleased to know, we now boast a dispensary! A far cry from your ministrations to the sick under a tree, isn't it?

I am very proud to say our dear church is nearing completion. We are now working on the interior and pews etc. Our black brothers and sisters are progressing remarkably well in school, and at their scriptures. The bible is now their favourite book. We have children who can recite whole psalms by heart and at least six trained and trustworthy assistants. I have arranged for two new white assistants to be here with Laurence when I leave.

I am sorely troubled by the problems facing you all at Barragan. It is difficult to see a solution. I feel that the mixing of far-flung tribes and the confinement of prisoners there is bound to lead to further trouble, although I believe it was always expected of blacks from that area. They are the only tribes that have banded together, and would have wiped out the settlement of Bracefield if the black troopers hadn't been shipped in large numbers from Sydney to quell them. Lucky for us that spears are no match for rifles, isn't it?

In the drives that followed, many blacks were forced from the mainland areas and even across the island into the sea. Hundreds perished, shot where they stood. I could not agree with that kind of treatment, but would have thought it to have been severe enough to dampen the spirit of even the most militant black. I have always said that the Kalangari Island blacks are not the same gentle people as our own folk here. They are physically different, being so much taller and well built, even their features are different.

All I can say is persevere in the Lord's name, and may you be given the strength to overcome your terrible loss Mother. I know that going back to Gildbourne and spending time with my dear sisters will help to ease your heartache.

All my love,

Your affectionate son,

Henry

Laurence booked a passage for Grace on the first available ship, which was due into Bracefield in two weeks.

Since that fateful day of Barney's death, Ellen had avoided Cob and pushed the worry of their mutual attraction to the back of her mind. So she was surprised to find him sitting outside the schoolroom, late one afternoon.

'Miss Grimshaw, may I speak with you a moment?' he rose to his feet, towering over her.

Not daring to stop and look at him, she hurried past saying, 'Not now Cob, I'm very busy. I have to see that the children are fed.'

'Just a moment, please,' his voice followed her.

She turned and looked into his face. Gone was the hard mocking look and in its place a compassionate sadness.

'I just wanted to tell you how sorry I am about your little brother's death. If only I had known he was out there. Maybe I could have stopped him in time. He would have grown up to be like you, that little boy.'

Tears welled in Ellen's eyes. A lump she couldn't swallow formed in her throat as she thought about Barney, and his love for gentle Rosie, who had been the one he shared his sweet baby secrets with. The tears flowed and she was helpless to stop them as for the first time, she really mourned her little brother's death.

Cob stood, hands thrust in his dungaree pockets, his red flannel mission shirt vivid against his dark skin. He shuffled his bare feet with embarrassment as Ellen stood gazing across the compound, tears streaming down her cheeks and dripping unheeded from her chin. Her shoulders shook as she silently sobbed.

'I didn't mean to upset you, Miss Grimshaw, please don't cry.' He rummaged in his pocket and pulled out a dirty old rag. He looked uncertainly at its grubby appearance, and was about to stuff it back into his pocket when she smiled through her tears. 'It will have to do Cob, I haven't got one of my own.'

He grinned sheepishly and handed it to her. She wiped her face, and as she gave it back, he blushed under the darkness of his skin.

She smiled at his embarrassment. 'Thanks for the cry, and the hanky, Cob. I needed both, I think. It's been a trying time lately, hasn't it?'

He lifted his eyes and searched her face. 'It's never easy in this place,' he replied in a guarded, but questioning, manner. 'I am sorry if I upset you, but I had to come and see if you were all right.' He started to move away.

'Why, Cob?' she whispered.

He looked down at her face, pink and flushed from crying. As usual, her black hair had escaped its combs, and hung in tantalizing wisps about her cheeks. Her simple calico dress reflected a solemn greyness into her blue eyes as she stared into his.

He shrugged his huge shoulders and looked away, unable to meet her gaze any longer. 'I should be going.'

Impulsively, she reached out and caught his hand. 'Please don't go. There's nobody around.'

He looked down at her white hand, gently resting on his large brown one, and pulled away as if it were a snake about to bite him. Ellen turned in utter confusion. The raucous clanging of the meal bell shattered the tension between them.

'I have to go,' Ellen said, and fled. *Why on God's earth did I do that?* she berated herself, as she ran across the compound.

Ellen spent the next few days trying to settle the seesawing emotions of her mother. One moment Grace was depressed the next angry and super active. Neither state gave Ellen much peace. Her mother had changed so much in recent years that sometimes Ellen felt she didn't know her anymore. The poverty, isolation and frustrations of the life they had been leading had made her bitter. She had after all, no security to speak of for a woman of her age. She was dependant for home and income on the whim of the church, whom she had good cause not to trust.

She had no choices. A destitute gentlewoman was not an enviable position to hold in this harsh land of stark reality and she was taking all her fears and frustrations out on the ones least able to resist, the blacks.

*

The day of Grace's departure dawned overcast and drizzly, reflecting her mood. Laurence and Ellen travelled with her to Bracefield and settled her on the ship before it sailed on the afternoon tide. Ellen breathed a guilty sigh of relief as they walked towards the lighter, waiting to take them back to the island.

'I shall have to be leaving soon myself, Ellen.' Laurence felt now was the time to broach the subject. 'Henry will be leaving on his expedition in a few months, and I should really be getting back and try to lighten his load, give him time to rest up. He is going to need all the strength he can summon for the trip he is undertaking.' He turned away and coughed into his handkerchief.

'Dear old Laurence,' Ellen smiled. 'You are always worrying about everyone else and their problems aren't you, but what about yourself? That cough of yours is getting worse, isn't it?'

'Oh, I haven't got time to worry about that. It comes and goes.' He brushed aside her concern. 'Ellen, before I go there's something I want to ask.' Laurence cleared his throat. 'You know that I have always held you in the highest regard, and well, we have the mutual interest of our work for the blacks in common. I think we could make a pretty good go of it, if we were to be married, don't you?' He turned his dependable face towards her, over-flowing with humble love and devotion.

Ellen was overwhelmed with pity. *Poor Laurence,* she thought, *I only wish I did love you.* She gazed out across the sea. The island loomed above the clouds like some majestic god, demanding her subservience. She shivered and thought of the impossibility of her attraction to Cob. 'I will consider your proposal, Laurence. That's all I can promise for now,' she said gently.

His face lit up, radiating happiness. 'It's more than I ever expected Ellen, that you would even consider having me. Thank you.'

He leaned over and reverently kissed her hand. 'I promise I won't push you into a decision. Take all the time in the world, just remember I love you very dearly.'

Ellen felt a cheat, using this poor fellow so badly. He deserved better, but she desperately needed some barrier to protect herself from her emotions.

Laurence lost not time in placing twenty of the younger girls, into service through the Bracefield diocese. Most were sent to outlying properties, where a well-trained black girl who knew her place, and cost only her food and clothes, was readily accepted. Some would go to decent people, whom they learned to love. Others would go to a fate much worse, being used and abused by lonely squatters, desperate for a woman, whose attitude was: "who cares what colour they are, when the lamp is blown out?"

Work permits, signed by their prospective employers made these girls virtual prisoners. These very permits, originally designed to protect them, and ensure liveable working conditions, only served in reality to enslave them. Having no redress or knowledge of the law, they had no choice but to remain, no matter what they had to endure.

Kalinga watched the miserable group from the veranda of the house. She had been smart enough to take over the duties of caring for the family, in the disruption following the removal of Rosie. She stood now, broom in hand, feeling a mixture of sympathy and contempt for these black girls, who were stupid enough to allow the white bosses to herd them up and send them off like cattle.

They stood ready for departure, a sorry group, faces scrubbed, hair cropped short, calico mission dresses starched and ironed, each clutching a meagre bundle of belongings.

As the girls were herded out across the mud flats to the waiting boat, mothers ran after them wailing and crying, only to be pushed back roughly by the police. The girls turned their tear-stained faces to take a last look at their homes and loved ones.

Brothers and fathers stood in angry silence, helpless as their families and tribe were once again torn apart. When the boat finally disappeared across the bay, they dispersed solemnly, each to brew on his own private store of bitterness.

Laurence took control of the mission, working hard to get the first crops in by Easter, which was when he would have to leave. All black labour was concentrated in this area.

Reverend Featherstone gladly handed over the reins. It was all too much for him; he pottered about bent and grey, fervently hoping that the church council would allow him to retire soon, away from this depressing place. He still wrote the expected reports for the mission publications, about the growing band of happy converts and their ability to recite whole chapters of the bible by heart, but he never mentioned the starvation, imprisonment or deaths. It was not what the church members wanted to read about, after their Sunday dinner.

With Grace away, Ellen took turns with Laurence at teaching the men in the evening classes. One of the pupils, Nugget, was an impish, wiry fellow, with a flashing smile and an irrepressible sense of humour. Cunning enough to keep himself well fed and clothed, when everyone else was half starving, he soon made himself indispensable to Ellen. Before long he was spending most of his days looking very busy, pottering about the house.

Every afternoon, after eating the leftovers from lunch that he scraped from the missionaries' plates, he would wriggle under the house between the stumps and make himself comfortable in the shaded darkness. If there were any chance of discovery, Kalinga would stamp her foot on the back step. In his own way, he manipulated every member of staff. He charmed Reverend Featherstone into giving him passes to Bracefield, and had no trouble extracting extra tobacco rations from Laurence.

As Ellen returned from her early morning ride, Nugget was sitting on the steps polishing the boots. She removed her saddle, and threw it over the veranda rail. Nugget looked up with a big grin. 'I'll polish your saddle, Missus Ellen, when I finish these boots.'

'Oh, thank you Nugget. It was marvellous along the beach this morning. The colours in the sands are absolutely beautiful.'

'Coloured sands been there a long time,' he agreed.

'They're amazing. I wonder where they came from in the first place.' Ellen sat down beside him on the veranda step.

'The old people say, way back in Dreamtime, very pretty gin Murrawar, fell in love with the Rainbow. He would come along to visit her, just before night-time. She was happy and sang to her Rainbow. One day Burrawilla, a very bad fella, come along an' steal Murrawar, make her his slave wife. Her beat her with a big bloody stick an' made her work all a time, while he sit under tree and polish his terrible big killer boomerang. That boomerang, bigger than biggest canoe tree, full of evil devils, very bad! One day Murrawar, run away from Burrawilla along beach. She look back an' see Burrawilla boomerang coming to get her. She fell onto ground screaming, call for Rainbow to come and save her. Rainbow, come racing along the sea to save Murrawar. Bad devil boomerang come spinning into the sky to fight brave Rainbow, and they bang together with big thunder.

'Soon bad boomerang was dead! But then Murrawar saw the poor Rainbow, was all broken up into little fella pieces in the sky. He fell along the beach and died. It's him you see there, all along the beach. Little bits of rainbow.' Nugget nodded wisely. 'Women go there to get sand, Missus Ellen, they put it on their heads before they go walkabout, so

Rainbow always love them and keep them safe.'

'That's a lovely story, Nugget.' Ellen agreed. 'The sands are a sort of lucky charm I suppose, we have those too.'

Ellen left him polishing the saddle humming happily to himself as she headed into the house. She was seated at the breakfast table reading a letter from Laura when Laurence walked in.

'Good news, I hope?' he asked as he sat opposite her. Kalinga wandered in and carelessly slapped a plate of bacon and eggs in front of him, and hurried back into the kitchen to eat the tasty bits she had reserved for herself.

'Yes, actually it is Laurence. Laura will be home for Easter. She seems to have had a wonderful time in Sydney too, by the sound of it.'

'That's good, I'm pleased you will have someone close by. I have to go. I can't stretch it out any longer. It's not fair to Henry, though leaving you will be the hardest part,' he said, taking her hand.

Ellen knew she should put him out of his misery. 'Laurence, about our talk the other day…' she began.

'No, Ellen, you don't have to feel obliged to give me an answer just because I'm leaving. I told you to take all the time you needed,' he interrupted.

'But Laurence…'

'Say no more, Ellen, please. There's really no need,' he insisted, dismissing her protest, afraid of her answer.

So Laurence departed too, and the house was empty and silent in the evenings. It was no use looking to Reverend Featherstone for company, he retired by eight-thirty as soon as the drill was supervised.

Ellen sat on the veranda, attempting some embroidery her

mother had started months before. The light was beginning to fade, making the delicate work too hard to see. Placing it aside, she watched the sunset dying behind the trees. Deciding to stretch her legs, she wandered aimlessly across the sandy compound where she saw a couple of dark figures sitting under a tree. The hum of quiet conversation reached her ears.

Drawing closer, she recognised the voice of Nugget and called out, 'Goodnight Nugget, thanks for clearing the long grass from around the house stumps today. At least we'll see the snakes now.'

'No trouble, Missus Ellen. I'll sleep on the veranda tonight again, there'll be no snakes, and nobody get in to scare you,' he promised with a wave of his hand. He had slept on the veranda every night since Laurence had left, and she had to admit, she felt more secure knowing he was there. She was about to leave when his companion moved out from the shadow of the trees.

'Evening, Miss Grimshaw,' Cob's voice greeted her.

Fighting down the usual butterflies, she took a deep breath. 'Hello Cob. I didn't notice it was you in the dark there,' she answered as casually as she could.

'Just having a quiet smoke with an old mate,' he informed her leaning against the trunk of the tree, and staring at her through the curling smoke rising from his glowing clay pipe. 'Mr Reid get back safely to his mission, did he Miss?' he enquired with just a hint of sarcasm.

'I suppose so, Cob, I wouldn't really know as yet,' Ellen replied, once again on the defensive. Unable to force herself to walk away, she picked nervously at a twig of dry leaves. Making conversation, afraid that he might leave, she said, 'Nugget was telling me the legend of the coloured sands you use Cob. Do the women really put sand on their head?' She moved closer.

'Yes, that's what the old people believe, so they still do it.'

'Do you believe it too?' she asked staring up into his dark face.

He held her gaze for a moment, feeling his belly churn, and his fingers curl at the urge to touch her. 'I think there's still plenty of magic in the sand,' he answered gruffly as he turned away to Nugget. 'See ya, Nugget,' he said and strode quickly away, his huge shoulders hunched, his hands shoved deep into the pockets of his mission dungarees.

Watching his figure receding into the night, Ellen asked, 'Have you known Cob long, Nugget?'

'Yes, Missus Ellen, since we were piccaninnies together at the camp, but he's been away a long time with his father, tracking with the white police.'

'Yes, I know,' she murmured absently, 'has he any brothers and sisters. Is he the only son?'

'Yes, Currie's wife died, a long time ago.'

'How did she die?'

'She was taken by a pearler man, Miss Ellen, he did very bad things to Currie's woman, she was so shamed she couldn't come back to her people.'

'You mean the pearler raped her?' Ellen shuddered.

'That's it, Miss. Cob's mother kill herself, she jumped off the rocks at the White Cliff.'

'Poor woman, but it wasn't her fault,' Ellen exclaimed at the unfairness. 'Poor Cob, how old was he then?'

'Just a little fella.'

'And Currie never married again?'

'No. He went with the trackers.'

Ellen took her leave of Nugget, and walked back to the

house. 'And we wonder why they hate us!' she murmured to herself.

Next morning, when she went into the store to collect her saddle, she found a tiny bottle sitting on her saddle blanket. Curious, she lifted it down and held it up to the light that crept through the cobwebbed window. The bottle contained, wave upon wave of coloured sand arched into a rainbow.

'It's a rainbow caught in a bottle, how lovely, my very own rainbow.' She cradled it gently in her hands. He knew. He did care. It was his way of telling her. Her heart pounded with excitement as she slipped the bottle into her pocket.

When she walked into the schoolroom for the men's lessons that evening, she immediately scanned the seats, looking for Cob. He was in his usual place but gave no indication that he had noticed her entry. Walking primly to the front of the class she began to write copperplate letters onto the blackboard. As she wrote each letter, the men chanted the name, as was the custom at the start of each class. As the letter Z resounded around the room, Ellen turned and caught Cob's eyes resting on her. He dropped his head hurriedly and pretended to be writing furiously on his slate.

She asked him to collect the slates as the other men left at the end of the lesson and he crept nervously round the emptying schoolroom like a naughty schoolboy. He dropped the slates on her desk and was making a bolt for the door when she spoke.

'Thanks for the present, Cob,' she placed the bottle before her on the desk. 'Now I have my own personal rainbow to protect me forever! Is that right?' she asked softly.

He stood with his back to her, hesitating before turning slowly, he spoke in a quiet voice, 'That's right, Miss Grimshaw.'

Silence hung in the air between them and now it was her turn to blush, she lowered her eyes and fiddled with her pen nib. 'It would never be allowed,' she whispered without looking up.

'And that's about right too, Miss Grimshaw,' he answered.

'My mother would never even think of allowing it,' she mumbled, embarrassed, still not daring to look at him.

'Neither would my father,' he replied, matter-of-factly.

Ellen's head jerked up in absolute amazement. 'Yes, that's right. Him too,' Cob's huge dark eyes looked miserably down at her.

The whole thing seemed so incredulous to Ellen that she began to laugh. 'Can you imagine my mother's face if I told her? Oh! And if I told her that your father didn't think that our family was good enough!' With these last words she bent over in laughter. 'Oh, just imagine it. Can't you?' She burst into further peals of laughter.

A big grin spread across Cob's face as he visualised Matron, bursting with indignation, as his father told her that her connections were not quite good enough for his son. He shook his wavy black hair. She came around the desk to him. 'I'm sorry, Cob,' she said pushing back her hair and wiping the tears of laughter from her eyes. Once again, Cob took out his grubby piece of rag, but this time, instead of handing it to her, he placed a large hand on the top of her head, and swivelling her head round to face him, wiped her cheeks and nose as one would a baby. Then, wrapping his arms around her, he held her tightly. Ellen rested against his chest, feeling a wonderful sense of safety and protection.

Taking her by the shoulders, he gently eased her away. She looked up at him wonderingly, studying his melting brown eyes with their long curling lashes. She traced a finger over his high chiselled cheekbones and down the straight nose with it's flaring nostrils. His mouth turned up at the corners in a sad smile.

'I have to go,' he whispered.

'But when will we see each other again?' she asked anxiously.

'We won't! We shouldn't. This is suicide for us both, you know that.'

'I know, but surely we could see each other, just once, maybe tomorrow.'

'I have to get more sand tomorrow. I'll be away all day. He refused firmly.

Suddenly a wonderful idea flashed into her mind. 'I could come with you.'

'How could you do that? You'd never be allowed.'

'No one will know, we could meet down the track away from here, and ride to the beach together. Could you get a horse?' she was excited now, like a prisoner planning her escape.

He turned the idea over warily in his mind. 'Yes, I could but where would you say you were going?'

Their heads drew together like conspirators. 'How about over to the timber camp for the day? I only have to tell Reverend Featherstone, and he will forget the minute I have told him. I'm sure he gets more vague by the day.'

'I think it's more vague by the bottle, actually, Miss, er Ellen,' he said hesitantly.

She laughed delightedly. 'You called me by my name for the very first time, do you realise?'

Blushing his rosy brown blush, he ruffled his hair shyly. 'Meet me by the scribble trees at, say, six in the morning.

They're used to seeing you go out at that time, so no one will really notice. I'll get one of the horses from the timber camp. I know the chap in charge of them. He'll lend me one.

'We'll go over the back track. No one will be around there on Saturday; most of the camp will be tied up with tobacco rations, and the football game. It's the assistants and native police against the camp boys but don't worry, I've made an excuse. It should be a real blood bath. It's the only time the camp boys can give those fellows a good hiding and get away with it. I've got to go now, see you tomorrow,' he said and hurried out of the schoolroom.

Ellen scarcely slept that night as excitement and fear mingling in her mind. Finally, she gave up trying, and sat watching the dawn slowly dilute the blackness of the night. Rising, she dressed silently, lifting each article and replacing it like a mime in a pantomime. She carried her boots to the bedroom door, and easing it open, she crept down the passage holding her breath at the kitchen door where she stopped to listen for the sound of Kalinga's breathing from her pallet on the kitchen floor.

Satisfied the black girl was asleep, Ellen tiptoed to the front door and peered along the veranda, to see if Nugget was sleeping there. 'No sign of him. Good!' she whispered to herself. The squeak of the veranda boards as she crept along, sounding to her ears as loud as a swinging gate in need of oil.

Reaching the shed, she whistled softly. The horse pricked up her ears at the familiar sound and, blowing gently in answer, walked towards her. Ellen stroked her neck and threw on the blanket. 'There you are my good girl,' she whispered. 'Stand still, that's right. Now your saddle.' Mounting lightly she moved the horse out at a quick walk, its hooves making little sound in the deep white sand.

She did not see Kalinga, watching from behind the trellis of the veranda, and Kalinga didn't see Nugget, who peered out from his snug resting place, under the house. Like Kalinga, he watched and wondered. *Miss Ellen was out early. It was still almost dark. Why was she creeping around?*

Pale yellow light silhouetted the trees as Ellen crossed the creek bridge and took the sandy track towards the scribble trees, where she pulled the horse up and moved into the bush off the track, to wait.

Fearing the worst, Kalinga ran across the compound to the camp just as Cob crept silently to mount his tethered horse.

'Where you goin' Cob?' she demanded as she tried to catch her breath.

Ignoring her he swung up into the saddle, she grabbed the rein at the horse's head. 'Where you goin' then?' She cowed before his glare.

'Get out of my way, Kalinga,' he snarled a warning.

'Don't go with her, Cob, please don't,' she sobbed, still hanging onto the reins. 'She'll give you big trouble. Don't go Cob, they'll get you,' she threatened as she was dragged along by the moving horse.

Cob reached forward and rapped her hard across the offending hand. Releasing her grip, she flinched back in pain, colliding with the horse's swinging rump. She fell to her knees and lay on the sand, wracked with pain and jealousy.

Cob was half inclined to turn back. Only a bloody fool would risk what he was doing, and now Kalinga knew, it was not a secret. He made a deal with himself. *If Ellen isn't there I won't wait, I'm not going to hang around.*

The snorting of Cob's horse was the first Ellen knew of his presence.

'There you go, creeping up on me again,' she joked.

'Shh! Don't talk too loudly,' he snapped already moving his horse out, 'and if we are stopped on the track remember, we only just met and you asked me to help you with a loose saddle, all right?'

'Yes, I understand, but we shouldn't meet anyone this early, should we?'

'Maybe some timber workers, who knows.' He shrugged, seeming disturbed about the whole thing.

Ellen had sudden misgivings herself. Had she pushed herself on him? Embarrassed, she followed quietly behind. They travelled in single file towards the rising dawn, until they reached a branch in the main track, which struck off at a steep angle north over the hills. It was rough and scarcely used.

Cob reined his horse. 'You'd better dismount and lead your horse up there. We don't want it going lame on you.'

Ellen obediently slid from the saddle and, began walking behind him as he rode his horse up the track. He slouched in the saddle, not looking round or giving any hint that he knew she was there. Struggling up the hill with the horse, she glared at his rough shirted back.

At the top of the hill he waited, silhouetted against the sky, as she scrambled up. 'Right, you can mount up again now,' he ordered.

Tears stung her eyes at the humiliation she felt. 'I'm not one of your bloody gins. Stop ordering me about,' she snapped at him. 'If you don't want me to come, just say so.'

Dismounting swiftly, he put his hands on her waist and almost threw her into her saddle. 'Use your common sense.

If your horse goes lame how do you explain being out here?
What if we run into the timber cutters?'

'I suppose so,' she mumbled, bewildered by his attitude.

They travelled in silence along the old overgrown track.
Ellen had no idea in which direction they were heading, and
could see nothing above the endless scrub. The track grew
narrower and more difficult to negotiate until at last, the trees
gave way to white sand dunes, formed into sculptured waves
by the wind. The horses plodded on through the deep ripples.

'Are we almost there?' she ventured to ask. They had not
spoken since they set off on the track.

'Almost,' he replied.

The dunes petered out suddenly, dropping into a lush,
heavily timbered, green valley. A swiftly flowing creek bubbled
over white sand and rocks, its banks filled with shady trees and
overhanging vines.

'We'll stop here and give the horses a drink, then we'll
follow the creek down to the beach.'

They stood apart, silently watching the horses nibble the
succulent green shoots near the water's edge. Hot and angry,
Ellen sat down and pulled off her boots and black stockings.
Tucking her skirt and petticoats up, she slid her white legs
into the shallows of the creek. 'Oh! It's icy cold,' she gasped
involuntarily. The strong current pulled at her ankles, washing
the sand from underneath her feet.

Cob sat on a rock watching her. 'You'll get yourself soaked.'

'I don't care,' she snapped back as she waded up and down,
looking into the water and swishing the sand up with her feet.

'Come on get out, we have to go,' he called, heading for
the horses.

She rolled up her blouse sleeves and undid the high lace

collar. 'Wait! Cob! What's wrong?' She waded after him, the hem of her skirts soaking as they half trailed in the water; her hair coming loose and falling over her face. She bent and swished the water up to him, soaking his dungarees.

'Hey, stop that! Get out,' he half-laughed, his worries fading at the ridiculous sight of her.

'No, make me!' she challenged sensing his mood change.

With one leap he was in the creek, causing a mini tidal wave that soaked her up to the waist. Gasping with the shock of the cold water, she frantically began to splash water at him. They shrieked and laughed, soaking each other until Cob overpowered Ellen and pushed her face down towards the surface of the water.

'Don't duck me! I give in! You win!' she screamed as she came perilously close to going under.

He pulled her back upright and they stood for a moment, water dripping from their clothes before they slid into each other's arms and clung desperately to one another.

Cob carried her out of the creek and lay on the grass beside her. All the tension of the morning was gone, and they lay smiling at each other.

'You're soaked you silly fool. Look at your skirt.'

'Yes, I know, and I don't care! Do you? She turned her head to look him squarely in the face. 'Are you sorry you came now?' she asked. 'You were earlier, weren't you?'

He was about to tell her about Kalinga but thought better of it. That was his problem. He would sort Kalinga out when he got back tonight. Ellen would only worry, and Kalinga wasn't going to spoil their precious day.

'I'm very glad I came,' he answered and rolled forward pinning her down as he kissed her. They held each other tightly, becoming lost in their emotion. Teetering on the edge of a much more serious commitment, they reluctantly eased apart.

'I think we'd better get going while we still can,' Cob said shakily as he brushed away the white sand that clung to her wet hair. Once more her arms slid around his neck as she tried to pull his face down to hers.

'Hey, stop it! I may be black but I'm still a man! You don't know what you're asking for,' he said desperately as he tried to untangle her arms.

'I think I've a jolly good idea,' she sighed.

Cob leapt to his feet and pulled her roughly up. 'Just look at you, sopping wet and covered in sand, throwing your virtue at a black. What would Mama say?'

Ellen gasped at the cruelty. 'Stop it! Don't spoil today, please.' She covered her face with her hands.

Pulling her hands down, he held her tightly to him. 'Oh Ellen, I'm sorry. I didn't mean it, but what the hell can I say? That I love you too? That no one will mind? That I am not really black? Look at me!'

She burrowed her face into his wet shirt. 'I don't care! I don't care what colour you are. I just want to be with you. I can't help it.' She sobbed helplessly.

'No, neither of us can help it, mores the pity, God knows we've tried.' Holding her to him, he patted her gently until her weeping subsided.

'Come on, let's go down and get some sand, shall we?' he suggested gently, leading her back to the horses.

The creek snaked between the hills until it widened out as it approached the beach. The basin formed a natural swimming pool, decorated with saltbush and creeping, purple flowering vines. The water formed deeply carved washaways as it poured into the sea. On the horizon the sea sparkled a deep cobalt blue, before curling into turquoise waves which crashed towards the shore and eddied in the shallows, a swirling mixture of ice green and white foam. Pinnacles of sand rose majestically from the beach, flashing their reds, yellows, and earth browns against the vivid blue sky.

Ellen took a deep breath of the salty air. The wind whipped her hair and pulled at her wet skirt. Her cheeks glowed and her eyes sparkled. 'This is glorious, absolutely glorious, but I'm starving already. I wish I could have smuggled some food out.'

He grinned, helping her down from her horse. 'Come on, you can work first and then we'll eat.

Tethering the horses to a piece of driftwood in the shade of some pandanus palms, they untied the sacks and set off to collect the sand.

By the time all the colours had been collected the sun was telling them it must be well into the afternoon. They carried the sacks back to the creek and piled them ready for leaving.

'Well now, I suppose I will have to feed you?' Cob smiled down at her ruffling her hair.

'Yes please,' she grinned. 'But how?'

'Hang on a minute. You collect some wood. I won't be long,' and he loped off up the creek towards the bushes.

Ellen found plenty of dry driftwood lying bleached and gnarled among the dunes, and soon had a heap piled ready.

Cob reappeared. She was momentarily shocked to see he had shed his clothes and wore only a laplap and carried a spear.

'Hope you don't mind the dress!' He winked at her as he strode past her heading towards the water.

'Hey, wait for me,' she called, setting off to run after him. 'Oh, damn this lot,' she cursed. Stopping, she undid the waistband and slipped out of her skirt. She pulled the strings of her petticoat until it too fell, with a swirl of white lace, to the ground. Determinedly she undid her blouse and dropped that too. She stood in only her camisole and knee length cotton bloomers. 'That's better,' she said with satisfaction, and ran barefoot and free to catch up with Cob.

He was in the shallows by this time, walking carefully along peering hard into the sea. Ellen giggled as she leaped the ripples and splashed towards him.

'Ssh! Be quiet! You'll scare off the fish,' he said over his shoulder, not looking up. She quietened down and crept up to him. 'What are you looking for?' she whispered.

'Flathead.'

'I can't see any.'

'Of course you can't. They dig in under the sand. You have to read the tracks.

He looked up; stark amazement registered on his face. 'Where are your clothes?'

'Back on the beach.'

'Go and put them back on, immediately!' he ordered with righteous indignation.

'Why should I? This is much better. There's no one here.'

'I'm here! Don't be so shameless.'

'You haven't anything on. I'm covered up. This is the same as my bathing costume, isn't it?'

'No, it's your underwear,' he blushed and looked away, embarrassed.

'Oh, don't be so stuffy. You're worse than Mother. Anyway I like this. It feels wonderful.' She skipped around him laughing.

'Well, if you're going to run around half naked you may as well do something useful. You can collect wongaries.'

'Oh good. How do I do that?'

He took her by the hand and waded into the shallows. 'Right, stand here and, as a wave comes in, twist your feet about in the sand. The wongaries are washed up by the water and you grab 'em, see?' He deftly picked up the little shellfish that floated towards the beach.

'Like this?' she asked as she did an exaggerated wiggle, more like a belly dancer.

'I suppose so,' he laughed, she whooped with joy as a wongarie floated by.

'I got one, look!' she shouted proudly, 'What do I do with it now?'

'Go and get one of the empty sacks and collect as many as you can.'

As she ran out of the water, he watched her go, pantaloons clinging wetly to her rump as she skipped over the sand. He turned back to the serious task of tracking the flathead, looking for the tell-tale ripples on the seabed where its fins had disturbed the bottom. He crept stealthily through the water, spear raised, ready to strike. Swish! The spear came down like lightning into the mound of sand that gave away the flathead's hiding place. Cob raised the spear with the frantically wriggling fish impaled on the end for Ellen to see. She waved back in a salute to his skill. He waded back to the beach to gut and wash the fish at the tide's edge and as he crouched, slitting open the fish, Ellen came prancing over.

'Look, I caught a heap.'

'Well, we won't get fat on your fishing I can see, but that will do for now. Come on.'

Cob made a small pile of the wood and, taking two soft sticks and some fine dry grass; he spun one stick into another until smoke began to rise. He blew softly on the grass until the smoke was fanned into a tiny flame.

'Cob, these are empty wongarie shells, aren't they?' she pointed to a huge mound of shells nearly. 'There must be thousands of them, how did they all get there?'

'From the old people eating them.'

'But there's so many, no one could eat that lot.'

'There are hundreds of mounds like that along the beach. The tribes all gathered here for the fishing festivals. Thousands of blacks camped along the beach here.'

Ellen looked along the miles of deserted shore and tried to imagine the crowds.

'Some say there would be at least three thousand attending each festival.'

'Where did they all come from?'

'All the inland tribes, and up and down the coast, some from as far as Brisbane and the Glasshouse mountains.'

'What did they do here? Catch fish?'

'Some did, but usually our tribe had the honour of driving the fish in with the help of old man porpoise.'

'The porpoises helped? Oh, come on!'

'No it's true. The man with the best eyesight would climb a tree on the beach, and watch for the shoals coming in. The other men would stand in the sea and watch for his hand signals. When the signal was given they would wade out very quietly, and stand with the nets stretched between them. One of the elders would call a special call and the porpoises would drive fish into the net. The porpoise was a very special totem to all the tribes here. My father has seen it. He used to be one of the best warriors in the great fights.'

'Great fights! What were they?'

'Like your football matches. It was sport to see who was the best spear thrower and wrestler. That's how my father got the big scar on his leg. Haven't you noticed it? He was speared.'

'Did they used to kill each other?' Ellen asked in horror.

'No, though accidents did happen. There were some rules; if one opponent was speared, then a fellow tribesman was allowed to spear the other fellow in the same place, just to make the fight fair.'

Cob raked the glowing ashes and dropped the fish on whole. He threw the wongaries around the edge. In a few minutes the shells opened, exposing the succulent flesh.

'Here, have some. They're really tasty.'

Ellen picked at the meat eagerly. 'I wish I'd caught more. They are delicious,' she said licking her fingers. 'If someone got killed in the fights, didn't that cause a real battle between the tribes?' she asked curiously.

'No, they were cooked and eaten! It was a great honour to eat a brave fighter. It was believed that the eater would gain the strength and skill of the dead one.'

'Ugh! Sharing him out like a good dinner.' Ellen curled up her nose in distaste.

'They didn't think so. Anyway it's all gone now, no more great fighting men or great tribes, it's all destroyed.'

Cob rose to his feet and pulled two palm leaves from a nearby tree. He laid them beside the fire and, scooped the cooked fish onto each leaf.

She watched him as he deftly peeled back the cooked skin and ate the steaming white fillets. She did the same. They sat eating the fish in silence, each engrossed in their own thoughts of the past. When they had finished Ellen took the scraps down to the sea and threw them for the seagulls wheeling overhead.

The sun was softly glowing over the sand dunes; the wind had dropped to a gentle breeze. She reached out her hand to Cob. 'Come on. Let's walk down the beach a while. It's so peaceful.'

With his arm around her shoulder and her arm around his waist, they walked slowly towards the quiet sea.

*

Grace piled her hand luggage onto the timber barge while one of the timber cutters carried her trunk aboard. She dropped wearily onto a seat in the shade of the wheelhouse. Her visit with Florence had been a disaster. She should never have allowed herself to be persuaded to go.

Not that Florence hadn't made her welcome, but all the time Grace could read in her eyes, the stark fear that she had come to take her two girls away. Now prim and straight-backed young ladies, the girls had presented her with samplers: "God is Love" and "Bless this House" all daintily stitched. They both played the piano beautifully, and entertained her dutifully with duet renderings of "The Trout".

After the first murmur of condolence, they avoided any mention of little Barney, nor did they mention the mission. They were like strangers to her, nodding politely, not wanting to become involved. Even when the girls said goodnight, it was a dutiful peck on the cheek for Grace, and a smile and a hug for Florence, who appeared embarrassed to receive such shows of affection, in front of their mother.

Grace had to face it. Florence was their mother now, any thoughts Grace may have had of bringing them back to

Barragan with her were soon abandoned, and after a week she excused herself, using a fictitious meeting with the Church Council in Sydney as an excuse. The trio eagerly accepted it.

Miserably, Grace had booked in at Mrs Moore's sister's boarding house, to await her return sailing date. Coincidentally, Mrs McGuffick and her girls were passengers too, and once they were over the shock of hearing about Barney's death, they helped to brighten her journey. Laura was bubbling over with excitement about a newly found suitor, a young and promising accountant who worked in her father's office in Sydney. Mrs McGuffick talked with Grace of the pending engagement, as the girls played deck quoits.

'Laura is so excited about her young man. It quite makes you wish you were young again too, doesn't it?' she commented.

Grace felt more inclined to disagree when she thought of her earlier life with Samuel Grimshaw, but murmured politely.

'I must say he suits the family well. Mr McGuffick thinks very highly of him at his office, and, not having a son of our own, he has ambitions of grooming the boy to eventually take over the business. It will be nice to have one of the girls getting married. Girls are always a worry, don't you think, Mrs Grimshaw?'

Grace became aware of Mrs McGuffick impatiently waiting for an answer. 'Oh yes, yes they are. Of course, my daughter Amy is comfortably settled now in Townsville, with a very successful husband. As for Ellen, well I do have hopes that she will marry Laurence Reid. He's a dear boy and quite devoted to the family.'

'Oh really! I had thought at one time that she would accept Andrew's proposal?' ventured Mrs McGuffick.

Grace fumed silently. She had never been told of any

proposal from Andrew and him so well connected. Really, that girl had no sense, imagine refusing such an offer!

'Well, girls will be girls, Mrs Grimshaw, and knowing Ellen, she will make up her own mind, in her own good time.'

Grace rose as the barge docked and tiredly made her way to the small boat that was to take her to the mission. What she needed was a cup of tea and a good sleep. Laurence would be gone by now, but Ellen would look after her.

The boat dropped her off near the track. Leaving her luggage to be picked up by one of the boys, she set off slowly up the incline.

I suppose I should have told them I was coming back, she thought as she struggled on, *but what does it matter? I don't want a fuss making, just a cup of tea and my bed.*

As she approached the house, the mission tea bell was clanging loudly. The black women smiled nervously at her and hurried away. The children bobbed a quick curtsey and disappeared. Exhausted, she stepped on to the veranda and called, 'Ellen, I'm home. Where are you?'

Nugget, who was just uncurling himself from his sleeping place to join the tea queue, stiffened at the voice and rolled his eyes. *Here was trouble and no mistake!* He scrambled out from under the house and crept away to find Cob and warn him.

Grace opened the fly screen door and entered the house. 'Hello. Anybody home?' she called again, flopping into her favourite chair and kicking off her shoes. Kalinga walked slowly from the kitchen wiping her hands nervously on her apron.

'Ah, Kalinga, put the kettle on girl, and make me some tea. I'm half dead. Where's Miss Ellen, have you seen her?'

CHAPTER NINE

Having stretched their one stolen day to its absolute limit, Cob and Ellen started to pack up the sand sacks. Ellen picked up her now dry petticoats and stepped into them, tying the drawstring round her waist. She was shaking the sand from her skirt when Cob came up behind her and wrapped his arms around her. 'You're very lucky, you know,' he said into her ear. 'You're the first girl I have had stripped down to her underwear and not seduced,' he nuzzled his face into her salty damp hair. She turned in his arms and smiled up at him.

'What stopped you? I think I would have been an easy victim.'

'His expression turned serious, he dropped her skirt over her shoulders and shook his head. 'It wouldn't have been right for us, that's all.'

'Why? Because I'm white?' she asked cautiously.

'Now you're the one doing it,' he pointed a finger at her. 'No! Funny but colour hasn't entered my head since this morning. I just mean that for you and me it has to be right. God knows why, but that's how I feel.' He shrugged.

Nodding her understanding, she fastened the skirt and pulled on her blouse. Then she remembered she had left her boots and stockings where she had taken them off, further up the creek. 'We'll have to go back for my boots.'

'Well, hurry up then, or it will be dark. How are you going

to explain being so late if anyone asks?'

'I'll say I stayed on at the camp for a barbeque and they escorted me back as far as the mission gates.'

'Up you go then. We'd better be off.' He helped her onto her horse, she leaned down and ruffled his hair as he stood below her.

'It's been a truly wonderful day, Cob, hasn't it? We have to go back to the real world again, but it won't be as bad now we both know, will it?'

'It will be hard to keep away from you,' he grinned wryly. 'Even with all your clothes on.'

She boxed his ears playfully 'Cheeky.'

'Seriously though, we must give no sign or hint that can make people suspicious of us, you do realise that?' His doleful brown eyes quizzed her.

'Yes, I know, but perhaps we'll have a chance to come here again, soon. That's something to look forward to, isn't it?'

'Come on, we have to go, worst luck.' He mounted his horse and led the way. They travelled as swiftly as they could along the deep sandy track, but night was well drawn in by the time they reached the scribble trees. Cob leaned out of his saddle and kissed her swiftly on the cheek. 'Goodnight, Miss Grimshaw,' he said softly.

'Goodnight, Munyabra. Remember, I love you,' she whispered back.

Humming cheerfully, Cob rode back to the camp where he dismounted and began to unload the sacks. At that moment, a voice whispered urgently to him from behind the bushes. 'Psst! Cob, it's me. Nugget. Over here.'

Curiously, Cob turned and walked in the direction of the voice. 'What's up, mate? Why are you hiding in the bushes?'

Nugget scurried up to him thrusting some money into his hand. 'You've got to clear out mate! Bloody quick. The old missus, she's back, she knows, mate! Kalinga told 'er. You're in bad trouble. She'll kill you.'

Cob stared at Nugget in amazement, momentarily too shocked to think. 'Oh God. Ellen's walking straight into it. I have to stop her.' He made for the horse but Nugget grabbed him from behind.

'You go up there now and they shoot you dead. She'll have the constables out.'

'But I've got to warn her!' Cob spoke through clenched teeth as he struggled with Nugget.

'No! You shoot through, go quick! I try to stop her.'

Without waiting for agreement Nugget bounded off. He ran at full speed towards the house, where he could see lamplight glowing in the windows. Skidding to a halt, he checked the shed first, praying to all the old people of the Dreamtime that Ellen would still be there, unsaddling her horse. She wasn't! The horse was already loose and wandering away across the compound; the shed door was locked. Turning again to the house, he watched helplessly as a dark silhouette crossed the lighted window of the veranda. He was too late!

'Mother!' Ellen blinked as she stepped into the bright light of the sitting room. 'What on earth are you doing back?' She moved forward to greet Grace, who sat stiffly in a chair facing her.

'Where have you been, Ellen?' her mother enquired stonily, her hands folded in her lap.

Ellen took a deep breath. She hated lies but knew she had to bluff this one out. 'Didn't Reverend Featherstone tell you? I went to the timber camp for the day. I was bored up here alone. We had a barbeque. Sorry I'm late, but the manager saw me home.' Her lies echoed mockingly around the tension filled room. A ticking clock counted the seconds as the two women stared at each other.

Grace was the first to speak. 'Oh yes?' Grace commanded icily.

'Would you like a cup of tea? Where's Kalinga?' Ellen asked nervously, backing towards the kitchen.

'Come back and sit down now! I have sent Kalinga out. The house is empty, there's just you and me.'

Terrified, Ellen sank into the chair facing her mother. Grace's eyes narrowed, and her lips curled with revulsion and she hissed, 'You dirty little whore, that's what you are, or worse! Not even the lowest whore would fornicate with a black!' Spitting her words like venom, she sprang to her feet and struck Ellen across the face.

Ellen went rigid with shock. 'Mother, don't. Please Mother,' she whimpered.

'Don't you "Mother" me; I know where you've been. Kalinga told me everything. You've been with that black bastard Cob, letting him paw you and spread his black filth inside you, you dirty slut!' she screamed. 'Then you think you can come back here and tell foul lies to cover up your disgusting behaviour. You wicked girl!'

Sobbing hysterically, Ellen cried, 'It's not true. It's not true. I didn't do those things. I didn't!'

'Then where have you been? Do you deny you went off with that black?'

'No! No! I did go with him, but not like you say. Not like that!' Ellen moaned at the horror of the accusation.

'Do you deny that he ever touched you? Dare you swear

on that?' Grace shouted, slamming the Bible on the table.

The blood drained from Ellen's face as she stared at the book in dismay. She knew she was beaten. She pleaded the truth. 'He did touch me, but not like that! He loves me, and I love him. Oh please Mother.'

'Ha! Love indeed! What would a cur like that know about love? Lust you mean. I knew it!' Grace paced the floor then swung back to Ellen. 'Don't think I am going to let you destroy this family with your demon ways. How could you do this to us? To me? After all I've sacrificed for you?' She towered over her daughter, face purple with rage.

Ellen shook as nausea flooded through her. Covering her mouth, she ran retching to her bedroom but Grace stormed after her, slamming open the bedroom door. 'Get up you wretched girl, get up and follow me.' Staggering, Ellen groped for her mother's arm for support but Grace dashed off the girl's hand with revulsion. 'Don't you touch me! I want none of your filth on me.' She marched out of the house across the compound. Ellen stumbled mutely behind her.

Nugget crouched, rigid with fear as he watched from his hiding place under the window. Grace stopped outside the red punishment cell. Unlocking the door, she grasped Ellen by her shoulders and pushed her inside. 'Get in,' she snarled. 'Or I'll have that black mongrel shot tonight, here, before your very eyes!' Ellen plunged into the darkness, she heard the cell door slam and the screech of the heavy bold as her mother locked the door.

Returning to the house, Grace administered herself a large glass of brandy with shaking hands. *What a shameful disaster! She must move fast to keep this quiet. If Church Council or the Bishop discovered the truth, Henry's career would be shattered; her own position lost! The family name would be disgraced beyond redemption. What if the McGufficks knew the truth? Or the rest of society in Bracefield? God forbid! And what of poor Amy? She would never be able to hold her head up in Townsville again. It could even destroy Edward's business. It must be kept secret. Nobody must know. Ellen had to leave, and quickly, but with a good excuse. There must be no questions asked, not a whisper of scandal. But how, dear God, how?* She tossed and turned for the rest of the night with no sleep and little in the way of an answer.

Ellen woke to see the sun filtering through the cracks in the timber walls. She raised herself stiffly onto her knees. Blinking, she looked at the dirt floor beneath her hands. Suddenly the whole horror of the previous night came rushing back to her mind. Covering her face slumping forward, moaning; 'Dear God what is going to happen to me now?'

Her hands touched her dress and the sour stench of dried vomit rose to her nostrils. She was filled with disgust. Her fingers touched her knotted hair, stiff with the salt water of yesterday. Her temples throbbed, her mouth dry and foul tasting. She looked around for water. Surely Mother would have left water. There was none. Her only hope was that Grace may have relented overnight and would release her this morning. Ellen shuddered at the very thought of facing her mother again and knew that there would be no reprieve.

*

Meanwhile, with the punishment cell out of bounds to the blacks, and Kalinga safely locked in the kitchen, Grace easily excused herself from taking up her duties, pleading exhaustion from the journey. Pacing the house she devised then rejected one plan after another, until at last, she was satisfied with a solution. She released Kalinga from the kitchen and propelled the girl by the arm into the sitting room. Kalinga stood, head bent, hands nervously wringing her apron. All night she had thought of her betrayal of Cob, but now realised the full enormity of her treachery. It would probably cost him his life. Humbly remorseful and desperate to save him at all costs, she stood before Grace.

'Kalinga, you did right to tell me of the bad things that wicked Cob Munyabra was planning to do to my daughter. You realise that he must be punished for his evil ways, don't you?'

Kalinga nodded dumbly.

'Do you want him to die, Kalinga, as he deserves?'

Kalinga shook her head vigorously, her eyes still downcast.

'I am a Christian woman, Kalinga, and do not wish to see a man die, but if anyone finds out about this wickedness, he will surely be hanged. Now, if you were to marry this Munyabra, be a good Christian wife to him, and teach him the error of his ways, could you keep silent about his wicked deed of last night? Forever, until you are dead, in order to save his life?'

Hardly daring to breath, Kalinga whispered, 'Yes Matron.'

Grace continued. 'My daughter must leave this dangerous place. She must go to where she will be safe from such dreadful fellows. I will see Munyabra and tell him of my decision. If he wants to live neither he nor you must ever tell anyone. Do you understand?'

'Yes, Matron. Thank you, Matron.'

'Right, go back to the kitchen and stay there until I call you.' Grace dismissed her. Kalinga scurried away, not daring to say another word in case the old devilwoman changed her mind.

*

Later, Grace went in search of Currie Munyabra. He was returning with the other men for the dinner break. She called him over. 'Munyabra, where is your son?' she demanded, hatred glistening in her eyes.

'I don't know, Matron,' he replied blandly, standing to attention, his worn tracker's uniform dusty from his work.

'Well, if you want him to live to see the sun rise tomorrow, you will tell him to be at my house tonight at ten o'clock. No one must see him come. If he doesn't attend, I will have every policeman and settler in the district hunting him down, like the dog he is. At ten o'clock, do I make myself clear?' Turning her back she swiftly walked away from the old man.

*

The bell had long since sounded for the dismissal of the drill class and the compound was now dark and silent. Ellen sat huddled in the punishment cell, with only the screeching of two possums fighting on the roof above her to keep her company. She had spent a miserable day in the stifling heat but now as the night set in the cell turned to bone chilling cold.

All day, she had waited to be released until finally, feeling totally degraded she had to relieve herself in the corner of the hut. Her mouth was parched and her limbs ached from sitting on the hard floor. She wondered if her mother meant to kill her slowly by starving her to death. She didn't care that much anymore. Perhaps Cob was dead already.

She started as the bolts were shot back loudly and the door swung open. Out of the blackness, a lamp flashed into her eyes, dazzling her.

'Get to your feet and follow me. Make one sound and you will be very sorry,' her mother's voice growled at her. Rising stiffly, Ellen limped after the light, across the compound towards the house.

Curling her nose up at Ellen's dirty, dishevelled appearance Grace came straight to the point.

'Your vile and disgusting perversions must not be allowed to lay Henry's life's work in ruins. To say nothing of myself, your sister and her husband. You must not be allowed to destroy this family!' Grace sat down, her stiff black taffeta mourning dress rustling loudly in the quiet room. Ellen stood in abject misery before her. 'Now you had better answer my questions truthfully, as your black's life depends on it!'

Ellen's eyes flickered into alertness. So Cob wasn't dead. Oh thank God! But where was he? In jail? She now listened more carefully to her mother's sarcastic, disdainful voice. 'Did that nigger penetrate your virginity at this time or at any other?' she demanded crudely.

Horror registered on Ellen's face and anger made her answer sharply, 'No! I told you before – no!'

'Watch the tone of your voice, girl. You are in no position to raise it to me. If I didn't think the gossips would get wind of it, I would have you taken to Bracefield and examined by a doctor, so be very careful.'

Fear and humiliation swept over Ellen.

'Next question. Did Laurence Reid propose to you while he was here?'

'Yes.'

'Did you accept him or refuse him?'

'Neither, I said I would think about it, but only because I

didn't want to hurt him,' Ellen whispered, wondering where this questioning was leading.

'Good. Then you will sit down and write, accepting his proposal with all the good grace you can muster. You will also tell him that you wish to be married immediately, so that Henry can perform the ceremony before he leaves. You will make it sound convincing. I shall be checking it. Do you understand?'

Ellen was aghast. 'I can't do that! I don't love him, Mother. Please don't make me do that!'

'Not only will you do that, you will also be a loving, Godfearing wife to Laurence, as long as you both shall live, or God help you! Just thank your lucky starts that you have escaped this disgusting episode so easily. Remember, and keep on remembering, this black animal you say you are so fond of will always be here on this island. He will not escape, if that's what you're thinking. He won't be able to, if he knows what's good for you, or his father. Do you understand my meaning, girl?'

'Mother, you wouldn't?'

'Wouldn't I? Just see if I wouldn't! Either you do exactly as I say or he will be hung, and you will spend the rest of your life in a lunatic asylum! And you know what they are like, don't you? I would have no trouble convincing a doctor that you were stark raving mad, and fornicating with the blacks at every opportunity, would I? You would have to be put away for your own safety, don't you see?' Grace sneered bitterly.

'Just let me and Cob go, Mother, we'd never trouble you or Henry again, honestly! We'd disappear and make a life for ourselves far away from here. Couldn't you please do that?' Ellen begged genuinely.

Grace laughed harshly. 'What, and have every Tom, Dick and Harry sniggering behind our backs about our whore of a daughter, who couldn't keep her hands off the blackfellas? You would have us destroy ourselves, and our position in the church for that? You really must be mad.' Grace stood like a judge passing sentence. 'No, Ellen, you have this one and only choice. Do you accept?'

Ellen knew she was trapped. Nothing would induce her mother to change her mind if the good names of Henry and the family were at stake. 'I accept,' she said with all the dignity she could muster.

'Right, go to your room, clean yourself up and write that letter. I will want to see it in one hour.'

*

Nugget slid down from the sitting room window where he had been listening to all that was said. He crept across the compound to hide in the shadow of the store shed to wait for Cob to appear.

Right on the stroke of ten, Cob walked silently toward the house, Nugget waylaid him with their old boyhood birdcall.

'What is it, mate? What's happening?' Cob whispered.

'Missus Ellen, she being sent away quick. She 'ave to marry Reid fella, or Missus Matron she 'ave you shot! And Missus Ellen locked up with crazy people. You done bloory stupid thing, Cob, muck round with 'er!'

'I didn't muck around with her. I've never been such a bloody gentleman in my life! Christ! If I was a big bloody boss cocky, it would be a different tale. They'd be all over me like a rash. The old bitch really said they'd lock Ellen up in the crazy house, did she? My God, they'd do anything! Did

Ellen say she'd marry that Reid fella, did she?'

'Didn't 'ave no bloody choice!' said Nugget.

'Oh! Hell! I've a good mind to just barge in there and get her. Let them all rot in hell.' In his anger Cob started to raise his voice.

'Shah! You get me shot too, if you keep that bloody row up.' Nugget grumbled warningly.

Cob paced up and down, trying to calm his rage before he had to face Grace. He knew that his pride caused him more trouble with the whites than anything else, but he was damned if he could crawl to the door and grovel for forgiveness.

What the hell! He had only taken the girl to the beach for the day. Admittedly things had got a little out of hand but nothing that he hadn't seen happen in their socalled civilisation every day of the week. But now, here they were, prepared to string him up, just because his skin was the wrong colour. He should just shoot through, now, while the going was good. Go bush, live off the land. Take up the old ways again. He'd tried their life all these years and, admittedly, when he was a little fella the police sergeants and their wives had been good to him. Treated him like one of their own. But you still couldn't bridge the gap between black and white. They wouldn't accept you as a man, as an equal. They only liked you when they could look down on you, patronise you, keep you in your place. If you dared to have opinions, dare to think for yourself, or touch anything they thought they might possibly want — wham! They had you strung up as a dirty nigger. It just wasn't worth trying! They're bastards, the lot of them, he thought bitterly. *But not Ellen, she wasn't like that. She cared for him as he was, black, brown, or brindle. She'd been prepared to go all the way with him, down there on the beach. He'd had a hard time refusing, but he'd meant what he said. He had wanted things to be different for them, and for one crazy moment, she'd had him half believing it was possible.*

What a fool he'd been! No way now could he just up and off, and leave Ellen to those pack of dingoes. The old bitch would do exactly as she threatened, have her locked up in the crazy house, if it meant saving her precious son's Christian dignity or her own. What bloody hypocrites!

Determined now, he walked to the house and straight up to the front door. As he raised his hand to knock, the door opened and Grace, turning her back on him and not speaking, walked to the centre of the room.

Cob followed her; glad he had changed from the rotten mission clothes and dressed in his good moleskins and white shirt. He had even polished his boots and they creaked as he stopped before the stiff-faced, black draped woman.

'I'm glad to see you had the good sense to come,' were her opening words. 'Don't think I underestimate your cunning, Munyabra, You saw the opportunity to destroy my family and all that we stand for here, by using my daughter's weakness and stupidity, her disgusting obsession with you blacks. Well, let me tell you Mister Munyabra, it is not we, but yourself and my half-wit daughter who will be destroyed, if one word of this foul escapade becomes known. Do I make myself clear?' She glared viciously at him.

Cob stood towering above her, the white emphasising the darkness of his skin. His eyes glinted dangerously, as he said quietly, 'Go on.'

'My daughter has agreed to leave this island immediately. She will be married by the end of the month and she does not wish to ever lay eyes on you again. Do you understand?' Not waiting for an answer she continued. 'You in turn will marry the Aboriginal girl, Kalinga. She has already agreed to this. Neither of you will ever speak of this incident again if you want to live. That is no idle threat "Mr" Munyabra.' She clenched her hands tightly under her bosom, her knuckles turning white. 'Don't think you can escape from this island. I'm sure you can imagine the rage of the settlers in these parts, if they believed a young white lady had been raped by a black heathen. We settlers are very nervous about such things, you know.

Of course, my poor daughter would be sent quite mad by the horror of it all and would certainly have to be locked away. I'm sure you understand.'

Cob pulled his earlobe as he stared straight into Grace's face, and said icily, 'Well "Matron" Grimshaw, I must say you are a credit to your race and religion. I would have expected nothing less of you. Ellen has more courage, Christianity and morals than you will have if you live to be a hundred, you evil old bitch.'

Grace's hand rose to strike him, but Cob gripped her wrist in an iron hold. 'Don't lady, just don't! Believe me, I would gladly swing for you,' he snarled, pulling her frightened face closer to his. 'I'll go along with your rotten scheme. You've got me this time you miserable old witch. But just remember, if you harm one hair on Ellen's head, just one, I'll get you, no matter where you are. And we'll see what you feel like after a pack of blacks have finished with you. Do you understand me, "Matron" Grimshaw?'

'I should have you shot here and now for this,' Grace gasped, her voice shrill with terror.

He turned, a sneer on his face, as he went through the door. 'But you won't, will you? Think of the family's name! Goodnight, "Matron" Grimshaw.'

*

Next morning, as the internees assembled in the compound for prayers, a bitter wind blew through their strange assortment of old clothes. Men blew into their cupped hands, women wrapped their arms tightly around their undernourished bodies. Children huddled together in the front rows like a litter of hungry, cold puppies, huge eyes staring sleepily from tiny drawn faces.

The Reverend Featherstone was enveloped in his thick worsted overcoat. Clutching a Bible with numb fingers, he droned on, not even listening to himself. He hurried through the service, intent only on rushing back to his house as soon as was decently possible, for a scalding cup of tea and tasty hot breakfast.

As Grace strode purposefully past the congregation, all heads turned, glad of any distraction. Ellen followed closely behind, shoulders back, head held stiffly erect, her severe black dress making her pale face seem even whiter.

Grace stopped at the Reverend Featherstone's side and waited as he mumbled through the last verse. Closing the Bible he looked up expectantly at her.

'Thank you, for those uplifting words Reverend Featherstone. I'm sure they give our brothers and sisters here new heart to go forward and do their Christian duty.' With that, Grace dismissed the Reverend and took command of the gathering. 'Now, I have some very happy news to announce this morning. Last night, our brother, Cob Munyabra, son of our much respected Currie Munyabra, came to my house to ask for the hand of my house girl, Kalinga, in Christian marriage. I am happy to say I had much pleasure in obliging him. Let's have the happy pair out front to congratulate them, shall we? Come out Kalinga and Cob, where are you hiding?'

Everyone stared as Kalinga slipped from the congregation and came to stand beside Grace. Her hair was neatly brushed and tied back with a red ribbon and she wore one of Ellen's castoff dresses. The dress was too small and the hem only reaching her calves exposing her thin brown ankles and dusty bare feet. She smiled shyly back at the gaping crowd, as she hung her head modestly. 'Now where is our bridegroom? Come along Cob, no need to be bashful!' chirped Grace with brittle joviality.

Cob stood apart from the grouped men, the collar of his old jacket turned up around his neck, against the cold. His hands were plunged stubbornly into his pockets as he glared out from under his pulled down, battered old hat.

Taking a step back, Nugget nudged him hard. 'Go on mate,' he urged, 'it's not worth swinging for.'

Cob turned his bitter face to his friend, he caught his father's eye, also delivering the same silent command. Shaking with suppressed rage, he took a deep breath and stepped forward. Grace began to clap and the congregation followed suit in ragged unison as Cob stepped over the children sitting at the front. His eyes, shaded by the curled brim of his hat, rested on Ellen who stood stiffly behind her mother watching him. He saw her lips tremble and watched a tear slide down her cheek before she hastily brushed it away.

'That's right, Cob, stand beside your bride. Don't they make a handsome couple everybody? How about three cheers to wish them luck. Hiphip!' Grace led the rousing cheers. The gathered blacks being happy to oblige with anything that stirred their numbing circulation.

With all the skill of a circus master, Grace continued the pretence. 'It seems that these two lovebirds are eager to tie the knot, so the ceremony will be performed on Wednesday, which gives us only a day to prepare. I'm sure Reverend Featherstone would agree to granting a half day holiday in honour of the occasion; is that no so, Mr Featherstone?' Grace nudged the old fellow who was lost in a daydream of steaming hot porridge and tasty liver and bacon. He started, 'Oh! Yes, Matron. Quite so, be delighted.' The children cheered, there would be no school that day.

At that moment, a little girl seated at the end of the row, stood up pointing towards the beach. 'Visitors come up, Matron Grimshaw,' she announced loudly above the general chatter. 'Look like Mr Marsden, sir coming. I see good eh, Matron?' she nodded in proud agreement with herself.

Grace froze. My God not him! Not now! It couldn't be! She could not bring herself to look. Frantically she tried to gather her wits. If he sensed one inkling of the true situation here he would have all the ammunition he needed. It would play right into his hands! He was still trying to prove them unequal to the job, and get himself reinstated. Her mind flew as she reassessed the situation, trying not to panic.

'By Jove, it is him,' said the old Reverend, squinting across the compound. 'Damn good eyesight, those blacks, can't deny that,' he said patronisingly.

Grace moved swiftly towards Cob and Kalinga who were standing centre stage, like nervous volunteers from the audience, ready to bolt at the first opportunity. Placing herself between them, she smiled a teeth baring smile and hissed quietly, 'Remember, Kalinga, not one word to Mr Marsden or he will be forced to arrest Cob; it would be his duty as

Protector.' Kalinga nodded vigorously, her eyes flicking nervously. Grace turned on Cob. 'Munyabra, look behind me, that's right!'

He stared over her shoulder towards Ellen who stood, despondent and humiliated, swaying slightly in a mammoth effort to keep herself erect. Her suffering was reflected in Cob's eyes as he sadly watched her. Grace pushed home her advantage. 'Haven't you done enough to her? How long do you think she will last in the asylum, Munyabra?'

Cob, flinched at the word. 'I'm playing your rotten game, aren't I? Leave her alone.'

'Just make sure you keep doing so,' Grace snapped.

She moved through the crowd to Ellen's side and whispered behind her handkerchief. 'Pull yourself together and smile! If Marsden gets one whiff of your disgusting behaviour we are all finished. Your bastard black included.'

She moved off swiftly, waving the handkerchief to Marsden and his companion as they strode into the compound.

'Good morning Reverend,' Marsden raised his pith helmet. 'And you, Matron Grimshaw. Allow me to introduce my son, Harry.' Harry smiled weakly, a fragile replica of the older man.

'Looks like we came at the right moment, why are you meeting? Not trouble is it?' Marsden asked almost hopefully.

Grace silently scorned his elegant tweed jacket and moleskin trousers, encased in polished leather gaiters. His suede-gloved hand clasped a liver knobbed stick, tucked neatly under his arm. *Just as Henry had said, another wealthy eccentric,* Grace thought, and found herself disliking the man just as Henry had.

'No, on the contrary, Mr Marsden. We were just announcing our first Christian marriage. Good news indeed, don't you agree?' she informed him briskly.

Marsden looked disparagingly down his long nose. 'Can't see the point in it myself. They haven't the vaguest notion as to the meaning of the ceremony. Saw some nigger babies being baptised once, while the fathers were at the back of the group pouring water over each other's heads and howling with laughter. Wonderful mimics these natives, don't you agree ma'am?' he sneered mockingly at Grace.

Grace's hackles rose instantly. 'May I ask what brings you to our mission Mr Marsden?' she enquired, giving him to understand by her tone that he was not welcome.

'I have come, dear lady, in my capacity as Protector. I am here to inspect the mission. I also require sixteen blacks, to take part in the Federal celebrations to be held in Brisbane this coming January. I do believe that Reverend Featherstone here is in charge of this mission station, Madam, so my request will be directed to him!' Marsden had effectively put Grace in her place and she seethed with indignation.

Poor old, Reverend Featherstone looked worriedly from one to the other, as the hostile atmosphere thickened. Grace was not about to be demeaned publicly by this domineering intruder. 'By what authority are you permitted to remove natives from this mission? Do you have authorisation from the Home Secretary?'

Marsden sighed condescendingly, tapping his cane on his gloved palm. 'Really, dear lady, I don't think you understand. If indeed it is any of your business, that is! I do not need authority from the Home Secretary, or anyone else for that matter. The government has decided to have a showing of Aboriginal culture in the celebrations. I am here to choose the ablest men. It's as simple as that!' He looked down at her as if she were some poor anthropological specimen. 'Now without more ado,' he said, dismissing her out of hand, 'ones I thought most likely would be…' He took a list from his pocket and proceeded to read it. 'Joseph, Charlie, Albert, Percy, Nugget, Cob.'

'You can't have him,' Grace interrupted sharply as Marsden read Cob's name.

'And why ever not, may I ask?' Marsden looked at in amazement, really this woman was too much.

'Because he is getting married on Wednesday,' blustered Grace on the verge of panic.

'I can't see what difference that would make. If you had more knowledge of the race, Madam, you would know that! We'll ask him if he wants to go, shall we?' Marsden challenged her and she was cornered. 'Call the black over, Reverend. We'll soon see who is right.'

The old fellow shuffled off shaking his head. Why they had to stand in the bitter cold arguing over a few blacks was beyond him. His breakfast would be ruined by now. Some people had no consideration.

Grace fought to keep her composure. Cob must not be allowed to leave the island! Once away, he would no longer be in her power. She looked around frantically for ammunition and spied Ellen standing alone a few yards away. 'Ellen dear, come and meet Mr Marsden and his son,' she called pleasantly. Ellen turned vaguely, her mind blank with misery.

'Come here, dear, and meet our guests,' Grace walked over and gripped Ellen's arm, her fingernails digging deep into the girls flesh. 'May I introduce my daughter, Ellen. Ellen, this is Mr Marsden, Aboriginal Protector, and his son Harry.'

'How do you do, Miss Grimshaw? How do you like living

on the island and working with the blacks? Hardly the life for a young lady, I would think.'

'I find it quite interesting, thank you, Mr Marsden,' Ellen answered parrotfashion, desperately wanting to run away and hide.

'Here comes the fellow, Cob, now Father.' Marsden's son sounded like his father. Ellen spun around, scarcely able to contain her emotions as Cob was led up by the grumbling old cleric. She felt a sharp stabbing pain as Grace's grip tightened on her arm in sharp warning.

Marsden greeted Cob. 'Good to see you again, Cob. How's mission life suiting you? I hear you're to be married soon?'

Cob peered suspiciously out from under his hat. 'That's right,' he answered shortly.

'Well, I have come to select sixteen of you fellows. I want you to represent your race at the Federation celebrations. This lady here says you wouldn't like to go, which I find very hard to believe. What have you to say on the matter?' Marsden asked confidently.

Cob's eyes shifted from Marsden to Grace, then to Ellen who was picking nervously at her gloves. Cob's heart ached for her. She looked so shattered and defeated. He couldn't cause her any more misery. 'Reckon that would be right Mr Marsden. Don't fancy having to make a monkey out of myself to amuse a mob of whites,' Cob answered rudely.

Marsden flared at the insult. 'Well, suit yourself, I'm sure! There's plenty here who would be glad to get away. Stay here if you like the damn place so much.' Marsden became childishly petty. He turned sulkily to Reverend Featherstone, 'Come along Reverend, let's have that cup of tea. We must not delay this lady, after all, we can't afford to waste the government's money,' he remarked snidely, hustling the old Reverend away. His son trotted after him like a well-trained dog.

Cob moved towards Ellen, but Grace smartly interceded. Roughly she pulled Ellen back. 'No, you don't. Get back where you belong Munyabra. You get back to the house Ellen and stay there.' She pushed the girl who staggered off with tears pouring down her face. Cob curled his lip in contempt. 'Bitch.' He spat as he turned on his heel and marched away.

Marsden created havoc for the old Reverend that day and the next. He criticised expenditure; he was disgusted with the food; he gave advice on every subject imaginable until Reverend Featherstone's head ached. As he retired that night, the old Reverend thought grumpily of Marsden's harassment. *Matron was no help to him either. She argued with Marsden at every opportunity, to the point where he had to keep them apart, just for some peace! She was spending all her energies organising this wretched wedding. Making such a fuss, when normally she never had a kind word to say for Kalinga or Cob. It was all very strange. Then, to cap it all, she announces that her daughter is going off to marry the Reid chappie from Bibiringda. Well, it had been obvious that the sickly-looking fellow was totally besotted with the girl, but to leave at such short notice, when they were so under-staffed, was very thoughtless indeed. One couldn't rely on the young these days!*

The old fellow removed his dressing gown and bent stiffly to flip off his slippers. As he eased himself into his bed, he heard a muffled conversation coming from the next room. Dratted Marsden and his son! Trust them to decide to stay over for the wedding, disturbing his routine and keeping him awake with their jabber. *The sooner I retire from this lot the better,* the weary old man thought, as he pulled the blankets over his ears.

'Why did you decide to stay for the wedding, father?' enquired Harry, as he straightened his trousers and lay them beside his father's under the lumpy mattress of the double bed.

'I don't really know, son,' answered Marsden, carefully shaving around his long side burns and under his pointed beard. 'I just have a feeling that something's going on. That insufferable Grimshaw woman is too eager to be rid of us. Nasty piece of work, that woman.' He wiped the cutthroat razor on the towel draped across his shoulder.

'Yes, I agree. The poor daughter seems to have a hard time of it. The woman barely speaks civilly to her. Not that she says much either, which is strange too. I was led to believe she was quite the belle of society in Bracefield. Hard to believe when you see her moping around, never a smile or a word, unless you wring it out of her. I wonder what happened?' Harry pulled on his nightshirt and scrambled into bed. He lay watching his father. 'The old Reverend chap says she's off to Bibiringda, to marry the assistant there. All of a sudden, he says, most annoyed about it.'

'Mmm,' Marsden mused, 'maybe that's the secret. She wouldn't be the first girl to make a hasty marriage, missionary's sister or not. That could just be it,' he decided.

Ellen sat on her bed surrounded by clothes set in neat piles ready to pack. She looked down again at the cable spread out on her lap. With sickening hopelessness she reread Laurence's reply.

DEAREST ELLEN – STOP – AM DELIGHTED
– STOP – WILL ARRIVE IN TOWNSVILLE
ONE WEEK AFTER YOU – STOP – HENRY
THRILLED TO PERFORM CEREMONY HAS

DELAYED DEPARTURE TO OFFICIATE –
STOP – NEW CHURCH COMPLETED WILL
LOOK BEAUTIFUL – STOP – DEAREST LOVE
LAURENCE

Even in the abrupt form of a wire, Ellen could sense his joy and excitement. Poor Laurence, little did he realise the deceit which was the basis of his happiness. How could she keep up the pretence throughout the ceremony and, God only knew, the rest of her life?

Tenderly lifting the little sand bottle from the dressing table, she thought wistfully of the day on the beach when she and Cob had collected the sand. Raising her eyes, Ellen studied her reflection in the mirror. A dark, sombre girl stared mockingly back, the dulled blue eyes rimmed with dark circles looked with scorn on the weak creature reflected. 'Well, Laurence,' she whispered, 'that's the rotten deal you are getting for your trouble. Look at her – spineless creature, isn't she, and in love with another man, a black man!

'What would you think of that? She hasn't got the guts to fight for him either, and she's allowed herself to be battered and cursed into submission. Just let him go! And now where is he? Being married to someone with black skin like his own.'

The pain welled unbearably and she slumped forward hugging the bottle to her. 'Cob! Oh my God, Cob!' she moaned, 'I know you've got to do it but I can't bear it. It hurts too much!' Still clutching the rainbow bottle she stumbled to the bed and threw herself onto the pile of clothes, wishing with all her heart that she could just die there.

*

The wedding had been a great success. Grace congratulated herself as she sat at the bridal table beside Reverend Featherstone, watching the newly married couple attempting to dance the Bridal Waltz, accompanied by Nugget on an old accordion. The rest of the mission people stood around the schoolroom laughing and clapping. Taking each other's hands the little children jigged around, copying the bride and groom. As he stiffly steered the glowing Kalinga around the small floor, Cob's face was expressionless. Kalinga worriedly watched his feet, trying to follow his steps. She was terrified of stumbling and embarrassing Cob, who knew all about these white weddings. In her experience, the groom just came to the gunya and took the girl, chosen for him by his uncles. They then went to the marriage bed, prepared by the girl's aunts. If the girl was tearful or nervous, they would sit with her for a while until she settled, or camp discreetly nearby to give her confidence. But that was all. Not like this, with the Reverend Featherstone saying words they had to repeat about plighting and trothing, whatever that meant! She had to admit that the dress Matron had given her was nice. All the flowers they had pinned into her hair made her feel really important. But Cob didn't seem to notice. He was tense and cold and hadn't smiled at her once. She set her mouth and stared down intently at his boots, wondering which foot he was going to move next.

Grace glanced across the table to where Marsden and his son were loudly discussing their plans. They would choose the biggest and strongest Kalangari Islanders for the Federation celebrations. They would oil their black bodies and dress them in traditional tribal dress – war paint, spears and shields. What a magnificent sight they would be. Really make the Brisbane ladies swoon!

'Stupid men,' Grace scoffed to herself. 'He wouldn't get any blacks from here if she had her way. Dressing them up, giving them ideas above their station, God! Hadn't she had enough trouble in that direction with Munyabra? When would these socalled academics realise the trouble they caused? They only came up with wild theories, let someone else do the hard practical work. Some even criticised the missionaries for teaching the blacks to read and write.

Why, she thought, *even Marsden himself, the hypocrite, screamed about keeping them primitive and untouched and now, here he was, wanting to make show ponies out of them.* She smiled a cold smile, nodding acknowledgement to him across the table. Well, thank goodness she had managed to keep Ellen away today. He had swallowed her excuse that she had too much packing to do as she was leaving tomorrow.

Couldn't risk Ellen making a fool of herself in front of Marsden. He was shrewd, that one. Come to think of it, he had been overly polite about the matter. What had he meant, when he said in his slimy way, 'Of course, dear lady, young girls can be so delicate before they marry, and all this rush too, the poor girl must be quite exhausted!' Well, thank God he and his shadow of a son were leaving on the afternoon boat. *After that I'll be able to breathe again,* she thought with relief.

*

Cob sat on a log smoking his clay pipe, staring morosely through the black night. Across the compound the softly glowing light of a lamp shone from Ellen's window. Taking the half empty rum bottle he drank a long swig.

'Come on, mate, cheer up a bit. It could be worse. You

could be swinging from a tree with the crows picking at you by now,' Nugget gave Cob a flashing grin as he tried vainly to lighten his friend's dark mood.

'I've got to see her before she goes, Nugget,' Cob replied tensely, not taking his eyes from the light.

'Jesus, mate! Don't start all that up again. Ya got away with it this time, but if ya try'n get to 'er now, they'll nab you fa sure.' Nugget nervously took the bottle and gulped the rum.

'I've got to try, mate. I can't let her go like this. She's the one for me, mate, always will be. That's just how it is. I've got to tell her before she goes.'

Nugget scratched his head in exasperation. 'Well, I dunno how ya gunna do it, mate, that old crow will be watching all a time. Kalinga bin waiting for you half a bloody night now. She'll come looking again soon.'

Cob rose and patted Nugget's shoulder. 'If she does, you cover for me, it's my last chance.'

'All right, but I'm not coming with you, you stupid black bastard. You get done good this time,' Nugget warned, watching Cob go.

No lights were visible from the front of the house. Cob felt safe in assuming that the old witch was in her bed, smug in the knowledge that she had witnessed his dispatch that afternoon. Creeping closer, he was grateful for the pitch black, overcast night into which he blended. Like a spirit skimming soundlessly over the dry grass, he moved without rustling a leaf. Birds slept soundly on, undisturbed, as he glided silently past.

Pausing, he listened intently for any sign of the constables before he moved swiftly to the back of the house. Crouching under Ellen's window, he balanced his toes on the lead capped stump and pulled himself up. His eyes travelled swiftly around the dimly lit room. Miserably he noted the half packed trunk, its open lid draped with dresses. The bed was strewn with coats and linen. He didn't notice the small, curled body of Ellen amid the disarray, until her foot moved as she rolled over in fitful sleep. Easing himself back down to the ground, he picked out a broom from among Nugget's discarded tools and tapped gently on the window with it.

In Ellen's nightmare dream, the monstrous face of Henry loomed over her accusingly as he mercilessly crammed red hot, burning wedding rings, one after another, along her tortured fingers. Screaming, she jolted upright, her heart pounding. The tapping at the window brought her back to reality. Sliding from the bed she stumbled towards the noise and lifting the sash, peered down into the darkness. Cob's face stared worriedly up at her, his arms outstretched. Without a sound she swung herself over the sill. His strong arms caught her, crushing her body to his, his mouth urgently kissed her lips, her wet eyes, and cheeks.

Cob gently lowered her to the ground. Still clinging together, they slid beneath the house and lay on the dry soft dusty sand under the cobwebbed floor timbers. No words were spoken as they made love, their bodies melting together in a last desperate bid to belong to each other.

Afterwards, Cob lay exhausted over Ellen's body. She stroked his long black hair and rocked him gently, feeling at peace with herself for the first time since she had arrived on this island. He gazed miserably down at her through the close dusty darkness. 'Oh God, Ellen, what have I done to you now? I didn't mean that to happen, honestly, I didn't,' he whispered, as his tears dripped down onto her face.

She cradled his head down to her breasts. 'Hush, Cob, hush, it's all right, really it is,' she crooned to him as one would to a fretful child. 'I wanted you too. I belong to you now no matter what happens to us.' Tenderly, she dusted a cobweb from his hair. They lay close, fondling each other, trying to imprint in their minds every curve and bend in each other's bodies, to store in their memories for the cold empty future.

'We could just go, Ellen,' Cob whispered wildly in her ear. 'We could make a break for it, go bush, I could look after us.'

'We'd be found, Cob, they couldn't just let us disappear Marsden would make sure there was a hue and cry and Mother would have to act, or admit the truth, and she couldn't do that. This is all we have, I'm afraid,' Ellen replied sadly, facing the inevitable.

Cob hugged her close. 'I do love you, Ellen. I came tonight to tell you, I couldn't let you go without knowing. There's nothing anyone can do to me that will change that. Maybe someday it will be all right for a black to love a white girl,' he said wistfully.

Ellen smiled at him in the darkness. 'That must be the longest speech you ever made, Mr Munyabra.'

'I think you're bloody right, Miss Grimshaw,' he whispered.

Time was their enemy now. As they watched, the blackness of the night faded into predawn. Soon they would have to say goodbye.

Ellen moved first. Crawling to the edge of the timbers, she waited for Cob to follow. 'Let's part now while we're calm. Be happy with Kalinga, Cob. But don't forget me. I'll never forget you. Try to remember us with love, not hate. Remember we've broken all the rules. Now we have to pay the price. When you feel sad, go to the coloured sands and think of me.

I will always have your love with me in my little sand bottle.'

Mutely their foreheads touched, then Cob lifted her in his arms and she swung back over the window ledge. 'Goodbye Mr Munyabra,' she whispered softly.

'Goodbye, Miss Grimshaw,' his soft voice cracked, before he melted away into the darkness.

*

Grace was surprised when Ellen appeared for breakfast next morning. She ate nothing, but sipped tea while Grace went over the arrangements. 'You'll have to be on the eight o'clock barge from the island, which will get you into Bracefield in plenty of time to be settled on the boat for Townsville before she sails. You'll stay with Amy and Edward until Laurence arrives. I would, of course, come with you, but I'm afraid, with things as they are, I really couldn't leave.'

'Don't worry about it, Mother, I will be quite all right,' Ellen said calmly putting down her teacup.

'Someone has to worry! Don't you realise how close you came to ruining us all? I had to do what I did to protect you! To protect us all. It's a mother's duty and don't you ever tell Henry about this! He must never know. He has enough problems on his mind at the moment and no useful purpose can be gained by distressing him, or your sister either. Just you thank your lucky stars, my girl, that I have managed to avert this disaster. I hope you have learned your lesson!' Underneath Grace's harshness was a small suggestion of reconciliation, mingled with relief.

Too proud to openly suggest that she and her daughter make up their quarrel, she waited for Ellen to beg forgiveness but Ellen sipped another cup of tea, showing no sign of contrition.

Angry that so guilty a party had rejected her generous gesture, Grace once more became aggressive. 'Don't you realise that if I allowed one inkling of what you have done be known, not Laurence – nor any other decent man would ever look at you. No man would want to marry a girl who defiled herself with a black. Oh! The very idea makes one shudder. God knows what would have happened if I hadn't stepped in. Just you be grateful! Then God may find it in his heart to forgive you one day.'

Ellen rose quietly, pushing away her teacup. 'God may, Mother. If He thinks there's anything to forgive, which I doubt, but what about your forgiveness? You're so righteous, aren't you? Doing your Christian duty, by these people. Yes Mother, they are people, just like you or me! You starve them, kidnap their children, strip them of their culture, rob them of their land, force your religion down their throats but you don't even class them as human beings, do you? Cob Munyabra is the most beautiful man I've ever met, but to you he is little more than an animal! You talk about brotherly love, but you don't mean a word of it, do you? I dared to love just one of them and I am treated like a whore! Don't worry; I'll marry Laurence as you order. I'll do my best to make him happy. That's the least he deserves for what we are doing to him. But don't ask me to love him because I love Cob, and I always will! There is absolutely nothing you can ever do to me that will change that.'

Grace sat speechless, Ellen straightened her shoulders and said with dignity, 'Now I will finish my packing and remove my abhorrent self from your sight.'

Later, Grace stood watching from the veranda, gripping the handrails for support as, straight shouldered, head held defiantly erect, Ellen strode down the track to board the waiting barge. She did not turn and wave to her mother and Grace would not allow herself to wish her daughter goodbye.

CHAPTER TEN

Unable to sleep, Ellen stood at the bedroom window watching the dark outline of Magnetic Island silhouetted against the rising sun.

The anguished numbness, which had paralysed her for the last week, was beginning to ease a little now.

She could smile at the antics of the brilliant green parrots, performing impossible acrobatics, as they competed for the nectar of the flame red blossoms that overhung her bedroom window. A brisk sea breeze ruffled her long nightdress and billowed the lace curtains.

She shivered a little as she stood deep in thought, trying to piece together the shattered remnants of her life.

Cob was lost to her, gone into the untraceable past, and now she had to find the courage to face Laurence, who was arriving today. He could no longer be banished from her mind; there was no escape.

He was taking her back to Bibiringda where she had no choice but to marry him, and make the best of it. It had to be faced.

She was startled from her thoughts as Amy swept briskly into her room. Now a plump well-corseted young matron, she was every inch the successful business man's wife.

'Edward has just left to take the first batch of contract labour down to the meatworks. He says they are a really rough lot. The captain of the ship that brought them from Sydney is charging for all the damage they caused on the voyage up, and threatening not to bring any more. Edward won't be back until late tonight. He is sorry not to be here to meet Laurence.' She chatted as she examined her sister's meagre supply of clothes.

Ellen breathed a sigh of relief. Not fond of her brotherinlaw's company at the best of times, at this time she found his loud brashness unbearable. She was glad he would not be here to witness her performance when Laurence arrived because, for all his faults, he was a very astute man.

'We'll have to go shopping today, Ellen,' Amy declared. 'You haven't brought a quarter of what you will need for your trousseau. Honestly, you seem as excited about this wedding as someone going to their own funeral!'

Ellen sighed wearily, 'I've already told you I don't need very much. The wedding is going to be a quiet affair at the mission. I thought I would wear one of the good dresses Mother made for me in Bracefield, that will do. I have all I need.'

Amy was astounded. 'You can't not have a wedding dress! What would people say? Your trouble is you've lived on those missions for too long! You mustn't let yourself go Ellen. You can't go back to Bibiringda and live as you used to, you were nothing but a little savage.'

'I'm not wasting money on a wedding dress, so stop brow beating me!' Ellen snapped back angrily.

Amy ignored her. 'I have already spoken to Edward, and he agrees with me. We can't have my sister going of to get married without a proper trousseau. What would the trades people here think? They are bound to talk; Edward has his position in this town to consider, you know. He's a member of the North Queensland Club now. We have to keep up appearances. He will be only too happy for you to buy what you need, on my accounts!'

Defeated, Ellen was dragged unwillingly through every shop in Flinders Street, where she was shown all the goods that according to Amy, she would desperately need. They were ordered to be delivered to the house by the cartload. Each purchase rang a deathknell, reminding Ellen of her inescapable fate.

All the friends and acquaintances Amy could muster heralded the docking of Laurence's ship that afternoon. They lined the wharf cheering and waving ribbons and horseshoes in greeting to the bridegroom to be.

Laurence squirmed with embarrassment as he descended the gangplank, to be borne off by the laughing crowd, making it impossible for any private conversation. For once Ellen blessed her sister's showmanship.

The following day Edward insisted on taking them on a tour of the Alligator Creek meatworks, pride and joy of his partner, Mr Cordingly, and himself. They travelled for hours along the dry dusty track until the sickening sweet smell of the cooking flesh signalled they were approaching the works.

Ahead, they could see a large group of buildings.

'We have three hundred men working here during the season,' Edward boasted proudly.

Work was in full swing inside the hot gauzed sheds, where some fifty men worked on the chain, in the soaring heat, stripped to the waist boning out the heavy carcases of beef. The massive joints were then taken to the boiling shed to be cubed by vicious looking slicer blades before being tossed into colossal steaming vats to be cooked. The meat was then passed to the cannery to be tinned and labelled "Bully beef".

Laurence was impressed by the size and efficiency of the whole operation. Nothing was wasted. The stock left after the fourth boil down was condensed and reduced into drums of beef extract, the offal was taken away and processed into fertiliser.

Outside they passed mountains of boiled bones stacked in the sun to bleach, before being exported for the production of buttons.

The air was filled with the sickly odour of fat being boiled down into tallow, which would be shipped off for candle making, nearby, stacks of fly covered green hides waited to be tanned into leather.

As they stood amidst the carnage, the stench of hot blood and boiling flesh made Ellen retch, and for a moment her vision blurred and she swayed light headedly. Amy and Edward talked excitedly with Laurence about the profits, which were returned from each lugger load of tins, and hides that passed down the creek in an unending procession, bound for Townsville harbour for transfer onto ships that were bound for Europe.

'We've thousands of troops fighting the old Boers now, you know. We have some excellent contracts with the military for bully beef and leather. It will be a good year for us,' Edward bragged.

Much to Ellen's relief, Amy's programme for the following day was such a whirl of traditional pre-wedding activity, that she and Laurence hardly had time to speak to each other, certainly no time to be alone. In the afternoon, a kitchen tea, where all the ladies brought Ellen gifts, gave advice about marriage in general, and gossiped about their own marriages in particular.

That evening a lavish dinner party was held in honour of the bride and groom.

Next morning, however, Laurence insisted they escape and walk to Queen's Park. As they strolled under the shady old Moreton Bay fig trees, Laurence reached out and took her hand. 'Amy means well I know, but we haven't had a minute together since I arrived,' He moved closer. 'May I kiss you, Ellen?' he asked.

'Of course you may, Laurence, we're to be married in a few weeks, aren't we?'

She closed her eyes as she felt his lips gently pressing hers. Unbidden, her mind flashed back to Cob's dark face above hers, holding her head in his hands, kissing her eyes, crushing her body beneath his. Frantically, she clamped her brain shut. *No, no, dear God, no!* She placed her arms around Laurence's neck and kissed him hard in return. Surprised, he pulled back in wonder. 'Oh Ellen! We are going to be so happy, I just know it! I'm a lucky man.' He bent and kissed her hands reverently. Looking down on his lowered head, she almost wept, *I'm not going to cheat you, no matter what I feel. I'll make you as happy as you deserve. You'll never know.* she vowed to herself.

On the last evening of their stay in Townsville, Ellen thanked Amy for all the wonderful, if slightly unsuitable gifts she had bestowed on them. Tissue paper and straw littered the dining room floor as they tried unsuccessfully to fit everything into the overflowing tea chests.

'Think nothing of it, Ellen. I'm just glad we could afford to give you a proper trousseau. How you can go back there, I can't imagine. Anyway, I've enjoyed all the fuss. I get lonely and bored with Edward working away so much, to tell you the truth. It would be different I suppose, if we had children.'

Suddenly she became wistful. 'I know I shouldn't complain. Edward gives me all I want, but it does seem strange that we haven't had a baby yet. All my friends here have a baby every year, just about.'

Ellen, put an arm around her shoulder. 'Have you seen a doctor, Amy?'

'Yes. He says he can't find anything really wrong, only time will tell and he tells me to keep busy and not get depressed.'

'Well, I'm sure he's right, you'll see, you will finish up with a dozen children. Come on, help me with the rest of this stuff or I'll never be ready in time for the boat tomorrow.'

*

Bibiringda had changed a great deal in the years Ellen had been away. She noticed it immediately she stepped from the *Goodwill*. Civilisation had taken over with a vengeance. The jungle had been eliminated, leaving vast tracts of cleared land.

Henry came striding up to greet her. 'How's my little sister?' he asked smiling down at her. He looked older, she thought, more distinguished. He had an air of authority about him now, as if he was used to being obeyed without question.

'I'm fine, Henry. Amy sends her love. Gosh, this place has changed. You've cleared so much more land.'

'Wait till you see the house, and the church, and the new dispensary. Your husband-tobe here has done a wonderful job.' He patted Laurence affectionately on the back. 'I could not manage without him, you know! I hope you realise how happy it makes me to have him join our family. You've made a very wise choice, Ellen.'

Laurence's thin face broke into a wide smile as he said, 'It's

I who am the lucky one, Henry, truly.'

Ellen quickly changed the subject as she started to walk up the track. 'I see the old cross that Father made is still standing,' she commented as they strode past the roughly hewn monument.

'Indeed it is. I will always preserve it here in memory of our founder,' Henry said piously.

Ellen looked up in surprise as a procession of twenty white-surpliced Aboriginal men strode solemnly down the track towards them, followed by a sea of black faces.

'Who are all these people?' she asked in wonder.

'My assistants, and your welcoming committee,' Henry said proudly. The mission procession halted, and the children, neatly dressed, and faces scrubbed, obediently lined up and sang a little song of welcome.

Smiling her thanks, Ellen searched the crowd, looking for familiar faces but could find none she recognised until King, a very old man now, dressed in mission clothes, his white hair carefully combed, stepped forward to welcome her. 'Goodness King, I didn't recognise you all dressed up like that! How are you! How are your wives and children?' She happily gripped his gnarled black hand in hers.

'I am a Christian now, Miss Ellen, only got one wife, like Jesus says,' he answered, shrugging his shoulders.

'Oh, I see, how nice for you,' Ellen turned to Henry in embarrassment. 'Where are the girls we had when we first came here?'

'Some went away into service, but the others are here, mostly married, with children now.' He called out a couple of names, and the young women came forward to shyly shake hands with Ellen. All the happy spontaneity and laughter seemed to have gone out of their lives now, and Ellen felt like a white stranger in their midst.

On reaching the cottage, she was delighted to see a pretty veranda had been added with a little garden planted out front, complete with picket fence. Ferns and flowers bloomed in profusion. Inside, the dirt floor had been covered with fine grey slate, brought from one of the nearby creek beds. Another room had been added, and real furniture now graced the parlour. 'Henry, you've done wonders with the old place!'

'I told you Laurence did most of it. I think he was hoping you'd say yes all along,' Henry teased his friend.

Wandering into the kitchen she sniffed appreciatively. 'What's that lovely smell?'

'Dinner. I thought you'd be hungry after your journey. I have everything ready, even a damper in the oven.' Henry took down plates and started to serve the meal.

'Where did you manage to get an oven?' Ellen asked, laying the table. 'Now this really is modernisation. I'm impressed.'

'Picked it up at a sale in Cairns. It goes like a beauty.' Henry proudly carried the piping hot, crisp bread to the table. The three talked as they ate, laughing as they reminisced about old times. Henry was full of excitement about his coming expedition and talked non-stop.

It was late. Ellen's eyelids drooped. She lost concentration and began to doze.

'Hey Ellen, wake up! I was just saying to Laurence, everything is organised for tomorrow.'

Ellen startled, 'What about tomorrow?'

'Your wedding, dear girl, that's what. It will have to be tomorrow. I have to leave Saturday. I've held off as long as I could, but the pack horses have been delivered and are waiting in Cairns.'

Ellen froze – her wedding! Tomorrow! The trap was set and sprung.

CHAPTER ELEVEN

Henry has been gone for a month now and life at Bibiringda settled back into its usual humdrum routine. The land grant of 80 square miles was now dotted with small villages and with such little interference from the outside world it now resembled a tiny feudal kingdom; it's king gone off crusading, while the prince consort was left to rule in his place. Each village was placed in the charge of a black knight loyal to the king. The population had now swelled to over 300 but Ellen found she had no opportunity to make friends with the Aborigines.

The new way of life was stifling; rules controlled everyone. Henry had trained his large band of assistants well. They were as strict disciplinarians with their own people as he was with them. The mission now boasted its own courts, where culprits were tried, convicted and sentenced completely outside any official legal system. White staff who volunteered their services these days stayed for only a few months and lived in small wooden houses close to the school and church. No whites were allowed in the villages.

With Henry's work being recognised and appreciated by the church hierarchy, funds were more forthcoming and the little kingdom's coffers, though not overflowing, were in a healthy state through Henry's careful management. Laurence was now spending his time, administering the mission's financial affairs, visiting each of the villages in turn, checking the crops each grew and the labour output of the tenants.

Ellen was lonely. She missed her friends, especially Laura, from whom she had received a very puzzled letter, demanding to know why Ellen hadn't seen fit to visit them before she had left to be married. Why had she changed her mind so suddenly about marrying Laurence? By the tone of the letter, Ellen could feel her friend's hurt at being snubbed, but being unable to answer her impossible questions honestly, she replied congratulating Laura on her own engagement and leaving the rest unanswered.

Time began to hang heavily on her hands. There was no need for her to volunteer for mission duties, apart from the social ones expected of her. She took to moping around the house, sewing, reading, and being depressed. She felt quite ill some days but put this down to the heat and readjusting to the tropical climate.

Laurence soon began to notice how listless she had become, and would rush through his work to allow him more time at home with her. He felt his own happiness was complete, he had his work, and he had Ellen. Their marriage may not be the passionate romance one read about but Ellen fulfilled his every need, though sometimes he felt she seemed far away, lost in a world of her own. He couldn't put his finger on it exactly; just somehow she seemed to have lost her sparkle.

One evening as they walked back to the house after the evening drill, he tentatively suggested that she might like to work at the dispensary again for a couple of hours a day to occupy herself. Half-heartedly, she agreed, and next morning rode her horse around the bay to where the new dispensary now stood. Groups of Aboriginals sat outside waiting, mostly women with young children. Inside the timber building two

Aboriginal girls sat rolling bandages.

They smiled at her shyly. The clean scrubbed wooden tables smelt strongly of carbolic soap. Rows of large brown bottles sat on shelves neatly labelled and orderly. A small spirit stove holding a pot of water bubbled away ready for the day's treatments.

A fat jolly half caste woman with slightly Asian features came bouncing up the steps, laughing over her shoulder as she shared a joke with one of the waiting women. She wore a simple cotton dress over which was wrapped a large white apron.

'Hello Missus Ellen! Good to see you come back to 'elp us again,' she called cheerfully.

Ellen studied her with puzzled expression.

'You remember me, Leena, I came to mission long time ago when we all little uns. I grow bigger un you, eh?' She gave a huge belly laugh, slapping her fat thighs.

'Leena? I wouldn't have known you. You've changed so much.'

For no reason, tears filled Ellen's eyes. This warm happy woman seemed to thaw a frozen spot in her heart. Leena patted her kindly and walked back towards the open door. 'Who first today then? You can come in now,' her voice boomed to the waiting patients.

As they worked through the queue of sick people, Ellen marvelled at Leena's skill. She spoke sharply to a mother not following her advice, joked and tickled small boys as they tried to spit out her medicines, but was as gentle as a butterfly with the hurting little bodies of the babies. She showed respect and dignity when she talked to the old people. The last patient of the day was a young girl. Ellen had noticed her earlier hanging back, away from the others, as each one had been called in turn.

The girl came up the steps now, looking scared and ready to bolt.

'Come on up, Kitty, let me see if your foot fixed up good now,' Leena good-naturedly pushed her down onto a bench. Puffing, she bent her huge bulk over to unwrap the dirty bandage around the girl's dusty foot. 'You not been washing it like I told you, eh?' she said accusingly 'You lucky this time, it's comin' good, but you are to wash it all a time in sea, till I tell you stop.' She looked up into the girl's face and studied it for a while. 'You feelin' sick somewhere else, Kitty?' she enquired suspiciously. Kitty hung her head, her lip trembled and a tear slid down her black cheek. 'Baby spirit, he come knock me up, Leena,' she confessed, wringing her hands.

'You know Rev'and Fader say there ain't no baby spirit no more!' Lena bellowed. 'You bin fornicatin! You wicked girl! Now God and Rev'and Fader will 'ave to punish you. You in big trouble, girl.'

Ellen stepped back as Leena heaved herself upright again. Poor Kitty shook as she sobbed quietly.

'Stand up,' Leena ordered the girl, and pulling open her dress Leena exposed Kitty's tender swollen breasts. Running her large strong hand over the girl's belly she confirmed her diagnosis. 'You knocked up, all right. That little fella, he bin in there a good time, 'im start shifting roun' soon.'

Ellen's eyes were round with wonder at the woman's skill. How on earth could she tell?

'Youse shift youself off now, an tell the fella youse bin fornicatin' along of that he 'as to get married alonga you on Sunday.'

Kitty pulled her dress back on and stumbled miserably out of the dispensary.

'What will happen to her, Leena?' Ellen enquired as she watched the poor girl wander off.

'She'll 'ave to stand up in church on Sunday an all mission get told she been bad and evil. She get shamed in front of everyone, then she 'ave to be married if assistants can find fella she get baby spirit from.'

'But you told her there was no baby spirit.'

'Rev'and Fader, he say there no baby spirit, but I don't know sometimes. Some of women they 'ave 'usband long time an' get no baby,' she replied, shrugging her shoulders at the mystery of it all.

'How could you tell she was having a baby. I thought only a doctor would know.'

'It show in 'er face, and 'er titties was gettin' ready,' Leena puffed as she bustled about clearing up after the day's work. 'An 'er bleeding time, 'im no come. She knocked up all right.'

After dinner that night Ellen told Laurence of poor Kitty's condition.

'Oh dear! I hate this to happen. It's so hard to instil morals into some of these young girls, though often it's the men's fault. They believe they still have a claim over the women by old tribal rights. Henry gets very angry about it. I will have to make an example of her, though I hate doing it,' he concluded.

'Surely there's no need, Laurence. I think she has suffered enough, judging by how unhappy she looked this afternoon, and she's so young, why I doubt if she would be fourteen.'

'It doesn't matter, Ellen. It's the only way to stop the others from following suit. They have to be more frightened of us than they are of the men.'

Angry at the unfairness of it all, Ellen pondered Kitty's fate as she showered in the outhouse next morning. *They wouldn't do that if it were the men who got pregnant,* she thought as she soaped herself with a flannel. 'Ouch,' she winced as her arm bumped against her breast. 'That's sore.' She checked her other breast and felt the same discomfort. She noticed too, how much larger her breasts seemed, the nipples were darker and swollen. *'Er titties was getting ready.* Leena's words flooded into her mind. Could she be pregnant too? Surely not! She looked at her breasts again. How else did Leena say she could tell? Ellen's own knowledge of such things was nil. The only information she had ever received was that babies were found under the gooseberry bush! *'Er bleeding, 'im stop coming.* Ellen's mind flicked over her own fluctuating cycle, *I can't remember when the last time was,* she thought. It was something she didn't take much notice of, and with all her other miseries being in much sharper focus, she had no idea. 'What if I am? It is possible, I suppose.' *Laurence would be pleased anyway.* It seemed a small price to pay for cheating him. She tried not to think of Cob, but sometimes she couldn't help getting the little sand bottle out and wondering where he was, how he was. Was he still thinking of her? Did he remember? *You bin fornicatin', you wicked girl,* again Leena's voice echoed in her ears. She froze. *Good God, that couldn't happen, could it?*

An icy cold shiver crept up her spine.

Could it happen the first time? She didn't know. *Could she have a black baby? Dear God, surely not. What would happen to it if it was? It would be a half-caste! Only the squatters' gins had those. She would be tormented and shamed like Kitty. No, not like Kitty. She was black. It would be worse, much worse.* Horrified, her mind raced. Laurence. *What would he do? Kill her? No. Poor Laurence, it would kill him. But Henry, and her mother?* She trembled with fear; they would destroy her and the baby too.

Mindless panic gripped her as she remembered her mother's rage. But this was much worse and there was no way she would ever be able to hide it, she was trapped.

There was no one she could turn to, no one she dare ask. Stifling her sobs with the towel she sank to the cold wet floor of the bush hut.

Hoping against hope that her period would begin, she waited another week before telling Laurence. Her opportunity arose one morning over breakfast when Laurence told her he had to make a trip to Cairns.

'I'm really sorry but I have to leave you here by yourself for a couple of days dear, I must get to the bank and sort out a few things. Also I thought I might call in to see the doctor. It's nothing serious, but this cough of mine is playing up again. I never worried much about it before, but I feel I should now I have you to consider. Can't have me getting sick on you, can we?'

Ellen saw her opportunity. Taking a deep breath, she blurted out, 'I'd better come too.'

'You? What's wrong darling? I've been thinking you looked a little pale lately, but I didn't realise you were feeling ill.'

'I'm not sick, Laurence, but I think I may be having a baby.'

'Having a baby? You? You mean us? Are you sure?'

'Well, no, not really, that's why I have to see the doctor,' she explained patiently.

'But I never thought. It didn't occur to me. I've been so overjoyed in having you, I can't believe I should be so lucky as to have you and a child as well. Wouldn't that be marvellous?' A big grin lit up his frail face as he came and knelt before her.

'I tell you, Ellen, I don't know what I have done to deserve all the happiness that's coming my way. I think it's wonderful, just wonderful.'

*

Sitting in the small hot waiting room, flicking nervously through old dogeared copies of *Punch* magazines, Ellen's palms began to sweat and her stomach churned. She wondered if it was possible for the doctor to tell. Should she confide her terrible fears to him? If only she could talk about it to someone.

Laurence came out of the surgery followed by the doctor, a small balding man wearing a dark suit with a dandruff spattered collar, and knees and cuffs shiny from wear.

'Please come in, Mrs Reid. I've finished with your husband now.'

Ellen looked at Laurence enquiringly; but he gave her a reassuring smile and stepped aside for her to enter.

'Now Mrs Reid, your husband has told me of the happy news you are hoping for, so please undress behind the screen, and we will soon be able to diagnose your condition.' The grubby little doctor, indicated towards a woven cane screen that partly hid an examination couch draped with a crumpled grey looking sheet.

After the examination, as Ellen replaced her hat and buttoned her jacket, he washed his hands in a none-too-clean looking basin. 'Everything seems to be fine, Mrs Reid. You should expect the birth to occur early next year. I'm afraid that means you will be carrying the child through the hottest months. I think you would be wise to consider returning south to your mother to await the confinement.'

Ellen's face paled. 'Oh no, I couldn't possibly do that.'

'Why ever not, dear girl? It's the wisest thing for both you and the baby. Medical facilities here are not good to say the least, and with you being so isolated on that mission of yours, it could be quite dangerous. Perhaps we should speak to your husband. I'm sure he will agree.' Without waiting for an answer, he called Laurence back into the surgery. 'Well, it's good news I'm happy to say, Mr Reid,' he exclaimed, slapping Laurence on the back.

Laurence stood speechless with a silly grin spreading from ear to ear.

'But as I have been trying to explain to your dear wife here, it would be much better for both her and the child if she left this climate, say in her sixth month, and went to her mother to await her confinement. You should both go. It would certainly help that chest of yours, Mr Reid. The medicine I have prescribed should give you some relief, but complete rest for six months would make a big difference. Well, what do you say?' He looked from one to the other.

The grin had disappeared from Laurence's face and he looked with deep concern at Ellen. 'Of course, she must go if it will make things easier for her, but I'm afraid it's out of the question for me. With Reverend Grimshaw away there is no possibility that I could leave my post. I have to stay, but Ellen dear you must go.'

'No, I can't, Laurence,' Ellen pleaded. 'I really don't want to. Please don't make me.' As she became quite agitated the old doctor looked at her in surprise. In his experience, most ladies in her condition would give an arm and a leg to be returning to civilisation for their confinements. It was well known that the risk of childbed fever and other complications increased in the tropics. He tried to persuade her, but she was adamant.

'I will not go, so that's an end to it,' she said finally.

'In that case I will book you a room in Cairns Base Hospital, but you will have to layin early. We don't want any storms or cyclones to prevent you from leaving the mission, do we?'

No. She couldn't do that, either. Everyone in Cairns would know. Somehow, she had to find a way to have this baby alone. If her worst fears were realised she would desperately need time to get it away, before they could take the child from her and quietly dispose of it to some far away mission; just another unwanted half caste. That could not happen if this child was one that she and Cob had created.

As the months passed, Ellen tried to learn as much as she could about childbirth. As her mentor she chose the unsuspecting Leena.

'How can you tell when the baby is ready to be born, Leena? How long does it take to come?'

'It just 'appen when its time, Miss Ellen, little fella will come when 'e good an' ready.'

Frustrated by the usual Aboriginal lack of the concept of time, Ellen would push for more detailed information. 'But how will I know when it's going to happen?'

'Don't really know for a white lady,' Leena felt sure there must be some difference, because of all the fuss they made. 'My people, she get all heavy down in her belly, then pains come in 'er back and all along of here.' She demonstrated in her own massive belly. 'Then she go to women's place near creek and waits for baby to come.'

'Does she manage by herself?' Ellen asked, maybe she would too.

'No! She's not by 'erself. Women stay by her all a time, not leave her alone.' Leena was disgusted at the very suggestion.

'How do you look after the baby when it's born?' Ellen pried.

'They rub 'im in cold fire ash an' mother's milk, then wrap 'im up good in paperbark. Little fella feel pretty good then.' The black woman sighed as if for the lost old ways.

'Don't you worry about it Missus Ellen. You goin' to Whiteman 'ospital. They fix you an' little fella up all good there.' With that she busied herself at the other side of the dispensary.

Rebuffed, Ellen fumed to herself. *How could I have lived so long and still be so ignorant? It's ridiculous!* She desperately tried to remember what had happened when Barney had been born, but realised she hadn't heard or seen a thing. Why she hadn't even known when her own mother was pregnant. The only inkling she had that something was about to happen had been when the neighbours had appeared and conversed in discreet whispers, before swiftly removing the children to their homes, where they remained until after the birth. *Why,* she realised with a shock, *I've never even seen a white woman breastfeed a baby and after all those brothers and sisters! Amazing! How did one breastfeed? How did you make the milk start? Did it hurt?* Questions without answers tumbled through her brain.

She searched out Amy's abandoned *Ladies Journal* and scavenged its pages for relevant information. The only worthwhile section she found, entitled *A Lady's Delicate Condition,* was hidden away at the back of the book. It discreetly suggested suitable clothes and foods for one in such condition, and made mention of simple crafts to do, to while away the time one had to stay indoors. Making the firm point that it wasn't considered good taste to be seen in public in such an embarrassing condition, the article concluded with a few long medical words, and that was the sum total of its information.

Ellen and Leena were preparing to close the dispensary after the usual afternoon of cuts, infections, burns and a lot of other minor ailments, when one of the assistants drove hurriedly up the track in the rickety old mission vegetable cart.

'Leena, get out 'ere, quick girl!' he shouted. Leena hurried out and Ellen followed more slowly, hampered now by the swelling girth of her seventh month. Inside the cart lay Kitty, her huge extended belly looking grotesque as it pushed out the cotton dress above her spindly legs.

'Wot happen to 'er?' enquired Leena, as she and the assistant gently carried the moaning girl into the dispensary and laid her on the examination bed.

'She bin 'elpin' on the sweet potatoes, she got a sack 'alf way onto the cart and she fall over 'urtin like and screamin'.' The embarrassed man babbled the information whilst backing hurriedly towards the door. 'Mr Reid said bring 'er 'ere, so I did,' and he was off before they could ask any more questions.

Ellen peered anxiously at the suffering girl. 'Oh, Leena, she looks awful! What can we do for her?'

'Nuthin much, she done bust 'er belly up. Get some water. We'll cool 'er down. That'll make 'er feel better, eh Kitty? You be good girl now, lie still, Leena make you all better.'

The frightened girl rolled her dark eyes and bit deep into her lip as the pain wracked her. She grabbed Ellen's hand and squeezed it hard.

'How is she, Ellen?' Laurence asked as he hurried up the steps, white faced and gasping.

'I don't know. Leena says there's nothing we can do,' she

replied wincing as Kitty's fingernails clawed deep into her arm.

'I want you to come away, immediately, Ellen. It's not good for you to see such things in your condition. Come along, dear. Leena can manage.' Laurence began to usher her towards the door.

'I can't leave her! The poor thing. Look, even gripping my arm seems to help her. I must stay.'

'Well, only until I can get some of the other women over from her village, then you must leave. I will not have you getting upset.'

Laurence, left to locate the girl's family. Ellen watched with keen interest as Kitty started to bear down, Leena lifted her gently in her arms and lowered her into a crouching position on the floor. After a few strong pushes, the tiny black baby slid into Leena's waiting hands. As Ellen helped the exhausted girl back to the bed, Leena gently wiped and wrapped up the tiny whimpering infant.

'She'll be right now, won't she?' asked the relieved Ellen, sure the miraculous drama was over, but her face paled in answer to her own question, as blood began to pour from the girl, spreading in a wide stain across the white sheet.

Leena anxiously kneaded the girl's stomach. 'It ain't coming like it should. It gotta come out an' I can't shift it!' Leena's voice now held a note of panic as she frantically worked sweat dripping from her shiny black face.

Abruptly, she heaved her huge bulk onto the table and dropped her full weight on the poor girl's stomach. Kitty screamed in pain and Ellen stared in horror as a large liver like object squelched onto the sheet. 'Good God, what's that?' she gasped.

'Got 'im. Bloory good show!' Leena yelled in triumph. 'That was baby's tucker in there, it had to come out or it would kill er.'

'I thought you'd killed her, Leena,' Ellen exclaimed as she sponged the exhausted girl. At that moment, a mewing wail of protest rose from the tiny black form in the basket, and looking at each other, Ellen and Leena both burst out laughing with delight and relief.

Next morning as Ellen lay propped on pillows sipping the tea Laurence always pampered her with, her mind dwelt on the events of the previous day.

She had her answer. Somehow she would have to start her own labour at a time when she could be sure she would be alone.

Christmas came and went. They received a curt note and card from her mother, and a rather envious letter from Amy, saying how thrilled Ellen must be about the baby. But no news of Henry. Laurence checked the telegraph line to the mission daily, privately convinced something was wrong. They should have had news weeks ago. He had contacted the Bishop in Sydney and everyone else he could think of, but the reply was always the same, 'No News.'

After another two weeks without a word, he determined to take action. He couldn't just sit around when his dearest friend and brotherinlaw could be dying out there. He approached Ellen, trying to make light of the matter. 'I think it might be time to take you to Cairns, Ellen. We don't want to risk anything, now, darling with only another month to go. Then I think I must start making enquiries about Henry. I do feel we should have heard by now. Once I know you are safe, I can spend more time away, getting some answers to my questions.

No one seems to know just where Henry and his party are, or what has happened to them.'

Ellen face drained of all colour. She dare not go. She wracked her brains for a feasible excuse. 'I couldn't bear to spend a whole month locked in that hospital, Laurence. It could be longer for all we know, weeks and weeks. I'm perfectly all right, and very healthy. Don't worry. You go for a few days and I'll wait until you return. Then I'll go to Cairns, I promise,' she wheedled, praying she sounded convincing.

'No, no. I would worry about you, and if anything should happen to you I'd never forgive myself. You pack up your things dear, while I organise everything and we'll leave on this afternoon's tide.'

Overcome with anxiety, Ellen paced distractedly seeking an excuse to stay, she daren't go, she couldn't go, she wouldn't go.

Standing at the open door, she saw Laurence hurrying back across the compound looking anxious and alarmed. 'Ellen dear, I don't want to frighten you but we will have to leave immediately. I've just received this telegraph from Sydney.' He held it out to her:

GRIMSHAW PARTY FAILED TO
RENDEZVOUS WITH PICK UP SHIP GULF
OF CARPENTARIA – STOP – NO SIGN OF
ARRIVAL FOUND – STOP – HAVE DOCKED
NORMANTON – STOP

The ship's captain signed it.

'But what could have happened, Laurence?'

He patted her hand. 'Now don't go thinking the worst,

anything could have delayed them, but I must get to Cairns quickly. I want to check with some boats that have just returned from that area. They may have some news.'

'You go, Laurence. I'll wait here. I'd rather stay in case any news comes in while you're away.'

Deeply worried about his dear friend, Laurence reluctantly agreed.

As she watched the *Goodwill* sail, Ellen knew it had to be now. This would be her only chance! She gently placed her hands over her distorted stomach and whispered, 'I'm sorry my little darling, whoever you are, but I have to do this for both of us.'

Walking back into the house she looked around for the heaviest object she could find. Deciding on the oak dresser, she took hold of the solid timber piece of furniture and heaved with all her might but her hands kept slipping and she failed to get a proper grip. That was useless.

What else? The bed with its carved head and foot was solid. Standing at the foot she lifted one end up as high as she could, again and again, until she felt her back would break but nothing happened. Beginning to feel quite desperate now, she went into the kitchen and filled the largest cooking pot she could find with water. It took several struggling efforts to raise it above her head onto the hook above the fire. She waited but still no pain. After repeating the process for half an hour she fell to the floor exhausted, sobbing with frustration. Something had to work it just had to! But what! Her only choice now was to go to the dispensary and coax or cajole another method out of Leena.

Hurrying out to harness the buggy, she stopped midstride. The horse! Of course! Laurence had stopped her riding it months ago, saying it was dangerous. Maybe that would do the trick! She had to try. She quickly saddled the horse and with the aid of a bale of hay, managed to heave her bulky body onto its back. Turning its head, she guided the animal out onto the beach. On reaching firm wet sand she whipped the horse into a fast gallop. Sea spray whipped through her hair, and for a moment she was back on the vast beach of Kalangari Island, with Cob's gentle eyes smiling at her his soft dark hair curling over the red mission shirt. Taking her feet from the stirrups, a sob of fear caught in her throat as she threw herself with as much force as she could from the back of the speeding horse. She spun in the air, her skirts flew up and wrapped around her face as she plummeted with a thud to the ground. Red hot searing knives of pain shot through her body as she rolled over and over on the hard packed wet sand.

For a time she lay stunned, unable to move, her breath coming in sharp painful stabs. When at last she tried to stand burning knives of pain shot through her again and she collapsed to the ground. She stared desperately across the sand dunes to the mangroves. She knew she was near the dispensary and somehow she had to get herself to Leena. The horse, which had bolted in fright, now walked slowly back, and put its head down nuzzling her curiously.

Taking a grip on the dangling reins she pulled herself to her knees whispering with pain. 'Come on, old thing, you've got to help me.' Holding the stirrup she struggled to her feet, clinging to the saddle to keep herself upright. Now the pain was constant, and almost unbearable, but she forced herself to stumble along beside the horse. Finally through a white haze of pain, the dispensary appeared before her. She toppled forward, striking her head on the rough timber as she fell.

Two large black feet appeared on the step above her head, topped by the swishing hem of a starched white apron. 'Leena! Thank God!' As two large hands reached down to her, Ellen smiled with relief, tasting warm salty blood that trickled into her mouth. She closed her eyes. It was over. What ever happened now, she could do no more.

Leena's huge bulk quivered with alarm as she struggled to carry Ellen's limp body into the dispensary. Placing the blood smeared girl on the couch she rushed back outside frantically calling for help. The compound was empty. Only the clicking sound of cicadas answered her cries.

'Oh Missus Ellen! What have you gone and done to yourself now. You're all broken up and poor little fella be no good now!' she sobbed as she gingerly peeled off Ellen's clothes.

Soaking wet, blood streaked pantaloons, confirmed her worst fears. 'Dear Jesus, you better get 'ere and help poor Leena now, in big bloory trouble.' She prayed to whoever was prepared to listen. Ellen's body arched as the pain from swift contractions wracked her body and Leena, grabbing a bowl of water and block of carbolic soap, washed the dirt and blood away.

'You all right Missus Ellen. Leena here, take good bloory care of you. Jus' stay alive till I gets this little fella born.' She babbled on as she swiftly examined the white girl, detecting the tiny baby's approaching head. Ellen could faintly hear her voice echoing down a long black tunnel beyond the pain. What was she saying? Struggling frantically to push back the engulfing unconsciousness that was overtaking her, Ellen heard the shaking voice say, 'It's a baby girl, Missus Ellen. Oh, but poor little bloory thing – she all wrong colour.'

Ellen collapsed as the black tunnel closed, swallowing her up.

CHAPTER TWELVE

The blackness lightened to a swirling grey, which lifted to a vision of entombed whiteness. Ellen's eyes flickered open and she gazed in wonder at the cocoon around her, until she vaguely realised that it was a mosquito net. Turning her head, she felt the cool starched cleanness of a pillowslip against her cheek. On stretching her legs she found them restricted by a tightly tucked sheet. Her chest hurt with each breath, and her head ached abominably. The heaviness of one arm made her look down to see it encased in plaster of paris.

'Ellen, Ellen darling, are you awake?' she screwed her eyes up against the pain as she turned her head in the direction of the voice. Laurence's face peered worriedly at her from the other side of the net.

'Sort of. Where am I?' she whispered back in confusion.

'It's all right dear. You're in hospital. You had an accident, remember?'

Ellen turned her head back to rest the throbbing ache. An accident – what accident? She tried to remember. Something stirred in her memory. The horse. Yes, that was it! She had jumped from the horse. She had to because of, 'The baby…' the words gasped out uncontrollably.

'It's all right, dear, it really is,' Laurence, swept aside the net and grasped her hand.

'But the baby, Laurence? I remember now. Leena said a girl… Her voice choked as she remembered Leena's other words *wrong colour*. She sank defeated onto the pillows. She had failed. They had seen her baby. 'What has happened to my baby?' she demanded, defiance now in her voice, as she waited for a holocaust of abuse to fall about her.

'I'm trying to tell you dear. Please stay calm. You've been very ill!'

'Laurence, don't pretend. Leena said it was the wrong colour. That's the last thing I remember. Tell me what they have done with my baby?' A scream rose in her voice.

'What?' asked Laurence totally confused. Thinking she must be delirious, he stroked her hair from her ashen face. He spoke to her gently. 'Now, now, Ellen dearest it's all right. Please be calm and listen to me,' he begged. 'The baby is alive, thank God, though the poor little mite has been fighting for her life these last two weeks. She was premature, Ellen, at least a month, possibly more, the doctor said. She was blue when she was born dear. That's what Leena must have meant. The cord had been wrapped around her throat. She nearly died, Ellen, and so did you.' A sob caught in his throat. 'I've been so frightened, Ellen. I thought I was going to loose you both. I'd sit beside her little cot willing her to live, and then I'd hurry here to you and do the same. It was dreadful. One night, I was walking down the passage when I noticed a text on the wall. It said "Oh ye of little Faith" and I knew then, that if I only had faith, you would live. I had the baby christened, Ellen, I had to. She was so ill. I named her Faith, dear. Is that all right? Do you like it? She is so tiny and beautiful Ellen. I had hoped she would look like you a bit but do you know, she gets more like me every day. You're bound to notice it.' Laurence could not keep the ring of pride from his voice.

Tears streamed down Ellen's cheeks as she lay back on

the pillows. 'Faith,' she murmured to herself. "Oh ye of little Faith".

'Now young lady, I want you to take my advice a little more seriously than you did last time.' The voice was stern. 'You've had a bad fall. Those broken ribs and arm won't mend in a few weeks. You will have to take things easy for a while. How's the concussion? Are you still having headaches?'

'Not often now, doctor, really, I feel much better thank you.' She turned her head as the door of her hospital room opened and Laurence walked in proudly carrying his daughter, her long lace gown and crochet shawl draped neatly over his arm.

'Ready to go, Ellen?' he beamed.

Watching him, she realised how confidently he was handling Faith already. He had spent every spare moment in the hospital nursery watching her while she slept, talking to her after the wet nurse had fed her. *I've missed out on so much already,* Ellen thought. Here she is, a month old and she hardly knows her own mother. 'I've just promised the doctor that I will do as I'm told, for a while anyway. Here, give her to me. She doesn't even know her own mother yet, do you baby?' She smiled down at the fragile little mite who looked lost in the overlarge gown and bonnet. Two bright blue eyes stared solemnly up at her, before the bottom lip began to tremble and the red faced baby began to howl miserably.

'Goodness me. What did I do?' Ellen faltered, terrified now of this demanding little creature, screaming in her arms.

'Here, give her back to me while you collect your things. She just doesn't know you yet, that's all.' Laurence retrieved the sobbing baby and held her expertly up to his shoulder, patting her back tenderly. 'There, there, little Faith, did Mummy frighten you?' he crooned, and with a hiccup the baby snuggled her face into his cheek.

Having settled Ellen and the baby carefully out of the breeze, Laurence hoisted the sail of the *Goodwill* and headed home to the mission with his precious cargo. When they arrived at the cottage everyone gathered around to welcome the new mother and babe, but Leena took firm control of the situation and shooed everyone away.

'Go on! Missus Ellen doesn't want you all hanging around waking the baby. Shoo! I'm taking care Missus Ellen's little baby. You can all see 'er later,' she decreed, appointing herself in sole charge.

She hustled the well-wishers out of the gate and took possession of the sleeping baby. Inside the house, presents awaited Ellen. Laurence had secretly handcarved a beautiful wooden cradle as a surprise, and Amy had sent an extravagant baby layette, accompanied by a wistful note asking that Ellen would soon bring little Faith to visit her Aunty Amy.

As Ellen sank thankfully into a chair, one of the assistants came rushing to the open door and tapped on it.

'Yes, what is it?' Laurence grunted, slightly put out by the unwanted intrusion to their home-coming.

'Wire just come in, Mr Reid.' He held out the folded paper.

Laurence read it and then whooped with delight. 'They found him, Ellen! They found Henry! Or rather he found them. He was camped on the beach waiting for the boat when it returned the second time. Halleluiah!' He grabbed Ellen and swung her around the room. They laughed hilariously together until he began to cough from the exertion. Choking and gasping for breath, he stumbled outside, where Ellen could hear him coughing until he vomited.

'Are you all right?' she asked anxiously as he walked shakily back inside, his hankie stained with blood, clasped to his mouth. Nodding his head he slumped into a chair.

'Are you still taking that medication the doctor gave you?' she fussed.

He lay with his head back on the chair and closed his eyes as he replied wearily, 'Yes dear, I take it regularly but I don't know why for what good it does me. I'll be all right in a minute when I catch my breath. I say though, it's great news about Henry, isn't it? He should be home in a couple of months.'

Henry received a welcome fit for a conquering hero. The women had sewn long streamers of brightly coloured bunting which was festooned from tree to tree all along the sandy track leading from the beach. Hundreds of mission inmates lined the route, dressed in their brightest and best, impatiently waiting to cheer and wave palm fronds as they had been instructed to do.

Lifted bodily from the deck of the *Goodwill*, Henry was born in triumph on the shoulders of his band of faithful assistants. The procession was headed by the mission's newly formed brass band, dressed in bright red uniforms, they proudly marched, bare footed and slightly out of step, blowing and banging their glistening instruments in a stirring rendition of hail the conquering hero.

The procession stopped at the school where a magnificent spread of tropical food was set out on trestle tables under the trees, ready for the party which would follow Henry's speech. Two small boys were already being dragged away unceremoniously by the ear after sneaking an early sampling.

Ellen watched as Henry, standing tall and assured, enthralled his attentive audience with snippets of his great adventure.

He wandered among them, patting backs, shaking hands, accepting their adulation without reserve, as though it was his God given right. Arriving at Ellen's side he gave her a quick peck on the cheek before turning his attention to the placid baby in her arms.

'Well, aren't you a little beauty? Do you have a smile for your Uncle Henry?'

Sapphire blue eyes solemnly scrutinised him from beneath the lacy frilled bonnet. Ellen could have sworn that Faith raised a delicate eyebrow to her before bestowing a condescending smile on Henry.

He was enchanted. 'She smiled for me!' he exclaimed with delight. 'She seems to know me already. Here, give her to me, Ellen, she wants to come to her uncle, don't you sweetheart?'

Ellen was secretly amused by Faith's instant conquest of her impervious uncle.

Carefully taking the baby and arranging her comfortably in his arms, he asked anxiously. 'You haven't had her christened yet, have you?'

Ellen nodded. 'We had to, Henry. She was so sick when she was born.'

His face fell with disappointment for a moment, suddenly brightening again as he addressed the baby. 'Well! We will just have to do it again then, won't we Faith? Properly this time, and you and I will have our photograph taken together, to send to your grandmother. Won't she be pleased?' Another smile blossomed in reply on the baby's face, and Henry was enslaved.

Retiring early, Ellen left her husband and brother deep in conversation. They talked long into the night. Henry described in detail his journey across the Cape York Peninsula to the mouth of the Mitchell River. He told of hastily abandoned Aboriginal camps they had found, the terror of grassfires lit by the fleeing natives as they tried to drive the unwelcome intruders away, sometimes trapping them in long grass which was high over the horses' backs. Hawks and crows would circle in their thousands as the fires approached, hoping for some charred remains.

After many adventures, the expedition had reached the coast five days late, in time to see ship's sails far out on the horizon to the south. They had fired rifles and made smoke fires, but they had little effect. They fired rockets, but the schooner had not returned. The now under-provisioned party had made a hurried journey back inland, leaving exhausted horses where they fell. In a state of near collapse, they had finally reached a line repairer's shack along the overland telegraph line, where they learned of the anxiety being felt for their safety. The government schooner had returned from Normanton two weeks later to pick them up from a new rendezvous point.

Laurence listened intently, feeling more than a twinge of envy and disappointment that he had been unable to share his friend's adventure. They discussed the problem of setting up a permanent mission in the area, and after a few more rums retired to bed.

Henry made his report to the Home Secretary, before once again resuming his position as head of the mission. Laurence found he was working even harder than ever and returned home each night exhausted, often too tired and sick to eat his supper. He would struggle into bed, trying to regain his strength for the next day always driven by a neverending feeling of inadequacy which forced him to try and match his friend's boundless energy.

Eventually Henry found time to send his mother the promised photograph of himself proudly holding his small niece, along with a graphic account of his adventures during his expedition. He was surprised at the speed of her reply and the bulky envelope which arrived in the next erratic mail delivery to the mission. In the same bundle of letters he found one containing the Bishop's seal, and opened it first. To his amazement he read that he was directed to travel poste haste to Kalangari to supervise the dismantling of the mission and the departure and resettlement of all inmates from Kalangari to Bibiringda!

Stunned, he felt quite unable to comprehend the reason for such a directive until he opened his mother's letter.

Dear Henry,

I was so relieved when I heard of your safe deliverance from the wilderness. I had been most distressed all those weeks pondering your fate. I am sure you will know how proud I am of your success and wish I could report the same success to you, but the situation here is deplorable.

Reverend Featherstone has lost all control, his lack of direction and discipline is leading to severe unrest among the blacks, I fear open rebellion if something isn't done soon.

I cannot assume the responsibility that is being thrust upon me. I am no longer a young woman and find coping with this constant insurrection just too much. It is having a very bad effect on my health.

My dearest wish is to be back at Bibiringda with you, and my dear little granddaughter. The photograph you sent me has pride of place on the mantelpiece. It's a wonderful likeness of you dear, and Faith looks the very image of her dear father. I would be happy indeed to be reunited with my family.

I hope, dear son that you will see fit to use all your influence to have me transferred back to Bibiringda, as speedily as possible, before my health suffers further.

I remain,

Your affectionate Mother

P.S. Joy of Joys, we have just received a wire from the Bishop informing us of your imminent arrival, to take charge of the closure of this miserable place. I am, to say the least, overjoyed and waiting impatiently for your arrival…

Love Mother

Ellen ushered Leena firmly out of the door. 'Off you go Leena, you are not taking Faith from her bed to nurse her. She can manage to go to sleep by herself very nicely thank you.' Ellen smiled as the big black girl stepped huffily down the garden path.

She joined Henry and Laurence who were sat together deep in conversation.

'We will have to set up a separate village for them somewhere. They certainly won't fit in with our blacks here. They will be a bad influence. It could cause us trouble.'

'Who will be a bad influence?' Ellen queried as she drew up a chair to join them.

'The Kalangari blacks,' Laurence answered her. 'They are to

come here apparently. Henry has just received a wire from the Bishop to say they are closing the mission.'

Conflicting thrills of hope and fear rushed through Ellen's body. 'How many of them are coming?' she asked as casually as she could manage.

'It looks like all of them,' Henry said grumpily. 'Just when we have things set up so well, and you're right Laurence, they will cause trouble. I've no doubt of that. Oh, by the way, Ellen, Mother is coming back too. She's had enough, she doesn't sound too well, either.'

From her cot, Faith began to wail. Ellen rose quickly, making her escape into the darkness of the bedroom. Picking up the sleepy baby she hugged the child close. 'He's coming, Faith, he's coming here. What ever will I do?' she whispered into the baby's soft curls.

CHAPTER THIRTEEN

Reining the horse the Aboriginal man easily swung his powerful body from its unsaddled back, at the same time lifting down the small brown child who sat before him. Hoisting the little fellow onto his shoulders, he began to climb the sandstone cliffs. High above the beach he stopped, he eased the child from his perch and they stood together, surveying the brilliant panorama below them.

'This is our place, Matheea. We belong here, like our old people, forever, since the Dreamtime.' He spoke softly to the child, who being too young to understand, looked up at him curiously before allowing his attention to be drawn back to the crashing waves rolling onto the beach far below them.

'This is the place of the big fights, Matheea. Thousands of our people came here. Your grandfather fought. We would have all been proud warriors then, though you wouldn't think so to look at us now, would you?' The toddler gave his father a happy grin and began throwing fistfuls of sand over the cliff's edge. 'She came here with me one day.' The man looked into the distance. 'What a day that was! She was a spirit too, in her way.' He smiled as he remembered. 'A white spirit in baggy wet bloomers! You should have seen her leaping about in the sea, she didn't give a damn then. But they made her go far away from everything she loved and cared about.' The little boy carried on tossing the sand heedless of his father's sad voice. 'She'll be up there where they're sending us; but she won't want to know us now, will she? She'll be well over the fling she had with a Kalangari Islander. Probably pretend she doesn't even recognise us.' His voice cracked at the thought. Suddenly his mind was made up. He caught the small child by the arm. 'Well, it won't matter a damn, will it, Matheea, because we're not bloody going! Come on son, we have some organising to do.' Swinging the boy back on his shoulders he purposefully wove his way back down the face of the cliff.

*

The campfire flickered bright in the darkness, lighting up the faces of the group gathered around it. Kalinga sat cross-legged, the little brown toddler at her breast. His soft dusty lips slowly slipped from her dark nipple as his head wilted over her arm in sleep. But she took no notice, her eyes being riveted on the face of her husband, as he outlined his plan of escape to his father and Nugget.

'I don't know how much longer we will be here, but my guess is only a few weeks. Grimshaw has all the buildings dismantled now. There is only the matron's place left standing, so it can't be long. Trouble is he's not saying! He knows damn well some of us will try to make a break for it, so the less we know the better he likes it. Kalinga, you keep your eyes and ears open at the house. You've got more chance than any of us to hear what's going on. Still, as long as we are prepared it won't matter. But one thing's for sure, we're going!'

Currie, now a little more grey, and a little more stooped, sat puffing on his clay pipe. He raised his eyes to Cob and slowly nodded in agreement. Nugget pulled a stick from the fire, knocking the sparking embers out on a rock before lighting his pipe with it. 'Too bloody right we are. I aren't bein' taken away from our island. No one wants to go, everybody bloody cranky 'bout it. The fellas talk of big fight,' he said menacingly and waved his pipe in the direction of the camp.

'It's no good to fight, Nugget. They'll just call in more police with more guns! That would suit them fine, save 'em the trouble of shifting us anyway. There'll be no fighting for us. We'll just clear out until they are gone, then come back to the island when the hue and cry has died down. Shouldn't be too long. Here's what we'll do.'

Taking a stick he began to draw in the soft sand. 'We'll each shoot through separately, and meet up there at Balbal Creek. Nugget, you still have your boat, take it down there and hide it. Do it soon, just in case we have to move quick. Kalinga, you shouldn't have too much trouble getting away from the house with all this shifting around going on. Take the baby and wait near the boat for us. It could take us men a while to get away, depending on how many troopers there are to dodge. Once we all make the boat we'll push off that night, get away as far as we can, and hide up during the day. Keep moving in darkness.'

'What if ya can't get away?' Kalinga asked worriedly.

'If things go wrong, and we don't turn up; take the boat and go to little Woody Island, wait there for us, but remember keep well out of sight. They may be searching. We will be able to swim over if we have to, later. The only thing we must decide now, is when.' Cob looked at each in turn.

'Can't be too soon for me,' Nugget grumbled. 'That old Matron Missus she bin workin' me like a dog, heaving them bloody great crates 'bout.'

Kalinga agreed. 'Hope we get out a this place mighty quick. I'm fed up of it.'

'We wait until the big boat comes,' Currie ordered, taking his pipe from his mouth.

'Why's that, father?' Cob enquired.

'Plenty of noise, plenty movin' 'bout, nobody know for sure where anyone should be. We slip out quiet then.'

Tension built as the ship's due date of arrival came and went. All the mission buildings were dismantled ready for loading. Mattresses, blankets, books, cooking pots, slates, were all crated and stacked down on the beach. The waiting gave the reluctant travellers time to voice their worst fears to each other. Rumours spread like wildfire each more horrific than the one before; the native tribes where they were going were cannibals, they would all be eaten. They would all be locked in the hold of the ship like the kanakas and drown in a cyclone. Fear fed upon fear. The mission inmates' resentment building to bursting point, Henry ordered two more platoons of black troopers shipped over from the mainland, bringing with them a plentiful supply of leg irons and chains.

At last the ship's sails were sighted from the lookout on the back beach. Grace rushed around organising the women and children, making sure all her own trunks and boxes were neatly labelled and stacked on the beach with the rest of the stores.

It took days to barge out the dismantled buildings and load them on the waiting ship, but finally with everything aboard, it was time to move the human cargo.

Black troopers were on full alert. Some were even stationed out in boats ready to catch anyone who decided to swim for it. The rest of the troopers swaggered among the milling crowds herded on the beach, their carbines at the ready.

Cob walked casually across to where Kalinga was working, packing food for the ship's journey. Matheea sat beside her, chewing happily on a hard tack biscuit. Picking up the baby Cob tossed him high in the air. Matheea laughed with delight as he landed, throwing his little arms around his father's neck and hugging him tight.

'You be a good boy for your mother, Matheea. I will see you soon. We'll go fishing in Nugget's boat. Won't that be good?' He placed the child in Kalinga's arms, and looked seriously into her eyes. 'This is it, Kalinga,' he said softly. 'Go as soon as you can. Be careful! Remember to hide well away from the boat until we get there, just in case.'

Kalinga grasped his hand. 'You be careful too Cob, don't be long. I will worry.'

Patting her arm he said, 'I'll try not to be, I have to go now and tell the others. See you soon.' Turning back into the crowd he soon found Nugget. 'Right, mate, see you at the boat,' he whispered as he passed.

He watched Nugget ease his way to the edge of the crowd and nonchalantly saunter off towards the main track, a paper parcel tucked under one arm.

Cob pushed his way through the assembled inmates looking for his father. Women were shouting hysterically for lost children, men huddled in nervous groups smoking and grumbling loudly. He searched the crowd but couldn't find him.

Suddenly, a young Aboriginal boy bolted towards the water, a shot rang out and he fell to the ground screaming! Panic erupted. Infuriated Aboriginals leaped at the trooper who had fired the shot, other troopers dashed to his assistance. Women screamed in terror and more shots were fired indiscriminately into the crowd by the outnumbered, panicking militia. Using their rifle butts as clubs the troopers struck out wildly: man, woman, or child it didn't matter.

Cob's anger burst into red rage too as, through the melee, he caught sight of a trooper viciously clubbing his father senseless with the butt of a carbine.

Hurling himself forward, he ripped the gun from the startled man's grasp. Swinging it high above his head he brought it down with all his might across the assailant's back. Now more troopers now came rushing back from the boats, firing wildly into the crowd as they ran.

Cob, shielding his father's body with his own, cowered with the other terrified Aboriginals trying to avoid the deadly flying bullets. He felt one strike his leg just as a carbine stock crashed down on his head from nowhere, rendering him senseless.

*

Cob regained consciousness, to find himself manacled to the rest of the battered and now subdued mission males. The terrified women huddled together, further up the beach under the watchful eyes of the troopers.

'Get these trouble makers on to the ship and locked below,' Henry barked to the sergeant.

The troopers abusively prodded the dispirited Aboriginals to their chained feet. Helping each other as best they could, they formed a ragged line. Supporting his father, Cob limped along with the rest, dragging the heavy chains through the sand. As they were half pushed, half knocked into the waiting dinghies, he knew that any chance they had of escaping was gone.

Nugget moved swiftly along in the rainforest shadows, unaware of the battle raging behind him. He began to feel quite confident, and taking to the centre of the track, he strolled along whistling quietly.

As his path skirted closer to the shoreline, his keen ears detected a splashing sound. Creeping closer, he saw a group of troopers mooring their boat and hurrying up the beach towards him. Smiling to himself, he nimbly shinned up the nearest tree where he sat hidden in the centre of a crows nest fern and watched them pass beneath him. Waiting until the sound of feet had faded, he slipped down and made his way back to the beach where he gleefully cut loose the troopers' boat and pushed it out into the strong flowing current.

Chortling to himself enjoying his dangerous game, he swiftly caught up with the marching troopers, trolling cheekily just behind them, listening as they gossiped and complained, quite unaware of his presence. As he approached Balbal Creek where his boat was hidden he gaped in stark amazement when he saw the battered little craft bobbing openly out on the water! The troopers pounced on it, laughing and jeering at the stupid black who had left his escape route so exposed.

From his hiding place Nugget cursed. Kalinga! The stupid gin. Skirting quietly round the creek he searched the undergrowth but found no sign of her. The troopers meanwhile, laughing loudly at their joke, had chained and padlocked the boat to a tree. Congratulating themselves on their sadistic sense of humour, they strode off, laughing uproariously.

Shrugging his shoulders, Nugget calmly undid his parcel and took out a sharp machete. It took him half an hour to chop through the tree, lift off the chain and retrieve the boat.

After vainly waiting for Kalinga and the others to arrive, he finally pushed off and paddled it undercover of the mangroves towards the anchored ship. Hiding under the overhanging trees, he watched as the manacled prisoners were loaded into the ship's hold.

With a shock he saw Cob stumbling along, dragging his injured father and knew at once their plan of escape was shot to pieces.

Quietly he paddled away. Under the protection of the falling night he took off alone to the mainland.

Terrified at seeing the troopers approaching earlier, Kalinga had fled in panic leaving the boat exposed. Taking Matheea deeper into the safety of the bush, she had huddled all night in the undergrowth, frightened and miserable, hoping desperately that Cob would be waiting for her. At dawn leaving Matheea hidden in a small hollow, she cautiously approached the creek mouth again. The boat was gone. The ratcheted tree told her that it hadn't just floated away. There was no sign of Cob. Retrieving Matheea she waited until noon before finally admitting to herself that she was alone now, he wasn't coming. He had told her to take the boat to Little Woody if he didn't come, but the boat was gone! Could she swim that distance, she wondered? Deciding that there was no other alternative, she wove a float of sorts from loose branches and, tying the baby to her back with vines, she entered the water, pushing the float before her. Checking the current with a floating stick, she pushed off aiming for the island half a mile away.

After twenty-four hours incarcerated in the hold of the still anchored ship, the rebels were given bread and water and taken up on deck to relieve themselves over the side of the ship. Cob examined his leg as he sucked in the desperately needed fresh air. The bullet had passed through his calf, leaving a ragged wound but luckily there appeared to be no infection. Trailing his shirt over the side he managed to soak it with seawater so he could bathe the wound, when a shout went up from a trooper on guard in the bow. He pointed towards Little Woody Island. 'Escapee off the port bow, Sir,' he shouted. Henry rushed over, shading his eyes to see a bobbing head struggling in the heavy surf a hundred yards off the island's mangrove shore.

'I can't make out what it is exactly.' Henry puzzled to the sergeant. 'Seems to have two heads! Don't shoot yet.' The prisoners shuffled in their chains craning their necks to watch the drama unfold. 'Look like a little fella on a big fella back, see that?' It little 'ead keep bobbing up, poor bloory fella look all done in, 'im not gonna make it if'n ya ask me.'

Cob screwed his eyes against the glare of the water, trying to see the object of everyone's concern. Sure enough the head rose again struggling desperately now to keep afloat. Then he saw it, a little face, mouth wide, gasping for breath, rising from the back of the swimmer. Suddenly he knew! Matheea! Kalinga! He had told her to make for little Woody if things went wrong. He held his breath, not even feeling the pain in his leg as he willed her every stroke. *Keep going, Kalinga! Hang on, Matheea!* He desperately prayed.

'My God!' he heard Henry shout, 'Look at that. Shoot man, shoot! Try and scare it away.'

Thrusting aside the men in front of him, Cob forced his way to the rail. A scream of horror stuck in his throat as he saw a shark's sinister fin cutting smoothly through the water, circling the exhausted swimmer. His brain flashed disjointed pictures before his horrified eyes. Kalinga's head sharply swivelling as she saw the fin come nearer and then disappear under the water; her arms flaying wildly, fingers clawing at the sky as she disappeared in a whirlpool of thrashing foam. No sound came from his gaping mouth as he watched his tiny son floating about helplessly before the next tumbling wave caught the baby on its breaking crest and sucked him under tons of crashing water.

'No! No! Matheea!' he screamed and beat his manacled fists upon the rails of the ship. 'Unchain me, you bastards! Let me go to my son!' He tried to hurl himself over the side, dragging his chained companions after him. Terrified, they clung onto the chains dragging him back, kicking and lashing out, he fought them with the strength of three men. Finally, they managed to overpower him and haul him back onto the deck.

'Quickly, lower a boat. See if they are still alive, and someone, shoot that bloody shark.' Henry barked out orders as the troopers ran in all directions.

*

Grace supervised the last of the women and children below deck. They had gone quietly despair being the only emotion they had left. They huddled together silently in their dark, dank quarters, bewildered at the loss of their home, and everything they understood. Returning to her cabin, Grace was joined by Henry 'Everything in order for you here, Mother?' he enquired after her comfort.

'It will do, dear. I don't care, as long as we can get away soon. What a dreadful two days this has been, I just want to get to Bibiringda and forget all about this awful place. Have they found any trace of Kalinga or the boy yet?'

'No, I doubt if there would be much left of Kalinga to find, and the child's body could wash up anywhere along the bay in these currents. I've called off the search. It's pointless. Munyabra seem to have calmed down a little but he's still chained. God, the man went berserk! Battered half the men chained with him. I daren't let him loose, in case he looses control again.'

'How's the father? Is he any better? I wish you would have listened to me, Henry, really I do. You should have sent them both to Brisbane with the worst offenders. They will cause nothing but trouble. Believe me, I should know!'

'Oh Mother, don't start that again. I've told you, they aren't criminals they have no record. I couldn't just send them without reason. I realise they have given you some discipline trouble in the past, but you really are making an awful fuss about it.'

Grace bit her tongue. She couldn't tell Henry her real fears or Cob coming into contact with Ellen again, maybe she was overreacting. It was two years ago now and Ellen seemed to be happily married and content with her little girl and Laurence. No point in dragging the whole dreadful episode up again. Ellen had most likely forgotten all about the black by now. Best put it down to a young girl's silly fantasy and if everything seemed all right, just forget it. *If that black causes me trouble again, I'll make short work of him.*

Henry interrupted her thoughts. 'You might be right about the father though, he's in a bad way, could die on the trip, can't lose any more of them, or Marsden will stir up more trouble. He'll have all his old lists out again, checking the names and demanding to know where they are, and what's been done with the money allocated to feed them. God, that man's a nuisance, you'd think it was his money instead of the government's. Yes, I'll send the old man back to the mainland before we sail. If he dies there, Marsden can't blame us.'

The ship docked in Cairns, the Kalingari inmates were quickly loaded into government barges and transported to Bibiringda where temporary camps had been prepared for them. Cob remembered little of the first weeks of the journey or the first weeks of his enforced resettlement. In his despair at the death of his son, he sat outside his humpy every night before a blazing fire, no matter what the heat of the day, conjuring up Matheea's happy little face in the glowing embers. He rejected any attempt by the others to draw him into their campfire circle. He ate what they gave him, lay awake while they slept and worked lethargically beside them, rebuilding the dismantled mission buildings.

Ellen disciplined herself to avoid the new arrivals. She hadn't gone down to the beach to see them disembark, terrified of seeing Cob and rekindling feelings she couldn't control. After the first stiff meeting with her mother, she had helped Grace set up home in one of the vacant cottages left by a group of retreating white assistants. It was on Faith that Grace now lavished all her attention. Finding no reasonable reason for withholding the child, Ellen allowed grandmother and granddaughter to spend many happy hours together. Grace would come for the girl early in the morning, taking her little hand while she toddled unsteadily over to Grace's house where special little puddings were cooked and waiting to be eaten, picture books read, Old Yorkshire nursery rhymes taught. Grace's joy in the child softened her attitude to Ellen so that gradually an uneasy truce developed between them.

Laurence worked from dawn until dusk supervising the

reerection of the Kalangari buildings. Henry had decreed that they should be made functional again as soon as possible in order to have the school and dormitory system working again, before the islanders could become even more restless and spread discontent throughout the whole mission. Having divided up the Kalangari men into working parties, Laurence was obliged to take on most of the carpentry work himself.

*

After working unmercifully in the sweltering heat to replace the school roof, Laurence staggered down the ladder, hot and sweaty, gasping for breath and sat for a moment to rest in the shade of the nearly completed building. He coughed fitfully, feeling the usual nagging pain in his chest. He knew he was sick and getting worse. The blood flecks in his handkerchief each time he had a coughing bout told him so. Most of the time his energy was sapped and some mornings it took a mammoth effort to even rise from his bed. He knew he should go back to the doctor in Cairns, but with all the work waiting to be done there never seemed to be time. Anyway what good would it do? His last prescription hadn't had much effect. *Maybe, I'm just making excuses not to go,* Laurence thought to himself. *If I'm honest I don't really want to know.* After his last serious illness, before he ever came to Bibiringda, there had been talk of consumption. They had said he would never be able to work again, but he had proved them wrong, look at all he had accomplished here over the years?

Perhaps he was overdoing it slightly. Once these poor souls were settled he would take a break, maybe even take Ellen and Faith on a holiday, have a good rest and get himself on top again. No use worrying about a silly cough when all these poor people had so many problems that needed his attention.

Feeling better for the rest, he began to study the progress of the building opposite. They were well on schedule and the dormitory would be ready to move into by the end of the week. Who was going to supervise it was another question. Grace wasn't keen at all. In fact, she didn't seem to have much enthusiasm left for any position suggested to her. She was quite middle-aged now and seemed to have found Kalangari too much for her. Laurence was sure that something had happened there to upset her but she wouldn't say what and if he asked Ellen she just changed the subject. Grace seemed to derive her happiness from having Faith with her and living independently in her cottage.

Rising wearily to his feet, he dusted off his hat and walked to where a group of island men were just about to raise one side of the dormitory. 'Make sure you've the right end there, or it won't fit. Remember both ends look alike but one is a bit out on the left hand side. Did you check the numbers painted on the timber?' he questioned the sweating blacks as they heaved on ropes to raise the gable end.

'It right one, Mister Reid, we checked it good but we got same trouble wid this one as other. She gone an' swelled up with all that seawater that got on 'er.'

Taking the rope, Laurence lent a hand to the struggling group. As they worked he noticed one fellow sitting behind the back wall, doing nothing. 'That fellow round the back there! What's he doing loafing when there's work to be done? Get him up here to help.'

'He not good, Mister Reid. He 'ad bad time afore we came 'ere.'

'Is he sick? Is that what you mean?' Laurence dropped the

rope as the timber wall was secured.

'Belly not sick Boss, 'im spirit be sick.'

'Well, hard work never hurt a sick spirit. Get him on his feet. Who is he?'

'Cob Munyabra, Boss. 'is wife 'n baby they got all eaten by shark. An' his father was bashed up too, had to stay at 'ospital. Cob no good after that, he all sad.'

'Cob Munyabra, you say? Doesn't sound like him. He was one of the assistants at Kalangari, wasn't he? Very arrogant too, if I remember rightly. All right, I'll go over myself and chivvy him along a bit, can't have men sitting around feeling sorry for themselves when there's all this work to be done. Leave it to me.' Laurence made his way over to where Cob sat lounging against the half finished walls, his long legs outstretched, covered by dirty crumpled dungarees, his battered hat pulled down low over his eyes. He gave no sign of being aware of Laurence's approach.

'What's all this, Munyabra? Why are you sitting here resting when your friends are working so hard? Are you sick?' Laurence stood over him waiting for an answer. There was none. 'I'm speaking to you Munyabra, do me the courtesy of a reply.'

Sighing wearily, Cob pushed back the wavy hat brim. He stared defiantly straight into Laurence's face. 'Yes,' he snarled. 'I'm sick all right! Sick of this place. Sick of being told what to do and where to go. Sick of you and everyone like you! Does that answer your bloody question, Mister Reid?'

Laurence's anger suddenly evaporated as he remembered his own anguish when he had thought he would lose Ellen and Faith. He viewed with concern the dull eyes, yellowed dark skin, his emaciated dirty condition. He remembered Cob as strong, virile and a strikingly handsome man. Pity welled in his heart. He knelt down beside the bitter, distressed Aboriginal. 'Look here, old chap, I realise you have been dealt a bitter blow and I understand how difficult it is for you to come to terms with, but moping around here, allowing yourself to get into this state isn't going to help you.'

'How would you know?' Cob spat back bitterly.

'Because I went through the same thing myself last year, I understand how you are feeling.'

Cob started. 'Your wife?' he said in a frightened whisper. *Dear God not Ellen too,* he prayed. 'Your wife, did something happen to her?' he urgently demanded again.

'Well yes, in a way, but not as bad as your terrible loss, praise be to God. She had a bad accident in her last month of carrying our child. It was touch and go at the time. I felt certain for a while that I would lose them both. So you see, I do understand.'

Cob closed his eyes, relief flooding through him. 'They are all right now, are they? Your wife and… the child?' The last words were spoken sadly.

'Oh yes. Fine now, thank goodness. You will have to come to the house soon and see them. Mrs Reid will be glad to know I have found you again. You were quite a protégé of hers at Kalangari, weren't you? She always spoke very highly of you, and your father. How's the old fellow these days?'

Once more anger flooded into Cob's voice, 'I don't know if he is alive or dead! He was beaten in the riot. They sent him away. I don't know where he is now.'

'Oh, I see. Well, that's not very good, is it? Tell you what, I'll make some enquiries and see if I can find out about him for you, if you like.'

Cob rubbed his chin and smiled. It was ironic. Here was the man who possessed the only woman he had ever really loved, trying to comfort and help him. Shaking his head he rose, towering above the frail earnest little white man. 'You're not a bad bloke, are you, Reid? I suppose that's something to be thankful for.' Cob turned and walked off towards the group of working blacks, leaving Laurence staring perplexedly after him.

*

'I ran into an old friend of yours today,' Laurence called casually as he towelled himself dry after having a good soak in the bush shower.

'Really, who was that?' Ellen enquired as she spooned stew from the black cooking pot into a tureen.

'Munyabra. You remember, his father was a tracker at Kalangari. He was one of the assistants.'

Ellen felt herself flush as she nervously spilled gravy over the side of the dish. 'Oh yes? And how is he?' she asked trying to keep her voice even.

Laurence buttoned on his shirt and sat at the table waiting to serve. 'Where's Faith?' he asked as Ellen set the tureen before him.

'She's having tea with Mother – again,' Ellen said, taking her place. 'She spends more time there than she does in her own home.'

'Well, it can't do any harm, and your mother seems to get so much pleasure from her. Between Grandma and Uncle, our little girl is getting quite spoiled. They both idolise her.' Laurence laughed as he ladled out the stew.

Ellen nervously pushed her food around the plate, unable

to eat. 'How is he?' she asked staring absently at the food.

'Who?' Laurence asked between mouthfuls.

'Cob Munyabra. You saw him today.'

'Oh yes. That's right – not good at all, I'm afraid. He looks appalling, poor fellow. Had the darndest luck. It was his wife and child that got taken by the shark as they left Kalangari. Remember, your mother mentioned something about it, but she didn't say who it was. Kalinga was the girl, you remember her? She was your housemaid for a while.'

Ellen violently pushed her plate away and covered her face with her hands.

Laurence looked at her alarmed. 'You aren't feeling ill, are you?'

Trying desperately to control herself, she whispered, 'No, no. it's just the thought of Kalinga having such a horrible death, and their baby too.'

'Yes, seems the child was tied on to her back for some reason, drowned, the poor little fellow. Munyabra's really upset, has let himself go to the pack. Looks half starved. I had a good talk to him this morning, tried to pull him out of it a bit. He always used to follow you around at Kalangari, remember? Very faithful these blacks if they become attached to you. I'll fetch him to see you tomorrow. Maybe you can raise his spirits.'

Suddenly irritated, Ellen snatched up the plates. 'I don't think there's any need to bring him here, Laurence. Really I don't!'

'But Ellen, you haven't seen the poor fellow. He really does need some kindness and the sight of a friendly face. I can't help remembering how I felt when I nearly lost you and Faith. I know it's different, him being black and all, but they do still have feelings, you know! Maybe not like ours, but I can't see that it would hurt you to show the fellow a little Christian kindness. He doesn't need to come into the house. You need only have a little chat with him in the garden, and he could see Faith, help him get over his own little one, that's all Ellen.'

'Oh stop it, Laurence, stop it! You talk about him as if he were a problem pet that might wet on the rug! There's no reason for him to come here. Leave him where he is, with his own kind!' Ellen cried, running from the room.

'What did I say wrong?' Laurence called after her. 'I'm only trying to help the poor chap.'

That they would meet again was inevitable, she told herself next day. It had to happen, and she might as well accept the fact and handle the situation like a mature woman. Most likely he had completely forgotten by now. Anyway it was all in the past and should be buried there. She would not allow it to upset her, she would act with dignity… Then why was she so terrified? Why had she already changed her dress twice today? Why couldn't she tear her eyes away from the clock? The hands creeping so slowly round its face that she had shaken it to see if it had stopped. *Damn! Damn! Damn! Please God, don't let him come,* she prayed. But she knew she was waiting, desperately hoping, that he would come – and soon!

The afternoon gave way to the early evening and she began to feel acute disappointment. *He wasn't coming! He had managed to talk his way out of it. Well, perhaps it was for the best.* She busied herself around the house to disguise her fretful mood from Leena who had managed somehow to claim Faith back from Grace. They were at the back of the house now, singing a happy bush song as she brought in the washing. Ellen could hear Faith's piping little voice providing an offbeat descant to the tune.

Laurence's voice calling from the gate startled her. 'We made it! Sorry, we're so late. I took Cob up to the telegraph for news of his father. Here you are dear, as I promised, an old friend come to visit.'

Ellen took a deep breath to steady herself and turned. There he was, looking shy and uncomfortable, just as she remembered him. But no! He was thin, his face was drawn, his once shiny black hair was now hanging dull and limp. He looked tired and empty. Her love for him overflowed in a desire to comfort him.

'Good evening, Mrs Reid,' he spoke quietly, his dark liquid eyes searching every curve of her face.

'Hello Cob.' She couldn't stop herself moving towards him, wanting to lay his head on her shoulder and soothe his pain. 'I was so sorry to hear about Kalinga and the baby,' she spoke with soft sincerity, and he knew she meant it.

Laurence coughed. 'Yes, well, we had some good news for Cob just now, didn't we Cob? His father is out of hospital and is living back on the island. So that was something good to cheer him up.' Laurence patted Cob's shoulder.

As they spoke Leena's huge bulk came sashaying round the corner of the house, clothes basket balanced on one huge hip, she rhythmically swayed to the beat of the song she was singing. Faith toddled behind her, pulling the peg bag by the string, singing and swaying her little bottom from side to side in imitation of Leena.

The three watchers burst into laughter, and a little of the tension between them was eased.

'This must be your little daughter, Mr Reid? She is so much

like you.' Cob squatted on his haunches as Faith approached but at the sight of the stranger she bolted behind Leena's skirts.

'Hello little one, have you been helping with the washing?' Cob waited patiently for her to regain her confidence. Cautiously a pair of deep blue eyes appeared from behind the calico apron. At the sight of them, Cob's heart stopped for a moment. *Her eyes! The very same!* He rose shakily still gazing at the little girl. 'You're very beautiful little miss. What's your name?' he enquired.

'Faith's her name,' answered Leena proudly. 'She's in my charge.'

'Well I can see you take good care of her. My name is Cob Munyabra.' He held out his hand to the beaming black girl. For once Leena was speechless. She smiled coyly, her eyes lowered, a giggle her only reply.

Turning back, Cob offered his hand to Laurence. 'Now I'll be going, Mr Reid. Thank you for taking the trouble to get me news of my father. Goodnight to you, Mrs Reid. It was good to see you again,' he said, searching her face for understanding. 'You have a beautiful little daughter and a very kind husband. I'm pleased things have worked out so well for you.' He took his leave.

Tears blurred Ellen's vision as she watched him leave. Did the old easy graceful stroll now hold a hint of weariness and defeat?

'He's a strange fellow, that one,' Laurence commented placing an arm around her shoulder. 'In one way he is as native as the blackest black here, yet when you talk to him you forget his colour, and he could be as white as you or me.'

'He's lovely fella, that one,' Leena purred from behind them, 'I 'ope he comes back an' see us again.'

Laurence laughed. 'I think our Leena's in love.'

Ellen began to hear a great deal about Cob's welfare. Desperate for good labour, Laurence began to train him in carpentry. 'He's really quite talented, you know, picks up the use of the tools so easily. I can give him a job to do and leave him to do it, knowing when I come back it will be done. Not like some of the others. Turn your back and they have vanished, usually under the nearest tree to roll dice. But not Cob, he's waiting for the next job.'

The rebuilding progressed well, becoming a race against the expected wet season that had so far failed to materialise. Clouds gathered over the ocean threateningly, but produced only the occasional shower. The red earth became hard packed, creeks that had always flowed abundantly from the mountains began to dry up to a slow trickle, the mission vegetables began to wilt, the cattle feed was getting scarce, and still there was no rain. The rainy season passed into winter, clear, cold and windy.

When Ellen wandered the rainforest tracks, the native grass felt like stubble beneath her feet as the drought began to take hold.

At the mission all water had to be carted in barrels from creeks further inland, and it became a precious commodity not to be wasted. Women carried bales of native grass miles to the cattle, which had become thin and poor. It was the children's job to ladle a measured amount of water on each vegetable plant in the paddocks after school each day. Once the novelty of the task had worn off, they became quarrelsome and irritable.

Each day, water was delivered to Ellen's house and had to be used sparingly. They no longer showered but sponged themselves down daily with water from a small enamel bowl. Once a week the old tin bath was hauled into the outhouse and filled with hot water. Faith would be bathed first, then Ellen would make the most of the few inches of sudsy water. Laurence was the last in the bath, taking a long soak to remove the grime of the week's work. Teeth were cleaned with the usual charcoal and salt, but only a small cup of water was used for this luxury. Washing was boiled in the copper, and the cooled water was then used to scrub the floors before being poured carefully onto the plants, as was the dishwashing water after dinner each night.

Everyone scanned the clear blue sky daily looking for a few telltale clouds, but as the winter progressed into an equally dry spring, it became obvious that there would be no relief that year. Henry discussed the matter with Laurence as they walked across the dusty compound after church. 'We are not going to get rain this year, not now, it's too late. We'll have to dig wells, one in each village, should have done it earlier, but who would have expected a drought.'

'I know,' Laurence agreed, 'Most of the Aboriginals can't remember drought in this area before either. Wells are the only answer, shouldn't have to dig too deeply but it's going to be a back breaking task.'

'Get straight onto it tomorrow, Laurence. I don't think we can afford to waste time. Let me know what equipment you'll need and I'll get it ordered from Cairns.'

'But I was hoping to take Ellen and Faith on a holiday once the buildings were up. To tell you the truth, Henry, I've been feeling a bit under the weather for quite a while now,' Laurence confided to his friend apologetically.

'Yes, I've noticed you haven't been looking too good. Ellen

mentioned it too. Go back to the doctors in Cairns, get him to fix you up,' Henry said matter-of-factly. Never having suffered a day's illness in his life, he had little patience with anyone who was sick and did not quickly recover.

'He doesn't seem to do me much good. I had thought of visiting Amy and Edward in Townsville, seeing somebody there. I suppose it will just have to wait until we get these wells down, shouldn't take long if we stick at it.'

'That's the spirit, old man, once we get the water problems fixed you and Ellen go, take all the time you need. I'll look after things this end.'

A water diviner was brought to the mission, and was soon striding purposefully across the dry earth with his tools of trade: a long piece of fencing wire, and a forked green stick. The mission children trailed behind him like the pied piper as he performed his magic.

'Joining of two streams here,' he muttered to himself, as he put aside the wire and brought the forked stick into action. Children and adults alike now watched in silent awe. Suddenly the green stick began to buck and jerk violently as if it was determined to escape his grasp. Muscles bulged on his arms as he fought to control the twisting serpent.

'Here she is,' he shouted loudly satisfied with his success. 'I'll tell you 'ow deep to go now.' Taking a firmer grip, he stamped each foot in turn, counting as he went, until on the count of fifty the violently shaking stick shot up into the air effortlessly pulling his strong arms with it. 'Fifty feet should do it, give or take a foot. Don't seem to be much rock around to give you any trouble.'

Six wells were marked in all and sure enough, water was found in the first three to be dug. The work wasn't too arduous during the cooler months of spring but soon the summer heat began to bear down, scorching the backs of the labourers. As digging on the fourth well began, work was brought to a sudden halt by a huge slab of rock.

'We'll have to blast it,' Laurence decided as he and Cob surveyed its monstrous size. 'We'll need sulphur, saltpetre and charcoal. I'll get it while you clear these chaps away. Send 'em home, don't want anyone hurt. You and I can manage.'

Having packed the explosive in the hole, Laurence lit the fuse and dashed to where Cob waited behind a tree some distance away. 'Right, get down Cob, it could fly a bit.'

They waited, heads down, hands over ears, for the expected blast. Nothing happened.

'Damn! The dratted fuse must have gone out. I'll nip over and light it again,' Laurence said, jumping to his feet.

'Wait,' shouted Cob reaching out to pull him back. The explosive blew and Laurence was hurled across the paddock. Cob scrambled over to where he lay covered in dust and rubble. 'Are you all right, Mr Reid?' he asked, easing an arm around the man's thin shoulders and holding him gently as he retched and choked.

'Are you hurt badly? Is anything broken?' Cob asked again as he dusted Laurence down.

'Don't – think – so,' Laurence answered between gasping and spitting up blood-filled mucus.

'Come on, I'd better get you home.' Cob lifted the shocked man upright, and supported him as they set off for the cottage.

Ellen rushed out as she saw them approaching. 'What on earth has happened?' she cried, as Cob half carried Laurence into the house.

'Nothing to worry about, Ellen, just tried to blow my silly

self up, that's all.' Laurence smiled wryly, his face caked with dirt. 'Bit too much sulphur and not enough charcoal, I think. 'He tried to laugh but only a wheeze escaped his throat. 'I'll be all right in a jiffy. Just give me a hand to the outhouse, Cob. I'll take a bath and to hell with the precious water. It's all this dust that's taking my breath away. Give Cob a drink, Ellen, he deserves it. I nearly blew him up too.'

Ellen poured a rum and had the glass waiting on the table when Cob returned. They sat uneasily facing each other, alone for the first time since Kalangari Island.

'He's a good man.' Cob indicated towards the outhouse with a nod of his head.

'Yes, I suppose so.'

'Are you happy with him?'

'As happy as can be expected, in the circumstances. It's not his fault. It's mine. Most of the time I feel as if I'm cheating him. Did you feel the same way with Kalinga?'

Cob drank the rum before replying, 'I suppose so, but that's all in the past now. I'll always be grateful to her for Matheea, even if I only had him for such a short time. It was worth it all for that.'

Ellen nodded. 'And I have Faith. I suppose in time, good comes out of even the worst situations. What will you do now, Cob.'

'Dunno, doesn't seem much point in worrying about it. I think I'll make a break with this place, once the wells are in. I feel I owe him that. He helped me through a bad patch.'

'Where will you go?' Ellen asked anxiously.

'It doesn't matter much, now that I know you are settled and safe here. I would be doing us both a favour to just disappear, wouldn't I?'

'But I won't know where you are, what's happening to you. Would you write to me sometimes, just to let me know?' She faltered and he saw all the feelings she still had for him written plainly on her face.

'For God's sake, Ellen,' he whispered softly. 'Let me go will you? I can't hang around here, seeing you with him all the time. If I stay, it will only happen again whether we want it to or not.' He reached out and took both her hands in his.

'He's a decent bloke, Ellen. He thinks the world of you. He can give you respectability, a good home, what would you have with me?' His dark eyes pierced her as his grip tightened.

'But I don't love him,' she whispered helplessly, tears rolling down her cheeks.

'I know, I know.' He grieved. 'But it's the only way! I almost destroyed you once, I won't risk doing it again. First chance I get, I'm going, Ellen. I have to.'

Biting her lip to suppress her sobs, she nodded dumbly. Laurence came back into the room, towelling his hair briskly. 'That's better. Amazing what a good bath can do. I feel tons better now and not too much bark knocked off either.' He saw Ellen's tear stained face. 'Hey, old girl, don't get upset. I'm all right, really I am. Look, see for yourself,' he came up close to Ellen for inspection.

Cob rose. 'Well, I'll be off then, if you're all right. Thanks for the drink, Mrs Reid.' He moved towards the door.

'Hang on Cob! Won't you have another drink with me? After all, it's not every day a chap tries to blow you up.'

'No thanks, Mr Reid, I really have to go, see you tomorrow' he called over his shoulder as he left.

'Well, would you like a drink, Ellen? You look as if you could use one. I'm sorry, I didn't mean to frighten you.' He brought two clean glasses and the rum bottle and placed them on the table.

'No thanks Laurence, really. It's nothing. I think I must be still a little run down, that's all. I feel very nervy lately.' She quickly wiped her eyes and straightened her hair. 'I'd better see about supper. Leena will be back with Faith soon.' She hurried into the kitchen to be alone with her thoughts.

Laurence followed her, rum glass in hand. 'Tell you what. As soon as the last well is dug we'll take leave, the both of us, and Faith. Go down to Amy's. She can prance you around all the shops in Townsville and I'll give you enough money to really splash out. Will that cheer you up, do you think?'

Looking up to answer him, Ellen glanced through the window to see Faith, approaching, her hand firmly grasped by her grandmother, and followed by a glaring Leena.

Laurence went to meet them.

'Oh Laurence dear. I've just come to bring Faith home. Did you know Leena's been taking her to the villages?'

'Yes Mother, Leena asked if she could,' Laurence answered her soothingly, placing a peck on her ruddy cheek.

'Well, I don't think it's good for her, Laurence,' she complained as she peeled off her gloves and sank into a chair. 'She needs the company of white children dear. Running around with all those blacks will cause her to pick up nothing but bad habits, mark my words,' she replied, looking sharply at Ellen. 'I thought I saw that Munyabra fellow leaving as I approached the house.' Her voice held a heavy tone of disapproval.

'You did, indeed, Grace,' Laurence agreed, still humouring her, 'and a good job too. He had to bring me home. I almost blew myself to pieces this afternoon,' he explained patiently.

'Oh dear, are you hurt?' Grace rose hastily to check out her favourite soninlaw.

'Now don't fuss, Mother, nothing's broken. Just gave me a fright, that's all, but it's a good job Cob was with me. He pulled me down just in time. Probably saved my life!'

'Well, that's as may be, Laurence, but I don't think you should be encouraging him to hang around the house. You know the trouble I had with that family, and I don't think Ellen likes having him here, do you Ellen?' she asked pointedly.

Laurence intervened. 'Now Grace, don't badger Ellen. She isn't feeling too well. In fact, I was just saying that when the wells are finished, I intend taking a holiday. We're off to Townsville to stay with Amy and Edward.'

'Are you taking Faith?' Grace enquired, quite put out. 'You don't have to, you know, I could care for her,' she suggested hopefully.

'Of course we are, Daddy wouldn't go without his little girl, could he darling?' he asked, kissing the tip of Faith's nose.

'Well, in that case, I'll come too,' Grace decided firmly, allowing for no argument. 'I will speak to Henry. He has just arrived back from Cairns actually. I saw the *Goodwill* heading in as I came past the beach. I suppose he will call in on his way past. I'll stay for tea with you, then I can speak to him while he is here.' She turned to Leena who was still stinging from Grace's sharp tongue. 'Here girl! Take Faith and give her a sponge down. You want to be clean and pretty for Uncle Henry, don't you dear?' she asked, propelling the child towards Leena. 'Here he comes now,' she said, as Henry accompanied by another clergyman, headed toward the house.

'Hurry up with the child, girl,' she harassed Leena, 'and

make sure she wears that blue dress I made her. We have company by the looks of it.'

Henry and the stranger entered the house. 'We're in luck,' he said to his companion, 'all the family are here. I'd like to introduce Reverend Wethersby! He is one of the others, I'm afraid, but a nice chap all the same, Wesleyan actually,' Henry joked. The grey haired middle-aged man shook hands with Grace and then with Laurence.

'Mr Wethersby has come to inspect our well system, Laurence. He is also suffering from drought, aren't you Mr Wethersby?'

The softly spoken fellow agreed. 'Indeed I am. The whole of the state is stricken. I've opened a small mission west of Cairns, with only a few children at the moment though. Nothing like the set up you have here, Mr Reid,' he said modestly. 'After talking with Reverend Grimshaw I realise the wisdom of introducing a reliable water supply as soon as possible, so I was very grateful of his offer of bringing me here to see how you are tackling the problem. Any advice you can give me will be accepted most gratefully. I haven't been out from the old country long. I'm a "new chum", I think the Australian expression is, and rather green, sorry to say,' he sat down apologetically next to Grace.

'We came with the first missionary fleet, so to speak, Mr Wethersby. You only have to ask. We have experienced it all, believe me,' she explained.

Wethersby stayed at the mission for a few days, listening quietly to all the information given to him and making copious notes for future reference. He inspected the flowing wells with Laurence and drew plans of their construction. Cob taught him the methods of digging and shoring they had used. He won Cob's respect when he peeled off his jacket, picked up a crowbar and worked side by side with him.

'It's no good just looking on. If you want to learn you have to get into it and get your hands dirty,' was his explanation to Laurence and Ellen as he sat sharing a pot of tea with them. 'That Cob fellow is a good worker, smart too. I could do with half a dozen like him to help me set up my place.'

'Yes, he is,' Laurence agreed enthusiastically. 'He's good at carpentry too. He's been my right hand man with the wells, I don't think I could have managed without him. Tell you what, we are nearly finished here now, and plan to go away on holidays soon, don't we Ellen? What if Cob was to come to you, giving you a helping hand to get you started. How would that suit?'

Wethersby's face lit up. 'I say, how jolly decent of you. With a chap like that to show me the ropes, I will be established in half the time. Are you sure you can spare him?' he enquired hopefully.

'No trouble, but I'll have to ask him if he wants to. Not one of your regular blacks, our Cob, is he Ellen? Had a bit of education when he was a boy, son of a tracker, spent a lot of time with whites. That's why he speaks English so well. I'll ask him tomorrow and see if he agrees.'

Ellen already knew what his answer would be.

CHAPTER FOURTEEN

Flinders Street was baked as hard as the rest of the drought stricken north. Clay, churned up by passing carriages, filled the air with dust, leaving a film of ochre powder on everyone's hair and clothing. It clung to the shop fronts and the sparsely leafed trees, and lay thick along the boarded walkways, making the whole town the same faded colour.

With relief, the gritty, hot travellers entered Amy's cool, shady veranda.

'Phew! If this heat doesn't let up soon I think I will go mad. Is it as hot at Bibiringda?' Amy asked, unpinning her wide brimmed hat and throwing it on the nearest chair. Undoing the top buttons of her dress she flopped her ample weight into a squatter's chair. Ellen carried the sleeping Faith through the French windows to a rug on the drawing room floor, where the cool breezes played over her hot little body.

'It's just as bad, dear,' she heard her mother saying as she returned to the veranda. 'The heat saps your energy until it seems an effort to draw breath. I had hoped it would be cooler here. I see you haven't had any rain, either. It's to be hoped we get a wet season this year and soon!'

Laurence lay back on the cane lounge, his eyes closed, resting his head on the embroidered cushion. He half listened as the three women discussed the crippling effects of the drought but couldn't force himself to join in. He felt so weary, bone weary. *God, I hope this Townsville doctor can perk me up a bit,* he worried to himself.

'And where's Edward, Amy?' He heard Grace enquiring. Amy's voice sounded bitter as she replied, 'Out west again, as usual. He's never home these days! He's trying to buy cattle to start the meatworks season, but he has serious doubts whether it will be worth bringing up the contract labour this year. Stock are dying by the thousands out there, there's no feed, even if the graziers manage to water them. They've tried taking the new sugar cane crops to hand feed the cattle but cartage makes it too expensive. The politicians are screaming for railways to be built to the inland cattle centres but, even if they succeed, it will be too late for many of the graziers. Most won't survive financially if the weather doesn't break soon.'

'Well, I'm sure Edward has a great deal on his mind right now, dear, he must be working very hard.' Grace sympathised soothingly.

'He always is, he's never home! I spend weeks just sitting here, waiting, then he dashes in, stays a few nights, and is gone again. All he thinks about is that wretched meatworks.'

Ellen looked closely at her lonely disillusioned sister. The drawing room was filled to overflowing with all the luxuries Amy had always craved; the beautifully polished parquetry floors scattered with fluffy sheep skin rugs, green velvet overstuffed settees matched by deeply fringed velvet curtains, gilt mirrors gleamed from walls covered in expensive, imported, heavily embossed wallpapers. Yet still she wasn't satisfied. Money couldn't buy the things she needed; a man she loved, and the children she didn't seem able to have.

Poor Amy, Ellen thought, *her only purpose in life is to spend money.*

Over the next few days, while Amy and Grace dressed Faith

up in frilly dresses and flowered straw bonnets and showed her off unashamedly at every local afternoon tea, unwillingly accompanied by Ellen, Laurence quietly made and attended his medical appointment. He sat now redressed and waiting nervously for the verdict.

'Well, Mr Reid,' said the doctor, 'I've given you a thorough examination and taken into consideration all the symptoms you have described to me,' he cleared his throat before continuing. 'I'm afraid there is little doubt, you are suffering from consumption, to give it its common term.'

'Consumption! How bad?' he hardly dared ask.

The doctor retreated to his seat behind the desk, absently shuffling his papers.

'Pretty bad, I'm afraid, Mr Reid, pretty bad.'

Fear now lurched in Laurence's heart. 'Is there some treatment you can give me?' he asked.

'Rest, complete rest and fresh air, lots of it!' the doctor replied positively.

'Will that cure me?' The question hung in the air between them.

The doctor's face assumed the professional mask he always used to proclaim the ending of a life. 'No, Mr Reid, I'm afraid it won't, things are too far gone for that, but it will help to ease you through coughing and conserve your strength.'

'You mean I'm dying?' Laurence asked in stunned amazement.

The doctor slowly nodded his head.

'When?' the word blurted unintentionally from Laurence's lips.

'We have no way of knowing, Mr Reid, with good care it could be quite a while. But quite honestly I would advise you to put your affairs in order.' No matter how many times he had to pass sentence it never became easier. The doctor rose abruptly as he felt his professionalism slipping and moved towards the door. 'I can give you some linctus to ease the coughing, use Friar's Balsam to inhale for the lungs. Next time you're down in Townsville, come and see me. Goodbye Mr Reid,' he said abruptly, shaking Laurence's hand.

In a daze, Laurence passed through the surgery door, mumbling his thanks. It wasn't until he was down the dark staircase and standing in the blinding sunlight that his brain truly registered the doctor's verdict. *I'm dying,* he told himself incredulously. *This can't happen, what about Ellen and Faith? I'll have to leave them. How will they manage without me? No! It's not fair. I won't let it happen,* he declared angrily. Eventually he found himself striding swiftly along the banks of the Ross creek with no idea how he had arrived there. Slowly his pace slackened as he came to terms with his fear. At last he sat on an upturned dinghy watching the suspension bridge open and close as sailing ships returned to their berths for the night.

He stayed long after the sweating wharfies had filed past him with their empty smoko boxes, heading off to beat the six o'clock swill, before the hotels bars closed.

Slowly the breathtaking beauty of the tropical sunset penetrated his denying brain and he wondered how many more times he would see it. He looked with new eyes at the sparkling ripples on the water, boats gently bobbing and swaying at anchor seemed to be waltzing together to the music of gently twanging rigging, as the evening breeze freshened. How many times had he looked and not see it at all? Precious time wasted, unappreciated. He thought of Ellen, her vivid blue eyes and wild flying hair; the sleepy face of Faith when she held out her little arms to be lifted from her cot; and the tears started, turning to deep choking sobs, as he crouched on the bank of the lonely river and cried out his grief.

While walking slowly back to Amy's house, he made his decision. He would not tell Ellen until they returned to Bibiringda. It would ruin her holiday for no useful purpose, and she was going to need all the strength she could muster in the near future.

Exhausted, he went straight to bed, leaving a message with the maid that he would not be down for dinner.

Next morning as he and Ellen lay in bed watching Faith tumbling over their outstretched legs he casually brought up the subject of returning to Bibiringda.

'But we've only just got here, Laurence. You mean you want to go back already? Aren't you enjoying yourself?' Ellen was puzzled by his sudden change in attitude.

'No, not immediately, of course not, I meant in a week or two perhaps. I feel quite guilty leaving Henry to cope on his own with this drought and all,' he lied uneasily.

'Stop worrying about Henry. He's more than capable of looking after himself. You should be worrying about yourself! You came here to rest and try and get better. Have you made an appointment with the doctor yet?' she scolded him.

'Yes, actually I called in yesterday while you were all flitting off to your tea parties,' he answered calmly.

'What did he have to say?' she asked, grasping Faith by the nighty just in time to prevent her falling headlong over the edge of the bed.

'Nothing much, just the usual medication to take.' Laurence evaded the question.

'Did he say what was causing all the coughing and your

constant exhaustion?' she persisted, taking the hair brush to Faith's blond curls.

'Not really dear, but he did give me some medicine and good advice.'

To avoid further questioning, Laurence left the bed and began to set out his shaving gear. 'I'll just call down for some hot water,' he said, pulling on his dressing gown and quietly leaving the room.

CHAPTER FIFTEEN

Cob rode beside Reverend Wethersby in silence. Not that there was any ill feeling between the two men. On the contrary, Cob quite liked the older man, and had jumped at the chance of getting away from Ellen. Best to go now while he still could, help the old man out, then shoot through. Where, he neither knew nor cared. He would make that decision when the time came.

They travelled inland from the tropical belt to the dry open plains country beyond. Striking off from the main track, they came finally to a shady campsite consisting of tents and a few poorly built humpies. A group of half-caste children came running eagerly to meet them. While the two men washed the dust of the journey from their hands and faces, the older boys tended their horses, a couple of teenage girls ladled stew on tin plates setting them down on an old wooden table, beneath some sparse gum trees.

As they ate the stew and charcoal covered damper with obvious relish, Reverend Wethersby explained to them how they were all going to help Cob sink two wells.

Later that night, as Wethersby and Cob sat making the most of the cool evening, with a last quiet pipe, Cob discovered more about the quiet balding man.

'I volunteered to come out to Australia after my wife and two children were drowned in a boating accident. I was minister to a wealthy parish, made a comfortable living, and was devoted to my family. I just couldn't face carrying on alone and grew more and more depressed. When the opportunity arose to do missionary work, I grasped it like a drowning man and here my ever growing new family surrounds me with a purpose for living again! They have given me so much I could never repay them.'

He smiled as the older girls brought the little ones over to say goodnight. He gave each child a kiss on the forehead and cuddle before saying a simple prayer over their bowed heads. Then it was a laughing, screaming, scramble as he chased them to the humpies to be tucked in to their beds.

Cob couldn't help noticing the love and respect in the eyes of the older boys, as they came to bid their benefactor goodnight. He spoke sadly of the children's histories, which were much the same, saving girls from the Chinese joss houses. He had taken in one family of five half-caste children left to starve when their mother died and their father abandoned them to return to his European homeland. Illegitimate toddlers taken from child mothers, too sick or ignorant to care for them and the same sad stories of abuse that Cob had heard a thousand times before. He sensed that these children would be some of the lucky ones. This man would obviously feed them his last crust of bread, and if necessary, defend them with his life. Already Cob felt an obligation to do the best he could to help the little group.

Work started with cheerful gusto when the diviner arrived next day. All the children wanted a job to do, down to the tiniest mite. The bigger boys swung picks, with more enthusiasm than good aim. While the girls shovelled away the dry broken soil. The younger children trotted about importantly fetching and carrying. Cob decided that the first well nearest the camp was the most urgent, and concentrated his efforts there. Reverend Wethersby organised a second well on the other side of the land grant.

It was slow back breaking work for the two men with only the help of the children, but day by day the holes grew deeper until timber shoring was needed to prevent caveins. Cob showed the older boys how to set up a sawpit and, using the horses to drag the trees over the pit, they split and cut more than enough timber to line the wells. In the back of Cob's mind was the idea of building a house for them before he moved on. Reverend Wethersby was delighted with his idea so, as soon as they had the first well finished, they abandoned work on the second well, in favour of a solid roof over their heads.

Cob patiently explained the use of the tools that Laurence had sent from Bibiringda and, in no time, the boys and Reverend Wethersby were happily planning and sawing. The girls hammered nails while the little ones dug out weeds and smoothed and polished the earth foundations. The rough timber framework rose proudly close to the little camp and at the end of each day's work the exhausted troop would head for the shade of the old table where kangaroo stew simmered constantly in the massive black pot over the fire. Every morning it was replenished with fresh meat, barley, and any available vegetables. It looked revolting as it was ladled onto the old battered plates, but Cob always enjoyed it and if the shiny breadpolished plates left on the table was any guide so did the others.

If anyone had the energy a game of cricket was usually played before the sun went down. Cob had fashioned a bat, bales, and stumps for the boys and Reverend Wethersby had sewn a kangaroo skin ball of sorts. Everyone joined in the fun, cheering and shouting if the old Reverend managed to bowl out Cob. After the game, the clergyman and his black advisor developed the habit of sitting together drinking tea and smoking while the children got ready for bed. A quiet friendship grew between the pair as they swapped yarns and discussed plans for improving the children's living conditions. The Englishman eagerly sought Cob's knowledge of the bush. He knew he needed all the advice he could get if he was to survive and care for his extended family in this wilderness. He also encouraged Cob to take the children out into the bush on Sundays to teach them bushcraft.

Cob taught them how to fend for themselves, how to catch goannas and snakes, where to look for witchetty grubs, how to track a kangaroo, how to rob wild bees hives, which berries were edible, which were poisonous; all the survival skills these half-caste children had been denied by being born out of the tribe.

*

Returning late one Sunday afternoon from one such trip, Cob and the children wandered happily into the camp eager to show off their haul of two goannas, suspended from a pole being carried between the two eldest boys, a bag of berries, and a good haul of witchetty grubs dug from a rotten log. The younger children ran ahead calling for the Reverend who had gracefully declined the offer of accompanying them in favour of a good book and a rest. They were surprised not to find him waiting for them, as he usually was, ready to listen to their adventures and admire demonstrations of the new skills they had learned.

As Cob brought up the rear of the little band, and laid his spears against the table, he noticed the fire had been allowed to go out, and the usually bubbling pot of stew was quite cold. Alarmed, he called the Reverend's name loudly. The children stopped their chatter as the tension in his voice told them something was wrong. After a quick check of the Reverend's tent, and finding his rifle and wallet still there, Cob checked the horses. Both were unsaddled and grazing on whatever dry grass they could find. He obviously hadn't left camp to visit anyone and, by the look of the sand around the track, no visitors had been.

Searching the new building, Cob picked up the tracks of a man leading out across the paddock to the other side of the land, towards the site of the second well. Cob ran the last hundred yards as anxiety began to churn his innards. At the site of the excavation his worst fears were realised. He saw an abandoned crowbar and short handled spade laying on the ground. He scrambled over the mounds of dirt and looked down into the nearly finished hole, only to see one side of the timber shoring had disappeared and the earth it had been supporting filled the well almost to the top.

'Dear God, if he's down there, he's finished!' Cob gasped as he carefully crawled to the edge and felt around in the dirt. Swiftly scooping away the top layer, he gently plunged the crowbar as far down as he could into the soft soil. He started as he felt the tip strike something hard. The timber shoring! It hadn't gone the whole way down the hole. Maybe, just maybe, the old fellow had a chance. If he was trapped down there the timber could have stopped the whole lot caving in on him. How deep was the hole dug now? About thirty feet, as far as he could remember. It was possible, if enough air had been trapped with him, but he couldn't last much longer if he had lasted at all. Crawling back from the edge Cob cupped his hands and shouted a long echoing 'Cooee,' into the empty bush. He repeated the call until the nearest of the boys appeared running across the paddock.

'Quick, go back to the camp, get me ropes and a lamp, some more spades and bring the other boys. I think the poor devil is down there. We don't have much time. Run, boy, run!'

The young fellow bounded off at top speed while Cob returned to the well and gently prodded around the cavein again with the crowbar. He could feel the timber stretching right across the hole, jammed as it had fallen forward. He began carefully shovelling away the fallen earth as speedily as he dare, taking care not to put any weight on the well's damaged sides. The other boys returned and together they desperately worked against time. It was getting dark before all the fallen timber was exposed. Cob lit the lamp and held it over the four-foot wide hole. As he had guessed the shoring was intact and jammed about twenty feet down.

Tying a rope to a nearby gum tree the boys lowered him into the dark hole. He shivered as he was lowered into what could be the Englishman's grave. Gnarled tree roots dangled against his face and earthworms burrowed hastily away from the light of the lamp.

'Careful now, a little more. Stop!' he called back up from where he dangled just above the fallen timber. Holding the light up against the darkness he checked the other shoring. It seemed to be holding all right.

'Lower down the other rope, I'll try and tie it onto the timbers,' he called, his voice echoing strangely from the tomblike walls. Struggling to relieve his weight on the rope he rested for a moment with his body wedged across the hole, toes clinging to the timber shoring. He felt the second rope strike his head. Reaching up he managed to catch hold of it in one hand while he groped around in the darkness for somewhere to hang the lamp.

Feeling a nail head poking out from the timber he lowered the lamp handle onto it gratefully. The lamp rocked at a crazy angle for a few seconds and he thought it would fall, but his luck held and it came to a sudden halt against the wall. A soft eerie glow reflected from the dark smelling earth close to his face, darkness below him and darkness above gave the feeling of being suspended in a timeless shapeless void, his world reduced to the small circle of lamplight.

He struggled to get the loose rope under the edge of the shoring; terrified that one bump would send it crashing down onto the maybe already dead man. The lifeline supporting him cut into the flesh under his armpits, gouging deeper and deeper as he swung about trying to twist his body down to reach the timbers. He could feel wet sticky blood starting to glue his armpits together. The pain was excruciating. Finally he had the rope secured as best he could and called to the anxiously waiting boys above to haul him up. Again the rope bit into his bleeding flesh as they lifted him out of the hole. The nearest boy handed him a cup of water, which he gulped down thirstily. 'Right now we have to try to pull up the timber, slowly does it, or we could have the whole bloody lot caving in.

'Heave! Slowly does it. It's moving I think. Right, heave again.' The timber rose terrifyingly, banging and crashing as it swung against the other shoring, no matter how careful they were. At last Cob could see it nearing the surface.

'Stop!' he called to his helpers. 'Two of you get around the other side, the rest of you hold it where it is. This is the hardest part. Take hold of that end you two. Gently now! Don't get too near the edge or you will be the next ones down there. Right, heave! It's bloody heavy but for God's sake, don't let go.'

The rough wood jarred sharp splinters into their hands as their skinny muscles strained to heave the heavy shoring over the edge and away to safety. Picking up the lamp, Cob held it out and called. 'Reverend Wethersby can you hear me?' His voice echoed down the dark chasm that lay at his feet. 'Reverend Wethersby, can you see the light?' There was no answer.

He shouted to the boys above, 'I'll have to go right down. He doesn't seem to be alive, but we have to be sure. Play out more rope.'

The tired boys, once again, strained their young muscles to support his weight, as foot by foot he was lowered, scrabbling with his feet against the walls to try to slow his descent. Clods of earth and stones came tumbling down into his face as the rope above scored the well's edge. At last he could feel the wall curving under his feet and he knew he had nearly reached the bottom.

Dangling the lamp beneath him, the dim light reflected a ghostly white face, half buried in the pile of dirt at the bottom of the shaft. Quickly untying himself he dropped the last few feet. Gently brushing away the dirt from the Reverend's face, he could find no sign of breathing. Feeling for a heart beat, he thought he could detect a faint flutter.

'I've found him,' his voice echoed around the dark shaft

walls. 'I think he could still be alive. Quickly, lower another rope.'

In their excitement, the boys rushed forward, the remaining shoring timbers creaked ominously and dislodged a shower of earth that tumbled with a roar down the shaft, crashing down on Cob's head.

'Get away from the edge, you stupid bastards, you'll have the whole bloody lot down on me!' he yelled up at them, covering his head with his arms as rocks ricocheted around him.

At that moment, a falling rock struck the lamp, exploding it with a blinding flash, blasting flames and shards of splintered glass into Cob's legs. His roar of pain rose like the bay of a dying animal from the bowels of the earth. The terrified boys above stood shaking with fright.

'Throw the damned rope down and be bloody quick about it,' he called to them in a broken voice. He managed to secure the rope around the inert body of the Reverend before slumping down against the shaft floor in almost intolerable pain.

He watched as the dangling body rose, blocking his only escape route from this hell hole, to the world above. Panic surged through him, suffocating claustrophobia made him want to reach up and tear the body back, to escape himself. Fighting for self control he closed his eyes and tried to beat down the awful fear. *Get me out, for God's sake, get me out,* he prayed silently digging his fingers into the soft earth wall to stop himself from screaming.

Half a lifetime seemed to passed before he felt the rope around him jerk and his own slow assent from purgatory began.

'Keep pulling, don't stop, get me out of here,' he whispered as he rose, half conscious and bleeding from the abominable black pit.

On the surface, he lay on his back for a few minutes, gulping down great lungfuls of fresh air, and sending silent prayers of thanks to the spirits for his safe deliverance.

The Reverend lay on the ground as the frightened boys hovered anxiously over him, unsure of what to do next. One had a wet a rag and was gently wiping Wethersby's face, another standing forlornly at Cob's side asked in a small voice, 'What do we do now, Cob? Reverend, he not moving or nuthin'. It too dark to see 'im proper. Is 'e all dead?' he asked, looking fearfully over his shoulder for any spirits that could be lurking about.

'I don't know, but we've got to get him back to the camp, quickly. Just give me a tick to get my breath and then we'll go.'

Rising unsteadily to his feet, Cob was so exhausted that he didn't even notice the stinging of a dozen cuts where splinters of glass had penetrated.

Hobbling over the dirt as best he could, he groped around in the darkness to find the timber shoring that had been cast aside.

'Here, a couple of you lads come and help me break a plank off this and lay the Reverend on it.' They rolled him onto the makeshift stretcher and, taking a corner each, four of the boys set off, carefully weaving their way over the dark, uneven ground. Cob staggered behind, helped along by a small boy who, too short to support the man's tall frame, held his hand anyway to comfort him as he struggled along.

As they wove their way, drunk with exhaustion into the camp, the older girls rushed forward to help, the boys carefully lowered the stretcher near the fire. Cob painfully eased himself down to examine the still form by the light of the flaming logs. Placing an ear to the Reverend's chest, he could detect an erratic heartbeat. He ran his hands over the Reverend's misshapen legs and knew at once that they were broken. He also found a nasty gash and huge swelling on the side of his face.

'It's lucky he's unconscious,' said Cob, as he carefully eased the crooked legs straight and splinted them with sticks and rags. Exhaustion now overtook Cob and he slumped forward feeling dizzy and faint.

'You all right Cob?' one of the girls asked. 'Here, I got you a cup a tea.'

'Help me up, will you?' Cob asked, taking hold of the girl's shoulder and heaving himself upright. 'Clean him up a bit and don't let them move him at all. Just put a pillow under his head and throw a blanket over him. Stay with him in case he comes to, but let's hope he stays out to it for the night. It will be best for him.'

He walked groggily across to where the boys sat huddled together on the ground, drinking hot black tea from tin mugs, too weary to even speak.

'You lads did very well out there tonight, you probably saved Reverend Wethersby's life,' Cob congratulated them. Lowering his mug, one of the tired youngsters looked up at Cob with solemn brown eyes. 'You did it, Cob, you didn't 'ave to go down there but you did. Thanks for saving 'im, 'e the only father we got.'

Poor little bastards, Cob thought as he looked round the frightened group of children. *He is all they've got. Have to get him to the hospital tomorrow, but I've got to get some rest first or I'll never make it.*

'You kids all get some sleep now, except the one who is to watch the Reverend. We have a big journey to make in the morning.'

CHAPTER SIXTEEN

'I don't see why Laurence is in such a hurry to go back! We've only been away a few weeks. I'm sure Henry will be coping,' Grace complained as she packed her bags. Amy sat on the bed nursing Faith, listening to her mother's complaints.

'I can't understand it either,' she agreed, upset at losing the company of her family so soon. 'He doesn't look at all well. You'd think he'd be glad to stay a bit longer and make the most of the break. After all, he's never really had a holiday from that place since he started. I don't know what Ellen thinks about it. She seems willing to go back early too. It's a pity. I haven't had much time with Faith,' she said wistfully, giving the little girl an even bigger cuddle. 'I suppose she will be ready for school before I see her next. Do you think Laurence would consider sending her here for her education when she's old enough?' she asked hopefully.

'I wouldn't know, dear,' Grace replied, slamming the lid of her case. 'You know, Ellen and Laurence, they have some strange ideas when it comes to rearing that child. I am determined though, she will get a decent education, and not have to live the life that you girls had.'

'Are you ready, Mother?' Ellen called from the hall. 'We will have to be going. The boat sails in two hours. Come on, Faith, let me put your bonnet on. Daddy's waiting downstairs.'

'Do you really have to go, Ellen, couldn't you and Mother

stay longer? I'm sure Laurence wouldn't mind,' Amy pleaded still holding the little girl.

'I suggested that Amy, but he wouldn't even consider it. He says he wants us to go back with him, but Mother can stay if she likes.'

'It's unlike Laurence to be so inconsiderate,' said Grace pinning on her hat. 'I'd rather leave with you. I don't like the thought of a long sea journey alone these days,' she said huffily.

Turning to Amy, she kissed her cheek. 'Goodbye dear, thank you for a lovely time as usual. Give my regards to Edward when you see him.'

'If I see him,' replied Amy sarcastically. She scooped Faith from the bed into her arms. 'Come on darling. Give me a big cuddle. You have to leave your Aunt Amy now, and she will cry big tears when you're gone, won't she?'

*

Ellen stood on the deck of the ship. She loved the early mornings, and would creep out of the cabin, leaving Laurence and Faith to sleep, glad to be alone with her thoughts. As the ship ploughed on before a strong wind, she remembered their first journey along this coast. Who would have guessed then what was to happen to them all.

They would soon be back at the mission, but it would not be the same. Cob would be gone with Reverend Wethersby, but after that, where would he go? What would he do? Would he forget her? She closed her eyes and tried to conjure up a mental picture of his face but the parts didn't fit. Would he haunt her for the rest of her life. No! It must' stop. She couldn't go on thinking this way, it was pointless and not fair to Laurence. He looked so ill these days, why on earth did he want to rush back to Bibiringda? She wasn't sorry for herself to be going back really. She could only take so much of Amy's life, and Faith would have been ruined if she'd stayed any longer. *I suppose I'd better go and get her dressed and ready for breakfast.* As she started to descend the gangway to her cabin, she saw her mother hurrying towards her.

'Thank goodness, there you are Ellen. I was just coming to find you. It's Laurence. I just popped into your cabin and found him having one of his attacks. He looks awful, Ellen, you'd better come quickly.'

The two women hurried to the cabin.

Laurence lay half out of the bunk gasping for breath. Coughing spasms shook him, wracking his wasted body as he fought to clear his lungs.

'Take Faith to your cabin, mother, I'll see to him,' said Ellen depositing the half awake child into her mother's arms. She held Laurence's frail shoulders and steadied him. 'It's all right try to keep calm. Lay back on the pillows and I'll open the porthole, see if some fresh air might help. Where's your medicine and the Friar's Balsam?'

He pointed to the leather shaving case on the cupboard top. She spooned medicine into his mouth and rang for hot water. While she waited, she set up a tent of sheets over Laurence's head. Pouring the balsam into the steaming bowl of water she placed it at Laurence's side. The steamy vapours filled the little cabin and after a while his breathing eased a little and he fell into an exhausted sleep.

She waited until she was sure he was not going to relapse into another bout of coughing before she quietly left the cabin, and went in search of her mother.

'I don't like the looks of him at all, Ellen,' Grace said

worriedly as they sat on deck chairs watching Faith play. 'What did he say the doctor in Townsville said about it?'

'Nothing much. He was pretty vague, just take the medicine and get plenty of fresh air! No different to the Cairns doctor, as far as I can see. I'd better get back to him now in case he has another attack. I'll be glad when we get to Cairns and I can get him out of that cramped cabin, it doesn't help.'

Laurence's condition worsened over the next few days. The spasms grew more frequent and his strength to handle them lessened, it was all he could manage to rise to a sitting position. When the ship finally docked in Cairns, Ellen would not listen to his begging protests and had him carried from the ship straight into a waiting carriage and driven immediately to the hospital. She and Grace waited a long time outside the room as the doctor examined him. When the doctor finally emerged, he motioned Ellen into the room, but blocked Grace following. 'You come with me, Grandmother, bring the child with you. We can have a little talk.'

Exchanging fearful glances, they did as he asked and Ellen quietly entered the sterile carbolic room, its pale green walls and sickly cream trim depressingly hospitallike. The only thing the room had in its favour was a huge window thrown wide open, giving a panoramic view of beautiful Trinity Bay.

Laurence lay grey and fragile against the pillows, he raised one hand weakly as Ellen approached. 'Come and sit on the bed beside me, darling, where I can see you, that's better.' He gazed fondly into her face.

'What does the doctor say, Laurence? He sent me in, but wouldn't let Mother or Faith come, what's happening?' she asked anxiously.

He took her hand. 'We have to talk, darling, just you and

me. I didn't want to tell you like this. I wanted us to be home in our own place, but it seems that is not to be.'

'Tell me what, Laurence? You're frightening me.'

'I'm afraid it's not good Ellen, oh damn, how can I put it? It's my health, love, it's not going to get any better. Do you understand?'

She resisted the thought stubbornly. 'No Laurence. I know you're sick, but there must be something we can do.' She stood and paced around the room angrily. 'We'll go to Sydney! The doctors here don't know anything. They're so out of touch and old fashioned.' She stood at the window, looking out to sea.

'Ellen, please come back and sit with me. Please.' he whispered, falling back onto the pillows, exhausted.

'I'm sorry, Laurence. It makes me angry. You went all the way to Townsville to see another doctor and get a second opinion, and he told you nothing. It's not good enough!' She came and sat beside him again, staring worriedly into his face.

He looked deeply into her eyes. 'He did tell me, Ellen. I'm dying dear. There's nothing anyone can do,' he said resignedly.

'No!' she gasped, tears springing to her eyes. 'That's not fair. You don't deserve that.'

He shook his head, laughing wheezily. 'I'm afraid it doesn't seem to count. Anyway, that's not quite true. It's you who have been good, so good to me. That's what I want to talk about now, to thank you for giving me so much these last years. Yourself and Faith, and a family, I couldn't have asked for more.' Raising himself he caught both her hands in his. 'I realise it hasn't been the same for you. I've always known you didn't love me in the same way as I loved you. But you gave me everything you could. I want you to know that you have made my life complete, Ellen. It will be very hard to leave, but I know I've been a very lucky man.'

'Laurence, don't say that. I do love you in my own way. It's just that…' she burst out sobbing unable to continue.

'Don't cry, Ellen, please don't cry. Let's make the most of what's left, shall we? I want to treasure every minute with you from now on. Could we do that, do you think?'

'Yes, yes, of course, Laurence. It's just that I need some time. I can't believe it! It's not fair, there has to be something, someone somewhere, who can help you.'

'I know how you feel. I felt the same at first, but I've had time to think now. I believe what they are telling me. There's no point in rushing around frantically, wasting this precious time, it won't do any good. I've decided what I want to do. I don't want to die here, in this room. I want to go home, Ellen, with you and Faith. If I have to die I want it to be there. Do you understand?'

'Oh Laurence, I don't know. There's no doctor at the mission. What if you need one urgently? Maybe it's better to stay here where there are people to help you.'

'But that's just it dear,' he said sadly. 'No one can help me, so what's the point in staying? I want to go home, Ellen,' he said in a lonely voice.

Struggling for control, she said, 'All right, if you think it's best for you, I'll speak to the doctor as soon as I can and see what he says.' She patted his hands and gently lowered him to the pillows. 'You rest now dear, you look absolutely exhausted. I'll fix everything, I promise, I'll come back and see you later.'

Kissing him, she walked quickly from the room. Closing the door behind her, she pressed against the wall and gave way to her grief. She sobbed quietly, resting her head against the cream paint. She was crying only for the loss of a dear friend, she knew it, and felt a cheat, a rotten cheat. He deserved a wife who would shed honest tears for the love of her man. He had friends enough to mourn him.

She wiped her eyes and was straightening her hair when she saw Grace and Faith coming back along the hall towards her. Her mother's face was crumpled, her eyes red rimed from crying. She held tightly onto Faith's hand, as if the child was about to slip from her grasp. The two women stood, dumbly facing each other, unable to find words to comfort each other.

Grace broke the silence. 'The doctor told me, Ellen. I can't believe it!' she said, shaking her head. 'Poor dear Laurence, of all people, he wouldn't hurt a fly. Oh! It's so unjust. He has everything to live for. Why him?' She sank weeping into a chair clutching the frightened little girl to her.

'Come on, Mother, don't cry. He doesn't want us to do that, you know,' Ellen said, awkwardly patting her mother's shoulder.

'How can you say that, Ellen? He's your husband. He's dying poor man. How can you be so callous?'

Ellen drew her hand away, stung by her mother's cruel remark. 'Because he just told me, that's how!' she replied, anger tingeing her voice. 'He wants to go back home to the mission and carry on normally with his life. He wants to be with us for the time he has left. I'm going to see he gets his wish, do you understand? I want you to take Faith back to Bibiringda as soon as possible. It's not good for her to see us so upset, you can prepare a sick room in the cottage, so that Laurence will be comfortable as soon as he arrives,' she ordered firmly. 'That's the way we can help him now, Mother, not by wallowing in our grief. 'She paced distractedly, trying to think. 'You will have to wire Henry and get him to come for you.'

'Oh dear, how am I going to tell Henry?' her mother's voice quivered. All at once she seemed much older and frailer. 'He will be so upset. Laurence is like a brother to him.'

'He will have to know, like the rest of us, Mother, and he will have to be just as strong. If he loves his friend I'm sure he will find a way. Now pull yourself together and do as I ask, if you really want to help Laurence.'

She watched the bent old lady and the small child walk down the hall and out of the building, disappearing into the hot sun of the street. She opened the door of Laurence's room and found him sleeping peacefully. Closing the door quietly, she set off to find the doctor.

She was soon lost in the long corridors each one seeming to lead nowhere. She approached a starched bustling nurse, and asked her directions, and was told to turn back the way she had come. Confused and distracted, she rushed around a corner and crashed headlong into a man hurrying the other way. He reached out his hands to steady her from falling. Regaining her balance she looked up into his face to apologise.

'Cob!' she gasped in disbelief.

'Ellen! What are you doing here? I thought you were in Townsville.' He kept his hold on her arms, alarmed by her stricken expression. 'What's wrong?' he gently shook her shoulders as she gaped at him, unable to speak.

'I… I…' she stuttered.

'Ellen! Tell me, is it the baby?' he demanded urgently. Gasping, she shook her head violently. All the fear and tension bottled inside came flooding out and she sobbed, unable to speak.

'Hey, steady on! Come and sit down a minute in here,' He opened a side door and showed her into a barely furnished room. They stood for a moment gripping each other's hands, staring into each other's eyes. Ellen threw herself into Cob's arms and buried her face into his shirt. He wrapped his arms tightly around her and held her close, waiting for her body to stop its violent shaking.

'Better?' he asked as he lifted her tear-stained face up to his. She nodded. He put his hand into his pocket and drew out a clean handkerchief. He held it up for inspection. She smiled at his expression and used it to dry her face.

'Now come on, sit down and tell me what's happened' he said steering her to an old horsehair couch in the corner. They sat close together, his arm still around her as she started to speak. 'It's Laurence, Cob. He's dying. He just told me, and I don't know what to do. He wants to go back to the mission. I was looking for the doctor when...' The tears started to flow again. She bowed her head in misery, unable to say more.

'Dear God, Ellen, what can I say? Is it that cough of his?' She nodded.

'I'm sorry, Ellen, really sorry. He is a decent bloke. I only wish there was something I could do.' Cob was genuinely upset.

'There's nothing anyone can do, only see that he is happy, and he won't be if we can't get him home.'

'Of course he should go home. Who wants to die away from their people? You're going to take him, aren't you?'

'Yes, that's what I need to see the doctor for, but I can't find him.' She bit her lip in an effort to control herself.

'Well, you're doing all you can then, don't cry.' His eyes were full of concern.

'It's not just that, Cob, it's the way I feel, inside. Oh, I'm devastated at losing my dear friend, but that's all I feel, Cob, a dear friend. Just how rotten and terrible am I?' she was shaking again.

'Stop that kind of talk, do you hear?' he ordered her sternly. 'You've done the best you can for him. He knows that. He's been happy with that, Ellen. You have to see it through now, play it to the end, for his sake. You can do it, you have to.'

'Yes, you're right, I know. I'll do my best. I didn't think I'd ever see you again. How did you know I was here?'

'I didn't. It was sheer chance I ran into you. I had to bring Reverend Wethersby in last week. He had a bad accident, poor fella. I'm just on my way to see him.'

Ellen shivered violently.

'Hey, are you cold?' he asked, drawing his arm more tightly round her.

'No, not really. It's just this whole mess I suppose. I feel so relieved now you're here.' She lifted her face to his and he gently kissed her.

'Nothing changes, does it?' she murmured, laying her head on his shoulder. 'I love you more now, than I did on the island. It just won't go away. It's as if I have the incurable disease, not Laurence.'

'I know, Ellen, it's the same for me, but what can we do? We are in a worse trap now than we were at Kalingari. There's no way we can destroy the last happiness of a dying man. You couldn't do it, I know, neither could I. But I tell you what, if anything does happen to Laurence it will be a different story then. I'm not letting you go twice, not if I can help it.'

Ellen put her hands on either side of his face. 'I love you, Cob Munyabra. I don't care what they say. If we do ever get another chance, it will be different next time, I promise you.'

They clung to each other, like two drowning people determined to spend their last seconds together. Then Cob released her. 'Ellen, we'd better go, someone may come. We can't afford to get caught together, not now.'

They stood, loathe to part.

'I'll tell you what,' Cob said, walking over to the door. 'I'd really like to visit Laurence. Do you think that would be all right?'

Ellen opened the door and peered down the empty corridor. 'Come on, there's no one around. You can come now if you like. I'll say I bumped into you; it's the truth anyway.'

They set off towards Laurence's room, Ellen in front, Cob walking submissively, slightly behind. She turned and beckoned him to walk beside her but he shook his head.

Ellen opened the door to Laurence's room and found him awake, looking peaceful and rested. He turned, smiling as she entered.

'Hello dear,' she said as she approached the bed, 'did you have a good sleep? Guess who I just bumped into in the corridor?' She beckoned Cob to come in.

'How nice to see you, old chap. Where did you spring from?' Laurence asked, genuinely pleased to see him.

Cob awkwardly approached the sicklooking man in the bed. 'Had to bring Reverend Wethersby in, Mr Reid. He's had a bad accident. Fell down one of the wells we were digging.'

'Poor chap, how dreadful, how is he?' Laurence asked, full of concern.

'Two broken legs and some head damage, but they say he will be all right in time.'

'That's bad luck, when he was just getting started. What's

happening to the children he was looking after?'

'I have them with me, I couldn't leave them out there when I didn't know if he would live or… die,' Cob faltered over the last word.

'No, of course you couldn't, but what will you do with them? How many are there?' Laurence enquired.

'Fifteen, counting the bigger boys. I suppose the older ones could fend for themselves, but I know the Reverend would want to keep them all together if possible.' Cob's deep concern for the children showed on his face.

'Don't worry' Laurence wheezed unevenly from the exertion of talking. 'Best thing to do is to take them to the mission at Bibiringda. I'm sure Henry won't mind, after all what's fifteen more when you've already got over three hundred?

A drop in the ocean so to speak.' Laurence smiled at his own joke. 'Tell you what, we should be leaving any day.' He looked at Ellen anxiously for confirmation. She smiled, nodding. 'Well, why doesn't Cob bring the children over with us? I'm sure we could squeeze them all on boat, what do you say, Cob?'

Cob glanced at Ellen before replying, 'Thanks very much, Mr Reid.'

*

Henry carried Laurence from the hired carriage onto the boat and laid him down on a mattress especially prepared for him, he called back to Cob, standing on the wharf surrounded by his new found family.

'Right Munyabra, let 'em aboard now. They'll have to squash themselves up in the stern and sit tight.'

Cob gave the word and the children climbed aboard, quietly finding a space and sitting down together, nervous of the overbearing minister. Cob followed Ellen down the gangplank, carrying the bags of tools belonging to Bibiringda.

'Everyone all right? Then we'll get going. I don't like the looks of that cloud building up, could be rain if my prayers are being answered, don't want to be caught out in the open sea, overloaded like this.' Henry and Cob handled the sails while Ellen squatted on the deck beside Laurence. As they sailed out of Trinity Bay and round the headland, the wind picked up and the sea became choppy, tossing the little boat about skittishly, The sky deepened and soon big shilling size drops of rain began to fall, one by one onto the deck.

'It's raining,' Ellen cried excitedly.

Everyone lifted their heads to feel the first drops of rain in over two years fall on their upturned faces.

The raindrops gathered momentum becoming a steady soaking stream. The children laughed as they let the water pour down their faces and trickle into their mouths, but very soon a cold wind began to pull at their soaking hair and clothes and the rain began to lose its appeal as they huddled together for shelter. Ellen tried her best to keep Laurence dry but the rain soon soaked the blankets she wrapped around him. She cursed herself for not having thought of more protection for him, but who would have expected rain after so long?

The sea's swell deepened as the wind became stronger, making the handling of the sails a difficult job. Cob and Henry battled to keep the little boat on course as the now driving rain made visibility poor. Waves began to break over the side of the tossing craft, sending sheets of cold salt water swilling across the deck, soaking everyone as they huddled in whatever shelter they could find. It seemed hours before the bedraggled little boat managed to limp into the mission's tiny bay and off load it's soaked, cramped passengers.

Henry directed Cob to carry Laurence to the house immediately, while he arranged places for the shivering children. Cob easily lifted Laurence and set off carrying him like a babe in arms up the track towards the settlement. Ellen followed behind. The rain had eased now, though the sky was still overcast. The shrivelled grass seemed to be lifting its dry brittle blades already as the life giving rain seeped to its roots. Raindrops dripped from the washed leaves of the overhanging trees which, cleansed of the heavy coating of dust, seemed to turn green again before their very eyes. The earth smelled rich and sweet.

'Sorry to be such a nuisance,' apologised Laurence as Cob stopped to adjust his grip.

'No trouble, Mr Reid. We're nearly there now,' Cob replied, quietly worried at the grey appearance of the wet, sick man.

Ellen moved quickly ahead to open the gate. As she did so the cottage door opened and Grace came out followed by Faith. She stopped short when she saw Cob Munyabra. 'That will do, Munyabra. Put him down we can manage from here, thank you,' she said tersely. Cob looked enquiringly at Ellen, who nodded, before he placed Laurence's feet on the ground and supported him until Ellen could take his weight.

'Thanks for the help, Cob, very decent of you,' Laurence croaked, his breath coming in sharp gasps. 'Come and visit me while I'm laid up, will you. I'm going to need some company,' he said, leaning heavily on Ellen as he tried to make it to the door.

'Yes, thanks Cob,' Ellen agreed over her shoulder. Grace

glared as she came forward to support Laurence's other side.

'No bother, Mrs Reid,' Cob replied, returning Grace's glare with an equally vicious one of his own.

'Good evening, Matron.' He half saluted in mock respect as he departed.

'What's he hanging around again for?' Grace asked suspiciously as they half carried Laurence inside and headed towards the bedroom. 'I thought he was gone for good. What's he doing back here?' she insisted.

'Ellen bumped into him at the hospital, Mother,' Laurence tried to explain. 'Poor Reverend Wethersby has had a very bad accident. He's laid up with two broken legs so Cob brought his little brood here, to stay with us, until he mends.'

'Mark my words. He's dangerous, Laurence. Get rid of him, a smart black is always dangerous,' she said and threw a threatening look at Ellen as they lowered Laurence onto bed.

*

The overcast weather continued over the next few days, though little more rain fell. A quiet stillness seemed to stifle the air, there were no breezes to ruffle the trees, and the birds and bush life grew still. An air of expectancy hung in the atmosphere. Ellen became completely preoccupied with Laurence's rapidly deteriorating health. Since the soaking he had received on the boat trip, he was hot and feverish. No amount of sponging cooled his burning body. He tossed restlessly, his breathing becoming increasingly distressed and he only seemed to rest a little more easily when Ellen sat with him. He would grip her hand and smile weakly as she quietly talked to him about nothing in particular. The sound of her voice seemed to have a calming effect on him, so she stayed beside his bed night and day, devoting her time absolutely to his well being. She sent Faith to live at Grace's house for the time being, away from the depressing atmosphere of the cottage, but insisted that Grace bring Faith to see her father every day. Faith would sit on the bed happily chattering to her dolls and sometimes slipping her little arms around his neck giving him a loving hug. She didn't seem to notice his sickness. To her he was still her adoring father.

Henry called one afternoon to sit with his friend. He had delayed the visit as long as possible, finally forcing himself to face the sickness and weakness that he found very difficult to cope with. He entered the bedroom uneasily. Ellen rose and offered him her vacant seat beside the bed. He gingerly sat down. Panic filled his eyes as she said, 'I'll leave you two alone for a while, so you can have a good chat. Would you like some tea, Henry?'

'Don't leave because of me, Ellen,' he said nervously. 'I just popped in to see how Laurence was doing.'

'Nonsense, Henry, stay and have a good chat. Laurence will enjoy that, won't you dear?'

Laurence nodded, his brilliant feverish eyes showing his pleasure. Ellen closed the door quietly behind her.

'Well, how's it going, old chap? You're looking much better,' Henry lied trying to be cheerful.

'Not too bad, mustn't complain,' Laurence replied with a wan smile. His smooth white fingers picked absently at the counterpane.

'Is there anything I can get you? No trouble to nip over to Cairns, if there's anything you need, no trouble at all,' Henry offered, being quite prepared to face any task rather than to sit and watch his friend die.

'There is something you can do for me, Henry, but not right now, later, when I'm dead. Will you promise to take care of Ellen and Faith for me, especially Faith, if anything should happen to Ellen, though God forbid it should. It would put my mind at rest about them.' Laurence lay looking into his friend's face waiting for a reply.

Henry lowered his head unable to meet Laurence's steady gaze. He pinched the bridge of his nose between his fingers as he tried to control his emotions. 'For God's sake, don't talk like that Laurence. You'll be all right. You'll be around for a long time to look after them yourself, wouldn't be surprised if you saw me out in the end. Don't be silly,' he rebuffed the implications of the request.

'Henry, please, it's no use pretending. I don't have time for that. Will you do it?' Laurence pleaded.

'You know I love that little girl as if she were my own,' Henry said. 'I'd never let anything happen to her, as for Ellen, I am her brother,' he choked, unable to go on.

'Well, that's settled then, now buck up and tell me what's been happening on the mission. I miss all the news now I'm confined to my bed,' Laurence cajoled Henry, trying to lighten the morbid atmosphere.'

When Ellen returned with the tea tray she found Henry away on his favourite subject, the expansion of the mission stations into the interior. Laurence's eyes drooped as he valiantly tried to keep awake.

'I think he may be a little tired now, Henry, perhaps we should leave him to rest. Come and have your tea with me in the parlour.'

'Oh! yes, quite, sorry old chap, didn't notice. Well, I'll be off now. Good to see you. Hope you'll feel better soon. I'll pop in again as soon as I can,' he murmured uncomfortably as Ellen showed him out of the room.

They sat for a while sipping tea. Henry, finally breaking the silence said, 'It's dreadful to see him like that, Ellen. I can't bear to look at him, I don't know what to say to him. It upsets me so much.'

'He was very pleased to see you, Henry. He has been asking where you were. I'm sure he enjoyed your visit, it's just that it tires him, trying to talk.'

'Yes, well, I'm not very good at these things.' Henry finished his tea and pushed his cup away. 'Better be going. There's heaps of work to do. I really miss Laurence around the place, hadn't realised how much I depended on him,' he said sadly, walking to the door. Ellen followed. As they strode together down the path Henry lifted his eyes to the sky.

'Don't like the look of this weather. It seems to be really building up. Could get a good storm before long,' he kissed her lightly on the cheek. 'I'll come again as soon as I can,' he promised half heartedly. 'If you need anything, let me know!'

She watched him, as he hurried away with an air of relief, and wondered how strong he really was.

Ellen woke frequently during the night, as Laurence relapsed into violent fits of coughing, and his breathing worsening after each bout. Eventually she stayed up, afraid to fall asleep in case she didn't hear him and he choked. She walked around the darkened house in an effort to keep awake, and went to stand at the opened door to breathe in some fresh air. The first grey shadows of dawn began to lighten the treetops and everything was silent and waiting. Threatening dark clouds banked solidly over the sea, tinged with foreboding rosy pink. It made her think of the old rhyme she used to say as a child:

Red sky at night, Shepherds delight,
Red sky at morning, Shepherds warning.

It certainly looked that way to her. She pulled her shawl tighter around her nightdress and watched fascinated, as the violent dawn fully unfolded, angry red now streaked the horizon as the massed clouds rolled in over the land. Small gusts of wind skitted across the compound, spiralling up dust and leaves into miniature BillyBillys as they frantically swirled off to nowhere. By the time Leena arrived the gusting wind had become stronger. It caught the door as Leena entered, slamming it back against the wall. Ellen, who had been dozing in the chair was jolted awake by the sudden noise.

'That wind 'im surely blowing up, Missus Ellen,' Leena commented as she stood before the kitchen fire fanning the dying embers and dropping small pieces of kindling onto them as they flared. 'I reckon bloody good storm'll come this way soon. I better get that washing in afore it's all blown away.' She bustled about, preparing the thin porridge gruel for Laurence's breakfast, while Ellen wearily made a pot of tea and sat with it at the kitchen table, her chin propped in her cupped hands.

'You look all done in, Missus Ellen? Did 'e have a bad night again?' Leena inquired looking at the girl's tired drawn face and tousled, unbrushed hair.

'Worst yet, Leena. I don't know what to do. He's only just managed to doze off. He fought for breath all night, and he's burning with fever this morning. I was hoping to get the doctor over from Cairns today, but with this storm blowing up it will be impossible to get the boat out. I am so worried. See what you think, when you give him breakfast, but don't wake him yet.'

'I don't like the look of 'im at all, Missus Ellen,' Leena said later, placing the shaving water and towels down on the kitchen table. 'not right in 'is 'ead, poor bloory fella, 'e all burning up, dun even know it was me, 'e kept callin' me your name.'

'What can we do?' Ellen asked desperately.

'I go in a little bit, get some fever vine, make 'im a strong dose. It quiet 'im down a bit.'

Leena left soon after. Ellen sat beside Laurence sponging his face as he restlessly tossed and turned. Ellen, hearing Faith chattering as the front door opened, rushed from the bedroom with her finger pressed to her lips.

'Ssh ssh, darling,' she whispered to the little girl, 'Daddy is a bit tired today love,' Grace looked at her enquiringly. 'He's not at all well today, Mother, its better if she doesn't see him.'

Happily accepting the decision, Faith pulled her grandmother by the hand. 'We go for a walk, Grandma.'

'In a minute, Faith, Grandma wants to just have a little peek in at Daddy first.' Grace slipped into the bedroom. She took one look at Laurence's flushed face, his skin drawn tightly over the sunken hollow cheekbones, and came quickly out again, her expression aghast.

'Oh, Ellen, he looks so – awful!' she whispered, finding it hard to express her dismay. She had had experience enough of death to know he was sinking fast. 'I'd better take Faith away. Send Leena for me if there is any change, will you?' she gestured over the child's head. They walked together down to the gate. 'You'd better get back inside, Ellen, it's going to rain again any minute. Goodness, this wind! It nearly bowled me over coming here. Come on, Faith, we'll have to hurry back to Grandma's house if we don't want to get a soaking.'

Ellen turned wearily to the sick room.

It was late in the afternoon before Leena return and began crushing a bunch of the vines and immersing them in boiling water.

'You just take a look out a window, Missus Ellen. It really coming down now,' complained Leena, as she stirred the evil looking concoction in a bowl.

Ellen was surprised to see heavy rain sleeting sideways across the compound, driven by a relentless buffeting wind. She had been so engrossed in trying to soothe Laurence that she hadn't realised that the weather was worsening.

Blowing on the hot medicine to cool it, Leena carefully carried it into the bedroom, and began to patiently spoon small drops into Laurence's mouth.

After a while the powerful herb began to calm his restless thrashing, and gradually he slipped into a deep sleep. They left him to rest, and returned to the kitchen. Leena pulled her still damp shawl over her head and prepared to leave.

'I'll come back in 'little bit time and sit with Mister Reid, so you can get some sleep, Missus Ellen,' she offered again.

'Thank you, Leena. I must admit I could do with it. I can scarcely keep my eyes open, 'Ellen agreed thankfully, as she opened the door for Leena. A blast of cold rain sprayed into her face, reviving her rudely. 'Goodness, look how wild it is out there now. Do you think you should go out in it?' she asked watching the wind viciously whipping small branches from the trees and hurling them wildly across the garden.

'I'll be all right, Missus Ellen, don't you worry none. I'll be back pretty quick,' she replied as she set off making a dash for it, remarkably nimble for her huge size.

Returning into the parlour, Ellen lit the lamps, trying to

ward off the miserable gloom that seemed to surround her. Collecting some sewing she went back to sit and keep her vigil at Laurence's bedside where, after a while, she began to doze.

Suddenly she was jolted violently to her feet by a terrifying crash as something struck the side of the house. She stood in confusion, not knowing what had happened, then she heard it! The deep rumbling roar of the wind, which gathered momentum to a spine chilling scream, as it violently blasted the cottage, making the tiny building shake to its very stumps. She ran to the window. A strange luminous glow lit the turmoil outside. She watched as huge limbs were ripped from tortured trees. and hurled into the air as if they were confetti. She screamed loudly as another branch slammed into the bedroom wall, but her voice was lost in the roar of the storm.

Deafening rain battered the shingle roof, in drumming percussion to the hideous wailing of the wind which grew louder and louder sounding like a thousand banshees, plucking and tearing at every loose nail and shingle, as if in a frenzy to destroy the house and snatch away Laurence's wavering spirit.

Trembling with fear, Ellen clamped her hands over her ears and squeezed her eyes shut.

Bang! Crash! The outside door flew open! She leaped up and ran out to see a ghostly black dripping figure lurching towards her into the house. She screamed hysterically.

'Ellen, it's me! shouted Henry pulling the soaking sou'wester from over his face. 'You've got to get out of here quickly! There's a cyclone nearly on us! I've just been for mother and Faith. Everyone is to go to the church. It's the strongest building we have. Hurry up! There isn't much time.' Just then a roar filled the air round them, throwing Henry off balance against her. The solid timber door flapped wildly on its hinges like a waving paper flag. Henry hurled himself against it with all his might, slamming it closed. He stood with his back holding it closed, shouting above the noise.

'Get Laurence up quickly, girl! You have to get out of here!'

'I can't,' she screamed back at him. 'He's worse, much worse. I think he's dying. I can't take him out there!' she sobbed desperately.

Henry pushed past her and went into the bedroom. He came slowly back out, tears streaming down his face. He wrapped his arms round his sister and clung to her for a moment. 'You're right Ellen,' he groaned, shaking his head. 'We can't move him now. Oh God, what are we to do? You must leave. I'll stay with him.'

'No!' she shouted. 'No! It's my place to stay with him. I can't leave.'

'All right, all right, Ellen, but this house just isn't built to withstand a cyclone. It will be wrecked with you both in it! Somehow we've got to hold it down. Look, can you hang on here, while I go and get some of the men? We will have to rope it down to the trees and pray to God it will survive. Will you be all right till I get back?' She nodded, biting her lip and trembling.

'I'll be as quick as I can, if the roof starts to go, get under the table or the bed. Cover Laurence with a mattress or thick blankets, anything you can find to protect yourselves with. I won't be long. Pack up what you can, just in case, and put the fire out.'

Terrified. she watched as he disappeared into the black whirlpool of rain and flying missiles, she ran into the kitchen and threw a pot full of water over the glowing embers of the fire. Before it had spluttered and died, she was back in the parlour pulling favourite photos from the wall and throwing them, along with books and ornaments into drawers and cupboards.

Taking the old wooden box that had been her father's, and now was filled with their personal papers and birth certificates, she pushed it under the bed for safety. She looked round, frantically trying to decide what else she should save when she heard hammering at the windows.

Henry hurried back into the house and caught her by the arm. 'Now listen,' he shouted above the raging storm. 'I've managed to get some volunteers. They are boarding up the windows now. We are going to rope down the house as best we can, then we'll stand by here with you, so don't be afraid.'

She breathed a sigh of relief and looked over Henry's shoulder, to where the men were now sheltering on the dark veranda.

One of them gave her a big encouraging wink. It was Cob!

No sooner were the ropes secured than the cyclone hit with its full vengeance. The noise was appalling. It screamed and howled as it tore at everything before it, the normal world ceased to exist as the holocaust raged. Ellen cowered on the bed beside the inert Laurence, praying for the horror to stop. The men clung to the veranda posts as the dreadful wind fought to rip loose their fingers and dislodge them. The house creaked and groaned as pressure built up inside it. Cob watched terrified as the ropes pulled taut to breaking point, trying to withstand the strain. One snapped, slashing open the face of the man beside him. There was nothing anyone could do to help him. To loosen one's grip now would mean instant death. Giant trees, ripped from their roots hurtled past them narrowly missing the house. Roofing iron and timber from the demolished cottages flew through the air like grotesque prehistoric birds before smashing clumsily to the ground. Debris crashed all around them.

As suddenly as it started the wind eased until it died altogether. Henry stretched up from his cowering position. 'Thank God, it's over!' he exclaimed with relief.

Cob grabbed his arm. 'No, Mr Grimshaw, it isn't. It's just the eye passing over. Quick, we haven't much time, check the ropes. I'll get on the roof and see how it's holding out.' He shinned nimbly up the veranda post and swung himself on to the shingles. He was worried to see how many had been lifted, even some of the main beams felt loose under his pushing foot. He climbed back down and went into the house.

Ellen rushed out to meet him. 'Is it over, Cob? Oh God! It was awful,' she shuddered, her face plainly showing her fear.

'This is only the eye, Ellen. We don't have long. It will be back again soon. Open up the back door. We have to release the pressure in here or the whole bloody place will explode!'

Unable to move, she stared at him horrified.

'Go on! Then get all the mattresses and quilts you can find, and put them over Laurence.'

Henry walked in just then, and the two quickly parted.

As she ran back from opening the back door, he stopped her. 'How's Laurence doing? All right, is he?'

She shook her head, unable to put into words her worst fears. 'Cob says to cover him with mattresses. He thinks the roof may go.'

'Right. I'll help you.' They dragged the mattress from the trundle bed and placed it over the still form of Laurence who sank deeper into oblivion unaware of the turmoil raging around him. They draped feather quilts carefully around his head and for a ghastly moment, Ellen thought he looked as though he was already in his coffin.

Cob rushed back into the room. 'Quick! Here it comes,' he shouted. Grabbing Ellen, he roughly pushed her onto the floor. 'Get under the bed, Ellen. Now! Don't come out for anything, do you hear?' He saw Henry glaring sharply at him. 'Mrs Reid,' he added quickly.

Sure enough, within a few minutes the screaming fury was unleashed upon them once again, even more horrendously than before. The house rocked violently, unable to take much more punishment, the soaking ropes began to slacken as they stretched.

'Get on to the ropes, for God's sake! The bloody house is going!' Cob screamed above the turmoil.

Suddenly one whole corner of the cottage rose from its stumps and hovered erratically in the air. Ellen, cowering in the darkness under the bed, felt the timber floor beneath her tilt crazily, and heard the furniture slide and crash together.

The window shattered and crockery tipped from the shelves. It seemed like the end of the world, the poor little cottage couldn't possibly hold together for even a minute more. The men fought with supreme effort as they clung to the sodden ropes and the house smashed back down onto its stumps and lay like a stricken whale.

'Thank God,' Henry gasped. 'I'm going in to check on my sister.'

He pushed the jammed door open and picked his way over the debris of fallen furniture and smashed glass to the bedroom. Lifting the mattress and quilts gently from round the still form of Laurence he looked anxiously into his face.

'Ellen?' he called softly. 'Ellen, come out.'

She pushed her head from under the bed and crawled out stiffly. 'Wasn't it awful, Henry,' she said reaching for his hand to help herself up.

He stood staring down at the bed. 'He's dead, Ellen. Laurence is dead!' he said in a shocked whisper.

CHAPTER SEVENTEEN

Raindrops glistened like jewels as they caught on the thick dark veil before Ellen's face, her boot heels sank into the sloppy clay piled up at the edge of Laurence's freshly dug grave in the little cemetery at Bibiringda. Faith stood obediently at her mother's side holding her hand, but she was unable to resist sliding her shoe toe around in the lovely little puddle of mud laying so close to her feet.

She jumped as Henry closed the Bible with a final snap. She watched with a child's curiosity as the Aboriginal pallbearers lowered Laurence's simple handmade coffin into the grave.

'Ashes to ashes, dust to dust,' Henry intoned, as he picked up a piece of wet clay and dropped it meaningfully into the hole. Faith watched her grandmother do the same, and then it was her mother's turn. Faith looked up hopefully, to see if she was to be invited too. On her mother's restrained nod she gleefully sank her small gloved hand into the gooey substance and hurled a nice big clod, thinking how clever she was to hit the hole so well.

People crowded around them shaking hands with her mother and patting her on the head. Her grandmother sobbed loudly, and had to be led away by her Uncle Henry.

Everyone seemed to be here, except her daddy; they had said he had gone to Heaven to sit with Jesus, but she hadn't seen him go! And the boat was still on the beach. *Maybe it wasn't far, and he had ridden the horse.* She clenched her gloved fist and watched the sticky clay squelch through the crocheted pattern between her fingers, and was quite disappointed when her mother peeled the soggy thing from her hand and wiped her clean with a handkerchief.

'Come on, Faith, we have to follow Uncle Henry and Grandma now,' her mother whispered close to her face, and she wondered why the others weren't supposed to hear.

Back at home everything was just as strange. Grandmother, though not crying any more, sat stiff and solemn, and sent her away when she placed her favourite nursery rhyme book on her lap. Her mother and Uncle Henry didn't even notice her when she stood on tiptoe at the table to look at the papers they were talking about. Rejected she sought out Leena, who was always ready with a laugh and a cuddle, but to her surprise she found Leena in the kitchen laying out tea cups and snivelling as she worked. Faith waited patiently, looking hopefully at the little tea cakes Leena was arranging on plates. Soon she was rewarded by a kiss and a half sob of 'Poor child,' plus the longed for cake. She took it out on to the veranda, and was about to pick out the currants when people who had been in the churchyard, filed past her silently into the house, all very sombre and dressed in black.

*

After the funeral guests had left, Ellen joined Henry and their mother on the veranda where they sat in cane chairs in silence. Ellen studied the damage wrought by the cyclone.

Hastily heaped piles of timber were all that remained of most of the cottages. Uprooted trees lay rotting where they had fallen, only those blocking the track had been heaved aside with the horses and chains. The rainforest had been stripped. Bare trees stood naked with broken limbs hanging pathetically from their trunks. It was as if Mother Nature had departed the earth, taking everything with her.

Henry's voice broke into her musing. 'We have to discuss your future, Ellen. Mother suggested that since her cottage is gone, she may as well move in here with you. It would be company for you both, don't you agree?' he asked. Not waiting for her opinion he continued, 'As you know, I have always handled Laurence's affairs so I don't have to check before I can tell you that he didn't leave you with much. Still be that as it may, you are quite safe here with us. You have the cottage and food expenses, which of course come out of Mission funds. We will be needing someone to run the children's dormitory soon, so I have decided to put your name forward to the church council. That will give you a small income!' Comfortable that he had met all his obligations regarding his widowed sister, he waited for her grateful thanks.

'Can't we discuss this later, Henry? I really don't know what I want to do yet. I need time to think things out.'

Grace turned on Ellen angrily. 'How can you be so ungrateful? After Henry has taken all this trouble to provide for you as a brother should. I can only hope that this is temporary lapse on your part, brought on by the death of our dear Laurence.' She sniffed and dabbed her eyes with her hankie.

Henry patted her knee 'Now, don't upset yourself Mother. I'm sure that Ellen is just overwrought at the moment.'

He turned in his chair to Ellen and said acidly, 'Take what time you need to compose yourself, Ellen, but do remember, I have a mission to run. I haven't the time to pander to your whims indefinitely. I did promise my dear friend that

I would be responsible for you and Faith, and I will meet that responsibility. We will say no more for the present. I'm sure I can trust your judgement, once you have had time to contemplate.'

'Pompous ass,' Ellen retorted under her breath. She rose from the chair seemingly calm. 'I think I'll go for a walk. I have a splitting headache. Excuse me, please.' She set off down the path past her devastated garden, and headed down the track to the beach.

Striding along the surf's edge she thought angrily of her future. How dare they? Again organising her life, making decisions for her, without even the courtesy of asking her opinion. Trying to trap her yet again into their suffocating mould. Squeezing and crushing her independence and initiative, until she would finish up just like them. *Probably try to marry me off to the next assistant; maybe it was one of the conditions of the post,* she thought cynically, *board and keep, plus missionary's sister. Well broken and trained! Never! Not again!* They had never asked her what she wanted. She stopped and stood throwing pebbles out into the sea. *Well?* she asked herself, *What do you want? Cob. Nothing else, just Cob. To be with him, to share his life, his other half, that was all. It was so simple. And why not,* she suddenly thought? Once you swept away all the hate, fear and hypocrisy, there was no valid reason left for their attitude. It was her life. And she alone would choose what she wanted to do with it.

They couldn't stop her!

Of course, it was so simple! Why on earth hadn't she realised that before? They couldn't stop her! She was of age. She was an adult. She could do it – if she had the courage. If Cob had the courage.

She would have to see him, talk to him, and tell him how easy it was. Joyfully she began to run along the beach, leaping over the eddying fingers of surf. She wanted to scream to the sky, laugh, and roll in the clouds. She was going to live at last!

She suddenly stopped, ashamed of her behaviour, how could she act like this when she had just buried her husband. *Oh, Laurence, I'm so sorry,* she sent a silent prayer to him. Would he understand? Yes, she was sure he would. She had kept her word, done the best she could for him, and now it was her turn. She knew he wouldn't begrudge her that, but she owed him respect, a decent mourning period in memory of his gentle kindness.

Feeling free and in control of her life for the first time, she retraced her steps to the cottage.

Next day the big clean up started in earnest. All mission hands were set the task of making the place habitable once more. The biggest loss was the dispensary, which had taken the full brunt of the cyclone and been almost demolished. Ellen and Leena spent most of the day scavenging through the widely spread debris, trying to salvage any undamaged or repairable items.

They piled any retrieved items they could find into the cart to be taken back to the church, which had miraculously survived undamaged. A firm memorial to Laurence's craftsmanship. It had been decided to set up a temporary dispensary there until the more urgent work of repairing the houses was finished and there was labour to spare for the rebuilding of the dispensary.

Grace had taken up residence in Ellen's cottage, without a byyourleave, assuming Ellen's silence to be acceptance of Henry's terms.

In reality Ellen was only waiting for a chance to speak alone with Cob. Her opportunity arose when Henry invited her to accompany him to Cairns. He was to order building supplies, she was to purchase new equipment for the dispensary. She was surprised when she saw Cob walking down the track ahead of her towards the *Goodwill* and quickened her step to catch up with his long strides.

'Cob,' she called, 'Wait for me.'

He turned at her voice, and a smile spread across his face. He waited for her to catch up.

'Where are you going?' she enquired as they walked together, keeping a respectable distance between them.

'I was just about to ask you the same, I'm going to see Reverend Wethersby. It's the first chance I've had since the cyclone.' he added.

'Good! Listen,' she said urgently. 'Meet me in Cairns. I have to talk to you.'

'Where?' he asked, intrigued.

'Somewhere Henry won't see us. I know! I'll come to the hospital when I've bought the supplies. He won't think anything of that. He will most likely go and visit Reverend Wethersby too, but not until later. He has heaps to do today. Shshh, here he comes.'

*

Once in Cairns, Ellen hurried away to make her purchases as quickly as possible, stopping only once to buy Faith a few ounces of her favourite sweets and a new doll to replace the one she had lost in the cyclone.

She strode briskly back to the hospital and made her way towards the Reverend's room. As she walked along the veranda checking the numbers above the open veranda doors, she saw Cob sitting on a flight of steps leading down into the hospital gardens.

Cob doffed his battered hat as he murmured, 'You see that clump of trees at the end of the path? There's a summerhouse there. I'll wait for you.'

Ellen walked around the hospital and back on to the veranda. Cob was gone. She made her way down the steps, along the path, and across the lawns. She found him leaning against the ornate wrought iron rails of a quaint gazebo, which nestled secretly under the entwined boughs of a massive spreading rain tree. He wore his moleskins and best white shirt, His black hair fell across his forehead as he leaned forward, his broad shoulders and arms spread across the railings.

'Cob we have to talk,' she said seriously as she mounted the steps, unpinning her hat and letting her unruly hair fall down around her shoulders.

'Talk? what's troubling you?' he asked opening his arms to her.

She came willingly into them. 'It's not Laurence. I can't do any more to help him now. It's us, Cob. You and me.' She looked seriously into his face. 'I've been thinking, we can do it! I realised down on the beach the other day we can just go. Call their bluff. They can't stop us, don't you see?'

He moved his hands from round her waist and placed them on her shoulders firmly. 'Hey hang on a minute, what are you saying?' he asked bewildered.

'You and me, silly fool, what else? It's so easy! We can go, clear out. You still want to do it, don't you?' Doubt now crept into her voice, as she saw the changed expression on his face. 'Don't you?' she repeated in a small voice.

'You know damn well I do. I haven't thought of anything else for years, but it's impossible, we both know what they'll do if we try anything again.' He turned and leaned over the railings, staring angrily at the ground.

'Cob, listen to me, please,' she pleaded moving closer to his side. 'They want me to take a position as teacher on the mission. Mother has moved in with me, they think they've fixed me up for the rest of my life. And they will have if we don't take the plunge now. This is our last chance to be together,' she implored.

'We can do it, Cob, Oh they may try and stop us if they find out beforehand, but once we're gone they won't dare! That's what we hadn't thought of. They won't want people to know… because that's exactly what Mother was fighting to prevent on Kalangari Island. The gossip will destroy them and that's the last thing they want. We have to call their bluff, can't you see?' she begged, pulling at his arm. He turned his head sideways to look at her, his face now deadly serious. 'Do you realise what you would be letting yourself in for?' he asked her roughly. 'God, Ellen, think girl, think! You don't know what it's like to be one of us. You have no idea how it feels to be patronised at best, and at worst, a dirty lazy nigger, on a par with the local dogs. Do you think that's what I want for you? You'd be treated like dirt, the MISSIONARY'S SISTER who fornicates with the blacks! Your own kind would despise you, my kind would scorn you. You wouldn't belong in either camp.' He pulled her close as if to protect her from the imaginary enemy.

'I would have a place, Cob, with you. It's the only place I want! All right, it may be as you say, but the alternative is worse. To slowly die inside, looking forward only to the day that I stop breathing, so the pain will go away. With you, I will be living, no matter how hard it may be. Without you is a living death. It doesn't seem such a difficult choice to me.' She sobbed as she buried her face into his white shirt.

He held her close stroking her hair. Suddenly he laughed loudly. 'Right girl! If you think you can take it, then let's have a go, what the hell, they can only hang us, eh?' He tilted her chin and kissed her hard. She clung to him as if her life depended on him, which in a way it did.

He now caught her excitement. 'All right then, that's settled. When do we go? And what about little Faith, she's coming too, isn't she?'

'Of course she is. I couldn't leave her, Cob. You don't mind, do you?'

'Mind? She's a beaut little thing, I only hope it won't be too rough on her, Ellen, we won't have anything to start with,' he reminded her, making sure she understood.

'That doesn't matter, we can always find work. I can get a position somewhere,' she said, brushing aside the problems.

'You work? No wife of mine is going to work! You can get that straight, right from the start, do you hear?' he thundered loudly.

'Wife? Will we get married, Cob?' she asked, genuinely surprised.

'Course we'll get married. What else!' he demanded.

She smiled happily at the thought, then her face fell. 'I don't think anyone will marry us, Cob. It's just not done, the squatters never marry their gins. It wouldn't be allowed. We'd never find a minister willing, would we?'

He nodded glumly in agreement. 'I hadn't thought of that. I suppose you're right, though surely there's someone out there who isn't so blinded with prejudice that he can't see what's right. Blimey, they are always eager to marry us blacks off to each other to save our souls! So they say. Bloody hypocrites! I'm sorry, Ellen. It just makes me so mad, that's all.'

'Well, I suppose we will have to get used to it. It's going to happen more than once so there's no point in allowing it to upset us. After all, it's our choice, so don't let it spoil things for us, Cob. We can be married without having a piece of paper to confirm it, can't we?'

'Sure can, Mrs Munyabra!' He burst out laughing again.

'Crikey, that's a mouthful isn't it?' They hugged each other giggling like two naughty school children in a secret conspiracy.

'When do we go?' he asked daringly.

She stopped laughing and said seriously, 'Not for a while. I feel I owe that to Laurence. It will cause enough bad feeling as it is. I don't want to sully his memory with the evil thoughts of other people.'

'Fair enough, he was a decent bloke, one of the few. It wasn't his fault he got caught up in this lot. Let him lie in peace. We've waited this long, we can wait a bit longer,' Cob agreed.

Ellen looked through the trees towards the hospital. 'I should be going, Henry will be here soon, and I am supposed to be visiting Reverend Wethersby. Have you seen him yet?' she asked scooping up her hair and pinning it back under her hat.

'Yes, I called in before you came. They were treating his legs so I was sent away. I said I'd be back later. You go first, then I'll follow, that way I get to see you for a bit longer,' he smiled, kissing her on her nose.

'Where will we go Cob? When it's time?' she asked wanting to stay and keep on talking of their life together, delaying breaking the spell, and having to face reality again.

He thought for a moment, then decided firmly. 'Back to the island, that's where we'll go. I can get a job on the timber. They know me, I shouldn't have any trouble. There's no whites there, so you should be left alone. We'll build a house away from the camp so no one can bother us. We'll be sweet, Ellen, just you see!' he enthused, the whole idea now taking a firm hold in his mind. 'All we have to do is wait, say six months, is that long enough?' he asked hopefully.

She smiled back reaching up on tiptoe to kiss his nose. 'That's long enough, Mr Munyabra, quite long enough.' She ran down the steps and out of the shelter of the trees. He watched her, a brave little figure hurrying away across the lawn.

'Six months,' he groaned to himself.

Ellen was seated at the bedside of Reverend Wethersby when Henry entered the room. He looked harassed, but strangely elated. 'And how are you feeling now, Reverend Wethersby?' he enquired cheerfully, stepping up to the bed and shaking the injured man's hand.

'I'm mending quite well, so they tell me, for a man my age. I've been very lucky. If it had not been for Cob I would be down that hole permanently. No need to dig me a grave, what?' He clapped his hand over his mouth, and blushed scarlet. 'Oh dear! Do forgive me, Mrs Reid. How dreadful of me to say a thing like that in your presence. They told me what had happened to your husband. I am so sorry,' he blustered on, in his embarrassment.

'That's quite all right, Mr Wethersby, I understand. I

know you didn't mean any disrespect,' she soothed him. 'Do continue.'

'Tell me, Reverend Grimshaw, how did you fare in the cyclone? Cob was in earlier, but they sent him away. He only had time to tell me my children were safe. It's so good of you to take them in while I'm laid up like this. I do appreciate it.'

'Only too pleased to be able to help, dear fellow,' Henry replied, 'but I wanted to speak with you about that with all the damage we have suffered from the cyclone, our resources are stretched to the very limit. I feel the best thing to do with those children is to send them south to one of the bigger missions. It will be quite a while before you are ready to resume your missionary work, even when your legs are fully mended, you will need to convalesce for a while. I'll see to it, don't worry. You can always start a new group when you're back on your feet.'

Reverend Wethersby was aghast. 'Oh no! Please don't do that. I couldn't let my children go to strangers! I may not be able to find them again if they are moved away. Please Mr Grimshaw, couldn't you just keep them for a few more weeks? I'm sure I'll be all right by then,' he pleaded.

'It doesn't do to become too emotional about these people, Reverend Wethersby,' Henry answered in a disciplinary tone. 'When you've been involved with them as long as I have, you will realise they have very little feeling of gratitude or commitment to us for what we try and do for them. They are just as likely to leave you, go walkabout without a by your leave or a word of thanks. Believe me, you are better to start afresh when you are right again,' he decreed putting an end to the discussion.

The older man now dug in his heels. 'I'm sorry Mr

Grimshaw but I cannot agree,' he said firmly. 'I trust my children; they trust me. I will not break that trust by sending them away. If you find it impossible to keep them with you then I'm afraid I will have to make other arrangements for them myself.'

Ellen interceded on the sick man's behalf. 'Perhaps we could manage a little longer, Henry, do you think? They are very well behaved, Cob Munyabra has made himself partly responsible for them. I'm sure they won't be any trouble.'

At that moment there was a tap on the door of the sick room, and Henry stepped over to answer it. 'Oh, it's you, Munyabra. Just wait outside. We are nearly finished.' He left the door ajar as he walked back towards the bed. Cob stood in the passage looking past Henry's retreating back over to where Ellen sat facing the door. He gave her a solemn wink, then hung his head like an obedient servant. She stifled a giggle.

Henry continued the conversation. 'I do not wish to appear unsympathetic, sir, but in light of correspondence I received today, I'm afraid my time and resources are even more pressed than I had thought.' He propped himself casually against the edge of the bed, his long legs outstretched. Ellen could tell he had news of some importance to impart. 'I have received a directive from the church synod in Sydney. I am to return forthwith to the Gulf of Carpentaria to establish a new mission on the land I recommended in my reports,' he announced, his voice rising with pride and suppressed excitement.

'Congratulations,' Reverend Wethersby said sincerely, 'you must be very pleased that they have such confidence in your ability. That's quite an honour I must say. I do understand that my children are an added burden to you at this time, but if you could just keep them a little longer?' he pleaded hopefully.

'A month is all I can possibly promise, Reverend. I have the mammoth task of rebuilding Bibiringda before I go, you know.' Rising, he paced the floor impatiently. 'We lost our new dispensary and quite a few cottages. I thank God and my dear departed brotherinlaw, that the church withstood the onslaught. What a great memorial to his dedication and craftsmanship. All repairs must be done before I leave, as I plan to take the labour force with me,' he stopped at the open door where Cob stood. 'In fact, I have decided to take you, Munyabra,' he announced pointing at Cob. 'Mr Reid always sang your praises as being a good worker, and I am going to need some trustworthy men with me.'

Ellen's eyes opened wide. 'How long will you be gone, Henry?' she asked in a tight voice.

'At least a year, dear,' he said, turning to face her. 'But not to worry, there is a replacement being sent to hold the fort so to speak at Bibiringda. With you and mother helping, the new chap should be able to keep things running smoothly enough till I get back.'

He turned back to Cob whose eyes were locked on Ellen's. 'Well Munyabra, what do you say to that, eh? Ready to move off on a big adventure?'

'The sooner the better!' Cob answered firmly, reading the concurring message in Ellen's eyes.

'That's the spirit I like to see in my men,' praised Henry, slapping Cob's back, and completely misconstruing the real implication of his answer.

'Well, Ellen, we must be going. I have a number of calls to make before we sail. I haven't time to let the grass grow under my feet now. I have a great deal of planning to do,' Henry enthused, in his mind's eye already off on his latest expedition.

'Thank you for calling, Mrs Reid and you too Reverend Grimshaw,' Wethersby said quietly shaking Ellen's hand.

Ellen smiled and made a hasty farewell as her brother waited impatiently at the door.

'All right, let's go. You too, Munyabra. I'll need some help loading the building materials, they're being delivered to the wharf.'

'Would it be all right if Cob stayed a moment longer, do you think, Reverend Grimshaw?' asked Wethersby politely. 'I'd just like to have a word with him, if you don't mind.'

'Oh yes, I suppose so, but don't you be too long Cob, I want to catch the next tide. Come along, Ellen.' He whisked her along the corridor without the chance of a backward glance.

'Come over here, Cob, and sit where we can talk,' Wethersby indicated the chair that Ellen had just vacated, The older man looked at him worriedly. 'I want you to do something for me, Cob, not that you haven't done enough already, but I want you to bring my children back to their home. I don't trust Reverend Grimshaw, he may dispose of them down south. Oh! I know he's a good enough man and very much respected, but he does seem to ride rough shod over other people's feelings sometimes. You've been with us Cob, you know that I love those children. I believe in some small way they love me too, despite what Reverend Grimshaw says. I'm all they've got Cob, and to tell the truth, they've all I've got too. Will you get them for me?'

'Don't you worry,' Cob said, consoling the lonely man. 'I'll keep an eye out for them, but I can't see how they can go back to the mission when you're laid up here.'

'But I won't be here, Cob, that's the point. I'm going to

discharge myself in a couple of weeks. That's when I want you to bring them back.'

'How can you discharge yourself, you're not right yet, your legs won't be taking you anywhere!' Cob argued.

'Then I'll get a bath chair to get about in. The children will look after me, once they are home again, and I will rent a carriage to take me back home. It's Grimshaw's attitude I'm most worried about. He may send them off before I can do anything about it. If I send him a formal request, you won't have any trouble removing them. Will you bring them back for me, please, Cob, in two weeks?'

'No trouble,' replied Cob rising to go, then a sudden thought flashed through his mind.

'No trouble at all Reverend. It will be a pleasure,' he called over his shoulder cheerfully, as he headed for the door.

CHAPTER EIGHTEEN

There was further opportunity to discuss the turn of events on the boat trip back to the mission. Once the *Goodwill* was at her mooring, Ellen was obliged to take herself on the beach, where her mother was waiting with Faith. Cob had to stayed on board to help Henry unload the building supplies.

Faith waited for her mother, beaming faced and expectant. 'Have you been a good girl for Grandmother?' Ellen laughingly enquired of the child, who nodded vigorously, knowing some treat would be in store for her after her mother's trip to Cairns. 'Then you must deserve a bag of dolly mixtures, do you think?' Ellen teased, giving the paper bag to the delighted child. Faith wandered along behind her mother and grandmother, as they walked back up the track towards the cottage. She was deep in serious contemplation counting the array of tiny jellies, little pink hearts, and pale green diamonds, unable to decide how many she would save for later.

'How's Reverend Wethersby getting along, Ellen? Did you call and see him?' Grace enquired as they walked together.

'He's doing very well, though he is worried about his children from the mission. Henry told him they would only be able to stay another month. He was quite distressed.'

'Well, we do have enough troubles of our own at the moment, don't we, with all this damage and everything?' Grace said, agreeing as usual with Henry.

'That's not the full reason, Mother. Henry has just received word he is to go back to the Gulf, to start the new mission there. He seems very pleased.'

Grace was visibly distressed at the news. 'How long will he be gone? Who will keep this place going?'

'He says he'll be away about a year, Mother, but a replacement is being sent to take over.'

'A year? Oh really, that's too bad. How is someone new going to run this place for a year without Henry's experience. It's quite impossible.' Her face set in a righteous anger as her temper rose.

'Henry did say he expected you and I to help out the new fellow.'

'Did he now? Well, I for one have no intention of killing myself with work at my time of life. We will remove ourselves from here and go to stay with Amy!' she declared angrily, walking faster.

Ellen knew she should try to prepare her mother in some way for her departure with Faith, she was sure that was what Cob had in mind when he answered Henry so eagerly. If they waited six months, Cob would be shipped out to God knows where. They would have to leave soon, and she felt obliged to try somehow to soften the blow for her mother.

'I may not be going with you, Mother. I've been thinking for a while now about getting out on my own. I will look for a position where I can take Faith with me.'

'Nonsense! Why on earth would you want do that? You and Faith have a perfectly good home with us! How could you even consider dragging the poor child around like that? She will be far better off in Townsville where she can mix with people of her own class. I never heard of such rubbish. Really!' Grace stomped off in disgust, leaving Ellen to follow, with Faith happily trotting at her side.

Ellen was working in the garden next day, pulling out broken plants and fallen tree branches, trying to rectify some of the devastation wrought by the cyclone.

Straightening up she pushed her hair from her eyes, to see Cob standing dutifully at the edge of the garden where the gate had once been.

Cob!' she whispered, looking nervously around.

'Good morning, Mrs Reid,' he said, doffing his hat, once again playing his Aboriginal servant role.

She walked across to him trying to match his casualness.

'Meet me tonight over by the wrecked dispensary. We have to talk. I have a way of getting us out of here,' he spoke quietly, pretending to be looking at the wrecked garden.

'How? When?' she questioned excitedly.

'Can't talk now. We're being watched, in case you haven't noticed! See you tonight, Mrs Munyabra,' he said, making a humble salute and striding away.

'What did he want?' demanded Grace, from the cottage door.

'Nothing, Mother, just wanted to know if I needed a hand with the heavier branches,' lied Ellen, surprised at her own glibness. It would be much more difficult getting away tonight though, she thought, looking at her mother's suspicious face.

'I won't have him hanging around here, Ellen,' declared Grace, making her way over the rubbish pile. 'He's still not to be trusted. I can feel it in my bones. He's up to no good, keep away from him,' she warned, intuitively.

Ellen retired early, but sat on her bed fully dressed until she heard the telltale creak of her mother's bed springs.

After checking to make sure that Faith was fast asleep, she

climbed quietly from her bedroom window, thankful for the timber shutters, which had replaced the glass smashed in the cyclone. She slipped silently from tree to tree, keeping in their shadow until well clear of the house, before taking the winding path that led around the bay. The waning moon gave her just enough light to find her way, but it wasn't long before she felt the first drops of rain on her face.

'Damn and blast,' she swore to herself. It would take her at least half an hour to reach the dispensary on foot. Why on earth did he choose to meet somewhere like that? But she knew the answer. It was built well away from the main part of the mission, its isolation being chosen by Henry in case of an infectious epidemic. As she trudged on, it began to rain more heavily. Her wet hair dripped down her neck, and her soaked dress slapped coldly round her ankles. 'How romantic!' she mumbled to herself as she sloshed through unseen puddles in the dark.

When she finally arrived at the dispensary, she couldn't help feeling a little frightened by its ghostly ruined appearance. She crept up the wobbly steps and picked her way across the gaping floorboards. And in a quavering voice, she called into the darkness, 'Cob? Are you there, Cob?' her voice echoed back to her strangely from the gloom.

A screeching flock of fruit bats flashed past her, one caught in her hair and she shuddered with revulsion as she tore it loose. 'Cob where are you?' her voice held more urgency now as her fear mounted. The steps behind her creaked loudly and she spun round, her heart pounding. 'Who's that?' she gasped as a dark silhouette loomed out of the darkness.

'Settle down, it's only me. Who did you think it was?' Cob called cheerfully, strolling easily towards her. Her fright turned to anger as she realised her own foolishness.

'Cob Munyabra! I've walked miles in the pouring rain. I'm soaked to the skin, then you try to scare the living daylights out of me! It better be worth it,' she threatened, her anger already starting to evaporate, as he came closer, grinning at her.

'Come here and I'll show you how much better it can get,' he teased, grabbing her and squeezing her hard.

'Stop it, you great ox,' she squirmed, gasping for breath.

He released her suddenly and held her by two fingers. 'Yuk! You are soaked, I should get you out of these wet clothes before you catch your death of cold, shouldn't I?' he asked suggestively beginning to unbutton her blouse collar.

Her eyes widened in alarm and he burst out laughing.

'You should see your face! Panic and rape written all over it!' he howled slapping his knee as he chortled.

'You pig!' she shouted, whacking him over the head.

He grabbed her flaying wrists and dropped a kiss on her protesting mouth. Arms around each other, they searched for a place to sit down. Finding a fallen beam they huddled together in the shelter of a half standing wall.

'I have a plan for getting us out,' he said, rubbing her cold hands.

'So you said. What is it?'

'Well, Reverend Wethersby has asked me to deliver his children back to him in two weeks time. He's worried that Henry will send them down south if he leaves them here any longer. So I thought I could smuggle you and Faith out with them. If we leave early enough, no one will be around. I can't see Henry being bothered to check, he's so wrapped up in his new expedition. What do you think?' he asked excitedly, his dark face close to hers.

'I suppose it could work,' she agreed cautiously, 'but where would we go?'

'With the children, back to the mission and Reverend Wethersby. And listen Ellen, I'm going to ask him to marry us!' he said proudly.

'Do you think he would?' She couldn't keep the doubt from her voice.

'I won't know till I ask, but he owes me one, and I think he likes me. We can at least try. He's the best bet we've got. What do you say? Would that be all right with you? Would that be good enough?' he asked anxiously, wanting very much to please her.

She smiled delightedly, stroking his cheek, 'It would be wonderful, Cob, just wonderful.'

They kissed passionately, forgetting the rain and the ruins surrounding them, Cob eased her away from him. 'That's enough, we are going to do things right this time,' he said firmly.

'You know your trouble, Cob Munyabra,' she murmured softly, 'you're too blasted moral!'

Each day Ellen smuggled some article of clothing out of the house and packed it away in an old bag she had hidden in the stable. She hoarded any money she could lay her hands on and fed Faith up on all the nourishing food she could persuade her to eat. Her mother was too upset at Henry's latest expedition to notice her strange behaviour. The two weeks crept slowly by, each seeming to her like a year as she waited anxiously to hear the date of their departure from Cob.

She caught only fleeting glimpses of him as he worked long hard hours on Henry's rushed, rebuilding campaign and she began to wonder how he would be able to get a message to her when the time came.

To her amazement he came boldly up to the front door and told her mother!

She held her breath when she heard his voice as Grace answered the rap on the door.

'Evening Matron, came to tell Missus Reid that the boat is going to Cairns first light in the morning, if she needs to go. I'm takin' Reverend Wethersby's mission children back.'

Ellen stifled the laugh that rose in her throat.

She tried to look unconcerned as her mother came back into the kitchen, 'That man's got a nerve. That was Munyabra again, said to tell you the boat is going to Cairns tomorrow if you need anything,' she announced picking up the knives and forks and stacking them to wash. After some reflection, she added in a puzzled voice, 'I always get the feeling that devil is up to something? I wouldn't trust him as far as I could throw him. Are you going to Cairns then?'

Trying to sound casual, Ellen answered lightly. 'I suppose I could. Faith needs new shoes. I was going to wait until next week but the weather could be against us by then.' She busied herself in the kitchen so as not to let her mother see her flushed face and trembling hands.

'He said they were leaving at first light, so you'd better be up early in the morning, if you want to go,' Grace called as she strolled from the parlour. 'Come to think of it, I may as well come too. I need some material. I could do with a new dress to take with me to Amy's.'

Ellen's heart pounded against her ribs. She had to stop her! 'Wouldn't you be better to wait until you got to Townsville mother?' she called back. 'There's always a better choice there.

I was looking in the drapers while I was in Cairns a few weeks ago, you've never seen such rubbish! And the prices! I really think you'd be better to wait.' She mentally crossed her fingers as she waited for her mother's reply.

'Didn't see anything suitable, for me, I mean?' Grace asked half-heartedly.

'No, nothing that would suit your good taste Mother, gaudy colours, and very little choice. They do say that the drapers in Townsville pick out all the best stock, and send the rubbish up here.' Scrubbing the pots with all her might, Ellen prayed *Please don't make her want to come, please. It's our only chance.*

'Yes, well perhaps you're right. I could do better in Townsville I suppose. Anyway, I don't really relish the thought of getting up at that hour.'

Ellen breathed a sigh of relief.

Deciding to bluff the whole thing out, she went to the stable and brought back the old canvas bag and placed it by the door.

'What are you doing with that?' Grace asked, looking up from her intricate Fair Isle knitting.

'It's just some old clothes I've collected from the mission supplies. I thought I'd give them to Reverend Wethersby for the children. He is going to need some help to get started again,' she lied.

Her mother accepted the explanation. 'Yes poor man. I'll see if I have a few odds and ends too.' Grace rose from her chair and headed for the bedroom.

'Another time, Mother! I can't carry anymore. The bag's full.' Ellen flustered, terrified her mother would look inside the bag.

Grace shrugged tiredly. 'All right, I can always send them

later. I think I will go to bed. Shall I put out the lamp?'

'No, not yet, Mother. I want to read for a while.'

'All right, well, goodnight. See you in the morning.' Grace walked off into her room looking weary and aged.

'Goodnight Mother,' Ellen called after her sadly, knowing that she wouldn't be seeing her again for a long time. There was no turning back now, she took out a pen and paper and started writing a note.

Dear Mother,

By the time you read this I will have gone away. I am sorry to do this to you, but you have left me no choice. I love Cob Munyabra. I always have and I always will. I know that hurts you, and you think it is terribly wrong, but it isn't for me, Mother. He is a good man and will always look after me, so don't worry. I hope for Faith's sake that one day you can find it in your heart to accept the situation. She loves you very much and will miss you. Please don't think of using threats like you did last time. They will not bring me back and will cause nothing but trouble and heartbreak for us all.

Thank you for all you have done for me.

Your loving daughter,

Ellen

She placed the letter in an envelope and left it on the kitchen table for her mother to find when she woke. 'We will be long gone by then, poor mother,' Ellen brushed away a tear and went quietly to her bedroom.

*

It was still quite dark when she rose and went to Faith. 'Come on, darling, wake up. We are going on the boat today,' she whispered, picking the sleepy little girl from her bed.

Faith rubbed her eyes and gave Ellen a cuddle. 'Are we going on the boat to go shopping?' she asked in a loud excited voice.

'Sh! Sh! Faith, you'll wake Grandma,' Ellen resisted the urge to clamp a hand over the child's mouth. 'We are going to be as quiet as little mice, aren't we?'

Ellen took a last look around the little cottage that had seen so many of her joys and sorrows. *Goodbye old place,* she whispered as she picked up the bag and crept outside, closing the door quietly behind them.

They reached the beach as the first dawn streaked the horizon with a pale band of gold. The *Goodwill* waited quietly in the bay, as if still fast asleep.

'Where are the children, Mummy?' Faith wanted to know as they stood alone on the beach.

'They will be coming soon, love, very soon,' she answered, more to convince herself.

Faith saw Cob coming down the track, with the children walking silently behind him. Her excited squeak of, 'They're coming, Mummy,' made Ellen start violently, and she realised how terrified she really was.

'Any trouble getting away?' Cob walked up to her and asked in a low voice.

She shook her head, unable to control her chattering teeth.

'All right, come on, we'll soon be out of here. Boys, one of you take Miss Faith, and you others help the girls, we'll wade out to the boat.'

He reached down and swung Ellen easily up into his arms.

'Come on, Mrs Munyabra, we're nearly there, keep your chin up.'

*

Grace rolled over in her cosy warm bed and drowsily pulled the blankets up over her shoulders, she sighed deeply as she settled herself to drift back into sleep once more. Suddenly, her eyes flickered open. *Damn,* she had meant to ask Ellen to collect the post. There would be a reply from Amy confirming their trip to Townsville. She closed her eyes again. *Ellen will check the mail, surely, but what if she forgets? It might be weeks before the boat goes over again. Maybe she hasn't left yet, I might catch her.* Wearily swinging her legs onto the floor, Grace drowsily groped for her dressing gown and stumbled into the parlour.

'Ellen? Are you up yet?' she called heading for her daughter's bedroom. The bed was made and the room was neatly tidied. *She's left already! Oh dear, I hope she remembers!* Grace automatically walked to the kitchen and filled the kettle. She stoked the fire and sat down at the table, waiting half asleep, for the kettle to boil. Her eyes flicked over the manila envelope before her. She pushed it to one side with her elbow as she rubbed the sleep from her eyes. *Goodness,* she thought, *it's becoming harder to wake up every day.*

These days, she rose as bone weary as when she had retired at night. Perhaps she would feel better after a long break in Townsville, and Ellen too. She seemed to be over the crazy idea of going away to find work, thank goodness. They both needed a holiday, what with Laurence's death and the cyclone. No wonder she felt so washed out.

The boiling kettle interrupted her train of thought. She rose and brewed the tea, bringing the pot to the table. She poured herself a cup, black and strong, and began to sip it appreciatively. Idly she flipped the envelope over, noticing for the first time it was addressed to "Mother" and was written in Ellen's hand.

She opened it curiously and lifted out the single sheet of paper. Her brow creased in a puzzled expression, as her eyes swiftly scanned the page. Suddenly her face turned deathly white.

A look of tortured anguish spread over her whole countenance and her bottom lip began to tremble as two large tears coursed down her rugged creased cheeks. 'They've taken my Faith away. Oh! Dear God, no!' she gasped.

Anger rose from her throat, spreading a crimson flush to her cheeks, her nostrils narrowed to a pinched white, her very hair roots tingled as rage burst upon her brain.

'No. Never. Over my dead body!' she screamed to the empty house. Heedless of her state of undress she ran from the house. Her grey plaits flapped wildly around her face, her uncorsetted body swung heavily as her bare feet pounded the dirt across the wide compound to Henry's house. Gasping for breath, she beat on the door with both fists. Dressed in his long combinations and still half asleep, he opened the door in alarm.

'Whatever is wrong?' he demanded as he stared into her ashen gasping face. 'Good Lord, come in and sit down quickly,' he helped her into his tiny office and lowered her into a chair. Hurriedly, he grabbed a bottle of brandy from the bookshelf and poured a good measure into a glass. Wrapping her shaking hands around it, he guided it to her lips.

Grace took a long sip, then another.

'Now try and control yourself, Mother. Tell me what's

happened for God's sake,' he ordered her sternly.

Grace drew in a deep breath and opened her mouth. She spat out the words as though they tasted of foul bile. 'They're gone! The pair of them, and taken my little Faith.'

'Who has?' Henry demanded angrily.

'That whore of a sister of yours, and her black bastard of a lover, that's who!' she screamed back at him.

Astounded, Henry gaped at her. 'You mean Ellen?' he asked incredulously. 'Ellen? And who?'

'Munyabra, the cunning rat! He's got our Faith!' Her voice rose hysterically again.

'Got Faith and Ellen? Why didn't you stop him?' he shouted back at her.

'How could I? I didn't know, did I? I thought I'd finished it once and for all! They must have been carrying on,' she stopped short, amazement written all over her face. 'I tell a lie! I did know, of course! Why that cunning mongrel! He was even brass-faced enough to tell me they were going. Yes, he did Henry!' She stared at him aghast. 'He came to my very door, I didn't realise, I never guessed.' Her face crumpled as the full impact hit her.

Henry gripped her shoulders, trying to force some sense out of her. 'What on earth are you talking about, Mother? What did you put a stop to? What's been going on, for Heaven's sake?'

'You have to stop them, Henry.' she said frantically grabbing his arm. 'You have to go after them. They've taken my little Faith. They will destroy her. Please, Henry, please!' she begged hysterically.

He brushed her clawing hands away. 'Stop it, Mother, do you hear me. Pull yourself together. I can't do anything until you calm down enough to tell me exactly what's been going on. What exactly has happened to Ellen and Faith? And what's Munyabra got to do with it?' The truth was slowly beginning to dawn on him, but he was desperately hoping for a more acceptable explanation.

As Grace sobbed to the end of her narrative, Henry paced the office floor.

'Why on earth didn't you tell me all this before, Mother?' he asked in a strained voice.

'I didn't want to worry you. I thought I could hush it up, and I did! Everything would have been all right if you hadn't brought that black devil up here. I begged you not to. I pleaded with you to send him away,' she glared at him accusingly.

'How was I to know? You should have told me everything then,' he defended himself. Already he could see the consequences of his sister's actions on his career and reputation.

'Who else knows?' he demanded.

'Kalinga knew. She told me, but she's dead now, and Currie Munyabra,' Grace answered dully.

'Thank God that's all. He's most likely dead by now too, 'Henry sighed with relief. Then a frightening thought struck him. 'What about Marsden? He was there at the time, wasn't he? Did he get wind of it?'

'No, I managed to keep it from him. You don't know what I went through! The strain and worry nearly killed me.'

Henry ignored her complaints as he tried to sort out the true situation. 'And you mean to say it's been going on again here under our very noses?' he asked incredulously. 'Even when poor Laurence was alive? I can't believe it, my poor dear friend, cuckolded by a black! My God, and you let him marry her, knowing what she did? How could you, Mother?'

he was now the accuser.

Terrified of her son's anger, Grace tried desperately to justify her actions. 'What else could I do? Who would have married her. He never knew, I swear. Go after them Henry, get them back before it's too late,' she pleaded.

'The damage is done, Mother, it's too late. She is no sister of mine anymore. I will never forgive her,' he replied flatly.

'But what about Faith? We can't abandon her. Think what will happen to the poor little thing. What could be happening to her right now, at this very minute. Henry please. You have to get her back,' Once again Grace was wracked sobs.

'All right, Mother. I'll get them back for you. Don't distress yourself further. Poor Faith will not suffer from the sins of her mother. I promised Laurence I would protect her, and I will. Now tell me, when did they leave and how?'

'They've taken the boat.'

'The *Goodwill?* The bastard! I'll kill him when I get my hands on him,' Henry roared angrily. 'I'll have to go overland. God what a journey! It could take me days.' He stormed out of the house still clad only in his combinations, to order the horses saddled.

CHAPTER NINETEEN

'I'll run up to the hospital and see Reverend Wethersby about transport for us. I won't be long, will you be all right here?' Ellen sat on the old bag at the quayside, surrounded by the patiently waiting children.

'Yes Cob, I'll be all right, but please don't be long, will you?' she glanced nervously looking around, expecting at any moment to see Henry and his assistants bearing down upon them.

'Just keep your head down and don't talk to anyone. These fishermen are a rough lot. See you soon.' Cob squeezed her hand and strode off. She watched his retreating figure disappear down the long timber wharf, feeling more and more afraid as he faded into the distance.

'I'm hungry, Mummy,' Faith wailed at her side. 'Can we have some dinner?' The eyes of the other little ones supported Faith's request.

'I'm sorry children, we can't have anything to eat yet,' she explained, 'but when Cob comes back we will buy some lovely fresh bread and meat and go on a picnic to see Reverend Wethersby. Would you like that?'

Satisfied for the moment, the children wandered off along the wharf. For a while they played hide and seek around the fish crates, forgetting their hunger. Ellen sat watching the sunrise higher in the sky wondering how much longer Cob would be. One of the boys was jostled into a stack of crates, rocking the pile precariously.

"ere! Get your grubby mitts off there, you little black bastards,' bawled a rough voice from the deck of a battered old ship moored nearby.

'These little buggers with you Miss?' the deckhand shouted to Ellen. Swinging his legs easily over the side of the boat, he dropped to the wharf. Leering into her face, his broken decayed teeth exposed by curled sneering lips. His breath stank of stale rum. 'What are you sittin' 'ere with all these little buggers for then?' he asked, wiping his greasy hands down the front of his dirty buttonless waistcoat.

'I'm taking them to a mission,' Ellen answered frostily. 'It was an accident. They won't steel your catch, if that's what you're worried about.' She averted her face, hoping he would leave.

'Oh well, that's all right then, as long as they're wi' you. Me names Charlie Watson. Pleased to meet you, Miss,' he said thrusting out a grubby hand. Wanting to get rid of him as quickly as possible, she gingerly shook the ends of his fingers and murmured. 'How do you do?' Suddenly, his grip tightened on her hand, holding her fast. 'Seein' as you're waiting 'ere like, 'ow 'bout comin' aboard for a little drink?' He ran his tongue over his revolting teeth, in lustful anticipation.

'No thank you,' she replied primly. 'Please let go of my hand.' Frightened now she tried to pull away.

'Aw come on, don't be shy,' he said coaxingly, gripping her arm and pulling her towards the gangplank. 'Get your hands off me, you drunken fool,' she half sobbed, as she struggled to get away.

A quiet voice spoke menacingly from behind her, 'Do as the lady says, or I'll break every bone in your body.' Spinning round, Ellen came face to face with Cob. She felt herself pushed firmly aside as Cob's fist flashed past her, sending the deckhand crashing into the stacked crates of fish, which went flying over the wharf's edge into the water.

An angry bellow rose from a porthole of the vessel. 'What the bloody hell's going on out there?' A balding red-faced man struggled up on deck, thrusting before him an enormous beer belly, which was supported by a wide thick leather belt that sat on his narrow hips. He waddled furiously down the gangplank waving his fist at Cob.

'You stupid black bastard. If you've got to 'it 'im, 'it 'im into the drink! Not the bloody fish it's more use to me than 'e is, any day.' He looked over and saw Ellen standing close by. 'Beggin' your pardon for the language, Miss,' he apologised, blushing scarlet.

'Sorry about the fish, mate,' Cob said, walking towards the scattered boxes. 'Here you boys. Help me pick these crates up, will you?' He called to the older boys who moved nervously forward to help, while the little ones peered out from behind the *bechedemere* baskets. Faith scurried over and hid behind her mother's skirts.

The fat captain kicked the inert drunk sprawled on the ground. 'Get your gear and shove off, ye drunken sod. I'll not 'ave the likes of you on my boat, go on, clear out.'

Heaving his belt back into place below the huge belly, the captain walked over to Cob. 'You can't get a decent day's work out of any of 'em these days. I'll be sailing the bloody boat by meself soon, 'he grumbled. ''ere hang on, you're Currie Munyabra's lad, aren't you?' he asked, staring up at Cob. 'You remember me, don't you, Captain Mullett from the *Falmouth Rose*. Seen you with old Currie around Broad Bay many a time. What ye doin' in these parts then?'

Cob glanced nervously at Ellen. 'Helping this lady here. Mrs Reid, may I introduce Captain Mullett.'

Ellen inclined her head to the rough old seaman whose weathered brown face creased in a wide smile.

'Did you get the transport, Cob?' she enquired, anxious to be away from the sea captain's prying eyes.

Cob shook his head, becoming once more the subservient Aborigine. 'Sorry, Mrs Reid, the Reverend left, signed himself out yesterday. We'll have to walk, I'm afraid.'

'Walk? All that way with these little children?' Her face fell.

'Sounds a lot of bloody trouble for nothing to me lad,' the fat captain commented. 'How about ye sign on with me for the trip down instead. I could do with a strong fella like you. You can finish up at Kalangari if you like, or stay on. I offer decent food, and I'll even give you a share of the catch. What do ye say?' he asked eager to strike a bargain.

'Sorry mate, I have to see these children safely home first,' Cob answered, declining the offer. 'But if you're going to be in dock here for a few days I'll be glad to take you up on it when I get back.'

'You're on lad! I've a few repairs that have to be done, got caught in that bloody cyclone I did, lucky to make it to one of the islands. I'll see you back here in under the week, right?' he asked offering his hand on the deal. Ellen stared at Cob astounded, he answered her glare with a wink.

'Right Mrs Reid, let's see if we can beg or borrow a horse for you to ride, then we'll be on our way. See you next week, Captain,' he called, taking her arm and steering her away.

'What the devil are you up to now, Cob?' she hissed at him as they walked off.

'I've just arranged our transport back to Kalangari, that's what,' he grinned down at her.

'But he doesn't know that Faith and I will be going, he won't take us as well,' she protested.

'Just leave it to me, will you? He won't have much bloody choice when he's ready to sail and doesn't have a crew! He may take a bit of persuading, but it will be all right. You'll see.' He marched off purposefully down the wharf, the ragged group of children running to catch up with him.

Ellen sighed in exasperation. Gripping Faith by the hand she lifted her skirts and hurried after him.

*

Henry and his two assistants had made good time. The stripped and depleted rainforest was not as difficult to move through as it usually was when lush and overgrown, although the horses could still only travel at walking pace over the mountainous terrain. The slower they moved, the more Henry fumed about his sister, who had brought this disaster crashing down on their heads. How could she? It was unspeakable! Especially for the sister of a man in his position, and with a black! He shuddered at the thought. Well, she was done for, finished, as far as he was concerned. God knows what she was, crazy, depraved? It was beyond his comprehension. What could make a civilised woman of her breeding defile herself in such a manner? But he had to save Faith. She was an innocent child caught up in this ghastly mess. He could not allow her whole life to be ruined by her mother's depravity. Yes, that was the only word to describe his sister's behaviour.

Well, if she wanted to be a black man's whore, so be it! but she would not drag his best friend's child, through the mire with her. He would kill Ellen first.

Angrily, he spurred his horse into the swollen creek before him, the spray splashed into his face as the poor horse struggled against the raging current.

*

The small band of weary travellers was once again on the road. Hungry and tired they trudged on as the sun rose strongly, promising another scorching day. The only transport they had managed to acquire was a miserable donkey, which had to be forced every inch of the way as it temperamentally tried to kick or bite anyone who attempted to hurry it along. By noon they had scaled the mountain range and were heading into the sparse, barren hinterland, where they stopped to rest under the shade of a rocky outcrop.

'Here, see if she will have a drink,' Cob said, passing the water bag to Ellen, who sat fanning Faith with a leafy branch. Dampening the edge of her skirt, she wiped the hands and face of the forlorn little child, in an attempt to cool her.

'I don't know if she is hot, or has a temperature. She looks feverish to me.' Ellen spoke in a worried voice, her hand against the child's burning forehead.

'Force her to drink as much as you can. That's all we can do for her until we get to the mission,' Cob replied brusquely, feeling inadequate. But there was no turning back now.

Avoiding the children's hungry stares he hustled them to their feet again, deciding to press on. With any luck, they would make the mission later that evening where a good hot meal and a bed would be waiting for them. Dumbly, they staggered from the shade of the rocks and scrambled back onto the scorching, dusty road.

As it was getting dark, Ellen managed to persuade Cob to stop for the night. 'I can't go any further,' she pleaded as she hitched the sleeping Faith into a more comfortable position on her shoulder. Her back felt as if it would break, and her heels were rubbed raw by her boots.

'All right. There's a creek over there. We'll camp by that,' agreed Cob, placing the two little ones he was carrying down onto their wobbly tired legs. Faith woke as Ellen sat down exhausted, on the grass.

'Are we going home now, Mummy?' the child asked hopefully 'I'm hungry, and I want my bath. Look, I'm all dirty,' she said in disgust, holding out her dress. 'Where's Grandma? Is she coming soon, Mummy?' Faith looked miserably around her. 'It's getting dark, Mummy. I don't like it here. I want to go home, 'she wailed.

'Hush darling, it's all right. We are going to camp out here tonight, won't that be fun?' Ellen tried to jolly her out of her miserable mood.

'But there are no tents. Where's the tent, Mummy?'

'We haven't got a tent, Faith. We'll sleep on the ground just like the little animals do.'

'I'm not an animal. I'm a little girl and I sleep in my bed. I want my bed,' Faith began to howl loudly.

Cob lit a fire and handed each child a thick wad of bread topped with a slice of corned beef. Faith pushed her share away crossly. 'I don't like that. I want my real dinner,' she sulked. Ellen retrieved the sandwich from Cob and offered it to her again. 'Come on, Faith, it's nice, really. Eat up or you will be hungry in the morning.'

The little girl lifted her vivid blue eyes to her mother, tears welled and overflowed down her pale cheeks as, frightened and lost, she sobbed. 'I want to go home. I don't like it here.'

Ellen's heart ached for her little girl, so confused, tired, and bewildered by the day's happenings. Feeling guilty at having put the child through such an ordeal, she cuddled her close and wrapped her underneath her shawl. Leaning back against a tree, she crooned softly until she felt the little body go limp in her arms.

She sat nursing the sleeping child, watching the stars get brighter and the moon slowly rise, its reflection rippling in the creek beside her.

Cob, having settled the other children down as best he could, threw some more wood on the fire, and came to sit down beside her. 'Poor little thing' Cob sympathised. 'She's not used to roughing it, like the others. They don't know anything else so it doesn't worry them. Only one more day and we should be there. Are you all right?' he asked, slipping an arm round her shoulders, she dropped her head wearily onto his shoulder, exhaustion flooding over her, and together they slept.

Next morning they rose at dawn to avoid the heat of the day.

Wearily, they struggled on with as many of the mission youngsters as possible clinging sleepily to each other on the donkey's back, led by Cob firmly griping its halter and forcing it along. The older children trailed behind, just managing to place one foot in front of the other, in a desperate effort to keep up. Ellen stumbled along under her burden of Faith dozing fitfully, her burning head against Ellen's neck. Cob offered to carry her to give Ellen a rest, but as he took hold of the child she woke screaming hysterically, and wriggled from his grasp. Hurt and disappointed, he handed her back to her mother, and they trudged on in silence.

As dusk fell Ellen saw a flickering light in the distance. 'Look, Cob, over there, it's a fire, isn't it?' she called excitedly.

'Where?' he strained his eyes. 'Yes! It looks right to be the camp. We made it, thank goodness!'

The children's pace quickened now as they realised they were nearly home, and it wasn't long before the flickering dot became a roaring, welcoming blaze. They ran the last few yards, calling the Reverend's name loudly.

He appeared, silhouetted by the fire furiously pushing an ancient wheelchair over the rough ground to meet them. 'Hello! Hello! Thank God you're safe. I've been so worried. Where have you been? Where's the cart?' he called, rolling his chair to a halt before Cob and the donkey.

'What cart?' Cob asked puzzled. 'I was told you didn't order one.'

'I ordered one from the fellow who brought me out here, paid him in advance! He was to meet you at the wharf. Didn't he come? The Blaggard! How on earth did you get here?' the confused Englishman asked, patting the faces of his children as they crowded round his chair.

'We walked, Reverend, and believe me it's a bloody long way! Next time, don't pay in advance. You're more likely to get your cart that way,' Cob informed him, only half joking. Ellen wearily brought up the rear, her arms ready to break.

'Oh, you have someone else with you?' exclaimed Reverend Wethersby, peering into the dusk as she approached.

'Good evening, Reverend, how are your legs now?' she asked in a low exhausted voice.

'Why, it's Mrs Reid. Goodness me! What are you doing here?'

Cob quickly interceded on Ellen's behalf, 'I think we are all too weary for explanations, just now Reverend. Can it wait until morning? Would you have a place where Mrs Reid and her daughter can sleep tonight. Her little girl isn't well. The journey has been too much for her.'

Reverend Wethersby was immediately concerned. 'Of course, I am so sorry. What a terrible time you must have had. There's only a tent, I'm afraid,' he said, embarrassed at not having decent accommodation to offer her. 'Come along, I'll show you,' He swung the bathchair round, and bumped and jolted off, leading the way across the darkening compound.

'Come on, Ellen, give her to me. You're done in,' Cob said taking the sleeping child. She handed Faith over to him thankfully. 'You'll feel better after a good night's sleep,' he promised, placing his other arm around her shoulders, steadying her as she groped her way along after the Reverend.

'Here's the tent, Mrs Reid. I hope you'll be comfortable. It's nothing much, I'm afraid.' Reverend Wethersby said, as he stopped beside the gloomy shadow on an old canvas marquee. 'You'll find a few of my things scattered around in there, but please make yourself at home. I'll send one of the girls over with some hot water for you presently and some supper.' For a moment a startled expression passed over his face as he saw the intimate way Cob supported Ellen. Ellen was too tired to notice; Cob wasn't.

'Thank you, Reverend Wethersby,' Ellen said gratefully. 'Please don't bother about food. Faith will just sleep, I'm sure, and I'm too exhausted to eat, but the water would be lovely.' She entered the tent and Cob followed, placing Faith down gently on the camp stretcher. Lighting the candle, Ellen looked around. The tent contained a rickety old table and a chair, a battered orange box, which served as a book case, and a well worn sea chest. A rope had been slung across one corner of the tent supporting the Reverend's meagre wardrobe of clothes.

'There's another stretcher behind the clothes, Cob,' called Reverend Wethersby from outside, 'and some blankets in the chest. I'll see about the hot water and a lamp.'

They could hear the wheels of the bath chair crunching in the dirt as he wheeled himself away.

Ellen slumped wearily onto the wobbly chair. 'What are we going to tell him, Cob?' she asked, dropping her face down into her folded arms.

'Don't worry, nothing tonight. There's no point. Wait until morning, then I'll have a yarn to him, tell him the truth. It's the only way.'

'And what if he sends us away?' she said, her voice stilted.

'Cheer up. He won't.' Cob promised.

Faith woke as Ellen began to remove her dirty clothes. She sat for a while in a daze, allowing her mother to peel off her dress and shoes. 'Where is this place, Mumma?' she asked fearfully, looking round the rough canvas dwelling.

'It's Reverend Wethersby's little house, dear. We are to sleep here tonight, you and I,' Ellen explained, trying to sound calm and cheerful.

Faith's bottom lip began to tremble. Tears welled in her eyes, and trickled down her scorched cheeks. 'Can't we go home, Mumma? Back to Grandma and Uncle Henry?' she pleaded, looking like a hunted little animal, frantically seeking safety. Ellen caught her breath; her mind flashed back. That look, the very same, she had seen it before. Where? When? The very same fear, the desperate need for security. It was Amy! That was it, when they first went to Bibiringda. Amy had been older than Faith but her distress had been identical! *I always thought that she was just like me, but she isn't. She hates all this. Dear God, what am I doing to her?* Ellen folded her arms round the terrified, lost little girl.

*

Henry and his assistants arrived in Cairns, after flogging themselves and their horses all the way. He now sat aboard the deserted *Goodwill*, which they had found neatly stowed, and safely tied to the wharf. They were exhausted after travelling the whole of the previous day and night, arriving at the empty boat amid the noonday bustle of the busy fishing port.

Stretching out on the deck, Henry rested. He tried to think what his next move should be. He would have to call at the hospital first, check and see if Reverend Wethersby was still there, and if he wasn't, well, it was a safe bet the birds had flown with him, back to the mission. And if he was? Maybe he could throw some light on where those two miserable wretches had shot through to. He would have to be careful how he broached the subject though, no good letting the old fellow get wind of the problem unnecessarily, or the gossip would be round Cairns like wild fire. Best play it down, until he saw how the land lay. Maybe the black mongrel had got the wind up, and dumped Ellen in Cairns. They were usually gutless when it came to the crunch. Well, if that had happened, he'd make her pay! She'd wish she'd never laid eyes on a black by the time he'd finished with her. She'd certainly not be looking in their direction again, that was for sure!

He rose, confident that he would have the whole mess cleared up by nightfall. Then he could proceed with the most important task before him, getting his latest expedition on the road. His eyes gleamed at the very thought of it.

'I'm going to the hospital to make some inquiries,' he told the two assistants, who were sitting quietly, awaiting his orders. 'One of you stay here, and if anyone tries to board the *Goodwill*, even someone you know, hold them until I get back. You,' he said, indicating to the other fellow, 'Take the horses to the livery and change them for fresh ones. We may need to leave immediately when I get back.'

*

Ellen woke and lay on the hard little camp stretcher, looking around at the musky, tobacco smelling, masculine domain. Her eyes wandered over the neatly stacked books, the rifle leaning against the sea chest, and up to the large patch of mildew spreading like a black pin pointed map across the canvas ceiling. Her eyes travelled to the Reverend's clerical clothes hanging limply from the rope. Would he marry them? Would he understand? Or would he be the first to abuse them? She felt already weak and hurt, as if the bitter condemnation was already being heaped on her head.

'For goodness sake, pull yourself together,' she chastised herself, 'Here you are, only one day into what you believed was what you most wanted on earth, and already you are overflowing with self-pity, and whinging like a whipped puppy,' she spoke sternly to her inner self. 'Get up, and start fighting if you believe it's worth fighting for.' Having made the decision she swung herself out of the rickety cot and reached for her bag to retrieve some clean clothes.

Her glance fell on the sleeping child in the bed close to her, the darkly smudged eyelids, sunburnt cheeks and a row of water blisters already forming down the tiny button nose.

Quietly, she dressed and slipped out of the tent.

Reverend Wethersby and the children were already awake and bustling about the camp. He sat in the bathchair holding steady a side of bacon, while one of the boys deftly sliced off even rashers with a wicked looking knife.

'Hello Mrs Reid, how do you feel now after a good night's sleep?' he enquired cheerfully, as she approached. 'Thought we'd have a celebration breakfast this morning, seeing it's our first day back together. I splashed out and bought some supplies on the way through Cairns. How about a nice plate of bacon and eggs to set you back on your feet?' he invited, cleverly catching each rasher as it fell, and flinging them into a huge black cast-iron pan, sizzling away on the brightly glowing embers of the fire.

'Sounds wonderful,' she smiled, the aroma of the frying bacon already tantalizing her empty stomach. 'Can I do anything to help?' she offered.

'Oh no, you're our special guest. We don't get many visitors. Just sit yourself down and one of the girls will bring you a cup of tea.' A shy girl jumped into action, and within minutes there was a tin mug full of piping hot black tea placed on the table in front of her. She sipped it gratefully as she watched the happy reunited family, each one cheerfully finding something that needed doing, and getting it done. The older girls were busily washing and dressing the little ones, in front of a large tin bucket that served them all. The boys were chopping wood, axes briskly swinging, while the younger ones jostled each other in their eagerness to pick up the split pieces and stacked them neatly beside the tree. They were more than happy to be back in the only place they had always called home.

Ellen saw Cob approaching from across the paddock, and

rose quickly to walk out to him. Reverend Wethersby didn't miss the bright expectation that lit up her face when she saw him. It only served to confirm in his mind his suspicions of the previous night. But being a patient man, he would bide his time and his tongue.

'Breakfast is ready,' he called loudly as the girls flipped eggs and crisp bacon onto the rows of tin plates. Hot steaming damper was dusted of ash and placed in the centre of the table next to the added luxury of an earthenware tub of creamy butter.

The hungry, laughing children hurried in to get their share. Everyone sat around managing as best they could, no one seemed to mind having to use only an odd knife, fork, or even spoon, to scoop their runny egg yolk onto slices of hot, butter dripping, damper.

As the meal ended and fragrant smelling coffee was being poured into tin mugs for the visitors, the Reverend laughingly produced his final indulgence, a stone jar of Dundee Marmalade. 'Couldn't resist it,' he grinned, liberally spreading the jam onto chunks of damper, eagerly held out by the children. 'Haven't tasted it in years, doesn't look like I'll be tasting much of it this time either,' he laughed, as the contents of the jar swiftly disappeared down a dozen chewing mouths.

'Right, you lot, that's enough for you now,' he said, pulling the metal seal back over the jam,' Bring your coffee over under the trees. It's peaceful there,' he invited Cob and Ellen. 'Sally, if little Faith wakes up, give her breakfast, will you dear?' he asked gently. The shy girl smiled back at him, nodding.

Ellen carried the coffee, while Cob pushed the Reverend's chair over to the paddock where they sat in the filtered sunlight of the ghost gums. Reverend Wethersby took out his pipe and carefully lit it, when it was burning to his satisfaction he turned to Ellen. 'I have a feeling that you didn't come all this way just to make a social call, Mrs Reid.'

Ellen only looked down at her hands.

'Perhaps you'd better tell me what it's all about then, Cob?' he invited.

Cob turned and faced the wise, sensitive man who had become his friend. He stated his case quietly. 'We want to get married Reverend. It's as simple as that! We've left the mission, run away,' he shrugged his shoulders, his dark liquid eyes troubled. 'We hoped you'd do it for us, Reverend, will you?' He looked without much hope down at the incredulous man.

'Now, hang on a minute Cob! You can't expect to drop that on me and have an answer by return! It will take some thinking about. Marriage is a very serious business at the best of times, but this? I never heard the like! Certainly, it's not something I could decide in five minutes.' He sat flabbergasted, allowing the full implication of what he had been told to sink in.

He looked from one to the other, aware of the anguish and pain they were both feeling. Cob went and sat supportively beside Ellen, taking her hand in his. 'It's not something we've decided in five minutes, Reverend. We've felt like this for years. We just couldn't take it any longer. They were going to send me away to God knows where. We had to make a run for it,' he tried to explain, Ellen gripped his hand, her face deathly white.

'Now let me get this straight,' Wethersby said, taking the pipe from his mouth and relighting it again. 'You say this thing has been going on for years. Yet you have both, in that time, been married to different people? I'm afraid that sounds like adultery to me!' He angrily drew on his pipe, looking at them both severely.

Shaking her head, Ellen burst into tears. 'It's not what you think, really it isn't! My mother found out about us. She made me marry Laurence and Cob had to marry Kalinga. We had no choice,' she sobbed, begging for justice.

'I think you'd better tell me the whole story, right from the beginning,' Reverend Wethersby said, sitting back in his cane chair and preparing to listen.

*

In the early morning shadows Henry's assistant led the horses back from the creek where he had been watering them, while the other rolled the swags and kicked dirt over the flickering campfire, extinguishing the only circle of light in the early morning gloom. Henry drank the last mouthful of his billy tea and tipped the dregs into the grass. He reached down and picked up his carbine from where it leaned against a tree. Breaking open the chamber, he checked the barrel and loaded it.

'Right,' he said, snapping the gun closed. 'We'd better get going.' Swinging himself onto the back of his waiting mount, he moved off into the predawn. The other two men tightened their horses' girth, tied down their swag rolls, and followed at a fast trot. They rode steadily through the mountains and out into the sparse dry hinterland, keeping up an even pace that quickly put the miles behind them. They missed the unmarked split in the track that led to Wethersby's mission the first time round, and had to retrace their steps many miles before again reaching the turn off. Henry swung his horse onto the little used path, knowing that his journey was nearly over. He was hot and tired, his sustaining anger now drained to a hard bitterness that he could taste in his mouth. Ahead he saw a small huddle of tents and humpies and, straightening his shoulders, he raised his chin, and rode into the camp at a brisk trot. His two assistants followed closely behind.

Cob was the first to hear the drumming hooves, Reverend Wethersby was in his wheelchair at the head of the table, his bible resting beside his hand. Cob clasped Ellen's aim tightly, as every muscle in his body stiffened. She followed his stare down the track. 'It's Henry,' she said in a frightened whisper.

'What? Where?' exclaimed Reverend Wethersby, swinging his chair for a better view.

'What are we going to do?' Fear mounted in her voice.

'Nothing!' answered Cob, 'Let's see what he is going to do first, shall we?' The reassurance in his voice, and pressure of his hand helped calm her panic.

Henry rudely rode his horse right up to the table and sat looking down at them with arrogant disdain. He slid his carbine from its sheath in the saddle, pointing it straight into Cob's face. He spoke with calm precision.

'TakeyourfilthyblackhandsoffmysisterMunyabra.'

Silence echoed in their ears as everything around them seemed to hold its breath. The playing children stopped statue-like in their tracks, the tension at the table paralysing them. They stared fearfully at Reverend Wethersby, waiting for his direction. He dare not take his eyes off the pointed rifle, fearing one flicker of movement would cause the death dealing weapon to explode. The spell on the frozen tableaux was broken by one of the horses blowing gently and scraping its hoof restlessly in the stony dirt.

Cob rose, very slowly, releasing Ellen's hand. 'All right,

Grimshaw let's talk this out, man to man.' He stared defiantly over the barrel of the gun, waiting for Henry's reply.

Still keeping the gun in position, Henry snapped, 'Get back from the table, Ellen, you too Wethersby!'

'No!' choked Ellen, grasping Cob's arm.

'Do as he says, Ellen. Now!' Cob ordered her not taking his eyes from the carbine.

She slid from the seat and pulled the Reverend's chair quickly with her, jolting him roughly across the uneven ground.

The Reverend shouted to the hovering children, 'You children, get to your beds, quickly!' They scurried off like frightened rabbits, pulling little Faith with them. While Henry's assistants warily backed their horses to a safer distance.

Left alone, the two men glared at each other across the table, the steely glint of hatred reflected in their eyes.

Henry broke the silence. 'I always believe in giving even a mongrel dog a fair trial, Munyabra, what have you got to say for yourself before I shoot you between the eyes.' He cocked his Carbine menacingly.

'That's the brave kind of talk I expect from you, Grimshaw, when you're safely tucked behind a gun,' Cob spat back at him across the table.

'You think I need a gun to beat the living daylights out of the likes of you, do you?' Henry hurled the rifle at Cob, as he leapt from the horse. Cob reeled back over the bench, loosing his balance. Taking the advantage, Henry dived across the table, and threw himself onto the flailing man. 'I'll put a finish to you once and for all, you bastard,' he screamed, sinking his fists into the writhing black man.

Dodging Henry's blows, Cob sprang to his feet and hit

Henry with a solid punch, sending the cleric sprawling backwards into the dust. Eyes blazing, he crouched, waiting for the next attack. Henry scrambled to his feet, blood pouring from a swiftly swelling cut on his mouth. The two assistants urged their horses towards the fighting men.

'No you don't! Get back, I say!' the old Reverend commanded, waving his fist at them. 'This will be a fair fight.'

The two men looked uncertainly at him and then at Henry, before swinging their horses away towards the paddock.

Henry lunged forward, but his agile opponent dodged easily, and caught him another vicious blow to the face. He did not go down but staggered to Cob feigning dizziness. Suddenly, Henry's high heeled riding boot shot out viciously kicking Cob in the groin. Cob's face turned a sickly mud colour, as he groaned and doubled up in agony. Swiftly, Henry brought both fists up under the anguished man's gasping mouth, cracking his head back in a fierce whiplash. Like a crazed terrier now, he flew straight for Cob's exposed throat, clamping it in an iron grip, forcing the choking man to the ground.

'Stop it! Stop it!' Ellen screamed, as Cob gagged and struggled.

'Shut up, you dirty nigger's whore!' Henry snarled at her, his face distorted in his lust to kill. The vile insult unleashed new strength in Cob and he fought the clawing hands from his throat. With pure loathing, he grabbed the figure before him, who now was not only his oppressor but also represented all those other faceless persons who had had the power to torment, degrade and humiliate his people for years. He systematically pounded his fists into Henry with all his might, and it felt good, oh so very good!

Finally, pulling the dazed man up by his clerical collar, he shook him like an old battered rug.

'You two-faced sanctimonious bastard!' he roared, pulling Henry's terrified face close to his own. 'Get back to your bloody mission where you belong. If I ever hear your filthy foul tongue speaking about my wife like that again I will kill you. Yes, I said, MY WIFE!' Cob spat straight into the upturned face.

Revulsion spread over Henry's whole countenance. 'Dear God, no! She never married YOU.'

'Yes!' Cob shouted back triumphantly, 'you're too bloody late, mate! She belongs to me now, and don't you ever forget it!' He tossed Henry to the ground in disgust. Shaking, he walked to where Ellen stood, sobbing and distraught and he folded his arms around her, holding her close, still seething with rage.

Henry pulled himself into a sitting position, spitting blood and dirt from his mouth. His bloodstained collar and the sleeve of his torn jacket dangled by a few threads, dirt caked his trousers.

Wethersby wheeled his bathchair across to help him up, but Henry turned on the man, snarling, 'You were in on this, weren't you? You married them!' he accused venomously. 'You stupid, interfering old fool! What do you know of black animals like him? They can't be allowed to marry white women – it's depraved! It's obscene! It's against the laws of God,' he raged at the elderly man.

Reverend Weathersby answered him in a low angry voice, 'And what would you have done, may I ask? Have them locked away so they could not offend the eyes of decent people, because they dared to have feelings just like every other normal human being? You, who professes to have given your life to their protection and well-being. Bah! Don't make me laugh. All you care about is your own hide and your high and mighty position. You don't give a damn how much you make them suffer, do you? As long as your lily white reputation gleams for all to see! "Let he who is without sin cast the first stone", Reverend Grimshaw. Do you have that right?'

'You are indeed a very strange Christian, sir, in my opinion, very strange indeed.' He swung his wheelchair away in disgust, and wheeled himself towards the two quaking assistants. 'You had better go and help your master up,' Wethersby said sarcastically.

Struggling for self-control he pushed himself over to Cob and Ellen. 'Come along you two, don't upset yourselves any more, he's not worth it.'

The three returned to the table. Cob righted the fallen bench and they sat down silently. The assistants pulled Henry to his feet. He brushed away their hands angrily, and tried to regain his dignity. Wincing with pain he limped across to the group at the table. 'Don't think you'll get away with this,' he threatened, 'I'll soon have this sham of a marriage annulled,' he sneered at them.

'Damn it, man!' Reverend Wethersby slammed his fist down on the table. 'Don't you ever give up? If two people can find a little happiness in this miserable world, why should they not be allowed to have it. Leave them alone. They want nothing of you!'

'I will not leave them alone. They have my niece. My best friend's child! If she,' he indicated his finger accusingly at Ellen, 'chooses to destroy herself in this bestial manner, then so be it! But she must not, I repeat, not, be allowed to destroy the life of that poor little child.'

Cob lunged forward, stabbing a finger viciously at Henry. 'I'm warning you, Grimshaw, don't you lay one finger on that child's head. Ellen is her mother. She will decide what's best for her, not you!'

They all turned as a tiny voice wailed from behind Wethersby's chair. 'I want to go home. Where's my grandma, Uncle Henry?' Faith stood alone and terrified, her tangled hair almost covering her tear stained, sunburnt, face, her dress crumpled and dirty above bare, dust covered feet.

'Good God! Faith!' Henry groaned. 'You poor little mite. Look at her! Just look what you've done to her already.' Hearing her name, the terrified toddler ran to her uncle and threw herself into his arms.

'I want to go home, Uncle Henry,' she sobbed, clinging round his neck. Ellen's face turned deathly grey, her heart seemed to swell and choke her.

'So you're doing the right thing by her, eh Munyabra?' Henry snarled, cuddling the miserable child to him. 'Not content with wrecking her mother's life, I suppose you intend to make sure she is dragged through the mire with you, too. What is this? Some plot to take your revenge on our family, or your white betters in general? I suppose you have some virile young buck in the tribe already selected for her, have you?'

Cob sprang to his feet ready to rip Henry apart, but Ellen placed a restraining hand on his arm, and spoke in a hollow empty voice, 'No Cob! No more!' she ordered despairingly, looking at her brother holding her beautiful delicate daughter.

She knew there was only one choice she could make. 'For once, Henry, you are right,' she said wearily. He turned to face her in astonishment. 'I have every right to do what I am doing. I was warned of what would be in store for me, and if your behaviour here this afternoon is anything to go by, Henry, then it will be a lot harder than I imagined. I am quite prepared to pay that price to be Cob's wife.' She twisted the wedding ring of the Reverend's dead wife on her finger. 'But you're right. I don't have the right to expect Faith to pay the same price. She will be better off with Amy. Henry, I want your word of honour as a clergyman, that you will take her to Amy for me, do you promise?' She fought to control the huge sob that rose from her very soul.

'No, Ellen, you mustn't!' Cob whispered urgently.

'Yes, I must, Cob,' she answered him tightly. 'Don't make it any harder for me, please.'

'You are a very brave woman, my dear,' Reverend Wethersby spoke quietly, 'I think you are making the right decision.'

His anger suddenly deflated, Henry answered, 'I promise you, Ellen, she will go with Mother to Amy's and be brought up as Amy's child.'

Ellen rose from the table and walked stiffly to where Henry stood. She held out her arms and he placed the child in them. Ellen cuddled the little body close to her stroking the soft golden curls. Then she lifted the toddler's face up and kissed her gently.

'You go home with Uncle Henry now, darling, back to your grandma, and all your toys. You'll like that, won't you?'

Faith smiled, nodding her head and slipping her little arms around Ellen's neck. 'You coming too, Mumma? Let's go home. I don't like this camping game very much, do you?' she confided, twisting a strand of Ellen's black hair round her finger.

Ellen blinked away tears, and took a deep breath to enable

her to control her cracking voice. 'I might just stay and play camping a bit longer, sweetheart, so you go with Uncle Henry, like a good girl.'

Faith pulled her finger out of the ringlet she had made, and said cheerfully, 'All right, Mumma, and you'll come home soon, won't you?'

Ellen handed her back to Henry, who placed her on the saddle of his horse.

'Yes, my baby, I'll be home soon. I'll see you very soon.' She turned away blinded by tears.

She couldn't watch as Henry mounted up behind the smiling little girl. 'Bye, Mumma, bye,' Faith called, waving her hand to everyone, like a departing princess. Henry turned the horse and spurred it out of the mission grounds.

'Bye Mumma,' Faith's little voice grew fainter as the riders moved swiftly away down the track.

'Goodbye sweetheart,' Ellen quietly sobbed to herself. 'Goodbye my darling! I promise I'll see you again one day, I swear. I love you, Faith. Oh God in heaven watch over her!' she prayed, as the rising dust of the horses hooves finally enveloped the departing travellers, taking them from her sight.

Next morning as Ellen slept, Cob carefully packed all Faith's belongings into the old canvas bag, then sat quietly beside her until she finally stirred. She sat up and instinctively glanced over to the other camp bed that lay empty and smoothed. She looked surprised for an instant, until realisation made her close her eyes and press her lips together.

'How are you feeling this morning?' Cob asked gently, coming to sit on the edge of the rickety narrow bed.

'I'm all right, Cob, really I am. It will just take some getting used to.' she twisted the loose wedding band on her finger.

'Cob?' she asked questioningly, 'You don't hate me for sending my own child away, do you?' Her blue eyes pleaded for his understanding.

'No,' he replied, sliding the ring back down her finger.

'It was the hardest thing I've ever done in my life, I had to let her go.' She'll be better off with Amy in the security of a settled home where things don't change too quickly for her to cope with. It's going to be hard being without her, but I know I did the right thing. She pulled her knees up and wrapped her empty arms round them as if to fill the space.

'Well, as long as you can think like that, Ellen, and you are at peace with your decision, time will heal the pain, you'll see.' He kissed her gently on the cheek, and put his arm comfortingly around her shoulder.

'Right now, it's to work for us two, girl. Up you get, you are going to work your backside off in the next few days. I want to try and get a roof on the shed for the Reverend and the kids before we go. I'd like to do that for them. You going to help me?' he asked throwing her the challenge, and hoping to God she accepted. He had every intention of working her to exhaustion. It was the best way he knew of to ease her pain.

*

When it came time to say goodbye to Reverend Wethersby, Ellen found she couldn't put into words the deep gratitude she felt for his understanding and gentle wisdom. She knelt before his wicker chair. 'I can never thank you enough for what you have done for us,' she said sincerely, squeezing his calloused hands.

'I don't want your thanks, dear, I only did my Christian duty, as I saw it. You're heading down a hard road, my girl, but it's one you have chosen freely and it's up to you and Cob to overcome the difficulties together. Just remember, he is a very proud man. His pride is his strength. Take away that pride, and you will be left with a hollow bitter shell. Love him, Ellen, but let him lead.' He caught her face between his hands and lent forward to kiss her on the top of her head. 'God bless you, dear girl, and give you strength.'

Cob walked over, dragging the belligerent donkey, the canvas bag and their other meagre belongings already strapped to its objecting back.

'Goodbye Cob old chap,' Reverend Wethersby said, with a catch in his throat. 'Thanks for the building job. We can finish it nicely by ourselves now. Good luck son and make sure you look after that pretty little wife of yours. Come back and visit us one day, won't you?'

Cob clasped the older man around the shoulders, as near tears as Ellen had ever seen him. Sniffing and damp-eyed, Reverend Wethersby hurriedly called over the waiting children to say their goodbyes. They crowded round; the girls shyly kissing Ellen's cheek, the boys pumping Cob's hand, grinning foolishly with embarrassment.

Ruffling the last boy's hair affectionately, Cob turned and lifted Ellen up onto the donkey's back. It was time to go.

Reverend Wethersby trundled the bath chair alongside as the children led the donkey, patting and stroking his neck and flanks. Finally, the chair stopped and the children gathered quietly around it.

'Goodbye my dear friends. God be with you,' Reverend Wethersby called after them. The children stood around him waving.

A lump stuck in Ellen's throat as she waved to the little

group gathered in front of their lonely camp. The raw timber roof of the nearly finished hut gleamed starkly in contrast to the shabby tent and the sagging bark humpies. On the ever-burning fire, the black stew pot still simmered. The ochre wilderness stretched away on all sides, fading to the pale purple of the distant mountains. This was the place of her marriage, a place she would never forget. She gave a final wave and turned to smile at Cob who appeared to be having the same thoughts. Taking a firmer grip on the stubborn old donkey's halter, he lengthened his stride, as their journey together now began in earnest.

RAINBOW IN A BOTTLE

Joan B. Cooper

ISBN 9781922175601   Qty

RRP   AU$24.99   .....

Postage within Australia   AU$5.00   .....

TOTAL★ $_____

★ All prices include GST

Name:..

Address: ....

....

Phone:..

Email: ....

Payment: ❑ Money Order ❑ Cheque ❑ MasterCard ❑ Visa

Cardholders Name:..

Credit Card Number: ....

Signature:..

Expiry Date: ....

Allow 7 days for delivery.

Payment to: Marzocco Consultancy (ABN 14 067 257 390)
PO Box 12544
A'Beckett Street, Melbourne, 8006
Victoria, Australia
admin@brolgapublishing.com.au

BE PUBLISHED

Publish through a successful publisher.
Brolga Publishing is represented through:
• **National** book trade distribution, including sales,
marketing & distribution through **Macmillan Australia.**
• **International** book trade distribution to
    • The United Kingdom
    • North America
    • Sales representation in South East Asia
• **Worldwide e-Book distribution**

For details and inquiries, contact:
Brolga Publishing Pty Ltd
PO Box 12544
A'Beckett St VIC 8006

Phone: 0414 608 494
markzocchi@brolgapublishing.com.au
ABN: 46 063 962 443
(Email for a catalogue request)